Taming Lady
TEMPERANCE

Books by Karen Witemeyer

A Tailor-Made Bride
Head in the Clouds
To Win Her Heart
Short-Straw Bride
Stealing the Preacher
Full Steam Ahead
A Worthy Pursuit
No Other Will Do
Heart on the Line
More Than Meets the Eye
More Than Words Can Say

HANGER'S HORSEMEN

At Love's Command
The Heart's Charge
In Honor's Defense

TEXAS EVER AFTER

Fairest of Heart
If the Boot Fits
Cloaked in Beauty

THE SECRET SOCIETY OF SPINSTERS

Taming Lady Temperance

For a complete list of titles, visit KarenWitemeyer.com.

Taming Lady
TEMPERANCE

KAREN WITEMEYER

BETHANYHOUSE

a division of Baker Publishing Group

Minneapolis, Minnesota

Published by Bethany House Publishers
Minneapolis, Minnesota
BethanyHouse.com

Bethany House Publishers is a division of
Baker Publishing Group, Grand Rapids, Michigan

Printed in the United States of America

Library of Congress Cataloging-in-Publication Data
Names: Witemeyer, Karen author
Title: Taming Lady Temperance / Karen Witemeyer.
Description: Minneapolis, Minnesota : Bethany House Publishers, a division of Baker
    Publishing Group, 2026. | Series: The Secret Society of Spinsters; 1
Identifiers: LCCN 2025026532 | ISBN 9780764244735 paperback | ISBN
    9780764246203 casebound | ISBN 9781493452613 ebook
Subjects: LCSH: Temperance—Fiction | Prohibition—Fiction | Prohibition—Texas—
    Fiction | LCGFT: Christian fiction | Fiction | Novels
Classification: LCC PS3623.I864 T36 2026 | DDC 813/.6—dc23/eng/20250616
LC record available at https://lccn.loc.gov/2025026532

Scripture quotations are from the King James Version of the Bible.

Cover design by James Whitney Hall; Image of woman © lldiko Neer / Trevillion Images

Published in association with Books & Such Literary Management, BooksAndSuch.com.

Baker Publishing Group publications use paper produced from sustainable forestry practices and postconsumer waste whenever possible.

26 27 28 29 30 31 32   7 6 5 4 3 2 1

But I say unto you, Love your enemies, bless them that curse you, do good to them that hate you, and pray for them which despitefully use you, and persecute you; that ye may be the children of your Father which is in heaven.

Matthew 5:44–45

Chapter
1

ALBANY, TEXAS
APRIL 1894

Casting a surreptitious glance over her shoulder, Noreen O'Sullivan tiptoed past the unoccupied Methodist church, then darted across Walnut Street toward the schoolhouse. Heart palpitations brought on by self-imposed skulking shallowed her breathing. She paused to brace her back against a pecan tree and steady herself before approaching the school.

Noreen had acquired many skills in the course of her twenty-seven years, but her arsenal had never included a talent for sneaking about in a clandestine manner. Yet the invitation someone slid beneath the door of her boardinghouse room two days ago had urged secrecy, so in a rare act of compliance on her part, she'd determined to make her attendance as covert as possible.

Giving in to the whims of others was not exactly a hallmark of her character. Noreen possessed little patience for people wielding power over others just because they could. She'd rather blaze her own trail than follow someone she didn't trust. It drove her mother to distraction. She begged Noreen to curb her defiant ways and practice biblical submissiveness. No man wanted to wed a woman who questioned him at every turn. Fine by her. She had no intention of becoming a husband's chattel. She'd submit to God and to the laws of the land as the Good Book urged, but she'd not kowtow to men simply because society considered them the only citizens worthy of a vote.

If something needed to be questioned, she'd question. If something needed to be opposed, she'd rail against it until things changed. Her brash attitude might make her unpopular, but she'd rather bear the stigma of being unliked than ignore the passion for reform burning in her chest. Noreen had seen firsthand what blind submissiveness had done to her mother, first with Noreen's father and now with her mother's second husband. She was a shell of a woman, timid, with no identity of her own. Noreen had no desire to follow in those footsteps. She might never have financial security, social standing, or children, but she'd have self-respect and her mission. It would be enough.

Reaching into her skirt pocket, Noreen fingered the edge of the invitation. Thick, high-quality paper. Finer than what one would find in the general store. Probably special-ordered from a stationer in Dallas or even a shop back east. Usually, she despised what she considered the putting on of airs by the wealthy when they flaunted their privilege in subtle displays, but she'd set aside her cynicism when she'd seen the sender's signature—Miss Hortense Lockwood, a woman Noreen had long admired.

Well into her sixties, Miss Lockwood had never married and never apologized for her single state. As sister to the local banker, she wanted for nothing financially, but instead of using her wealth as an excuse not to involve herself in the plight of those beneath her standing, she was the first to volunteer to help the needy. She'd nursed sick children through the night to allow mothers to get some much-needed sleep, she hosted a widows' tea every week in her home to encourage the elderly ladies in town, and she chaired a church committee that organized meals whenever a family in the area suffered a loss. Miss Lockwood might not be as outspoken as

Noreen, but she was a reformer at heart, one who cared "for the least of these" as Jesus had taught. A lady the entire town esteemed.

And she'd personally invited Noreen to join a new society of ladies. "Ladies uniquely positioned to aid in the betterment of their community" had been the precise wording. Her. Noreen O'Sullivan, bane of the Albany Town Council's existence, had been invited to join Miss Lockwood's organization. She'd worked hard to build up an immunity to social ostracism, so the warmth that flowed through her upon receiving the invitation had caught her off guard. It felt good to be included. Especially when this new society might very well be an answer to her prayers. If she could convince Miss Lockwood and her ladies to take on the cause of temperance, she might finally make headway toward closing down the Salt Fork Saloon, a feat she'd been unable to accomplish on her own, despite numerous attempts of increasing zealousness.

Pushing away from the tree in the schoolyard, Noreen stole a quick glance back toward the street to ensure no evening strollers were about, then scurried the rest of the way up Schoolhouse Hill and eased open the door of the two-story frame building that served as the Albany public school. She hated arriving late, but it couldn't be helped. When one of the kitchen staff went home ill, Mrs. Winslow had needed Noreen to stay and prepare the dessert service. Hopefully, she hadn't missed anything of vital importance.

Noreen moved through the foyer as quietly as possible, not wanting to disrupt the goings on in the classroom ahead. Ignoring the staircase that led to the secondary room on the upper floor, she entered the room where her good friend Martha Evans taught and looked around for an unobtrusive place to sit among the ladies who had answered Miss Lockwood's call. Spotting a friendly face at the back of the room, Noreen aimed herself in that direction, relieved she'd not have to suffer the awkwardness of sitting beside someone less tolerant of her outspoken nature. Jane Cowan might crave invisibility for herself, but she supported her friends and their dreams without equivocation.

Jane had yet to notice Noreen's approach. Her chin was tucked toward her chest as if she were trying to hide. Poor thing. She'd likely be as grateful for Noreen's company as Noreen would be for hers. Noreen lengthened her stride. However, three steps into the room, it dawned on her that Jane wasn't ducking her head out of shyness.

". . . ask you, O Lord, to bless our endeavors . . ."

Good gravy. They were *praying*. Noreen halted at once and bowed her head where she stood.

"May we be vessels in your hand, prepared for good works, and eager to serve those around us in a manner that brings you honor and glory. In the name of Jesus we pray, amen."

Standing behind the lectern at the front of the classroom, Miss Lockwood lifted her face at the conclusion of her prayer. Her gaze immediately landed on Noreen. One brow raised slightly from behind her spectacles, but she quickly softened the censure with a smile. A rather thin smile, but the expression was more welcoming than the scowls Noreen usually collected from displeased townsfolk.

Thankfully, the woman didn't call her out for her tardiness, just turned to address the group of roughly a dozen ladies who'd gathered in the schoolhouse that night. Her smile brightened as she did so.

"Take a look around the room, ladies."

Noreen dove into the small desk next to Jane, hoping no one had seen her before she claimed a seat. Martha spied her, of course, since she was at the front of the room next to Miss Lockwood, but her friend just smiled, her eyes alight with good-natured teasing. Jane's eyes, on the other hand, widened like those of a frightened fawn. When she realized Noreen was the one bursting into her quiet corner and not a stranger, however, she relaxed.

"I'm glad you're here," Jane whispered, a sweet smile adding a radiance to her face that her shyness usually hid. "Miss Lockwood doesn't seem quite so intimidating now."

Jane's temperament was as opposite from Noreen's as one could get. Quiet, bookish, and wanting nothing more than to go unnoticed. Many mistook her bashfulness for blandness. Nothing could be further from the truth. Jane was the kindest, most selfless person Noreen had ever met. Not to mention wise. She could see things from multiple perspectives instead of just her own and had saved Noreen from making regrettable decisions in the heat of the moment on more than one occasion.

"The women in this room are your sisters," Miss Lockwood was saying, her voice carrying with all the authority of a minister preaching a sermon. "We are different ages and come from different backgrounds, but we share something in common, something beyond mere womanhood. We are all spinsters."

Noreen bristled as Jane squirmed in the next seat over, her face reddening in shame.

"I see your discomfort with that term, and I share it. *Spinster. Old maid. Maiden aunt.* I've been called them all, even to my face. The terms are used to denote our difference from other women. To declare us strange or inferior because we lack husbands. Over the years, I've learned to let go of the hurt those terms inflict and to seek value not in the opinions of others but in the eyes of God. But in recent months, a desire has stirred within my breast to reclaim the term *spinster* and transform it into a badge of honor. Single men are not looked down upon in society, so why should single women be ashamed of their unmarried state?"

Noreen's heart swelled to hear such a prominent woman espouse the beliefs she herself held. "Amen!"

Heads swiveled to stare at her. Noreen held hers high, unapologetic. Miss Lockwood nodded, approval in her eyes. Approval. From a leading member of Albany society. Mother would've swooned had she been present.

"Is this a suffrage meeting?" one middle-aged lady called out from a seat near the front. "I don't hold with militant women marching in the streets and causing a ruckus. It's unseemly, and I won't be a part of such an organization."

Several heads nodded in agreement, causing Noreen to frown. Did these women not care that they had no voice in selecting the people and laws that governed them? All citizens deserved to be heard regardless of gender, skin color, or financial status. Miss Lockwood would set her straight.

"No, Bertha. This is not a suffrage society."

What? Noreen's frown deepened.

"I'm not proposing we form a group to support any particular political or social agenda. What I hope to create is a sisterhood that supports each other and our community. Some of us live as spinsters by choice, others ended up on this path due to the twists and turns of an unpredictable life. No matter your story, every woman in this room can relate to the unique hardships you face. The pinch of loneliness that strikes in the dark of night, the ostracism that comes from living on the periphery of other people's families, the frustration of not being taken seriously because we have no husband to defend our ideas, and the shame that comes from the careless words or disdainful glances from others that imply we are unnatural or broken in some way."

The words punctured Noreen's chest and deflated her rigidity, leaving her slumped in her seat. Had Miss Lockwood peered directly into her heart? How else could she have described with such accuracy the secret insecurities and heartaches that Noreen battled in the darkness of her private thoughts? Surely, *she* didn't suffer from such emotional distress?

"You are not the only one to feel such things." Miss Lockwood's gaze landed on Noreen for a heartbeat as it swept the audience, and Noreen felt as if salve were being rubbed into the raw places that had just been exposed. "We have all experienced the pinch of those particular pangs. However, I have not brought us together tonight to commiserate and complain. No, my sisters. I wish to encourage and empower you. For you are of special worth in God's sight, and he has work for you that no one else can accomplish."

She lifted an open Bible from the lectern and began to read. "Hear the words of the apostle Paul. 'The unmarried woman careth for the things of the Lord, that she may be holy both in body and in spirit: but she that is married careth for the things of the world, how she may please her husband.'" She set the Bible down and gripped the edges of the lectern with both hands, her eyes lighting with fervor. "We have a freedom to care for the things of the Lord that married women do not possess. I propose that we form a society to do precisely that. To careth for the things of the Lord and for each other. A secret society known only to its members. I do not propose secrecy because I am ashamed of my spinster sisters but because anonymity will grant us freedom from public censure. The Lord himself promised that righteous deeds done in secret will be rewarded by the Father.

"Now, I don't expect anyone to give an answer tonight. I ask you to pray about it and give it careful consideration. Those who choose to join will make a commitment to be a supportive sister to each member and to uphold the standards of the organization as stated in the packet that Miss Evans will now distribute." Miss Lockwood nodded to Martha, who rose from her seat and began handing out papers as if the ladies in attendance were part of her grammar school class.

"Each of these packets contains a brief biographical sketch of an unmarried woman who made a positive impact on our world," Martha said as she handed papers down the rows of seats. "Women like Clara Barton, Charlotte Brontë, Susan B. Anthony, Jane Austen, and Nellie Bly. Some were quiet in their influence, others were more outspoken. But each chose to stand for what she believed to be right and was willing to overcome the obstacles the world stacked in her path."

Martha arrived at the back corner of the room and pulled a set of papers from the bottom of her stack. "I saved these for the two of you." She handed the first packet to Jane. "I thought you might gain inspiration from Louisa May Alcott. I know how much you enjoyed *Little Women*."

Jane flushed with pleasure as she accepted the papers. "I might just read the novel again in her honor this week."

"How many times will that make?" Noreen teased.

Jane ducked her head. "Eight."

"How can you enjoy a story when you already know everything that is going to happen?" Noreen adored Jane, but she didn't always understand her. "Doesn't that make it boring?"

"Not at all. It's like visiting an old friend. The pleasantest of company." Jane folded her papers and slipped them inside the cover of a book that had been hiding in the folds of her skirt.

Of course. Jane never went anywhere without a book.

Noreen returned her attention to Martha. "Who did you save for me?"

Her friend offered a smug grin. "Someone I thought you might appreciate."

Noreen took the papers and flipped to the second sheet, her midsection aflutter. She scanned the top of the page. A name she knew well jumped out to greet her. Swallowing a delighted squeal, she beamed a smile at Martha. "Frances Willard?"

Martha winked. "The president of the Woman's Christian Temperance Union."

A woman Noreen idolized and strove to emulate.

"This is *perfect*."

Martha tapped the remaining papers against Noreen's shoulder. "I know." Martha made her way back up to the head of the class, and Miss Lockwood regained the audience's attention as she went over the society standards.

Noreen only listened with half an ear. She was too busy scanning the information Martha had pulled together on Frances Willard.

She'd been president of a college for ladies? Noreen hadn't known that. Hadn't known that she'd worked a brief stint as the director of women's meetings for Dwight L. Moody, either. Ms. Willard's experience as a renowned lecturer came as no surprise, though. One of Noreen's greatest dreams was to hear her speak in person. Yet she hadn't realized the woman had spoken in every state in the Union in 1883. Noreen had only been sixteen at the time, without means or opportunity to travel to wherever the woman had stopped in Texas. But if she ever came to Texas again, Noreen would travel as far as necessary to meet her hero.

Noreen reached up to touch the small bow she wore pinned to her bodice over her heart. A white ribbon to symbolize purity, the badge of membership in the Woman's Christian Temperance Union.

Her passion. Her calling. A calling she'd renew tonight. For Frances. And all the families, like her own, that had been destroyed by the evils of liquor.

She'd grown lax of late. Hadn't protested in nearly three weeks. Had allowed the patrons of the Salt Fork Saloon to fall back into complacency. Well, no more. Time to set the drunkards of Albany on the path to redemption.

Chapter 2

Deputy James Paxton moseyed down Second Street on his evening rounds. All was quiet around the courthouse square. As usual. Weeknights were pretty tame in Albany. Weekends, too, for that matter. Just the way he liked it. He'd gone nearly two weeks without arresting anyone. Letting Donovan Farley sleep off his drunks on a jail cell cot didn't count. After Farley tripped over a rock last year and busted his arm on his way home from one of his drinking binges, his wife told him not to come home until he could see straight. Farley's vision was questionable on a good day. Add a half-dozen shots of whiskey to the mix, and he'd be lucky to find his own boots. If a jail cell cot kept the man in good graces with his wife, James didn't mind putting him up for the night. As long as he kept the contents of his stomach where they belonged. Sheriff Adair didn't take too kindly to his jailhouse smelling like regurgitated liquor, and James wasn't overly fond of floor scrubbing.

A couple of decades ago, this part of Shackelford County looked vastly different. Rowdy cowboys working the cattle trails to Dodge City, adventure-seeking soldiers stationed at Fort Griffin, buffalo hunters, gamblers, and outlaws of every sort made the area home. Old-timers even talked about the days when Doc Holliday and Big

Nose Kate lived in The Flat, the locals' name for the town of Fort Griffin that sprouted up below the military garrison. It had been one of the most lawless places in the West. Vigilance committees sprouted up to try to preserve the safety of the ranchers, farmers, and merchants in the area, but lynch mob justice was still murder in James's book. Thankfully, Albany won the county seat away from Fort Griffin and helped establish some stability in the area. And when the railroad bypassed Fort Griffin in favor of Albany, people of The Flat dispersed in search of greener pastures.

Thank God for men like Henry Herron and William Adair—men who'd worn the badge and helped tame this land. James aimed to follow in their footsteps one day and wear the sheriff's star himself.

His steps slowed as he turned his gaze upon the three-story limestone courthouse sitting in the center of town. The impressive edifice never failed to inspire him. Solid. Steady. A symbol of justice and righteousness. His chest expanded. Yep. That's what he wanted to be a part of—a system that valued righteousness, that offered protection and created peace.

God had been training him for this work since the day he was born. The middle of five kids, he'd been negotiating truces and curtailing crises for years before he left his father's ranch outside Breckenridge, Texas, to work as a deputy for Sheriff Herron five years ago. He hadn't had enough experience to run for sheriff when Herron retired in '90, but there'd be another election in a couple of years, and James intended to throw his hat into the ring. Not that he didn't like working for Sheriff Adair. He did, but he didn't want to be an underling forever.

Leaving the courthouse behind, James ambled north on Main. If trouble planned to come callin' tonight, that's where it'd start. Most of the downtown area stood quiet after business hours, but this stretch of two blocks echoed with raucous voices, music, and the occasional impromptu bout of fisticuffs. Billiard hall, saloon, hotel, and railroad depot—all within a few strides. If a man wanted entertainment, games of chance, or a place to wet his whistle, this was where he'd be. Which was why James passed most of his evenings patrolling these two blocks. His pappy had always said that an ounce of prevention was worth a pound of cure. Sure proved true in law enforcement. All the sheriff required of him during night shifts was to make a couple of rounds of the business district, then be on duty at the jailhouse in case someone required his services. Easy enough since he lived there. Yet over the last two years, James had started putting in regular, after-dark appearances at the Salt Fork Saloon and the billiard hall a few doors down. He never lingered too long—having a lawman on the premises tended to be bad for business in those particular establishments—but a well-timed entrance had a rather remarkable cooling effect on hot heads. The number of assaults on the books in Albany had dropped by twenty-five percent since he'd begun the practice. A fact that could aid a fella's campaign when election time next rolled around.

What would *not* help his campaign was the thorn in his backside ignoring his warnings and continuing to harass law-abiding citizens. Citizens with influence, and more importantly, votes. James's jaw tightened as he transformed his mosey into a march and lengthened his stride to hurry past the darkened fronts of drug stores, cobblers, and grocers on his way to his target. The irate woman jabbing a pointed finger toward Milton Taggert's chest.

"I will not make myself scarce, Mr. Taggert. I will make myself heard. I have the right of free speech, and I will exercise that right wherever and however I choose. I choose here and now."

The finger jabbed toward the ground to emphasize her point, easing a bit of James's anxiety over the likelihood of said digit being snapped in two by the irate tavern owner. Milton Taggert had moved to Albany from The Flat after the railroad came through and had a roughness around his edges that didn't bode well for single-minded women too blinded by their ideals to identify the danger right in front of them.

"My customers have rights, too," Taggert growled. "Like the right to spend their evenings as they see fit without being insulted by some sour-faced, teetotaling old biddy who wouldn't know a good time if it bit her on the nose."

Miss O'Sullivan's stubborn chin ticked up a notch. "The demon drink you serve only offers the illusion of fun, but it's a lie, and we both know it. In truth, it steals a man's sense and his morals, leading to crime, cruelty, and an immeasurable amount of stupidity."

James chuckled inwardly at that, ducking into the shadows as he neared. The woman had grit. And a valid point. Not that he expected her zealous sermonizing to sway the burly man glowering at her like a grizzly bear on the boardwalk outside the Salt Fork Saloon.

"If liquor is such an abomination, why did that Jesus fella you're so keen on turn water into wine for a wedding party?"

Noreen O'Sullivan blinked. Her lips parted but no rejoinder sprang forth.

Taggert's arms unfolded. "That's what I thought. Drop this obsession and go home, O'Sullivan. You got no business here."

Yes, go home, lady. Please. No need to escalate this into something ugly. Even as the plea formed in his mind, Noreen O'Sullivan's eyes narrowed, and her finger rose back to pointing position.

"Proverbs twenty verse one: 'Wine is a mocker, strong drink is raging: and whosoever is deceived thereby is not wise.' Ephesians five verse eighteen: 'And be not drunk with wine, wherein is excess; but be filled with the Spirit.' Galatians five verse twenty-one . . .'"

The woman kept firing her Scripture bullets, paying no heed to her increasing peril. Her ammunition bounced off Taggert without making a dent, yet the more she fired, the angrier he became. When the man took a threatening step forward, James stepped out of the shadows.

"Evenin', Taggert."

The saloon owner pulled up short and whipped his face toward James, jaw tight and eyes blazing. "You gonna do somethin' about this, Deputy?" He jerked a thumb in Miss O'Sullivan's direction. "This Bible thumper's been out here for the past twenty minutes haranguin' my customers and disturbin' the peace."

Miss O'Sullivan pivoted toward James, her back ramrod straight and her eyes as fiery as Taggert's. Not a good sign. "I'm on a public street, exercising my freedom of speech. There's no law against such activities."

Taggert spun to face her, his fists clenched but thankfully not raised. "What about the law of human decency? You're a public nuisance!"

"And you're a threat to public safety, filling men with liquor with no care as to how the drunkards you create will treat their wives and children when they get home." Miss O'Sullivan's voice cracked slightly, and for the first time James suspected that temperance was more than a social issue to this reformer. It was personal.

James wedged himself between the two before they could start taking swings at each other with something more damaging than words.

"All right. That's enough." He kept his voice calm and measured, hoping to defuse some of the tension. "Taggert, I'm sure you have customers to tend. I'll see Miss O'Sullivan home."

"What if I'm not ready to go home?" She took aim at James with a pair of glistening brown eyes that bore a striking resemblance to shotgun barrels.

James held his tongue and forced his gaze away from the compelling woman. He eyed Taggert instead, making it clear he'd not tolerate anything other than retreat. The owner of the Salt Fork exhaled a disgusted breath but complied without arguing. He backed off a few steps, then pivoted and shoved the flat of his hand against the batwing doors, sending them flying inward with a squeak of hinges.

James returned his attention to the woman before him and offered his arm. "Shall we?"

"We shall not," she declared as she stretched her arms behind her back and laced her fingers in protest.

A smile snuck onto his face, though he did his best to keep it on a tight rein, doubting his amusement would go over well. Noreen O'Sullivan was wound as tight as the black curls that had sprung free from their pins to dangle about her face in a defiant yet oddly fetching manner.

"You know, I actually agree with much of what you were saying."

Her eyes widened slightly. "You do?"

Before he could answer, lines of suspicion formed between her brows, erasing the momentary vulnerability. "I won't be placated, Deputy Paxton. And I won't succumb to your charms, so aim that smile of yours elsewhere."

She found his smile charming? The notion made his grin grow, no doubt the opposite of what she'd intended. When her eyes narrowed, he had to bite the inside of his cheek to keep from chuckling. The woman sure was contrary. But James found her fascinating as well. Hard not to with all that passion and purpose zinging around beneath her surface.

"I'm not placating you, Miss O'Sullivan. I meant what I said. I've seen a lot of senseless damage done by fellas who were too drunk to think straight. Liquored-up cowboys firing off their weapons and endangering townsfolk, petty arguments turning to fistfights, men taking their anger out on their wives and kids."

A slight tightening around her eyes at that last statement supported his hunch. She'd been hurt by someone who drank too much.

"Then why don't you do more to stop it?" she demanded, her hands emerging from behind her back to gesticulate in the air between them.

"I do what the law allows me to do. I patrol. I anticipate. I step in when I can."

"That's not enough!"

He shrugged. "Maybe not. But let me ask you something. How many men did you keep from entering the saloon tonight?"

Her militant shoulders sagged just a hair. "None. But that doesn't mean my words aren't planting seeds that will bring about a harvest of change eventually."

"Anything's possible, I suppose." James weighed his next words with extra care. "But it's difficult for seeds to take root in folks whose hearts are hardened with anger toward the one doin' the sowing."

Her thick, dark brows lifted slightly, giving him a peek of that vulnerability he'd spotted earlier, but like before, a glimpse was all he got before she slammed the door.

"You don't understand." Her hands waved him off and her feet followed suit, her dark blue skirt snapping in sharp movements as she strode off in a huff.

James fell in beside her, stretching his long-legged stride to keep pace with her shorter, choppy steps. He didn't bother saying anything more, figuring she wasn't up to listening at the moment anyway. Besides, she was leaving the Salt Fork. That's what mattered. And not just because he'd told Taggert he'd take care of the situation. It was in her best interest, too. The woman had no care for the consequences that could come from riling the wrong fella. She might be a burr under his saddle, but he didn't want to see her hurt.

She picked up her pace when they reached the courthouse square, as if she thought she could outdistance him. James bit back a smile. She'd definitely worked up a full head of steam, but he matched her gait easily enough. A fact that obviously annoyed her, for she threw on the brakes and spun to face him.

"I am fully capable of seeing myself home, Deputy."

He nodded. "I don't doubt it."

"Good." She sniffed, then took off at a more normal pace.

He flanked her.

She halted again and glared at him, raising one of those thick eyebrows. "Good *night*, Deputy."

He made a show of gazing up at the few stars that were making their presence known in the darkening sky. "Yep. A right fine evening."

He smiled at her then, and her feathers ruffled so violently he half expected to see her feet leave the ground.

"Perhaps I've not made myself clear. I do not need, nor do I wish to be forced to endure, your escort."

"I'm sorry you find my company so tedious."

"It's not that."

Was that a blush crawling across her cheeks?

She blew out a harried breath. "I promise not to return to the saloon tonight, all right? There. Your duty is dispatched. You can cease trailing me about town as if I were a dangerous criminal. I'm sure you have more important things to do with your time."

James shrugged. "Can't think of any."

"Oh for pity's sake." Noreen O'Sullivan grumbled something under her breath about muleheaded lawmen, then took off like a trotter in a harness race.

James scurried along at her side, allowing several feet of space to separate them so as not to encroach too much on her independence. When she stomped up the steps of her boardinghouse porch, he hung back at street level and watched her grab the knob and yank the door open.

"Good night, Miss Noreen."

As he'd hoped, she tossed a glare over her shoulder at him. He smiled, grabbed the brim of his hat, and dipped his chin.

She made no comment, just disappeared into the house and closed the door with unladylike force.

James shook his head as his grin stretched wide. The man who hitched his wagon to that spitfire would never be bored, that's for sure. 'Course he'd have to tame her first. An unlikely prospect when the filly in question would rather trample a man than sacrifice her freedom.

Good thing he was too busy building his credentials as a future sheriff candidate to bother with unbroke fillies, or he might actually be tempted to try his hand at gentling that one.

Chapter
3

The nerve of that man! Interfering in her business. Restricting her freedom. Smiling at her as if he actually *liked* her. Despicable, deceitful man. He might bamboozle other women with his calm demeanor and dry wit, but she saw through his façade. Deputy James Paxton had cared about one thing tonight—getting her away from the Salt Fork and preserving the peace for Milton Taggert and his saloon full of liquor lovers. And he'd succeeded, dragging her away like some kind of criminal.

Noreen wiped her shoes on the rug inside the boardinghouse entryway as if trying to wear a hole in the weave.

"You better not be in trouble with the law again."

Noreen swallowed a gasp as her chin lurched upward and her gaze landed on the disapproving frown of her landlady. "Mrs. Barker, you startled me."

The woman prowled around the lower floors of the house with the stealth of a cat. And with her teacup in hand, and her mention of the law, Noreen had no doubt she'd been sitting by the front parlor window, spying on whomever happened by. Especially her tenants.

"Maybe you'd hear better if you didn't slam doors and attack my rug like a grater on cheese."

Noreen swallowed the sarcastic retort that sprang to mind and forced an apology through her tight throat instead. "Sorry, Mrs. Barker."

She couldn't afford to lose her room here. It was the only respectable place in town for female boarders and therefore the only alternative to her stepfather's home. Her mother might have chosen to tie her life to Arthur Clevenger, but Noreen had made no such vow, and the moment she'd found employment, she'd escaped from under his roof and under his thumb.

Mrs. Barker raised a brow as if doubting the sincerity of Noreen's apology, not an unwarranted reaction. "I only rent to women with good morals, Miss O'Sullivan. You run afoul of the law, and you're out on your ear."

Oh for pity's sake. "I am not a criminal, Mrs. Barker. I'm a reformer endeavoring to make this community a better place. A safer place. All within the bounds of the law, I assure you."

"If that's so, then why did Deputy Paxton deliver you to my door? And don't try to feed me any nonsense about him courtin' you, 'cause I won't believe it."

"Of course he's not courting me." Though an inexplicable pang jabbed her chest at her landlady's assumption of the impossibility of such an occurrence. Was she really so repellent that the idea of a man wanting to woo her was unfathomable? Noreen shoved the depressing notion aside and focused on the issue at hand. "Deputy Paxton happened across me in town." No need to specify where. "And being the gentlemanly type, he insisted upon walking me home."

Mrs. Barker sniffed. "That does sound like something the deputy would do. He's such a nice young man. Always ready with a smile and a willingness to lend a hand."

Her expression softened into something that almost looked . . . dreamy. Noreen couldn't recall ever seeing such a wistful look on the middle-aged woman's face.

"Reminds me of my Percy, God rest his soul. That man had a heart of gold. Needed it to put up with my persnickety ways." Her mouth curved at the corners, and a shadow of a dimple appeared in her left cheek.

Noreen nearly lost her balance while standing on flat feet. Mrs. Barker had a *dimple*?

The miraculous dent disappeared in the next heartbeat, however, returning the widow to her normal prudish state.

"Well, get on with you, then." Mrs. Barker shooed her toward the staircase with the hand not holding her tea. "You're the last one in, as usual. I need to lock up for the night."

More than happy to escape the judgmental glances and unflattering repartee, Noreen bid her proprietress a tepid good-night and hurried up the stairs to the small room with the slanted ceiling next to the bathroom. It was the cheapest space in the boardinghouse, cramped and noisy when water ran through the pipes, but it was home, and the moment Noreen crossed the threshold, a layer of stress fell from her shoulders.

No critical attitudes could find her here. No whispers of pity or condescension could penetrate the walls. No maternal disappointment or paternal bullying would spring at her from behind the dresser, and no angry saloon owners with fisted hands stood ready to silence her with physical force.

Here in the privacy of her room she could drop her bravado and admit that if Deputy Paxton hadn't been there to intervene, her debate with Milton Taggert could have ended very differently. Noreen sighed as she crossed to her washstand and unfastened the top few buttons on her high-necked blouse.

Growing up with a drunkard father who possessed a mean streak that could slice with cruel words or bludgeon with backhanded blows depending on his mood, she knew the dangers of pushing too hard. Of making herself a target. But coming away from the spinster society meeting, she'd been too full of renewed zeal to exercise caution. She couldn't imagine Frances Willard backing down. She'd stand for what was right, no matter the personal consequences.

As Noreen poured water from the ewer into the chipped porcelain basin, Deputy Paxton's voice rang through her memory.

"How many men did you keep from entering the saloon tonight?"

She dipped a washcloth into the lukewarm water, squeezed it out, but failed to lift it to her neck.

In all of her passion-fueled protesting over the last few years, she'd never stopped to consider whether her reformation efforts were actually producing progress. All of her focus had been on proclaiming truth. Not on getting people to *hear* that truth. As much as it galled her to admit, the irritating deputy might have a point.

Noreen ran the damp washcloth over her neck and face, letting routine guide her hands so her mind could wander down new paths. How did Frances Willard fight for temperance? She used her political connections and social standing to bring awareness to those with the power to enact change. Politicians. Newspapermen. Writers. She lectured to women's groups and organized those who shared her beliefs. One woman might be ignored, but hundreds standing together had a voice.

Noreen draped her washcloth over the drying bar and reached for the folded papers in her skirt pocket. She might not have any political connections or social standing to exploit, but thanks to the Lord's perfect timing, she now had a group of women willing to stand together to better their community. All she had to do was convince them that temperance was a worthy battle to wage.

The following afternoon, in the lull between the lunch and dinner crowds at the Albany Hotel, Noreen washed dishes, handing off the freshly scrubbed place settings to the young kitchen maid at her side. Luella accepted the plate and swirled her dish towel over its surface with vigor. The girl was only fifteen, but she worked hard and gave Mrs. Winslow no reason to regret taking her on three months ago.

Luella came from a difficult home life, something Noreen understood far too well. The girl's father, Claude Templeton, was one of the farmers who frequented the Salt Fork, drinking away funds that could be better spent on providing for his wife and daughter. When Martha came to Noreen at the end of the winter term with concerns about some bruises she'd spotted on Luella's wrists, Noreen had taken the girl on as a personal project—finding a way to keep her out of the house after school while earning her own funds so she and her mother could have a way to escape should the need arise. It had taken some fast talking to convince Mrs. Winslow that the hotel would benefit from having an extra pair of hands in the kitchen, but after the first month, Luella had more than proven her worth.

"Noreen, I'm going to check on the table linens for the dinner service," Mrs. Winslow called, one hand on the swinging door that led from the kitchen to the dining room. "When you are finished with the dishes, start prepping the vegetables for the salads and side dishes. Lu can peel potatoes for the mash."

"Yes, ma'am."

Mrs. Winslow pushed through the door and disappeared from the kitchen. The moment the door swung closed behind her, Luella turned an eager face toward Noreen and practically bounced on the balls of her feet.

"So . . . which spinster profile did you get?"

The plate Noreen had been washing slipped from her fingers to clatter against the metal basin. "How do you know about that? It's supposed to be a secret."

"Oh, it is. But Miss Evans let me help with the research. We met every Saturday for the last month to work on it." Her eyes shone with excitement. "It was so inspiring. Learning about women who make a difference in the world all on their own, without a husband or father telling them what to do. I had no idea there were so many. Miss Evans says there are likely hundreds more. We just don't know about them because their stories aren't flashy enough to end up in newspapers or history books." Luella collected the plate from the dishwater and smiled. "Women like you and Miss Evans."

The girl's adoration soothed the places inside Noreen's spirit that had been rubbed raw over the years from those who looked down on her with disapproval, dislike, and even scorn. Her heart softened and stretched, letting her sisterly feelings for the girl fill even the forgotten corners. If she could make a difference in Luella's life, assure her that she was enough all on her own, Noreen would consider her life a success, even if Congress never passed prohibition into law.

"It just goes to show how trustworthy Miss Evans believes you to be that she would let you in on our secret." Noreen nudged Luella with her shoulder, then retrieved the soaking flatware from the bottom of the sink and dropped it into the basin of rinse water.

The girl beamed at the compliment. "I wish I could be a spinster, too. I asked Miss Evans if I could join the society, but she said I was too young." Luella's face fell. "Miss Lockwood's rules state a woman has to be twenty-four before she can be considered for membership. That's so old! I'll have to wait nearly a decade!"

Noreen stifled a wince at the *old* comment and chose not to take offense. To a fifteen-year-old girl, nine years surely felt like an eternity. It was more than half her life, after all. Noreen dried her hands on her apron and reached for a second dish towel. "I guess we'll just have to dub you a spinster-in-training."

Luella's smile returned in full force. "Do you mean it?"

Noreen chuckled. "Of course. Though we can't let the other spinsters know. Wouldn't want them to think we were breaking the rules."

"I won't say a word. I swear!"

"I suppose we can let Miss Evans in on the secret since she already told you about the society. And possibly our friend Miss Cowan." Jane might balk at the rule bending, but she had such a heart for children that Noreen couldn't imagine her protesting Luella's inclusion once she understood what a difference their mentorship could make in the young girl's life.

Luella launched a hug attack, grabbing Noreen around the waist and squeezing tightly. "You're the best!"

Not quite sure how to handle this unexpected burst of affection, Noreen held her arms wide for a moment before allowing them to curl slightly around Lu's back. It had been a long time since someone had hugged her, and it caused a strange burning at the backs of her eyes.

Then, in a blink, it was over. Luella pulled away and started bouncing again, as if her joy didn't know how to sit still. In contrast,

Noreen could barely move, too unaccustomed to affectionate displays to navigate the treacherous territory with any kind of confidence. She cleared her throat and busied herself with drying flatware.

"Which famous spinster did you get?" Luella asked as she shifted her towel around to find a dry spot.

Noreen managed a smile. "Frances Willard. She's the president of the WCTU."

"I don't remember that one." Luella's eyebrows arched as she reached for a group of spoons. "What's WCTU?"

"The Woman's Christian Temperance Union." Noreen scrunched the bib of her apron to one side so that Luella could see the small white bow she wore pinned to her bodice. "Members wear a white bow of purity, like this one, and dedicate themselves to promoting the prohibition of intoxicating liquors. Miss Willard founded a state organization in Texas as well and even helped us bring a prohibition referendum to the polls in 1887. Unfortunately, it failed to pass." A scowl tugged Noreen's mouth flat. "If women had been allowed to vote, I suspect the outcome would have been much different."

Not wanting to dwell on unpleasant thoughts when they had such little time to talk openly, Noreen forced a brightness into her tone and turned the conversation around to Luella. "If you were able to pick one of the reports you helped research as *your* spinster inspiration, who would you have chosen?"

"That's easy. Clara Barton." Luella's hands stilled, and her voice grew wistful. "The Angel of the Battlefield. Her whole life is about helping people, especially those who are unable to help themselves." Luella shook off the dreaminess and shot a grin toward Noreen. "Did you know that she was named head nurse for General Butler's unit in the War Between the States even though she had no formal medical training? That's how big of an impact she made by taking care of wounded soldiers. Then she convinced President Hayes to create the American Association of the Red Cross and has been the president of the organization ever since. I want to be a nurse like Miss Barton. Helping folks heal, making their lives better."

Giving others what she needed so badly for herself.

Noreen placed a hand on the young girl's shoulder. "I have no doubt you'll be the finest nurse in Texas one day." If she ever escaped her father's confining hold. Noreen would need to talk to Martha about putting together some kind of scholarship fund to help Luella continue her studies beyond the secondary classroom.

Luella smiled, but shadows lingered in her eyes, the curse of a child who understood that reality rarely lived up to one's dreams. "Did you know that Clara Barton actually came to our town once? After those three years of drought in the '80s. Mama said Miss Barton set up her headquarters in Albany as she toured the surrounding counties and brought clothing, household goods, and tools to the farmers' families who'd been devastated by lost crops. Mama said only a woman would think to bring things for the families. All the men thought about was the seed they needed to replant. I was only eight and don't remember much about it, but I still have the shoes I got from the Red Cross that year. They're plumb wore out, but Mama told me to keep them so I could remember the woman who brought hope to a land that had none."

A woman who brought hope. That's who Noreen wanted to be as well. A woman who made the world a better place. But even Frances Willard had failed to get her prohibition referendum passed in Texas because men alone held the right to vote. Yes, rallying the spinsters would make it more difficult for the town council to ignore the plight of those negatively impacted by drunkenness. But that might not be enough. She might need another ally. One well-liked and respected around town. One who appreciated the value of sobriety. One capable of growing facial hair.

Jane's father occasionally assisted the cause by preaching a sermon on the dangers of overindulgence, but his concern centered on the spiritual needs of his flock, not on promoting a political agenda many considered divisive. And Noreen didn't want to risk a rift developing between herself and Jane by pestering the parson too often.

That left only one trouser-wearing candidate on Noreen's list of possible advocates—Deputy James Paxton.

Chapter

4

James milled around the churchyard after services Sunday morning, shaking hands and jawing with the farmers and ranchers who came to town infrequently. As the son of a rancher, he felt more at home among the men with cracked leather work boots than those sporting polished Oxfords. Spotting his mentor, Henry Herron, chatting with the preacher near the church steps, James meandered that direction.

"How is your wife fairing?" Brother Cowan was asking. "I didn't see Alice next to you this morning."

"Bertie was feelin' poorly. Alice stayed home to tend to her."

"Sorry to hear that. I'm sure Jane missed having her in Sunday school. Jane always speaks highly of your young'uns."

"And they, her." Henry grinned. "They love Miss Jane's class." He glanced over at James, no doubt catching the movement of his approach from the corner of his eye. Once a lawman, always a lawman—at least regarding instincts and vigilance. His smile widened. "James! Good to see you, Deputy."

He extended his hand, and James clasped it gladly. "Henry. How are those Herefords treating you?"

"Better than the outlaws I used to spend my days roundin' up. I much prefer dodging kickin' hooves than flyin' bullets."

James chuckled. "Can't argue with that. Calving going well?"

Herron nodded. "Had two drop this past week. Got a couple other heifers showing signs of bein' near their time as well."

"Sounds—"

"Deputy Paxton." An unwelcome voice broke into the conversation. "Might I have a word?"

James did his best to hide his frown as he glanced toward Arthur Clevenger, owner of Clevenger's Emporium and self-proclaimed mayoral candidate for the next election. James could understand a man having political aspirations—he did, himself, after all—but Clevenger's ingratiating manner got under James's skin. He was one of those fellas who hobnobbed with those in power to elevate himself instead of standing on his own two feet. Night and day different from his headstrong stepdaughter, who didn't care who she vexed or what personal consequences she might suffer in her quest for reform.

"Come out to the ranch on your off day," Henry offered in parting, his gaze glowing with sympathy and just a touch of glee that he was no longer the one whose time was not his own. "I'll show you the herd, and Alice will fill your belly with some decent grub for a change. I remember how sorry your cooking skills are." He thumped him on the back, and James grinned.

"How do you know they haven't improved since you hung up the star?"

Henry's eyes glittered with suppressed laughter. "Boy, you couldn't fry a potato without nearly burnin' down the jail. If your skills had doubled, they still wouldn't be worth a plugged nickel."

James chuckled, well aware of Clevenger's growing impatience beside him. "True. I'll stop by on Wednesday."

"See ya then."

"Deputy." The title burst from Clevenger the moment the last word fell from Henry's tongue. "I really must speak with you."

Biting back a sigh, James pasted a pleasant expression on his face and turned to the man who cared more about his own agenda than another's conversation. "Clevenger. What can I do for you?"

The man's mouth pinched beneath his thin mustache. "It has come to my attention that my wife's daughter might have been involved in some . . . unsavory activities a few nights ago. I wanted to apologize on her behalf and to assure you that her mother and I do *not* condone such bold behavior. I will be making my feelings on the subject known to her today when she comes to Sunday dinner."

Nothing like a warmhearted family meal filled with lectures and accusations. No wonder Noreen chose to live at the boardinghouse instead of with her parents. Or *parent*, singular. Good old Arthur made it quite clear that he wanted no association linking him to his opinionated stepdaughter.

Cautious of others who might be near enough to overhear, James kept his voice boringly pleasant so as not to draw undue attention. "I found nothing unsavory in Miss Noreen's activities last Thursday. She might have been sharing opinions that weren't particularly popular in the vicinity where she'd chosen to linger, but there was nothing illegal nor unseemly in her conduct."

"It's good of you to take that stance, Paxton. I appreciate your discretion. Heaven knows Noreen has none." He laughed as if he thought himself quite funny.

James didn't join in.

"Her mother and I have done our best to curb her outspokenness and redirect her political leanings, but that girl has a mind of her own, I'm afraid."

Yes, James figured Clevenger *was* afraid of Noreen having her own mind. Afraid of how her choices might reflect on him and impact his political machinations.

"I actually find her quite admirable," James said, taking pleasure in the shock that widened Clevenger's eyes. "It takes a lot of courage to stand for what you believe when others strive to undermine you, silence you, or even persecute you. Reminds me of Peter and John in Brother Cowan's sermon this morning, standing firm in their mission even when the high priest ordered them to quit tellin' folks about Jesus."

Clevenger opened and closed his mouth at least three times before he managed to get any words to spill out. "Surely you're not comparing Noreen to the holy apostles?"

"Nope. Just her courage. And her dedication to her cause." The woman's methods might need some adjustment, and her delivery could use a little less vinegar, but no one with working eyes and ears could doubt her zeal.

The man's face reddened, and he just couldn't seem to get the drawbridge of his jaw to crank upward.

"Maybe take it easy on her at lunch today." James touched the brim of his hat and eased away from the unpleasant man. "She has enough opponents in town. Might do her good to have a few more allies."

"I'm glad to hear you say that." A familiar feminine voice echoed directly behind him. "For I've been meaning to discuss that very matter with you."

James's stomach clenched. He slowly pivoted to discover Noreen O'Sullivan standing a mere three feet from him.

Surely, Noreen hadn't been there the whole time. He would have noticed. He was a trained observer. James sorted through his memory and confirmed a total of four ladies in his vicinity when he'd approached Henry Herron a few minutes ago. And none of them had wild, curly hair or eyes that snapped brown fire when they took aim at a fella.

That reassurance offered little comfort, however. For this woman was on a mission. A mission that apparently involved him. He swallowed and steeled himself for what was to come. The tenacity he'd just admitted to admiring was about to bury its teeth into his leg, and he wasn't at all certain he'd be able to shake free.

Butterflies assaulted Noreen's belly the moment James Paxton's eyes locked on hers. How had she never noticed how blue they were?

More to the point, why was she noticing their color *now*? This was no time to get distracted by attractive male attributes. Broad shoulders, lean musculature, and a rugged jawline had absolutely no bearing on the present circumstance. She'd do well to remember that fact.

"Might I have a word with you, Deputy Paxton?"

James dipped his chin in consent at the same time her stepfather heaved a dramatic sigh. "For pity's sake, Noreen. Leave the man alone. He has more important things to do than listen to you rant about closing the saloon."

Noreen bristled, but before she could offer a retort, the deputy shot Arthur a pointed look. "I'm fully capable of deciding how to spend my time, Clevenger. I don't need you screening my appointments for me."

Noreen pressed her lips together to keep the shocked laughter from exploding out of her throat.

"I didn't mean . . ." Arthur tightened his jaw, apparently realizing he would only make himself look worse if he offered excuses.

He turned his frustration on Noreen instead. No surprise there.

"Your mother needs your help with dinner. I'll not have her working herself to the bone because you're too busy with your personal schemes to give a thought to her health."

If you're so concerned with Mother's health, why don't you hurry home to help her? She bit back the words, even though they begged to be spoken. She knew from experience they'd have no effect. Besides, she really did intend to help her mother. Preparing Sunday dinner was one of the few times she and Mama could talk without Arthur overshadowing the conversation.

"I won't be long," Noreen promised.

"Perhaps we can chat on the way to your mother's house," Deputy Paxton suggested. "I'd be happy to see you home."

Again.

They both seemed to hear the unspoken word, for something that looked very much like teasing glittered in the deputy's eyes.

That man and his obnoxious charm. Good grief. She'd almost shared a smile with him. Thankfully, she'd stopped herself in time.

"A very practical suggestion." Hopefully, her no-nonsense tone sufficiently hid the crack in her armor. Yes, she needed him as an ally, but she'd not have him thinking he could sway her just because he'd stood up to her stepfather.

Though that *had* been rather wonderful. And rare. Not even her mother spoke up on her behalf.

Noreen shored up the softening places inside her and coated them with a layer of steel. She couldn't afford softness. Too much was at stake.

He gestured for her to lead the way, so she did, winding through the slowly dispersing congregants. Once they'd put some distance between themselves and the churchyard, she slowed her gait slightly and allowed the deputy to come alongside.

"So what did you wish to speak to me about?" he asked.

Such a simple question, yet it tied her belly in knots. She'd intended to blurt out her request as she walked so she'd not have to look him in the eye, but the breeze her hurried steps generated seemed to blow through her mind like wind pouring through an office window to scatter papers all over the floor. Her thoughts swirled in disorganized chaos, making it nearly impossible to grasp anything intelligent.

Thunderation. She couldn't have this discussion with her faculties flying about all willy-nilly.

Noreen jerked to a halt in front of the blacksmith shop and turned to face Deputy Paxton. The man had good reflexes; she'd give him that. He only took half a step before he recognized her stoppage and reined in his forward momentum. Pivoting to face her, he met her gaze, nothing but patience and curiosity gleaming in his eyes.

"I've been thinking about what you said the other night," she began, her voice shaking only slightly. "About the lack of results my reform measures have produced to this point."

"And?"

Noreen swallowed. "And it occurred to me that someone who understands the masculine mind might prove to be an invaluable asset in this endeavor. Someone who could advise me what techniques to employ to motivate men to change their ways."

"I . . . uh . . ."

Was he *blushing*? Noreen had never seen Deputy Paxton nonplussed. Not even while taking down that pair of outlaws who held up the bank last year.

"Surely there's another fella who can advise you. Your stepfath—no." He shook his head, erasing his own suggestion. "I don't reckon he'd be too interested in helping." His face brightened. "What about the parson? Aren't you friends with his daughter? A minister is bound to have recommendations about gettin' folks to turn from their wicked ways."

Noreen frowned. He wasn't supposed to pawn her off. Yet here he was squirming like a worm desperate to avoid her hook. Maybe Mrs. Barker had been right about Noreen's ability to repel men.

Logic had served her well thus far in life, so she set aside the twinge of hurt his evasion caused and focused on making her case.

"Sermonizing doesn't seem to be working for me, as you've already noted. And I'm not precisely in a position to pay calls on these men at their homes as a preacher might."

His brow furrowed. "No, I'd definitely not recommend private visits."

Stiffening her spine, Noreen dug out the ammunition she hadn't expected to need for this conversation. But James Paxton was just a man, after all.

"You've admitted to agreeing with my position, Deputy. So why won't you support my efforts? Are you afraid of what people will think of you? I hadn't thought you a coward."

His eyes hardened, and Noreen instantly wished she could put that particular bullet back in her gun.

"You want my advice? Fine. Here's tip number one. Insulting a man rarely results in getting him to do what you want. It nearly always goads him into doing the exact opposite."

Moisture tickled the backs of her eyelids, but she held it at bay with a trio of rapid blinks. "You're right. I should not have called you a coward, especially since it is quite apparent by your years of service to this town that you are anything but. I apologize."

His jaw unclenched slightly. "Apology accepted."

She searched his face, and when his eyes softened, she dared to believe him.

He exhaled a heavy breath. "Look, Noreen, I do agree with a lot of what you stand for, but I see many more shades of gray from where I operate than your black-and-white perspective will allow. And if I'm being completely honest, I *am* concerned about how the people of this town perceive me. I hope to be sheriff one day, and if I alienate half the voting populace by publicly supporting your saloon eradication mission, my chances of accomplishing that goal turn to dust."

"They wouldn't if women had the vote."

"But they don't. Not yet." He turned his gaze toward the court-house square for a moment before refocusing on her. "It's my duty to uphold the law, even when the law allows for things that offend my morals. It's also my duty to protect the citizens of Shackelford County, whether they are saloon owners, reformers, or anyone in between. I have to be impartial. Or at least as close to it as I can manage. Any law-abiding person in this town needs to be able to depend upon me to do what is lawful and right. If I don't hold their trust, I can't hold their respect, either."

Noreen's spine lost a good deal of starch as he spoke. She should be angry that he didn't want to help her, yet her admiration for his principles overshadowed her disappointment.

Never had a man spoken to her with such honesty and open-ness. Certainly her father and stepfather never had. They'd been too busy ordering her around or ignoring her entirely to bother with such depth of sharing. Deputy Paxton, on the other hand, spoke to her as if he considered her his equal, someone worthy of his trust.

It made her wish she could actually *be* worthy of his trust. Of his good opinion. But a man as dedicated to the law as James Paxton would despise her if he ever discovered the sins of her past. God might forgive, but in her experience, people rarely did. Not when it came to murder.

Chapter
5

W ho's the nice young man I saw you walking with?" Mama asked the minute Noreen came through the back door.

Her smile was so annoyingly hopeful that Noreen turned her mouth down the same degree in the opposite direction just to balance things out.

"Not a suitor, if that's what you're thinking." Noreen grabbed the extra apron from the hook near the door, fit her head through the opening above the bib, then tied the strings around her waist. "And Deputy Paxton's not all that young. He's at least thirty."

"Well, you're not all that young yourself." Mama turned back to the stove and the gravy she'd been whisking when Noreen came in. "Seems to me thirty and twenty-seven fit together quite nicely."

Noreen sighed as she collected the pot of boiled potatoes and poured them into a colander that was waiting for her in the sink. Mama always left the potatoes for her to mash. The arrangement served them both well. Noreen had an excuse to smash something—an excellent outlet for the frustration that invariably beset her when visiting her mother and stepfather—and her mother ended up with well-creamed potatoes for the dinner table.

"Mama, we've been over this a hundred times." She exhaled heavily enough to flutter the ruffles on her apron bib. "I don't need a man to take care of me. I'm fine on my own."

The whisk slowed its cast-iron scraping. "But are you happy?"

Noreen dumped the drained potatoes back into the hot pan and moved to the wooden worktable. She glanced toward the stove, and a genuine curiosity pushed aside her normal defensiveness. "Are *you* happy, Mama?"

The hint of a shadow passed over her mother's lined face. "I'm content, and, yes, at times, I would classify myself as happy."

At times. Times that were rare and far between as far as Noreen could tell.

"Now, don't go pitying me, Reenie." Mama pushed the gravy skillet to the back of the stove and covered it with a lid. "Arthur has been good to us. In fact, he was an answer to prayer. I was barely older than you are now when your father died. I had no money, the bank was fixin' to take the farm, and I had a daughter to feed and clothe. I needed a provider, and the Lord sent Arthur. A man who attended church, who owned his own business, and—most important to me at the time—a man who abstained from strong drink."

Mama's gaze carried the weight of haunting memories. Noreen shared many of them, but she'd likely never know the full extent of what her mother had suffered. Father had been a brute when he drank, and when the farm began to fail, his drinking—and his temper—worsened.

"Arthur isn't perfect," Mama said as she checked the green beans simmering in a small pot, "but he takes care of me, and if you ever found yourself in need, he'd take care of you, too."

Noreen didn't share her mother's faith in the goodness of Arthur Clevenger's heart, but she had to admit that the man *had* kept food on the table, clothes on their backs, and a roof over their heads. It was too bad that in return he expected subservience and the forfeiture of any opinions that differed from his own. Mama might have a nice house and pretty things, but her spirit had shriveled from years of emotional drought.

Noreen contemplated her mother as she pummeled the potatoes.

Long ago, Noreen had vowed never to surrender her identity to a man. She refused to become her mother, trading independence for security. Yet hearing Mama talk about being near Noreen's age when she was left on her own with no way to provide for a child stirred an empathy she'd not experienced before. She knew how difficult finding work as a single woman could be. Adding a child to the equation would complicate things a hundredfold.

Perhaps Mama *hadn't* taken the easy way out by marrying the first man who came along. Perhaps she'd chosen the only viable path open to her at the time. Noreen couldn't even imagine having a child to take care of in her current circumstances. She barely managed to provide for herself. Perhaps it was time she stopped judging her mother for her choices and started extending grace.

Releasing her grip on the masher, Noreen moved to the stove and wrapped her arms around her mother from behind, resting her cheek against the back of Mama's head. "Thank you for taking care of us all those years ago. I'm sorry if I've acted ungrateful for the sacrifices you made."

Her mother's body quivered as she let go of her spoon and squeezed Noreen's arms where they rested at her waist. Affection had never had room to flourish with Fiery Finn O'Sullivan at the family helm. And after his death, Noreen hadn't wanted any connection. Any softness. She'd withdrawn and hardened herself, determined to rid her heart of all vulnerability. As if that were possible. Yet in the midst of this odd backward embrace, a pleasant warmth moved through Noreen that she hadn't felt in years. The warmth of family.

"Ramona!" A door slammed at the front of the house, and Noreen's mother jumped.

Pulling away from Noreen, she grabbed the bean spoon and started stirring with a vengeance.

"Better finish those taters," she said as she lifted the edge of her apron with her left hand to give her eyes a quick swipe. "Arthur will be wanting his Sunday dinner."

Arthur's dinner could wait a few minutes in Noreen's estimation.

Some things were more important than a man's eating schedule, like rare moments of emotional closeness between mother and daughter. But Noreen complied with her mother's request and smashed with renewed frustration. As much as she wanted to encourage her mother to stand up for herself and not worry so much about bending to Arthur's every whim, she bit her tongue. She could leave this house after the dishes were done. Mama lived here. She'd sworn Arthur had never hit her, but there was more than one way to inflict wounds, especially on the soul.

"Is your daughter here?" Arthur's footsteps pounded in the hall. "I warned her not to dawdle with the deputy, but that girl is obstinate enough to defy me out of spite."

Noreen rolled her eyes. Nice of him to confirm her absence before making free with the insults. Although, her presence had never inhibited his criticisms before, so he likely would have said much the same had he been standing directly in front of her.

"Noreen's here," Mama called as she poured the beans into a waiting serving bowl.

Arthur strode into the kitchen, sans hat and coat, the accoutrements no doubt hanging from a hook on the hall tree in the entry way. "Good, I intend to have serious words with her. You'll not believe what this girl of yours has done now."

Noreen scraped a heaping spoonful of butter into the potatoes, then sprinkled salt and pepper liberally into the mash. "At seven and twenty, I'm hardly a *girl*, stepfather. You really must stop addressing me as a child."

Arthur's eyebrows dipped into a sharp vee. "I'll stop addressing you as a child when you cease acting like one. I swear, Noreen. You are the most selfish, willful female I've ever encountered. You give no thought to how your actions will reflect on others or what repercussions they might carry."

Not in the mood to listen to her sins recounted ad nauseum, Noreen took up the bowl of perfectly seasoned potatoes in one hand and the bowl of green beans in the other and backed through the swinging door that led into the dining room.

"Don't walk away from me when I'm talking to you, girl."

Noreen gritted her teeth. Sunday dinners in the Clevenger household were rarely enjoyable, but this one was gearing up to be especially unpleasant.

Not trusting herself to say anything that wasn't dripping in vitriol, Noreen set the bowls on the table, turned to face her stepfather, and braced for whatever disparaging remarks he considered his duty to impart.

"Edward Thompson threatened to take his business to Wilson's Mercantile this morning. Thompson's one of my most loyal customers, and he's leaving because *you* keep accosting him outside the Salt Fork. That little stunt you pulled on Thursday night was the last straw. He says he'll no longer do business with a man who continues to allow his daughter to cast aspersions on his character."

"Oh, Noreen." Mama brought in a platter of ham and placed it at the head of the table. The disappointment in her voice hurt more than Arthur's overblown complaints. "Tell me you didn't go back to that saloon."

Her mother, of all people, should understand why she felt so passionately about the cause of temperance. Yet she'd never supported her mission. She'd taken Arthur's side from the beginning, pleading with her to stay out of trouble and quit making herself a target.

"She most certainly did." Arthur jabbed an accusatory finger in Noreen's direction. "Not only did she risk her reputation—and *ours*—by visiting an unsavory part of town in the evening, she saw fit to harangue several prominent members of the community. Edward Thompson related to me that Noreen called him a criminal and accused him of destroying his family."

Mama moaned softly, her shoulders curling in on themselves.

"For pity's sake." Noreen crossed her arms over her chest. "I did *not* call Mr. Thompson a criminal. I simply stated that liquor is the beverage of criminals, and that truly respectable men would not seek to imitate the behavior of felons."

"So you insinuated that he was not respectable. Marvelous." Arthur exhaled loudly, his disgust evident. "Thompson sits on the city council, Noreen. He's one of the most respectable men of our community."

Noreen jutted her chin. "Not in my estimation."

"Well, your estimation isn't worth a hill of beans. You insist you're not a child, yet you're incredibly naïve about how the world works. Making enemies of people in power has consequences. What if Thompson not only removes his patronage from my shop but encourages his friends and colleagues to do the same? I'll be ruined! The emporium will fail, and we will be destitute. Is that what you want?"

"Of course not. But someone has to take a stand against Goliath. We can't all cower on the sidelines hoping the giant will simply tire of his taunting and go home. Someone must confront the evil of strong liquor and cut off its head before it destroys civilization. Families are suffering. *Children* are suffering." Children like Luella. And like Noreen had once been. "I can't ignore them. I won't."

"'Before it destroys civilization'? What rot. Liquor has been around since the time of Noah, and civilization is still here. It doesn't need your paltry efforts to keep it from collapse. It will survive just fine on its own."

"Will it?" Noreen uncrossed her arms and advanced on her stepfather, too full of righteous indignation to proceed with caution. "Let's look at Noah, since you brought him up. A righteous man. Chosen by God to save humanity and every animal that walked upon the earth. What became of him when he drank the wine of the vineyard he planted? He became drunk and shamed himself with nakedness. And when his son happened upon him and told his brothers, did Noah take responsibility for his nakedness and repent? No, he cursed his son for not covering him. And not only his son but his grandson and all future descendants of that line. Where is the righteousness in that? It was Noah's sin, yet his son bore the brunt of his curse. Is it not the same today? Parents drink, they behave poorly, then take their shame and anger out on their children. Cursing them. Beating them. Destroying their future."

"Worthless brat! You're nothin' but a millstone around me neck." Her

45

father's voice rang through Noreen's head, and an ache throbbed in her jaw at the memory of the backhanded blows that had sprawled her upon the floor.

Tears flooded her eyes, but she was too angry to bat them away. "Liquor is a poison that corrupts righteousness and manufactures cruelty. Civilization is already broken. I'm just trying to fix it."

"You're an unhinged fanatic." Arthur took a step back, shaking his head. "There's no reasoning with you. *You're* the poison, Noreen. Slowly killing this family with your radicalism. Our only chance to survive is to cut you off like a gangrenous limb." He sighed, then squared his shoulders and braced his legs apart. "I'm going to have to ask you to leave. You're no longer welcome in this house."

Mama gasped. "Arthur, no."

But he paid his wife no attention. Caring only for his own desires. As usual.

Noreen hesitated, the little girl inside of her hoping her mama would say something, do something to support her daughter.

However, Ramona Clevenger said nothing. *Did* nothing. Just let her head droop forward in defeat, her surrender nearly rending Noreen's heart in two.

It seemed liquor wasn't the only thing with the power to destroy families. Betrayal did a bang-up job, too.

Chapter
6

James scraped charred potato from the edge of the skillet, then hissed when grease popped from the pan to the back of his hand. Sucking in a breath, he released the handle of the frying pan and swiped the burning spot against his shirt. Maybe Henry had a point about his cooking skills. He'd just wanted something warm to go with the ham sandwich he'd picked up from the café after walking Miss O'Sullivan to her mother's house.

With Sheriff Adair investigating a string of cattle thefts down near Moran, James was currently the only lawman in town. And since the sheriff wasn't a fan of night duty, James had volunteered to take up residence at the jailhouse, leaving him in charge of his own meals.

He raised a brow as he considered the sliced potatoes and bits of onion littering his cast-iron pan. Mmmm. Half raw and half burnt, just the way he liked them. James shook his head, the lie as impossible to swallow as his supper was bound to be. Even for him, this was abysmal. That's what happened when a fella spent too long pondering a certain curly-haired woman, her request for assistance, and the political quagmire sure to follow should he agree.

With a sigh, James pushed the pan of pitiful potatoes to the back of the stove to keep them from fossilizing further. Maybe he should just give up on the troublesome mess and be content with his sandwich.

Movement in the street beyond the open jailhouse door caught his attention. Was that—?

Potatoes forgotten, James grabbed his coat from the back of his office chair, shoved his arms into the sleeves, then snatched his hat from the coatrack by the door and fit it to his head as he jogged into the sunlight.

Noreen O'Sullivan. He recognized the dark green calico she'd worn to church that morning. What was she doing running down the road on this side of town? He'd thought she was eating with her folks. There was nothing out this way except the grist mill.

Clevenger!

James's jaw tightened as he hoofed it down the street. The insensitive clout. So caught up in his own agenda he gave no thought to his stepdaughter's feelings. Noreen might be a bit on the prickly side, but anyone with half an ounce of common sense could see that her barbed spines protected a bruised heart. If James recognized it, how much more aware should a family member be?

James stretched his stride, gradually closing the distance between him and the surprisingly fleet-of-foot woman he trailed. Not wanting to holler and draw undo attention from anyone who might be nearby, he waited until he was less than five yards away to call to her.

"Noreen."

She cast a startled glance over her shoulder, and James's gut hardened like a knot that had just been yanked tight. Tears streamed down her face. Tears. On Noreen O'Sullivan's face. The grittiest woman he'd ever met, the one who stood toe-to-toe with Milton Taggert without flinching, had been brought to tears. James's normally cool head erupted in flames, but he batted down the worst of them to focus on the woman in front of him. The one currently trying to shoo him like an unwanted fly.

"Go away, Deputy. I've no need of your services." Loud sniffing ensued, followed by a jig of jutting elbows as she attempted to wipe her face while trotting with increasing speed toward the millpond.

"Noreen. Slow down, would you?"

She kicked into a canter. Ornery woman.

"I just want to help you." James sprinted forward and cut into her path, forcing her to a halt. She tried to bolt in another direction, but he was onto her game and dodged side to side to block her as if she were a goat set on escaping her pen.

"Why can't you just let me be?"

Never had he heard a more broken sound than her tear-clogged plea. His heart throbbed in his chest as he dug out a handkerchief from his jacket pocket and extended it toward her. "'Cause it's my duty to help the good folk of Albany in their time of need." Though the compulsion that had demanded he give chase felt a mite more personal than simple duty now that he'd corralled her and witnessed the evidence of her distress.

"I'm not one of the good folk of Albany."

She accepted his handkerchief, mopped her eyes, then blew her nose. Her nostrils made a rather robust honking sound, but he was too concerned about her well-being to find any humor in the instrumentation.

"I'm a selfish, willful, unhinged fanatic bent on destroying my family."

James leveled a stern look at her. "Those sound like Arthur Clevenger's opinions, not yours. They certainly aren't mine. So why are you speakin' them as if they're truth?"

She raised her chin but refused to meet his gaze. She stared off toward the pond instead, fighting to pull together scraps of composure. Gradually, her quivering lower lip firmed, and the pools shining in her coffee-colored eyes receded. Her shoulders lifted as she drew in a breath, and James found himself holding his as he waited for her to respond.

Would she trust him enough to open up? Or had his evasion of her proposal earlier today demoted him in her estimation?

"Arthur kicked me out," she said, her voice flat. "And my mother did nothing to stop him."

A hammer slammed into his chest at her pronouncement.

"His association with me is causing him to lose business. He's afraid he'll lose favor as well—favor with the men in this town who hold the power to advance his political career." Her head turned, and her eyes brushed over his. "An increasingly common concern, I'm discovering."

Her well-aimed arrow jabbed him somewhere between his conscience and his pride. The very idea of her viewing him in a similar light as Clevenger stuck in his craw like a sideways fishbone. Yet he couldn't argue her point. His motives might be more noble than Clevenger's, but the end result was the same.

His motives *were* more noble than those of Clevenger, right? Beneath Noreen's gaze, he was no longer so sure.

James took a small step toward her. "I'm sorry."

She sighed, and some of the starch leaked from her spine. "I'm not homeless. I haven't lived under his roof for nearly a decade."

"But it's not about the roof."

Her attention fell to the ground between them. "No, it's not."

She didn't elaborate, but she didn't need to. She'd already revealed the truth. *"My mother did nothing to stop him."*

James's parents had always supported him, even when they disagreed with his choices. His father had raised him to take over the family ranch in Breckenridge. His mother had tried to pair him off with no fewer than three different local gals, making no secret of her desire to see him married and on his way to producing grandbabies for her to dandle on her knee. When he told them of his plans to work as a lawman, they didn't exactly rejoice. In fact, they spent the next several weeks trying to talk him out of it. But when they saw how serious he was about it and how important it was to him, they accepted his choice and never said a word against his chosen vocation again. Had they turned their backs on him . . . nothing would have cut deeper.

"I don't know why I came here," Noreen said, sharpening his

attention on her. She stared out over the surface of the placid millpond. "I didn't want to interrupt Jane or Martha. Brother Cowan always has guests to the house after services, and Martha rotates eating Sunday dinner with different families of her students." She glanced back at him, but she failed to hold his gaze for more than a heartbeat. "I didn't intend to interrupt you, either. You shouldn't have followed me out here on a fool's errand."

He grinned. "You're not calling me a fool, are you, Miss Noreen? I might have to take offense at that."

One corner of her mouth twitched upward at his teasing, and his entire chest lightened at the sight.

"No, sir. Someone once warned me that offended gentlemen were likely to become obstinate. You're mulish enough already."

He chuckled. "Fair point." Thankful to see some of the sass and spark returning to her eyes, James tipped his head back toward the heart of town. "I've got a skillet full of poorly cooked potatoes and a ham sandwich I'm happy to share if you haven't eaten. Nothing fancy, but it will keep your stomach from rumbling."

She hesitated, so he leaned close and offered the first enticement that came to mind. "I'll let you look at the new wanted posters that came in the mail yesterday."

Even as he dangled the ridiculous bait, it surprised him how much he hoped she'd agree.

A genuine smile blossomed on her face, banishing some of the red from her eyes. "How could I possibly resist the chance to ogle two-dimensional felons?"

A laugh burst from him. The woman sure had an entertaining way of stringing words together. "Well, they do tend to behave themselves better than the three-dimensional variety."

She snickered softly, and James counted it as fine an accomplishment as when he'd captured his first cattle rustler.

"I'm glad to know they won't disrupt our meal."

James held his hand over his heart. "I'll be sure to keep them in line." After dipping his head in what he hoped was a gallant manner, he gestured toward the road behind them. "May I escort you to the Jailhouse Café?"

Noreen nodded, one of her dark curls springing free of its pin to bounce behind her ear as her chin bobbed. "You may."

They walked back to town at a relaxed pace, a nice change from the frenzied scurry that had brought them to the millpond. Neither of them spoke during the return trip, but the silence between them radiated more peace than awkwardness. He rather enjoyed it. Once they made it back to the jailhouse and she saw the state of his potatoes, however, her tongue loosened.

"Oh dear. This is worse than I anticipated." She fingered the skillet handle as if afraid she might be contaminated by the contents.

Heat flared in James's face, but he hid it by turning to the wall to hang up his hat. "You can take the sandwich," he said. "I didn't make it, so it's bound to be edible. I've got an iron stomach after years of eating my own cooking."

"Don't worry. I can fix this."

Without asking permission, she started rummaging through the shelf that held his meager cooking supplies. She also unwrapped his sandwich and started dismantling it. He opened his mouth to stop her from destroying the one edible item in the room, but then he recalled that she worked in the kitchen of the Albany Hotel. Maybe she could salvage something from his mess.

In truth, she did more than salvage. She created a masterpiece. After removing the burnt edges of his potatoes, she added some bacon fat, chopped ham from his sandwich, and fresh onion slices. She stirred and flipped with magical precision until everything was golden-brown and sizzling. She portioned the hash onto a pair of tin plates he'd wiped down for her, then surprised him by grabbing the sandwich bread and laying it flat in the skillet drippings and taking it back to the stove until it formed a delicious crust. He dipped out water for her and poured himself a cup of overly strong coffee, then sat down for a meal that would have warranted a white tablecloth had they been anywhere but the jailhouse.

"This looks amazing." His stomach growled in agreement, earning a delighted laugh from the chef.

"I couldn't let you eat half-cooked potatoes. Not after you've been so kind to me."

James pulled the desk chair over to the worktable for her and held it while she sat. "I'm not sure that chasing you down and infringing on your privacy merits such tasty favor, but I'm not fool enough to turn down a well-cooked meal. Or the pleasure of sharing it with such a lovely companion."

She blinked at him as if he'd taken her aback, but before he could figure out how to get his foot out of his mouth, she gestured for him to sit and folded her hands as if waiting for him to say grace.

He cleared his throat, a jolt of nervousness zipping through him. He didn't usually pray aloud with anyone but family, but he supposed he could manage something simple. Bowing his head, he closed his eyes and spoke from his heart. "Thank you for this food, Lord, and for sending someone with the skill to prepare it properly. We're grateful for your provision, not only to satisfy our physical hunger but our spiritual and personal hungers as well." *Heal Noreen's hurt, Lord. Fill the empty places in her heart with your Bread of Life.* "May we honor you with the lives we live and the choices we make. In your holy Son's name, amen."

"Amen." Noreen's soft echo of his closing settled on his heart like butter soaking into warm bread.

Not wanting to consider the ramifications of that particular observation, he grabbed his fork and tucked into his food. Salty, crunchy goodness filled his senses, and a moan escaped him before he could rein it in. "This is delicious!"

A pleased smile lit her face as she raised her own fork. "Glad you like it."

She didn't say more until he'd cleaned every bite from his plate and leaned backward in his chair to pat his satisfied belly. Man, but the woman could cook. He muffled a contented belch, then reached for his coffee.

"I could cook for you on my nights off, if you like. I don't work

Sundays or Wednesdays." Why was she dipping her head as if she were suddenly feeling shy?

"Miss Noreen, I'd eat your cooking any day of the week."

"Perfect," she said as she reached for his empty plate, her eyes gleaming. "That will give us plenty of time to strategize my new approach to closing the saloon."

And just like that, the savory meal he'd consumed turned to rocks in his gut.

Chapter
7

"Oh, Noreen, I'm so sorry." Jane leaned forward on the chair in her parlor and clasped Noreen's hand, her eyes gleaming with heartache on her friend's behalf after hearing the recounting of Sunday's unfortunate episode.

Noreen had waited to fill her friends in on what had transpired until they met for their weekly Tuesday afternoon tea. Thankfully, the sharp sting of hurt had dimmed to a dull ache after two days. Unexpected flares of anger occasionally burst upon her, but Noreen had been doing her best not to succumb to bitterness. Prayer had been helping, but additional motivation had arisen from a surprising source. A smiling, good-natured deputy who was quick with a laugh and even quicker with a kind word. Somehow in the last few days, his opinion had started to matter to her, and the thought of disappointing him bothered her more than her stepfather's callous treatment.

Martha's teacup clinked as she set it on its saucer. "Has your mother reached out since then?"

Noreen nodded as she squeezed Jane's hand. "She stopped by the hotel kitchen this morning during my breakfast shift to apologize. She didn't stay long and wore a scarf draped over her head as if trying to hide within its folds. It wouldn't surprise me if Arthur has forbidden her from associating with me in any capacity."

"Her poor heart must be breaking," Jane said. "I can't imagine being separated from one's own child."

"That's because you'd never willingly allow such a travesty to happen." Martha set her cup and saucer on the small table in front of her chair and aimed an indignant look at Jane, who perched on the sofa next to Noreen on Martha's right. "Even as mild mannered as you are, you'd fight to your last breath for your child. Any of us would. It's our duty and our God-given privilege to love and protect the children in our care."

Noreen laid a hand on Martha's arm. How her heart swelled in her chest to have the support of two such loyal friends. "I appreciate your outrage on my behalf. I have to admit that I felt quite the same in the moment. The little girl inside me longed for Mama to speak in my defense, to defy her husband and declare that I am welcome in her house whenever I wish to visit. But once the feeling of betrayal faded, I remembered that I wasn't that little girl anymore. Unlike your pupils, Martha, I'm a grown woman. I don't need my mother to fight for me. I can do that myself."

"And you have us." Jane's fierce look reminded Noreen of a kitten imitating a mountain lion. It was utterly adorable and completely genuine at the same time.

"That's right," Martha agreed with a teacher tone that brooked no argument, "and we'll never abandon you."

"Thank you both. I don't know what I'd do without you."

"Lord willing, you'll never have to find out." Martha pushed to her feet and began pacing the room, her face a study in concentration. "I've never been terribly fond of manipulative men who use their power to get their way. But it makes me wonder why your mother capitulated so easily." She paused her pacing and turned a concerned glance Noreen's way. "You don't think he will harm her, do you?"

"Not physically, no. That is one thing my mother will not tolerate. She told him before they married that if he ever laid a hand on either of us she'd leave him. But there is more than one way to assert an unhealthy dominance, especially over a woman who believes it is her Christian duty to bend to her husband's will in everything."

Jane's brow furrowed. "But isn't that true? Ephesians 5:24 says that 'as the church is subject unto Christ, so let the wives be to their own husbands in every thing.'"

"Yes, but have you noticed that sermons preached on that topic fail to go on to the next verses? The ones that stipulate that husbands are to love their wives as Christ loved the church, giving himself up for her. Sacrificing himself for her good. Not subjugating her opinions and will in order to promote his own. Verse twenty-nine states he is to nourish and cherish his wife as the Lord does the church."

Martha chuckled softly. "I see you've given this some thought, Noreen."

She shrugged. "Yes, well, my mother and I have had a few debates on the topic over the years. Especially when she decides to nag me about marrying. I've told her that as soon as I find a man who loves me as Christ loves the church, I'll be subject to him in marriage. Until then, I'll hang on to my freedom."

Jane shifted on the sofa. "Do such men exist? Christ was perfect, and his love is perfect. That seems like an impossible standard to achieve. Not even my papa, a man of the cloth, can claim perfection."

Noreen offered a cheeky grin. "Hence why I'm still single."

"You're terrible." Martha jostled Noreen's shoulder, amusement thickening her voice. "But not exactly wrong."

Noreen joined Martha's laughter, and even Jane smiled, but at the back of Noreen's mind a thought stirred. *Could* there be a man out there who might come to love her in such a nourishing, cherishing way? One who would put her needs above his own as Christ did for the church? She'd never credited the existence of such men, but Deputy Paxton was starting to challenge her assumptions. Oh, he'd never love *her* that way. She annoyed him far too much, and the secrets she harbored would destroy any goodwill she managed to build. Yet the fact that he existed meant that others might as well. A radical paradigm shift for a staunch spinster to consider.

Martha circled around to her chair and reclaimed her seat. "Have you ladies made your decision about joining the society?" Her gaze darted from Noreen to Jane and back again as if she were actually nervous about their answers.

"Of course we're joining. Right, Jane?" Noreen looked to her friend for confirmation.

Jane nodded, though her slow chin bob lacked Noreen's adamancy.

Martha's perfect posture sagged a bit in relief. "Oh, good. I've been on pins and needles since the meeting last Thursday. Hortense and I have such hopes of encouraging a sisterhood among ladies in similar circumstances. In fact, the reason she sought out my partnership was because she recognized the close friendship that exists between the three of us. She claimed we inspired her."

Noreen sat a little straighter. Who would have guessed that someone as respected as Hortense Lockwood would find inspiration in something in which Noreen was involved? What a novel experience.

"I should probably warn you that I promised Luella she could be a junior spinster. When she told me that she'd helped you gather research for the reports on impactful single women in history, I figured it wouldn't hurt to offer a little more comradery. She's so young, but she's in desperate need of a community she can count on. She doesn't get that at home, and she was so excited by the prospect."

"I think that's a great idea," Martha said. "She's such a bright student, but she has trouble making friends her own age. And with no siblings at home, she's a bit adrift. She wouldn't be allowed to attend the meetings, of course, but maybe we can look for other ways to involve her. I might even be able to save her a handkerchief."

Jane reached for the teapot and refilled her cup. "What's this about a handkerchief?"

Martha's eyes danced. "You'll have come to Thursday's meeting to find out."

Noreen sat forward. "You're going to keep us in suspense?"

"Patience is a virtue, Noreen."

"One I don't possess." She sat back with an exaggerated huff, crossing her arms over her chest.

"Consider it a chance to practice," Martha teased. "You might need it the next time you take on Milton Taggert."

Not if her secret weapon came through. And she intended to see that he did. She'd spent all day yesterday planning the perfect menu to present to him tomorrow in order to gain his cooperation. If fried chicken, glazed carrots, yeast rolls, and her famous mashed potatoes didn't put Deputy Paxton in her debt, nothing would.

James peered out the jailhouse door on Wednesday evening and spied a willowy woman marching his direction with purpose and a basket filled with what were sure to be tasty vittles. Instead of purring in anticipation, though, his stomach clenched in dread. Whatever delicious meal she'd prepared, it came with a giant string attached. One that could easily hog-tie his career aspirations if he didn't handle it right.

Noreen must have spotted him, for her face brightened, and she raised a hand in a cheerful wave. Which caused his stomach to flip-flop around like a landed fish on its last breath. Dread. Delight. Discombobulation. He could do without all the acrobatics in his midsection. 'Course that was business as usual when Noreen O'Sullivan was around.

Why'd he have to pick *this* woman to be attracted to? She could ruin him. Yet she could also spice up his plain-potato existence. Just as she'd taken his pitiful taters and turned them into a feast, he got the feeling she could do the same thing with his orderly life. He just wasn't sure if he wanted his simple life complicated to that extent. If she'd even have him. She was married to her reform work and gave no indication she'd entertain a suitor made of flesh and blood.

He pushed to his feet, strode to the doorway, and leaned against the jamb as she approached, hoping he looked nonchalant. He lifted his gaze from her face to scan the surrounding streets, a cowardly part of him hoping to uncover an excuse to avoid her. Not only because he had no idea how to help her cause without damaging his career, but because she looked far too fetching in pink gingham. Where were the no-frills white blouses and dark skirts she usually wore? She hadn't dressed up for him, had she? His heart gave an extra hard thump. Surely not. She wasn't the feminine wiles type. Maybe she was behind on her washing. Yeah, that made sense. He'd donned Sunday duds on a weekday more than once when he'd run out of clean clothes to wear.

"Deputy Paxton." Her smile widened, and a gentle flush painted her cheeks as she drew to a halt in front of him. "I hope you're hungry." She lifted the basket between them, and the unmistakable aroma of fried chicken immediately set his mouth to watering.

He straightened away from the doorjamb and politely tugged on the front brim of his hat. "Miss Noreen." Figuring speaking as little as possible might be his best strategy for this encounter, he stepped aside and motioned with a sweep of his hand for her to enter.

He followed her in, casting his gaze safely past her distracting form to the wanted posters tacked to the notice board on the office wall. Maybe he should find someone to arrest. The lack of privacy might discourage her from trying to rope him into her plans. Or at least provide a somewhat valid excuse for him to escape to the cells upstairs.

After setting her basket down on his worktable, she sauntered over to the jailhouse stove and took down the tin plates they kept for feeding prisoners as if perfectly at home in her surroundings. The woman had cooked one meal at his stove and now moved about as if she belonged there. Worse yet, she made it far too easy for him to imagine her there on a regular basis.

"Would you like coffee with your supper?" She helped herself to the towel hanging from a nail beneath the shelf, folded it over her hand, and took up the coffeepot as she turned to face him, the question reiterated in her eyes.

"Sure." He turned toward his desk and retrieved his cup that still had a few dregs in it from an afternoon spent working on reports documenting the arguments and scuffles he'd intervened in so far this week. He dumped the dregs into the spittoon Sheriff Adair kept in the corner between the back of the door and the edge of his desk, then plopped the cup on the table.

Noreen's smile faltered as she beheld the unwashed cup, but she rallied in a blink and poured coffee into the vessel without further hesitation. She did make a point to wipe out one of the cups from the shelf before she filled it with water from the pail he'd filled at the pump a couple of hours ago.

She remained blessedly nonverbal as she unpacked the supper she'd brought—a feast of crispy chicken, creamy white potatoes, glistening glazed carrots, and yeast rolls as big as his fist.

Man, he was in trouble. The wafting aromas had already started seeping into his brain to erase his reasons for not getting involved with this woman.

"You shouldn't've gone to such trouble, ma'am." She *really* shouldn't have.

"Nonsense. I enjoyed cooking for a particular person instead of faceless hotel patrons. It was a nice ch—"

The explosive crack of gunfire shot a bolt of electricity through James, crystalizing his focus in an instant.

"Stay here!"

Drawing his revolver, he ran out into the street and headed west to the heart of town, praying he'd not find anyone dead.

Chapter 8

What he found was utter chaos. Following his ears and the swelling crowd of onlookers pouring out of homes and businesses, James crossed the courthouse square to Main Street and found his way to the epicenter in front of the Albany Hotel.

"Go back to your homes," James called as he pushed through the crowd, slightly alarmed at the number of men brandishing shotguns and rifles with dinner napkins still tucked into their collars. "If you did not witness the incident, I need you to clear the area." He shouted to be heard above the cacophony, but only a handful paid him any mind. Curiosity proved too strong a draw.

"You heard the man," a commanding voice called out behind him. A commanding *female* voice. "Back inside. You'll learn all the details soon enough. Zeke Carlson! Yes, you. Get those two boys of yours and start herding folks back toward the square."

"Paxton?" The local rancher met James's gaze through the crowd. He wasn't one to take orders from a woman, but the fellow was reliable. A good choice for crowd control. Something Noreen had obviously recognized at once, even in the midst of all the confusion.

James met Carlson's gaze. "I could use the help."

The rancher nodded and immediately took charge. "Brent! Leonard!" He signaled his nearly grown sons by raising a hand above his head and rotating it in a circle. "Time to turn the stampede. Drive 'em back to the square. Deputy's orders."

James winced a bit at the loud dismissal of Noreen's role, but she didn't react to the announcement. Instead, she'd worked her way over to an imposing older woman actively shooing one of the Carlson boys away from her.

"I am not a heifer to be herded, young man."

"No, but you *are* a leader in this community, Miss Lockwood," Noreen countered as she stepped in front of Brent, freeing him to round up other strays. "Your example will be a powerful force for good. The last thing we need is for another weapon to discharge in this crowd. Think of the children. We must minimize their danger. Will you help me? Mothers will listen to you more readily than to me. Please. Deputy Paxton will soon have things in hand. Let us not add to his burden."

Her voice faded as James wended his way through the crowd, but he glanced back into the throng once he pushed his way onto the hotel boardwalk and picked out her face from the dozens swimming through his field of vision. Once he caught her eye, he nodded his thanks. She dipped her chin in return even as she steered Hortense Lockwood back toward the square, a handful of other ladies following in their wake.

He'd told her to stay behind, but for once, he was glad she'd ignored his advice. Noreen possessed steady nerves and an abundance of common sense, two critical assets in a crisis. She'd assessed in a heartbeat what needed to be accomplished and unabashedly delegated assignments to those well-qualified to carry them out. Undaunted by those who might discount her efforts, she waded into the fray anyway, not looking for commendation, only results. Precisely the type of unselfish, level-headedness a man in his line of work appreciated.

What he didn't appreciate was half a dozen people swarming him as he stepped back down into the street, all flappin' their gums and pointin' fingers at someone else in their hurry to justify themselves.

"His dog attacked my chickens . . ."

". . . came out of nowhere . . ."

"Someone's gotta pay for my busted window!"

". . . them flutterin' flappers spooked my . . ."

"That ain't how it happened . . ."

"I could have been killed!"

James holstered his revolver and whistled with earsplitting precision. The people hovering around him backed away a step and fell blessedly silent.

"You will speak one at a time and not until I address you, is that understood?"

The three youngest of the bunch responded to his authoritative demand with humbled nods, but the others went right back to pleading their cases. James slashed his hand through the air like a butcher wielding a cleaver and narrowed his gaze.

"Enough!" The clamor died. "Test me again, and I'll throw you all in the clink, where you will stay until Judge Lynch can sort out this mess." He drilled a look into each person, and while Mr. Gaines, the hotel manager, looked disgruntled and Mr. Freeman glowered back while clutching his blacksmith's hammer, they all managed to hold their tongues.

"Good choice. Now, first order of business. Freeman, has anyone been injured?"

James had examined the street while being harangued upon his arrival and hadn't noticed any obvious casualties. Not of the human variety, anyway. Four or five crates that had once housed chickens had toppled from the back of an overloaded farm wagon and broken open. Hens of all colors and sizes squawked and fluttered about while a pair of boys who likely belonged to the wagon ran around trying to catch them without much success. Boards from the lumber shed lay scattered in the road in front of the carpentry shop across the street as if they'd been dropped in a hurry. Unsettled by the chickens, the wagon's team stomped and snorted, as did a pair of saddle horses hitched at the hotel rail.

The blacksmith met James's gaze and shook his head. "Naw. The fool woman managed to miss anything vital."

"The hotel's front window is *quite* vital," Mr. Gaines muttered.

James chose to ignore him. Instead, he turned his attention to the one female in their midst, a gray-haired woman who stood barely five feet tall. Her weathered skin and chapped hands bespoke a life of hard work, and the shotgun gripped in front of her warned she'd not be one to back down without a fight.

"Ma'am? Did you discharge your weapon within city limits?"

"I did."

"Endangering public safety in such a manner is a jailable offense, ma'am." He extended his palm toward her. "I'm afraid I need to confiscate your weapon."

She held tight to the gun. "Thievery's a crime, too, ain't it? By law, I got the right to protect my family and my belongings. That's all I was doin'."

"Hand me the shotgun, ma'am, then tell me what happened."

Reluctantly, she loosened her grip on the weapon and allowed James to take possession of it. The barrel was still warm. One shell spent, the other waiting in the chamber. James removed the second shell and stuffed it in his coat pocket as the woman started recounting the events that led up to the shooting.

"This fella's dog ran out into the street and startled my team. The horses bolted, and we hit a rut that nearly threw me outta my seat. Bounced my hen crates right outta the wagon and busted them all to pieces. Poor birds were in a panic as it was, then that thievin' hound come back around chasing and snapping, stirring 'em up even worse. I hollered at him to leave them be, but he paid me no mind. Well, I wasn't about to let him eat my chickens. Not with my grandchildren lookin' on. So I grabbed my shotgun and aimed for the sky, hopin' the boom of the gun would scare the varmint away."

James waited for her to continue her tale, but she offered no further explanations. Just stood stiff and defiant before him, much like another woman he knew.

"How exactly did a shot aimed for the sky end up going through the hotel window?" No one's marksmanship was *that* poor.

The woman stubbornly refused to answer, so James turned to one of the young men he recognized from the M. T. Jones Lumber Company. "Reed, you see what happened?"

"Yessir." The fellow nodded, his eyes wide as if afraid James might find a reason to haul him off to jail if he didn't cooperate. "One of them scared chickens landed on her head right as she was fixin' to pull the trigger. The dog givin' chase rammed into the lady's backside at the same time. Me and Jonesy were laughin' about it till her gun exploded, and the hotel window shattered. That's when we dropped our load and ran over to see if anyone had been hurt."

James had to fight to keep his own lips from twitching as he pictured the events unfolding. Working to keep his stern lawman façade in place, he turned to the hotel manager. "Gaines, any damage besides the window?"

"Eight terrified guests who were in the lobby at the time." He gave a disdainful sniff in the grandmother's direction.

"Were any of them injured by buckshot or flying glass?"

The man sniffed again, then shook his head. "No. Thankfully, most of them had been preparing to enter the dining room and were not near the window when the shot was fired. I shudder to think what might have happened if anyone had been seated on the settee directly behind the glass. She could have killed someone with her carelessness!"

"If that dog hadn't knocked into me, your precious window would still be in one piece!"

"My dog was just doin' what dogs do. It was your fault for shootin' when you had no business." John Meyers, who had been obediently silent up until that point, jumped in to defend his hound, who was squirming in the boy's arms, no doubt wanting his freedom restored so he could engage in another round of chase-the-chicken.

James cleared his throat with meaningful force, not about to let this group get out of hand again. Guilty looks accompanied closed mouths. "All right. Here's what we're gonna do. Reed, grab Jonesy and help the youngsters round up the chickens. If the crates that are busted can be fixed temporarily with a nail or two, see to it. The sooner we get those chickens contained, the sooner things will settle down around here."

"Yessir." Reed bounded away like a schoolboy who'd just been let out for recess.

"Meyers, find a length of rope for your dog and keep him tied up until the chickens are penned."

"I got something at the smithy that'll work," Freeman volunteered.

James nodded. "Perfect." He pointed a look at Meyers. "Stay close to the smithy for a while. I'll need to get an official statement from you before I let you go. You too, Freeman."

Both men murmured their agreement.

"Gaines, get that glass cleaned up and board your window. I'll check back with you tomorrow to get an estimate on the damages."

Once the men departed to take care of their assigned tasks, James turned back to the tiny, gray-haired woman in front of him. Her posture sagged, and her already petite size seemed to shrink even further. Gentling his voice, James leaned her empty shotgun against a nearby hitching post and pulled out a notebook and pencil from his pocket. "What's your name, ma'am?"

"Edna Hanover."

James made a note. "You kin to Elijah Hanover?"

She hugged her arms around her middle. "He's my son. Them two boys are his nephews." She nodded her head in the direction of the two youngsters herding hens. "Their ma and pa passed last month. Influenza. Elijah is takin' us in."

"I'm sorry for your loss, ma'am." Losing a child, a home. Was it any wonder she was determined to lose nothing more, even a bunch of silly chickens? "I'll escort you out to your son's place myself after I finish up here." If it was up to him, he'd let her go with a warning, but the law had to be administered equally. If a liquored-up cowboy had fired his weapon in town, he'd be facing a hefty fine or three days in jail. James couldn't ignore the crime just because he felt sorry for the perpetrator. "I'm afraid I will have to arrest you after we see to your grandsons, though. Elijah can come back to town with us and pay the twenty-dollar fine. You'll be free to go until Judge Lynch calls your case. He'll render a decision about the damages owed to the hotel. You can be home tonight before nightfall."

Mrs. Hanover shook her head. "Elijah can't afford to throw away twenty dollars. He's already taking on three new mouths to feed when he can barely feed the five he's got. I'll take the jail time, Deputy. How many days should I expect?"

"Three, but surely that won't be necessary." Great galoshes. He did *not* want to be the man who locked up somebody's grandmother in the same cells that held cattle thieves and outlaws. What would Sheriff Adair think when he got wind of it? "Why don't we wait and talk to Elijah? I'm sure we can work something out."

"This is my problem to deal with, and *I'll* decide what action needs to be taken." Her eyes narrowed, and James found himself reaching for the shotgun he'd set down a moment ago just in case she took it into her head to beat some sense into him. "I know my own mind, and neither you nor my son will talk me out of it." She pushed past him. "Now step aside and let me have a word with my grandsons before you drag me away in irons."

James bit back a moan as he moved out of her way. Drag her away in irons? He prayed that turn of phrase didn't show up in the *Albany News*. He might not have to worry about Noreen O'Sullivan ruining his chances to be elected sheriff, after all. Apparently, he was perfectly capable of blackening public opinion of his fitness for office all on his lonesome.

Chapter 9

By the time Deputy Paxton returned to the courthouse square, most of the crowd had dispersed. John Meyers had come through fifteen minutes ago with tales of a trigger-happy grandma who'd nearly shot his dog. There'd been chickens and a broken window involved somehow, and the boy seemed particularly put out by the fact that the deputy had made him leash his dog. A few of his neighbors cheered to see the energetic pup curtailed, spouting woes of dug-up gardens, spooked horses, and chewed shoes credited to the hound's penchant for mischief.

With their curiosity assuaged, people returned to their homes and their interrupted dinners, eager to discuss the evening's events. Noreen felt a similar craving for food and conversation, especially since her dinner companion would have the best details to share. However, when he finally put in an appearance, he wasn't alone. A stone-faced woman in a faded red calico dress strode by his side, a travel bag in her hand. She lifted her chin high, even if it barely reached the deputy's shoulder, but it was the glistening film in her eyes that grabbed Noreen's sympathy. How many times had she worn the same expression? Displaying a brick wall to a world that stood against her even as her heart crumbled like old mortar within her breast.

As the pair drew near, Deputy Paxton veered toward Noreen, his blue eyes void of their usual sparkle. "Would you be willing to assist me with a delicate matter back at the jailhouse?" The intimacy of his lowered voice caused her stomach to flit, but his need of her assistance clenched her cooperation in a heartbeat.

"Of course."

Noreen fell into step beside him, holding back the flood of questions that begged for release. No one spoke again until they reached the jail. The deputy ushered the older woman into the office and offered her his chair, then unlocked the gun case on the far wall and set the shotgun he'd been carrying inside. After locking the case, he took off his hat, ran his hand over his sand-colored hair, and exhaled a heavy breath.

"Noreen O'Sullivan, meet Edna Hanover. Mrs. Hanover is going to be staying here for the next few days."

He'd arrested her? Didn't infractions like this usually carry a fine instead of jail time? No one had been hurt, after all. Noreen would have been affronted on the woman's behalf had the deputy not looked so utterly miserable about the situation.

Noreen offered an uncertain smile. "Mrs. Hanover."

The woman speared her with a sharp gaze. "You his wife?"

Noreen's lungs seized for a moment, causing a series of coughs to erupt before she managed to recover enough to speak. "No, ma'am. I'm, uh . . ." His friend? Associate? Thorn in his side? "His cook."

The deputy's brows rose at her response, and the start of a smile quirked one corner of his mouth. The man was laughing at her! Warmth heated Noreen's cheeks, but the ire she expected to flare fizzled. She liked seeing a spark of his good humor returned. Liked even more the fact that she'd aided its appearance. A rather unexpected development.

"And a fine cook she is, too." He winked at Noreen, setting off an alarming quantity of quivers through her abdomen. "Fried chicken's on the menu this evening. Why don't the two of you help yourselves while I fix up some proper accommodations. I'll grab something from the café later."

No, he would not. He'd be eating the meal she'd fixed him, and that was that. She and Edna could get by on smaller portions. Noreen had made enough for him to have seconds, anyway, so it should stretch for three people easily enough. She'd not argue with him, though. He had enough on his mind at the moment. Like how to make a barren jail cell fit for a female occupant.

Noreen gestured for Edna to take a seat at the worktable and started dishing up modest-sized portions of the chicken and fixings onto one of the tin plates. Glancing over the lady's head, she caught Deputy Paxton's eye. He tipped his head to the side in silent request for her to join him. She placed the filled plate in front of Edna, smiled encouragement to the older woman, then excused herself to meet the deputy over by his desk.

He placed a hand on her elbow and tugged her close, bending his face near hers to murmur in her ear. The intimacy of the position had her heart beating out an irregular tattoo, but she willed her mind to concentrate on his words instead of his touch.

"Would you check her bag for me?" As he spoke, Noreen's gaze fell to the floor next to Edna's chair, where a battered leather travel bag sat. "I can't let her take it into the cell without checking it for weapons, but I don't want to embarrass her by digging through her unmentionables."

A strange sensation permeated Noreen's chest. Warm and pleasant and completely foreign, at least when it came to her interactions with men. He *trusted* her. Believed her capable. Wanted her assistance. She'd not let him down.

"Of course. Is there anything else I can assist with?"

His hand fell away from her elbow, and she immediately missed his touch. She had to fight the absurd urge to lean closer to him to replace what had been lost.

"Mrs. Hanover came with me of her own volition, so I doubt she'll be making a run for it, but if you would keep an eye on her while I try to rig up some kind of privacy screen in her cell, I'd appreciate it."

"Does this mean you're deputizing me, Deputy?" Noreen teased, hoping to lighten his mood a little more.

A full-blown grin stretched his cheeks and brightened his eyes. Not even a commendation from Frances Willard could have left Noreen more gratified at that moment.

"I suppose I am. Temporarily," he amended, his mouth straightening into a nearly serious expression that failed to knock the amusement from his gaze. "Don't think you can go around arresting folks all willy-nilly after this."

"Oh, there will be nothing willy nor nilly about it," she said with a saucy smirk. "I'll set up shop directly outside the Salt Fork Saloon and apprehend any visibly inebriated men who emerge on a charge of public drunkenness. I'm sure they will all respect my newly gained authority and comply without complaint." She laced her tone with enough sarcasm to keep Deputy Paxton from taking her seriously. "Although, I suppose it would be unkind to burden dear Edna with foul-smelling, ill-mannered company, so maybe I'll forgo that plan for the time being."

"Wise choice." The warm humor in his gaze combined with his nearness made her heart palpitate with alarming, yet not unpleasant, rapidity.

Their gazes remained connected for a suspended moment, then released when James dipped his chin and moved away to see to his duty.

Noreen watched him round the corner and disappear into the stairwell that separated his personal quarters from the main office. His footfalls echoed softly as he climbed the stairs to the prisoner accommodations. Certain he was out of earshot, she returned her attention to the dangerous felon nibbling on a chicken leg at the deputy's table. Noreen dipped out a tin cup of water and placed it near Edna's plate.

"Is it all right if I go through your bag? It must be checked before it can be allowed in your . . . room." *Cell* was far too depressing.

"Deputy Paxton thought you might prefer that a woman go through your belongings."

"Suit yourself. Nothing in there but a change of clothes and a few personal items."

Edna continued picking at her food as Noreen retrieved the travel bag from the floor and swiveled to place it on the sheriff's desk. Taking care not to rumple anything more than necessary, she felt around each corner and layer, pulling out anything she couldn't immediately identify. A nightdress, some underclothes, a spare skirt and blouse, brush, hairpins, and a couple of handkerchiefs filled most of the space. A Bible lay at the bottom of the bag along with a framed photograph of a man, a woman, and two boys standing in front of a farmhouse. Nothing that could be considered a weapon.

After packing everything away where she'd found it, Noreen joined Edna at the table, taking the seat across from her. She spooned tiny portions onto her plate to ensure plenty remained for the man scraping furniture around above their heads.

Noreen closed her eyes to offer a brief blessing over her food, then picked up a fork and smiled at the woman drawing lines through her mashed potatoes instead of eating them.

"I can warm those up for you if they're too cold." Noreen tried a bite herself and scrunched her nose. Not exactly the way she'd intended to serve them. They'd cooled to room temperature after sitting out for the last half hour.

"The taters are fine," Edna ceased drawing with the tines of her fork and stabbed them into a carrot instead. However, she made no effort to lift it to her mouth. "Guess I ain't hungry. Too much regret swimming around in my belly."

Not sure how to reply, Noreen tore off a bit of a roll and popped it into her mouth.

Edna released her hold on the fork and leaned back in her chair with a heavy sigh. "I never shoulda taken that shotgun in hand. Shoulda left it under the wagon seat where it belonged. All I did was add to the burden my family's already carrying. Had to leave my grandsons in the care of strangers while they wait on the deputy to drive 'em to my son's place. Shameful is what it is. And Elijah? He's bound to do something foolish like try to scrape together funds he don't have to pay my fine. Well, I won't have it." She banged the flat of her hand against the table with enough force to set the plates to rattling. "You hear me, Deputy?" she shouted through the ceiling. "You make it clear to my son that paying the fine ain't an option. He's not even to come see me until my release on Saturday."

"Yes, ma'am" came the call from the stairwell.

Noreen set her roll back on her plate and reached for her water. "Do you think your son will honor your wishes?" Heaven knew none of the men in Noreen's life would do so. Not if they disagreed with her choice of action.

A mindful nudge brought a certain deputy to mind. Perhaps not *all* the men in her life would disregard her wishes. That is, if one considered James Paxton to be *in* her life. What, precisely, were the qualifications for being in a person's life? Quantity of time spent in each other's company? Level of familiarity? Frequency of personal encounters? James's involvement had certainly been increasing in each of those areas of late.

"Elijah won't like it," Edna muttered, harnessing Noreen's wandering attention, "but he'll go along."

"You're blessed to have a son who respects you."

A hint of a smile briefly softened Edna's face. "That I am. His father saw to that, God rest his soul. And not just because he took the boys to task whenever he caught them sassin' me. It was the example he set. Treating me like an equal. Givin' me space to be who I wanted to be, supporting my decisions, and never sayin' a word against me in their hearing." Tears suddenly welled in her eyes. "When I think of how disappointed Randal would be to see how I handled things today . . . it cuts me to the quick."

Noreen set aside her cup and covered Edna's hand with her own. "It seems to me that a man like you describe would be quick to forgive a mistake made with good intentions."

It was the mistakes made with bad intentions that were unforgiveable. But Noreen pushed thoughts of her past aside and did her best to offer Mrs. Hanover encouragement through a squeeze of her hand.

"You're right. Randal wasn't one to cast blame." She sat a little straighter. "Your deputy reminds me a little of him."

Her deputy? James wasn't her anything. Yet that didn't stop a little thrill from vibrating through her at Edna's assumption. And what was she doing thinking of him as *James*? It wasn't as if he were an intimate friend. Though their recent interactions had taken a rather personal turn.

"Sensible. Kind. Able to take charge in a way that demands respect."

Noreen couldn't argue with Edna's assessment. James was all those things. Not to mention dutiful, honorable, and quite handy to have around when a woman got into trouble over her head.

"All right, Mrs. Hanover, we can get you moved in now." James rounded the corner, brushing some dust off his trousers as he came. "You can bring your food with you."

Edna rose to her feet as he moved past, leaving her plate and fork behind but taking one of the yeast rolls with her. She collected her satchel, then strode toward the stairs with dignity and aplomb. Noreen followed, her curiosity piqued. She'd never seen where the prisoners were kept.

When she reached the top of the stairs, she glanced to her left and found a collection of cramped cells, barely large enough for a man to take more than a step or two. In contrast, on the right side of the stairwell sat a large cell that extended the entire length of the building and included a chair, small table, and likely a cot, though she couldn't see past the blanket that the deputy had tied to the top of the bars closest to the stairs to confirm. This must be where they kept long-term prisoners. Or women who'd managed to get themselves arrested.

"I'll announce myself whenever I come upstairs," James explained to Edna. "But I'll need you to step into the open area where I can see you before I deliver any food or other amenities."

"I understand." Edna stepped across the cell's threshold as if it

75

were a hotel room with unfortunate steel rod décor. "Thank you, Deputy." She plopped her bag atop the table, then pivoted to face him. "Please see to my grandchildren now, if you would. I'll be fine."

"I'll stay with her until you return," Noreen volunteered.

James looked at her in surprise. "You don't need to do that. I can get one of Zeke's boys to watch things." He eased the barred door closed, then turned the key in the lock. A chilling click echoed off the ceiling. A shiver skittered down Noreen's spine.

James ushered her back to the downstairs office and placed the keys in the top drawer of the sheriff's desk.

"I don't mind. I have been deputized, after all."

He smiled but still hesitated to agree.

"Please, James. Let me help."

It wasn't until his eyebrows arched that she realized she'd used his given name. She raised her chin. So what if she had? He'd called her Noreen on more than one occasion. Only fair that she be given leave to address him in the same fashion.

"It might be rather late when I get back."

"Just stop by Parson Cowan's house on your way out of town and give Jane a message for me." Mind spinning, Noreen hurried to the desk and found a sheet of paper in one of the drawers. She scribbled a few instructions, folded the page, and handed it to the deputy. "No one will give a second thought to the parson's daughter and her friend doing some charity work."

She might have oversold things just a bit, but where was the harm? Mrs. Hanover needed a friend tonight, and Noreen needed a distraction from her deteriorating relationship with her mother. What possible trouble could two spinsters and a grandmother get into?

"You have nothing to worry about," she said with a broad smile as James tucked her note into his pocket. "Everything will be fine."

Chapter
10

Everything was most assuredly *not* fine. Feminine chatter echoed through the jailhouse, bringing a frown to the face of James's companion.

"I thought you only locked up one woman, Paxton." Sheriff Adair brushed past James and pounded up the stairs to see for himself. James dogged his heels, trying to think of an adequate explanation for what they would find, but since he wasn't precisely sure what that would be, he had little to offer.

The sheriff reached the top of the stairs, then turned to glare down at James. "Why's the parson's daughter behind bars? She don't exactly strike me as the criminal type."

Noreen jumped out of the chair she'd positioned outside Mrs. Hanover's cell and spun to face them.

"Sheriff Adair. You're back."

"Observant of you to notice." Adair used a thumb to push the brim of his hat higher on his forehead as he strode forward and took in the scene. "Was riding in to see my family before heading out to Fort Griffin to track down a lead on the rustlers I'm chasin' when I ran into Paxton coming back from the Hanover place. He told me about the shooting. Didn't tell me we'd turned the jail into a henhouse."

The sheriff shot an irritated glance over his shoulder, and James mentally winced. His ignorance of the goings on in his own building didn't exactly portray him in the best light. As he struggled to formulate a response that didn't make him sound completely thick-headed, Noreen addressed Adair. A frightening prospect, since one never knew what might come out of her mouth when addressing a male authority.

"Now, Sheriff, you should be commending Deputy Paxton, not taking him to task. He's handled a delicate situation with great diplomacy. Not only did he provide privacy for Mrs. Hanover in an otherwise inhospitable space, but he personally delivered her grandchildren into the care of their uncle. He also arranged for Miss Cowan and me to keep Mrs. Hanover company until he returned, knowing, as he did, how worried she would be for the welfare of her charges until he reported back."

Actually, he hadn't really given that much thought, but now that he considered the notion and saw Edna's questioning gaze raking his face for an answer to that very question, he recognized the truth of the situation.

He dipped his chin toward the woman seated near the table with a pile of mending in her lap—mending that hadn't been there before he'd left. "Tom and Lionel are safely delivered, ma'am, as is your wagon and all your chickens. I explained the situation to Elijah, and he said he'd see you bright and early Saturday morning."

Mrs. Hanover nodded. "Thank you, Deputy."

"My pleasure, ma'am."

Well, his argument with Elijah hadn't been too pleasurable, what with the man yelling at him for putting his mama behind bars for breaking a bit of glass. She wasn't a criminal, for pity's sake. It had been an accident. James didn't blame the man for being upset. He'd be fighting mad, too, if the situation had been reversed and his mama was the one behind bars. Still, he hated being made to feel like a villain when he was enforcing the law.

"Ain't you that temperance woman who's always stirrin' up trouble at the saloon?" Sheriff Adair scratched at his beard as he narrowed his eyes at Noreen.

Her smile flattened, and a spark of ire lit her gaze, sending warning bells gonging in James's head.

"Observant of you to notice." Noreen shot back the sheriff's earlier words in blatant challenge.

He stiffened. "You hankerin' for a cell of your own, young lady?"

"You would imprison me unjustly?"

Gads! This was going downhill fast. "Noreen," he murmured from behind her, "I don't think—"

A book slammed, drawing everyone's attention. Jane Cowan rose from her chair inside the cell—a chair that looked suspiciously like the ones in his office. She offered a tremulous smile as she clutched a copy of *Little Women* to her chest and took a single step toward the door. The *locked* door, he was happy to note. Wouldn't do for his prisoner to be dawdling about in an unsecured cell.

"Sheriff Adair," she said, "you must be tired after your long ride. Let me cut you a slice of my mama's peach pie. I know it's one of your favorites."

Jane smiled shyly as she tucked her book under her arm and reached for the half-empty pie tin sitting on the table next to Mrs. Hanover. Holding the pie in front of her to give Sheriff Adair an unimpeded view, she approached the bars.

"Mama sent it with me when she heard about Mrs. Hanover's incarceration. It is our Christian duty to minister to those in prison, yet it's not proper for a woman to tend to a male prisoner's needs. So when Mama learned of a female in the jailhouse, she encouraged me to come and support Miss O'Sullivan's ministry to the less fortunate."

Noreen pressed close to James's side and slid something into his hand. The key to the cell. He took the hint and moved forward to unlock the door and let Miss Cowan out.

"Jesus himself said that when we feed the hungry and visit those in prison, we are ministering unto him." Jane stepped out of the cell, and Noreen moved forward to take the book from under her friend's arm. The table knife balancing on the edge of the pie tin rattled louder the closer she came to the sheriff. "I'm sure you don't mean to oppose such a charitable endeavor." She held the pie out toward him, strategically positioning it just below his nose. "Do you?"

Sheriff Adair frowned at Miss Cowan, but his gaze soon shifted to the pie, and his jaw clenched. The sheriff did love his pie, and the parson's wife had won a blue ribbon at the Albany Independence Day picnic for her peach pie last year. If James recalled correctly, Sheriff Adair had served as one of the judges, making this particular dessert the perfect weapon to wield in an attempt to win the sheriff's favor. Apparently, the unassuming Miss Cowan possessed a rather cunning mind.

Adair huffed as his fingers closed over the edge of the pie tin. "I guess if your mama sent you, I won't object, but don't be making a regular practice of lingering." The sheriff grabbed the knife and sliced off a large wedge of peachy goodness, then lifted it straight from the tin, not waiting for a plate. "Prison ain't meant to be a social shindig, you know. It's meant to be miserable, so a man will reconsider his life choices." He chomped off a bite from the end of the slice. Ecstasy flashed across his features before quickly retreating behind his usual stony façade. His gaze darted toward Mrs. Hanover. "Or a woman," he said around his mouthful of pie.

"Mrs. Hanover has already expressed remorse," Noreen informed them, the sass noticeably absent from her voice thanks to the calming effect of her friend's earlier interruption. "Perhaps in light of this you would see fit to shorten her detainment period?"

"That so?" The sheriff raised his handful of pie again but stopped it just short of his mouth. He glanced into the cell. "You sorry for shooting a gun off in my town, Miz Hanover?"

The widow rose from her chair, setting aside the mending items she'd been sewing. "I am."

Adair nodded. "Good. Be sure to tell that to the judge when he weighs in on damages. In the meantime, get used to your new home, 'cause if you ain't got the funds to pay the fine, you'll be staying here for the full three days." His head swiveled, and his gaze targeted James with pinpoint accuracy. "Ain't that right, Deputy?"

"Yes, sir." He knew his duty. The law was the law, and he was paid to uphold it. Even if this felt like one of those go-and-sin-no-more moments, he didn't have the authority to extend mercy. Only the judge could do that. James prayed he would.

"Good." Sheriff Adair tipped his head toward the extra chairs cluttering the area. "Now, ladies, I want you to close down this here quiltin' bee or whatever you've got goin' on and head home. It ain't fittin' for you to be here after dark, and sundown's headin' this way mighty quick."

Noreen turned a pleading look on James, but he made no argument. His silence led to a narrowing of her eyes and a tightening of her mouth that sizzled a warning through him much like the electricity that collected in the air right before jagged lightning bolts shot from the sky. What did she expect him to do? He couldn't gainsay the sheriff. Not if he wanted to keep his job.

Just go along, he tried to communicate with his gaze. Not every battle needed to be fought on the front lines. Some were better waged with diplomacy and patience.

Thankfully, she held her tongue, but she punctuated her verbal silence with the scrape of chair legs against the floor and the clang of dishes being packed with little care. If looks were bullets, his hide would be sporting several new holes.

In contrast, her friend moved about the cell like a shadow trying to escape notice as she collected the mending items from Mrs. Hanover and placed them in a flour sack. James did what he could to assist, toting the extra chair downstairs after handing off the key to the sheriff.

Once everyone was back in the office, Sheriff Adair licked a bit of peach filling from his hand, then dusted his palms together to dislodge any clinging crumbs. "Thank your mama for the pie. It hit the spot."

Jane ducked her head as she scuttled past. "I will." She stopped suddenly, as if she'd just remembered something, then swiveled to set the pie tin on the table she'd just hurried past. "I'll leave the rest of the pie here so Deputy Paxton can have a piece as well."

A grumbly female voice murmured something about him not deserving pie, but James chose to ignore it.

"That's very kind of you, Miss Cowan." He dipped his head in her direction. "Thank you."

She nodded. "Mama and I can retrieve the baking dish tomorrow when we pay a call on Mrs. Hanover." She glanced back at the sheriff. "If that's all right with you."

Adair waved his hand in front of his face as if he were shooing a fly. "As long as it's a *brief* visit and the two of you don't pitch tents in here, I ain't got no objection."

An audible huff echoed near the doorway.

"Thank you, Sheriff." Miss Cowan turned to leave, then paused and took a step closer to James. Leaning in, she whispered, "Noreen fixed a supper plate for you and placed it in the warmer above the stove. She wanted to make sure you had a chance to eat after your trip to the Hanover farm."

She'd saved back food for him? James shot a glance toward the door, where Noreen stood, arms crossed, toe tapping. She met his gaze long enough for him to tug on his hat brim in thanks, then jerked her head in the opposite direction and stepped out into the street. Ornery woman. Yet thoughtful too.

And expressive. A smile tugged one corner of his mouth upward. A man didn't have to guess what she was feeling. She made it quite plain. Wasn't always fun, but it was honest. A fella could figure out right quick where he stood. And where James stood at the moment was squarely in the doghouse.

"Can you believe the nerve of that man?" Noreen tramped down the street as if she were personally in charge of flattening the ground. "Kicking us out as if we were vermin underfoot. He had no right."

"Actually, he did. He *is* the sheriff. The jailhouse is his jurisdiction."

Noreen shot a glare at her friend. "Must you always be so . . . amenable? For goodness' sake, Jane. Doesn't it make you angry that poor Edna is there all alone?"

"She's not alone. I slipped her my copy of *Little Women.*" Jane smiled, as if having a book was all a person needed to be content. Perhaps for Jane that was true, but Edna didn't particularly strike Noreen as a big reader. "And Deputy Paxton is there," Jane continued. "He'll look out for her."

Argh. Deputy Paxton! The traitor. Making her feel needed and appreciated one minute, then standing back and doing nothing to stop her being evicted in the next. "I doubt we can count on him. His principles seem to crumble the moment someone with more authority enters the picture."

Jane took hold of Noreen's arm and tugged her to a halt. "That's not a fair assessment."

"No?" Noreen flung an arm out in the direction of the jailhouse. "He didn't say a single word in our defense when Sheriff Adair ordered us out. Just stood back and let it happen. Even helped us on our way."

She'd looked to him for help. Practically begged him with her eyes. And what had he done? Nothing. She never should have expected more from him. But she had. Her mistake. One she'd not be making again.

"What good would have come from him speaking up?" Jane had the nerve to ask. "You and I both know Sheriff Adair isn't the type to change his mind once he makes a decision. If anything, when challenged, he just digs his heels in deeper. Mr. Paxton would know that. Had he argued for us to stay, he would have risked damaging his relationship with his employer, and for what? To make us feel better? We were planning on leaving after he returned anyway. The only difference was that we didn't leave on our own terms."

Noreen sighed, and her chest deflated as her friend's words defused some of her indignation.

Jane reached for her hand and gave it a sisterly squeeze. "Perhaps this ejection hurt more than it should because it followed so closely on the heels of what happened with your stepfather."

"I . . ." Noreen peered into Jane's gentle eyes and saw a truth she probably never would have seen on her own. "I hadn't considered that."

Perhaps James wasn't the complete villain she was making him out to be. Perhaps her lingering hurt over her mother's silence had colored her perceptions. Time would tell, she supposed.

Linking her arm through Jane's, she started the two of them walking again, this time at a more sedate pace. "How did you get to be so wise?"

Jane grinned up at her. "By reading books, of course."

Noreen chuckled. "Of course."

If only there were a book on how to earn a man's esteem and gain his willing assistance without endangering one's heart in the process. Such a manual would prove exceedingly instructive.

Chapter
11

"All right, ladies. Let's come to order." Hortense Lockwood clapped her hands to capture the attention of the women who had gathered in the schoolhouse on Thursday evening for the first official meeting of the Shackelford County Secret Society of Spinsters.

Noreen frowned at the heading on the charter she'd been handed at the door. There were far too many *S's* being employed in their group's name. It made her think of hissing snakes. Jane had been delighted with the alliteration, but Noreen would have preferred some rearranging. Perhaps Secret Albany Spinster Society. Then they could be known as SASS. A much more feisty and determined acronym. SCSSS sounded like someone had just let the air out of a pneumatic bicycle tire.

"I'm gratified to see that so many chose to accept the invitation to join our society," Miss Lockwood said after the room quieted.

Noreen counted fourteen ladies in attendance, in addition to Miss Lockwood and Martha at the front of the room. Sixteen secret spinsters. She fought against the urge to roll her eyes. These *S's* were really getting out of hand.

"Miss Evans and I have drafted a charter for our organization. Each of you should have a copy." Miss Lockwood held up a sample sheet.

Noreen dipped her chin to examine the charter. It had been written out by hand instead of produced by the local printer. A necessary precaution for a secretive organization. The handwriting didn't look like Martha's, however, and it differed from the more flourished style used on the original invitations. Perhaps Martha had enlisted Luella's assistance. If so, the girl had done an excellent job of keeping the details to herself. She'd not said a word at work this week. Though even if she had, there was no guarantee Noreen would have remembered. She'd been rather distracted by family issues and her schemes to win Deputy Paxton's cooperation. Schemes that had come to naught, thanks to the untimely chicken crisis.

". . . few basic tenets." Miss Lockwood's voice pulled Noreen from her thoughts. "Membership shall be open to any unmarried woman aged twenty-four or older living in Shackelford County."

Noreen smiled to herself as she recalled Luella's despair over the minimum age requirement.

"Members shall be women of good character who will support their society sisters and serve the larger community. Should a member harm one of her society sisters with slander or malice, her membership will be revoked. Should a member act in such a way as to bring disgrace upon herself, and by association, her society sisters, her membership will be revoked. Should a member choose to marry, her membership will be retired in good standing."

Noreen leaned close to Jane and whispered in her ear, "What? No tar and feathers? We can't let the traitors off that easy."

Jane smiled, her eyes lighting with amusement even as she gave Noreen's shoulder a gentle nudge to discourage any further discourse. Always the parson's daughter on her best behavior. It would be annoying if she weren't such a sweetheart.

"The society will select one project each month as our service to the community. We encourage all members to engage at some level with each project, but the requirement is to participate in at least four per year to maintain active membership status."

Noreen's heart rate picked up speed. This was why she'd joined. To harness the power of numbers in her quest to rid the town of its saloon. Energy thrummed through her limbs as she readied herself to nominate her project. The fingers on her right hand tingled, eager to shoot into the air as soon as Miss Lockwood opened the floor. But their founding mother seemed more interested in spending time on boring details like meeting dates and introductions. Having sixteen people stand and talk about themselves took *forever*.

Noreen tried to hurry things along by making her own introduction as short as possible. "Noreen O'Sullivan, age twenty-seven. I live at Mrs. Barker's boardinghouse and am employed at the Albany Hotel." She started to sit, then remembered one other pertinent piece of information. "I'm also a member of the Woman's Christian Temperance Union."

Jane kept her introduction brief as well. Or tried to. She spoke softly, leading an older member sitting near the front of the classroom to interrupt and request that Jane speak up. Face aflame, Jane apologized and began again, her voice louder, but trembling this time. She offered only her name, age, and relationship to her parents before ducking back into her seat.

Noreen immediately reached over and clasped her friend's hand, hoping to lend her strength in the same way Jane had lent her own to Noreen last night when Sheriff Adair had shown up unexpectedly. Had Jane not been there to smooth things over with the obstinate lawman, Noreen might have found herself keeping Mrs. Hanover company behind bars.

When the interminable introductions finally concluded, Noreen once again readied her arm for flagpole duty. She intended to be the first to nominate a project idea. The sooner she could rally her new troops, the better. Her hopes lifted when Miss Lockwood yielded the podium to Martha, then shriveled when her friend opened a small wooden box and announced she had a gift for everyone.

Patience, Noreen. You'll get your chance.

Despite the internal reminder, Noreen still fidgeted in her seat and struggled to focus on what was being said. Until Martha mentioned her by name. Like a naughty child caught in the act of misbehaving, Noreen immediately straightened her posture and focused all her attention on the speaker.

"My good friend Noreen O'Sullivan sparked the idea." Martha caught Noreen's gaze and smiled. "Some of you might have noticed the white ribbon she wears pinned to her bodice."

Noreen lifted a hand to touch the bow.

"Most people in town likely have no idea what that ribbon symbolizes. However, should a member of the Woman's Christian Temperance Union see it, she would immediately recognize the significance. Not only that, but a bond of sisterhood would spring up between the two of them even if they were strangers to each other. That ribbon is a symbol of shared values and of belonging. Miss Lockwood and I wish to give the members of our society the same blessing."

Martha reached inside the box and pulled out a white linen square edged with a thin border of white lace. Noreen leaned forward. Aha! The mysterious handkerchiefs that Martha had alluded to a couple of days ago.

"Each member will receive a handkerchief that has been embroidered with forget-me-nots." She folded the handkerchief into a triangle to show where a cluster of blue flowers had been stitched on one corner. "When you receive your handkerchief today, we encourage you to embroider your initials near the flowers and to make a habit of carrying this hankie with you in a pocket or purse. We chose forget-me-nots because we wanted an emblem signifying that you are not forgotten. Not overlooked. Not unappreciated. Each of us was created for a specific purpose, one not tied to marriage and the production of children. Our Lord has not forgotten us, and we will not forget each other. We will use the talents we have been given to serve a calling higher than ourselves and to minister to one another. Therefore, if any of you is ever in need of assistance, you have only to send your handkerchief to another member, and your society sisters will come to your aid."

Noreen's eyes misted slightly as the significance of the handkerchief soaked into her heart, dissolving her impatience as an agenda greater than her own flowed through her. An agenda of sisterhood. She looked around the room with new eyes as Martha handed each lady a handkerchief. No one hurriedly stuffed the linen into her pocket. Each lady examined the handkerchief with care, tracing the embroidered flowers with a fingertip or smoothing out the entire square upon her lap. A thread seemed to weave throughout the room, stretching from handkerchief to handkerchief and bonding each spinster to the others as the gifts were distributed.

Martha smiled at Noreen and Jane as she reached the back of the room and handed each of them a handkerchief. Noreen accepted hers with near reverence. She'd spent so much energy over the years convincing herself that the opinions of others didn't matter. If she angered half the town in her temperance crusade, so be it. The work was more important than conforming to societal expectations. If her family turned their backs on her, she'd soldier on. If no man ever desired her companionship, she'd find fulfillment in her reform work.

Yet as strong as she tried to be, her feet often felt as if they were made of clay. If she hadn't had Jane and Martha to lean on, she would have crumpled long ago. God had fortified her spirit through their friendship, and it seemed he was fortifying her again by widening her circle of support.

"Thank you." She murmured the words to Martha, but her soul sent even more gratitude heavenward.

Looking at the ladies around her, Noreen no longer saw faceless numbers she could rally to her cause. She saw women who carried their own hopes and dreams. Women who deserved to be seen as more than mere pawns in Noreen's battle against the saloon.

Shoe heels clicked softly as Miss Lockwood stepped up to the podium once again. "We will now open the floor to solicit suggestions for our monthly service projects. Have you noticed needs in our community that we can meet?"

Noreen hesitated as her priorities shifted. She still wished to recruit aid for her cause, but perhaps she should wait to see what projects other people suggested. Only, the room remained silent. No one wanted to be the first to speak.

"Miss Cowan."

Jane stiffened in her seat next to Noreen when Miss Lockwood called her name from the front of the room.

"As the daughter of one of our local ministers, perhaps you are aware of some needs that the rest of us are not yet privy to?" Miss Lockwood smiled in an encouraging fashion toward Jane, but Noreen knew her friend would need more than a smile for her to find her footing. Especially since all the other ladies had turned in their seats to stare in her direction.

"I . . ." Something—likely terror—strangled Jane's voice, keeping any words from escaping into the room.

Noreen shot to her feet. "Just yesterday, Miss Cowan and I worked on mending a few of the items donated to the church poor box." Jane's mother had suggested they bring a sack of mending items to the jail to help pass the time in a productive manner while visiting with Edna. "The Cowans have collected about two trunks' worth of items. Many are in need of patches, buttons, and repaired seams. Jane and her mother work on mending the items here and there as they are able, but if we gathered as a group, each lady bringing her own sewing kit, I imagine we could get through the entire supply in a single meeting." Noreen looked to Jane. "Do you think your father would let us meet in the church?"

Jane nodded.

Noreen turned back to the group. "Those who aren't skilled with a needle could bring snacks or perhaps help organize the clothing as the mending is completed."

Miss Lockwood nodded. "An excellent suggestion, Miss O'Sullivan. That is precisely the type of activity that would be well-suited to this group."

Her mouth suddenly dry, Noreen kept her feet. "I have another suggestion to make, if I may?"

"Go on."

"I would like to organize a temperance march. It need not be only our group that participates, since that might reveal our society. We could invite other women—and men—who recognize the role liquor plays in the moral decay of our society. It would be a peaceful event. Perhaps just a march around the square, then up to the Salt Fork Saloon. We could distribute temperance pledge forms and end with a prayer meeting in front of the saloon. Many temperance crusaders have found success with such events. The more the community stands together against the distribution of alcohol, the more likely we are to convince the mayor to declare Albany a dry town. If that happens, crime rates will drop, home lives will improve, and our community will be a safer place for everyone."

Miss Lockwood's enthusiasm dimmed considerably as Noreen spoke. "I will make a note of that suggestion, Miss O'Sullivan. Perhaps the society might consider it for a future project. I think it might be best to focus on something a little less . . . ambitious for our first endeavor, however." She swung her gaze away from Noreen and focused on the rest of the group. "Does anyone else have a suggestion?"

Feeling as if she'd just been chastised, Noreen sat back down, her shoulders slouching.

"Don't worry," Martha whispered from behind her. "I'll see that your temperance march gets on the ballot for our next meeting. You might have more supporters than you realize."

"You should give her a chance to share her heart with the group, Martha," Jane said before turning her gaze back to Noreen. "If you tell your story, you're sure to sway the group to your side. People can overlook facts and figures when they wish to avoid something uncomfortable, but a compelling story will grab their hearts and win their sympathies."

Tell her story? Could she do that? The only people she'd ever told were Martha and Jane, and only after they'd been friends for several years. She couldn't tell a room of mere acquaintances. She glanced down at the handkerchief she'd laid upon the school desk in front of her. These ladies weren't just mere acquaintances any longer, though. They were sisters now. And if a story would win them to her cause, she'd have to find the courage to tell it.

Chapter 12

James nearly nodded off twice during the sermon on Sunday. Thank heaven he was sitting in his usual spot at the back of the church when his head nearly fell into his lap the second time. That meant his only witnesses were Brother Cowan in the pulpit and three-year-old Mary Green, who'd woken him from his unintentional nap by banging her rag doll against his knee.

He should have had a full night's rest after releasing Edna Hanover into her son's care yesterday morning, but a storm blew in last night and brought a tree down on Clyde Weatherby's house. Thank God no one had been hurt. He and Clyde and a couple of Clyde's neighbors worked through the night to clear away the debris and rig up a few tarps to keep the worst of the rain and wind out of the house. The covered back porch had taken the brunt of the collision, which was a mercy. The roof and walls sustained minimal damage, leaving the structure sound enough for the Weatherbys to continue living there. A pair of windows had been busted out, and the tree had left a sizable dent in the roof above the kitchen, but the repairs shouldn't be too costly.

Shifting away from the pew end, hoping it would be harder to drift off without the secondary support, James returned his attention to the preacher. He'd absorbed about two minutes of Cowan's discourse on the witless nature of sheep and the humbling ramifications of that observation when combined with Christ's declaration of being the Good Shepherd, when little Mary Green climbed down from the pew and made a dash for freedom. Not one to allow a prisoner to escape so easily, James slid his leg out to bar her path. She attempted a brute force maneuver first, pounding his leg with her fists. When that didn't work, she changed tactics and tried to duck beneath the barrier, but James anticipated the strategy and plugged the hole with his opposite boot. This earned him a cherubic glare that made him grin.

The grin proved to be a miscalculation on his part. The tiny outlaw hurled her rag doll straight at his head. James bit back a chuckle as he dodged the projectile. Only to discover that it hadn't been thrown in a fit of pique as he'd assumed. It had been a clever ploy to distract him from Mary's next breakout attempt. The little hooligan was tunneling for freedom on her hands and knees beneath the pew. Thankfully, she'd made a critical error and tunneled forward instead of back, allowing James to make a quick dive, snatch her about the waist, and reel her in. She flailed and kicked as all foiled escapees do, but she was no match for the cunning lawman who'd taken her into custody. Not until her face scrunched and her mouth began to open. Scream imminent, James did the only thing his sleep-deprived brain could think to do to stave off disaster for them both—he blew in her face.

Mary blinked, shook her head, and stared at him as if no longer sure where she was. James stood her on her feet and blew in her face again as he released his hold on her waist. This time she giggled, the sound finally drawing her mother's attention away from Mary's year-old brother, who was climbing all over Mrs. Green's lap.

"Shh, Mary," her mother whispered before darting an apologetic glance toward James. "Leave the deputy alone."

James smiled and whispered back, "She's no bother."

In truth, she'd probably done him a favor. Kept him awake and on his toes. Kind of reminded him of another stubborn female intent on going her own way.

His gaze strayed to the front of the church to a slightly unruly dark-haired bun nestled against a slender neck. A simple straw bonnet decorated with a green bow perched somewhat precariously atop the barely contained curls as if ready to abandon ship at a moment's notice. Rather like the woman herself who seemed to be having difficulty sitting still. Unlike the perfectly composed young woman at her side. Of course, Jane Cowan had much more experience sitting in the front row and ignoring the scrutiny of the churchgoers than Noreen did. Until this week, Noreen had sat in her mother and stepfather's pew, comfortably anonymous in the middle of the congregation.

As James watched, a pair of bonneted heads two rows behind Noreen bent together. A heartbeat later, Noreen shifted in her seat. James frowned. Were those ladies talking about her? Had Noreen overheard something unkind? Something rather fierce sprang to attention in his gut, but before he could analyze it too closely, another female demanded his attention.

Mary's foot kicked his boot as the little girl moved to stand in front of him. She waited for him to look down at her, then shoved her arms up and out in clear demand. James glanced at Mrs. Green, but the young mother was too busy with the baby to pay her daughter much mind. Not wanting to endanger his delicate truce with the runaway toddler, James complied and scooped Mary up and sat her on his knee. Unhappy with that position, however, she climbed him like a ladder until she had both feet poking his belly while she peered over his shoulder, likely eyeing the church door and planning her next escape attempt.

He hadn't had much experience holding youngsters. Especially little girls. The experience had an odd effect on his brain. Implanting family man type desires that had no business sneaking up on a fella out of the blue. Especially when the imaginary children they generated bore a striking resemblance to a certain curly-haired firebrand sitting in the front row.

Nope. Not gonna go there. Noreen O'Sullivan was trouble with a capital *T*, and any attraction he felt for the woman needed to be squelched. Just because she cooked like a dream, held fast to her beliefs despite widespread opposition, and could tease him out of his worries when the occasion called for it didn't mean she was a good match for him. All right, so those attributes *were* elements he hoped to find in a wife someday—some very far away day—but not when they were tied to the same woman who picked a fight with over half the voting populace of Shackelford County.

Thankfully, the call to stand and sing the invitation song interrupted his ill-timed musings and drew his attention back to where it belonged—on worship. During the closing prayer, he added a silent apology for his distraction as well as a petition for an extra dose of wisdom as he navigated the unfamiliar currents he found himself floating in. Instinct warned that there'd be plenty of rapids before he reached the still waters promised in the psalm.

"Down!" Mary pushed against his chest the moment the final *amen* was spoken, as if the word were a starting gun to a race.

"Go ahead," Mrs. Green said. "Paul will look after her." She nodded toward her eldest son, who'd been sitting between her and her husband.

The boy was probably only six or seven, but he seemed just as eager to run for the door as his little sister. Placing one knee on the bench, James lowered Mary over the back of the pew, giving her a head start since her brother still had to get around his father. She squealed with joy and pumped her little legs, narrowly beating Paul to the door. She still had to wait for him to open it for her, but the triumphant gleam in her eyes made it clear that she savored the rare victory.

James grinned, glad he could play some small part in her success. Too bad grown-up victories were so much more complicated.

He wandered through the sanctuary, greeting friends and neighbors and asking after their kin. A good lawman needed to stay well-informed regarding the people in his town if he wanted to serve them to the best of his ability, yet that wasn't his main motivation for making the rounds. He genuinely liked these folks and cared about what was going on in their lives. Especially after the storm they'd had last night. He'd likely need to ride out to some of the area farms and ranches over the next few days to see how those living outside of town fared.

After getting an update on Mr. Holman's colicky horse, James stepped between a pair of pews to allow a family to move down the aisle. Turning to make his way to the other side, he found himself face-to-face with Noreen O'Sullivan.

Her sudden appearance shouldn't have surprised him. He'd been subconsciously tracking her movements as he made his way through the crowd and knew that he'd entered her general vicinity. Still, he'd not been mentally prepared to find her standing less than a foot away. Especially not wearing that contemplative expression.

"Are you feeling well? You look tired."

The woman would never be accused of coating things with too much sugar.

"I *am* tired," James admitted. "Only got a couple hours' sleep after helping Clyde Weatherby get a fallen tree off his house."

Her eyes widened. "Good heavens. Is everyone all right?"

James nodded as he rubbed a hand down his face, the thick stubble he encountered reminding him that he needed a shave. "No injuries, thank the Lord. A couple busted windows and some roof damage, but nothing that can't be fixed."

"I remember waking up to thunder last night and hearing the wind howl, but I didn't realize the storm had been that bad. I'm so glad no one was hurt."

"Me too. It could have been much worse."

Noreen dropped her gaze, almost as if she were . . . nervous? That couldn't be right. She had the stiffest backbone of any woman he'd ever met.

"Did Edna's son pick her up as promised yesterday? I wanted to stop by and see her one last time, but the hotel was short-staffed, and I couldn't get away."

Surely, she wasn't nervous about asking him about Mrs. Hanover. There must be something else.

"Yep, Elijah showed up bright and early to collect her. Brought the boys with him."

A smile touched her lips but failed to take up permanent residence. "Good. I'm glad she's back with her family."

James waited, but she didn't say more, though everything about her indicated she wanted to.

He glanced around. Most of the congregation had exited the sanctuary. A few pockets of people lingered inside, but no one stood close enough to overhear their conversation.

Still, James lowered his voice for good measure. "Just spit it out, Noreen. Whatever it is, I want to help."

Even if it had to do with her temperance work. He couldn't get involved directly, of course, but he could advise her on how to make a stand without running afoul of the law. Maybe he could find a way to minimize the risk she took upon herself. Making enemies of powerful men was a dangerous business, a business in which Noreen excelled.

"I want to apologize," she said, her gaze not quite reaching his eyes.

"What for?" He wracked his sluggish brain, trying to come up with a situation that warranted an apology, and came up blank.

Finally, she raised her chin enough for her eyes to meet his. "I've been selfish. You were exceptionally kind to me last week, and in return, I've done my best to bribe you into helping me close the saloon even after you shared your reasons for remaining neutral. I didn't respect your wishes as a friend should. Instead, I pressed my agenda onto you, trying to manipulate you into doing what I wanted as if you were a chess piece on a game board and not a person with aspirations as meaningful as my own. You deserved better from me, and I'm sorry."

James took a moment to absorb her words, recognizing that they'd not been easy to say. It took a lot of courage to admit to a personal failing, a courage he didn't often display himself. Hard to admit to flawed motivations when his pristine reputation was what kept him employed. He confessed his failings to God, but rarely, if ever, did he confess them aloud to another.

"If I accept your apology, do I have to give up you fixing dinner for me on Wednesdays and Sundays? 'Cause I was really looking forward to not eating my own cooking tonight." He grinned as he teased, hoping she'd see that he harbored no ill will. In fact, his respect for her had only grown.

A smile bloomed across her face and lit her eyes in a way that made him slightly light-headed. "I think the dinners can be negotiated."

"Good. Then apology accepted."

"Excellent." Her eyes sparkled, and her posture took on the vivaciousness he'd come to associate with her. "Would six o'clock be a satisfactory delivery time tonight?"

"Sounds perfect."

Still smiling, Noreen backed up a step. "See you then."

"Yep." He fingered the brim of his hat in salute. "Oh, and I'm ready to help you with that project you've been asking about if you still have questions."

He hadn't thought it possible for her smile to grow any larger, but she proved him wrong.

"I have quite a number of them, actually." The expression on her face nearly stole his breath.

When had Noreen O'Sullivan become such a staggering beauty? The truth hit him as she practically danced between the pews on her way back to her friends. Joy. Joy had transformed her. A joy he'd played a part in creating.

Heaven help him, but he wanted to see that joy on her face every day, even if regular interactions with the Temperance Terror ended up being a disastrous election strategy.

Chapter
13

Noreen arrived at the jailhouse at six o'clock sharp, a cold supper of ham sandwiches, deviled eggs, and sliced carrots in her basket and optimism in her heart. James Paxton was actually going to help her!

She'd wanted to cook something much finer for him to show her gratitude, but the stores were closed, so she had to make do with what Mrs. Barker had on hand in the boardinghouse kitchen. Thankfully, her landlady had the necessary staples to bake a pound cake. The recipe made enough for two loaves, so Noreen left one behind for Mrs. Barker to serve to her boarders that evening along with a few coins to cover the cost of the ingredients she'd utilized.

"Right on time." James met her at the door with one of his customary smiles and held out a hand to take the basket from her.

Unused to chivalrous offers from men, she found her cheeks warming as she relinquished the supper basket.

"I'm afraid it's just simple fare this time." She followed him inside and nearly stumbled over her own feet when she spied the old worktable.

He'd set out plates, forks, and cups for two.

She darted a sideways glance at him as he set the basket on the edge of the table and started taking things out. He didn't *act* like this was anything special. And it wasn't like he'd used a tablecloth or picked wildflowers to stick in a jar. Yet her heart fluttered as she tried to interpret the significance.

Had he been looking forward to sharing a meal with her? Did he view tonight as a . . . romantic encounter?

The very possibility of such a consideration made her stomach tighten in an unsettling manner. Good heavens. Did she actually *want* him to consider their meeting in such terms?

For pity's sake. The man had merely set the table. He was probably hungry and wanted to speed things along. Only a dreamy-eyed woman would read anything more into it. Noreen was far too pragmatic to fall into that trap.

Or so she'd thought. The palpitations vibrating through her chest cavity suggested her immunity to such things might be weakening.

"Is this a cake?" He unwrapped the napkin from around the small loaf, then held it near his face and inhaled deeply through his nose. "Mmm. It's even slightly warm."

He turned a grin on her that stirred those annoying palpitations into a frenzy, like bees in a jostled hive. Everything inside her buzzed.

Bees sting, Noreen. As do unfulfilled dreams. Remember that.

It might be tempting to look at this kindhearted man and start wishing for more, but only a fool would waste time wishing for something destined to stab her through the heart should she achieve it.

Friendship. Yes, she'd hope for friendship between them. Allies who enjoyed a platonic comradery without the expectation of sharing every secret. Such a relationship would be pleasant, indeed. Safe too. No reason for him to come to hate her if he never learned the truth of her past.

"After you promised to help me, I wanted to do something to show my appreciation."

He broke off a corner of the cake and popped it into his mouth, then closed his eyes as he enjoyed his pilfered goods. "Mmm. Remind me to put you in my debt more often."

A startled laugh tickled her chest. "Deputy Paxton! I thought you a law-abiding citizen and here you are stealing bites of cake right before my eyes. I'm shocked." She tried to sound prim, but she couldn't seem to restrain the smile that kept stretching out her pursed lips.

He chuckled, and the dancing light in his blue eyes sent delighted tingles coursing through her midsection. Heavens, but the man was handsome when he laughed. Something about his lightheartedness drew her in, made the weight of her burdens lift slightly from her shoulders. Filled her spirit with dangerous levels of optimism.

"No man is perfect, Miss Noreen." He flipped the napkin back over the top of the cake as if to remove temptation. "I'm afraid you've found my weakness."

"If cake is your only weakness, sir, you are a far better man than most."

His expression sobered. "Cake's far from my only weakness. I also suffer from regular bouts of selfishness." He turned his back on the table and faced her fully. "You apologized to me this morning, but it's been on my heart the last few days to apologize to you. You sought my help, and I turned you away, more concerned with ingratiating myself with the voting populace of Shackelford County than aiding one of the people I took an oath to serve and protect. I let my ambition direct my steps instead of trusting the Lord with that duty." He found her hand and clasped it, once again becoming a thief as his touch stole her breath. "I'm sorry, Noreen. You deserved better from me."

Noreen blinked, not trusting her senses, yet his earnest expression was no mirage. He meant every word he said. Every beautiful, affirming, completely wonderful word.

She couldn't recall a single time her father had apologized to her or told her she deserved better from him. Not even the time he'd broken the special teacup Grandmother had handed down to her. In the midst of one of his drunken episodes, he'd just yelled at her to stop blubbering before he gave her a real reason to cry. Arthur wasn't much better. He might not have broken any of her childhood treasures after she and Mama came to live with him, but he concerned himself more with pointing out her flaws than admitting to any of his own.

"Thank . . ." Her voice creaked like a rusty hinge, so she cleared her throat and tried again. "Thank you for saying that. It . . . it means a lot to me."

"Well, you mean a lot to me." His eyes flew wide open, and he dropped her hand as if it had suddenly burst into flame. "As a friend, and . . . you know . . . a member of the community."

The man's gaze darted about the room like a hunted rabbit in search of a hole to hide in. Choosing to be amused instead of offended, she grinned as she turned to face the table and removed the lid from the dish holding the deviled eggs.

"Well, as a member of the community, I'm grateful for your consideration. As your cook, however, I think we should set aside this discussion of apologies and focus on eating this food before the ants march in and carry it off."

James regained some of his equilibrium at her teasing. "Sensible woman, my cook."

Noreen tossed him a glance over her shoulder. "She hates to see food go to waste."

"A crime for sure." He stood straight and tall, puffed out his chest, and jabbed his thumbs beneath his suspenders to give them a pompous stretch. "As a professional crime opposer, I'd be falling down on my civic duty if I allowed such a travesty to occur."

Noreen chuckled, enjoying his playful spirit. Between her job at the hotel, her temperance work, and her uneasy family situation, she rarely took time to let go of responsibility and just . . . play. Her weekly teas with Martha and Jane provided wonderful companionship and sisterly support, but their get-togethers didn't usually include much laughter or silliness. James, with his ready smile and droll humor, had a way of lightening her mood and reminding her of the joy to be found in letting go of one's worries.

After unwrapping the brown paper from the sandwiches and placing three deviled egg halves on his plate and one on hers, she set the carrots within easy reach and claimed her seat on the far side of the table. James removed his hat and set it on the sheriff's desk behind him, then joined her at the table. Folding his hands in front of him, he bowed his head. Noreen did the same.

"Lord, we thank you for this food and for the strength and health it provides. I'm extra thankful not to be eating my own sorry cooking tonight, and I ask you to bless Miss Noreen for her kindness in preparing this meal."

Eyes closed and head bowed, Noreen grinned at the deputy's way of mixing formal reverence with a more relaxed conversational style.

"Grant us wisdom, discernment, and courage as we strive to serve you each day, and help us to reflect the love of Christ to all who cross our path. In Jesus's name, amen."

"Amen." Noreen lifted her head and reached for her sandwich as the final words of his prayer rummaged about in her brain.

He'd said them with such ease, as if they were a regular part of his prayer life. And as she considered her interactions with him in recent weeks, she found plenty of evidence pointing to the Lord granting his petition.

"So tell me about your family," Noreen said as she picked up her sandwich. "Any other lawmen in the bunch?"

James chuckled as he shook his head. "Nope. I'm the odd one out in the Paxton clan. My oldest brother, Joshua, went into business with my dad running the family ranch. He and his wife built a house a stone's throw from my folks and filled it with kids. Four at last count, though it wouldn't surprise me if more popped up over the next few years. Sometimes I think Josh and Judith are competing to see who can provide the most grandchildren." His eyes danced as he talked about his siblings, and Noreen suddenly craved hearing more about them.

Were they all as carefree and lighthearted as James? Were family gatherings filled with laughter and fun? How she had envied her classmates with siblings who teased each other, stood up for each other, and trusted each other even when they were at odds.

"Judith is your sister?" She probably should have waited for him to stop chewing before asking, but he didn't seem to mind. Just hurried along his swallow, then obliged her with an answer.

"Yep. Bossiest big sister a kid could have. We all celebrated when she had her first baby, figuring she'd turn her attention to running little Abel's life instead of ours. Somehow, she still manages to tell us all what to do, though, even with three young'uns of her own. Jethro's still mad at me for taking the deputy job and leaving him and Joanna to put up with all her interferin' ways. But he's got Dora now to act as a buffer, and that wife of his ain't afraid of letting Judith know that Jethro is *her* responsibility now, not Judith's. You shoulda seen the sparks flying over the Christmas dinner table last year. Whew doggies. I'd rather shoot my way out of a den of outlaws than try to broker peace between a pair of strong-minded women. Thankfully, Joanna chose that moment to announce that she was expecting her first babe, and all attention turned to her, exactly as she prefers." He grinned, his love for his family obvious.

Trying to keep the siblings straight as he described them proved a challenge since the Paxtons had opted to give all their children names that started with the same first letter.

"So you're the middle child?"

James nodded as he took a drink of his water. "Yep. Been playing the peacemaker most of my life. Guess the Lord wanted to give me plenty of practice before I became a professional."

"I suppose my childhood prepared me for my vocation as well."

Why did she bring *that* up? Mercy. No topic was guaranteed to throw a damper on an evening faster than talk of her father. And they'd been having such a lovely chat, too.

He looked at her, interest shining in his gaze. "How so?"

She waved off his question. "Forget I said anything. Tales of my childhood aren't nearly as entertaining as yours. I'd rather hear more about all those nieces and nephews you have."

"I'll be glad to regale you with tales of the Paxton pollywogs over dessert, but I'd like to hear more about you. If you're willing to share, that is." He leaned back and raised a conciliatory hand.

"If you'd rather not, that's fine, too. Just say something about the weather, and I'll take the hint." He winked, making it clear there'd be no hard feelings, no matter which option she chose.

An observation about last night's storm perched on the edge of her tongue, but she found herself oddly reluctant to speak it into the room. She fiddled with her napkin, took a sip of water, then picked up a carrot stick and tapped it against the edge of her plate enough times to probably make her dinner companion wonder if she'd decided to converse in Morse code.

He turned to his meal, giving her time to decide. No pressuring. No taking the decision into his own hands by introducing a new topic. No impatient glances or heavy sighs. He'd ceded the reins to her and appeared content to wait and see which way she would direct the conversation.

"I was raised on a farm outside of Cleburne."

James set his fork down and gave her his full attention. It should have made her more nervous, but somehow it had the opposite effect.

"My father had been injured during the War Between the States. It left him with a limp, which made working the farm difficult, but he made do. The war left him with other scars, however." She dropped her gaze to her plate. "Ones that couldn't be seen. Mama said that was what led him to drinking. He was trying to block out the memories. But then he fell from his horse and reinjured his leg. So he started drinking during the day to deal with the pain. The more he drank, the less he worked. The less he worked, the more the farm deteriorated. The more the farm deteriorated, the more he had to drink to escape the shame of his failure. It was a vicious cycle, and it turned him into a vicious man."

"He hit you."

It wasn't really a question, but she nodded anyway. "Sometimes. Mostly he yelled. Degraded us. Blamed us for his troubles. It almost made me glad when he took himself off to the saloon for a few hours, except for the fact that I knew he'd come home in worse shape than when he left. On a good night he would pass out in bed. On a bad night . . ." Noreen swallowed. No need to go into those details. James was a lawman. He'd likely seen the aftermath of a drunken rage.

His hand covered hers, bringing her head up at the tender contact. "I'm sorry, Noreen. No child should ever experience that kind of abuse."

"No, they shouldn't." The trembling in her hand stilled, perhaps from the comfort of his touch, or it could be the resolve rushing anew through her veins. "That's why the temperance movement is so important to me. I want to spare families the heartache I endured. Liquor destroyed my father, destroyed our family. It needs to be outlawed."

James leaned back in his chair, taking the warmth of his hand with him. "In my experience, outlawing something doesn't stop it from happening."

Noreen pulled her hand down into her lap and rubbed the spot where his fingers had rested. "I know. I'm not so naïve as to think that prohibition will solve the world's problems, but it *will* remove the temptation for many, and that will make a difference."

It had to.

James shifted in his chair again, bringing his elbows to rest on the table and his gaze to rest upon hers. "So how can I help you make that difference?"

Chapter
14

Even though James had suspected her history, hearing her recount it and watching her posture wilt while she did so enraged his sense of justice. He wanted to crawl backward through time and stand between the spunky young girl with the pointed chin and rambunctious curls and the bully of a father who'd struck her with both words and fists. Even knowing the man couldn't physically hurt her any longer didn't quench the fire burning in James's chest. For he saw the scars she bore. The hurt and mental anguish she carried.

Yet he also saw her incredible strength. To rise from such a harsh experience and become an educated, independent woman who refused to live life as a victim. Instead, she dedicated her energy and passion to improving society and fighting for the protection of women and children who faced the same adversity at home that she'd suffered.

Even now, her eyes glowed with zeal as she pushed her plate aside and met his gaze with a directness more common from a man.

"I read about the benefits of temperance rallies in *The Union Signal*, and I'd like to conduct one here in Albany. I've wanted to do one for years, but I never felt like I had enough community support to make an impact. However, over the last week, things have changed, and I now believe I'll be able to gather a substantial number of participants. Enough to make a political statement and garner the attention of city officials."

James just hoped she didn't end up garnering the wrong kind of attention. Most of the city council members already considered her a nuisance.

"What do you envision happening at this rally?" he asked.

She smiled, and the light that entered her eyes proved infectious. Not only did he smile in return, but he found himself catching a bit of her enthusiasm as her animated hands drew shapes in the air while she described the scene.

"I picture us meeting at the schoolhouse on a Saturday afternoon, gathering signs, and practicing our temperance hymns. Then we'll line up and begin our march." She turned her attention toward the door as if waiting for her imaginary parade to process past the opening. "We'll sing our way down Walnut Street, circle the courthouse square, then turn back up Main Street until we reach the Salt Fork Saloon. We'll distribute temperance pledge forms along our route and invite others to join our band.

"Once we reach the end of our route, we'll serenade Mr. Taggert and whomever happens to be patronizing his den of iniquity with some inspirational songs to encourage wayward souls to repent. Then we'll conclude with a prayer meeting and disperse around suppertime."

Her voice fell away, but it took a minute for her to turn her attention from the doorway to refocus on him.

"What do you think?"

James grinned. "I think you've given this a lot of thought."

"I have. But not from the perspective of a lawman." She leaned toward him, the bottom of her ribs pressing against the edge of the table. "Are there impediments I need to be aware of? Steps I need to take to ensure the safety of those who march with me?"

James appreciated the questions, especially since they would make his job easier as well as allow things to move more smoothly for her. And she didn't look at him like someone who expected to be given blanket permission to do whatever she wanted. In fact, she reached into a pocket of her skirt and pulled out a tablet and pencil, ready to take notes on whatever information he shared.

Unfortunately, not everything would be easy to hear, but she seemed a practical-minded woman, so he figured she'd want him to shoot straight.

"I can assist with the safety aspect, but you need to understand that my duty to protect extends to Taggert and those frequenting his establishment as well." Despite their growing friendship and his compassion for her mission, he couldn't give her preferential treatment. If he did, he'd be just as corrupt as those lawmen who let themselves be swayed by bribes or threats from powerful men. "I will guard your protesters, but if any of them cross the line and engage in acts of vandalism or personal attacks, I will step in to defend the Salt Fork."

She nodded, no disappointment readily apparent in her gaze. "I expected as much, but I'll make a note to remind the group to leave their rotten vegetables at home."

She looked down to scribble on the page in front of her, her mouth twitching slightly at one corner.

James fell a little bit in love with her at that moment. Not only because she believed him to be a man of integrity and didn't try to manipulate him away from his neutral position, but because she was learning to find humor while pursuing her temperance work, something he'd not seen from her before. In the past, her reform work had always operated with a level of passionate seriousness that teetered on the edge of anger. It had lent her a bitter air that had drawn his pity. This Noreen, whose passion and purpose were fueled by hope instead of anger, drew him in an entirely new way. One that had nothing to do with pity.

"What else should I know?"

The rally. Right. *Get your mind back on business, Paxton.*

"It might be best to place a notice in the paper a few days before. Let people know what's coming ahead of time so the businesses along your route won't complain about you interfering with their customer traffic."

Her pencil flew over her paper. "And we might even recruit people to the cause. Brilliant!"

James sat a little straighter. Rather nice to be considered brilliant by an intelligent woman.

Her pencil slowed, and her head came up, wrinkles forming across her brow. "But won't that warn Mr. Taggert we're coming? What if he tries to stop us somehow?"

"I'll be there to ensure he doesn't do anything illegal." Like brandishing the shotgun the fellow kept behind his bar. "But really, it's better not to take Taggert by surprise. A cornered animal is more likely to strike out wildly without thinking through the consequences. On the other hand, if he knows you're coming, his response can be premeditated and calm. Less chance of things escalating into violence, which takes priority in my book. Though, you're right about giving him time to plan. I imagine he *will* try to counteract your march somehow."

Noreen grew thoughtful. "I suppose I'll just have to prepare myself for some undermining tactics from that quarter and resolve not to let it derail me. Because you're right. The safety of my ladies comes first."

"You have proven to be quite resilient in the time I've known you, so I have no doubt of your ability to handle any scheme Taggert might cook up."

A bit of pink colored her cheeks as a smile blossomed at his praise. The expression had a softening effect on her features and made it downright difficult to resist reaching across the narrow table to cup her face and stroke that pretty blush with the pad of his thumb.

Deciding he'd best distract his hands before they got him into trouble and added a whole new layer of complication to the friendship developing between him and Noreen, James grabbed the cloth-wrapped pound cake and sawed off a thick slab.

He chanced a quick glance in her direction, then immediately ordered his gaze back to the cake. "Want some?"

Half a sandwich remained uneaten on her plate, but it seemed rude not to offer.

"I'm impressed you waited as long as you did to claim your dessert." Her wry tone made him laugh at himself.

James shrugged. "I warned you it was weakness of mine." And he suspected he was quickly developing another. One with big brown eyes and a smile that set his heart to pattering in his chest like summer rain on a tin roof.

"Since you're serving, I'll take a small piece."

He carved a slice about half as thick as his own and set it on the edge of her plate.

"Thank you."

James nodded, then forked a large bite into his mouth. Mmm. The inside tasted even better than the outer crust he'd snitched earlier. Only thing that would make it better was—

"Coffee?" Noreen had risen and retrieved the pot from the stove a couple of feet away and stood with the spout positioned over his empty cup.

"Please."

She was not making his resolution to think of her in friendly terms very easy to keep.

After filling his cup, she returned the pot to the stove and resumed her seat. "Does this mean we're done discussing the rally?"

James took a sip of the steaming brew as he pieced together his answer. "When you settle at the saloon for your prayer meeting, you cannot block the entrance or impede anyone from going in or coming out. Probably shouldn't block the walkway, either. And since you'll be on Main Street, you'll need to allow enough space on the road that a wagon and team can get through without the driver having to worry about running anyone over."

"If we have enough participants to clog the street, I'll be overjoyed." Her pencil fell from her fingers as she turned hope-filled eyes on him. "Do you really think that many people will attend the rally?"

For her sake, he hoped so. For his sake? Well, it'd be easier to manage a small group than a crowd that could turn mobbish at any moment, but the longer they talked, the less he cared about making things easy on himself.

"'With God all things are possible.'"

Noreen nodded. "Something tells me I should start praying about this now. It will likely be a month before the event takes place, but I'll pray that hearts will be opened to the temperance message."

"You might pray for Taggert, too." James's heart thumped hard against his ribs as he anticipated her reaction. He'd been thinking about this ever since he'd found her going toe-to-toe with the saloon owner, but he hadn't known how to bring it up. Until now.

"Pray for Mr. Taggert? Why?" Her face scrunched at the distasteful notion, then all at once it cleared. "Oh yes, I should ask the Lord to block his attempts to interfere with the rally. Good thought."

"No, Noreen. That's not what I meant." James sighed as he straightened, abandoning the last of his cake.

A guarded mask fell over her face, banishing all the softness he'd been admiring. "What did you mean, then?"

"When I told my dad that I'd taken this deputy position, he pulled me aside and gave me some advice that I've done my best to follow over the past five years. It hasn't been easy, but it tends to keep the regret at bay."

"And you think I'm in need of this same advice?"

He cringed inwardly at the primness of her tone. Gone was the warmth, the teasing, the comradery they'd been enjoying. Her hackles had been raised, and he was bound to get jabbed by a few of them before this was over. Nevertheless, he plunged in with both feet.

"I think *everyone's* in need of this advice. Pretty sure that's why Jesus included it in his Sermon on the Mount."

Her brow furrowed slightly, and he continued before the tiny opening in her defenses slammed closed.

"My dad warned me against viewing myself as better than the criminals I battle. Yes, it's my job to bring them to justice and to protect others from their wicked deeds, but they are still people. People loved and cherished by God. They might hate me and despise what I stand for, but I can't let their feelings dictate mine. I've been called to love my enemies by a God who died on a cross for his. To do good to those who hate me by the one who healed the severed ear of his accuser. To pray for those who persecute me by the one who asked his Father to forgive those who spat on him, scourged him, and hung him on a tree."

Noreen's eyebrows slashed downward as her mouth tightened. "I don't harbor hatred in my heart for Mr. Taggert, if that's what you're trying to say." Her hands stabbed the air like jousting lances. "I'm not fond of the man, but I don't wish for any harm to actually befall him."

"Okay. But do you pray for his good?"

Her arms crisscrossed her midsection like a shield. "Not when his good brings harm to others." Her voice cracked, and so did James's heart. "The more he and his saloon prosper, the more destruction drunken men bring home to their wives and children. That is *not* the Lord's will." She pushed away from the table and jerkily grabbed up her notebook and the empty supper basket.

James lurched to his feet. "I'm not suggesting you pray for his saloon to prosper, Noreen. I'm speaking of what is good for him spiritually. Forgiveness. Mercy. Salvation."

A tear fell from her left eye as she pushed past him and strode for the door. "He doesn't deserve salvation."

James made no move to stop her. He simply stated the truth. "None of us do."

Noreen stormed out of the jailhouse without a backward glance, her woundedness on full display. He ached for her. And prayed for her. That the Lord might heal the places James was unable to reach and make all things work for good in her life. That she might be blessed with joy and peace and be freed from the shackles of her past.

You know what she needs better than I do, Lord. But if there's anything I can do to help, I'm ready and willing. Just show me what to do.

Chapter
15

"Are you taking food over to the jailhouse again tonight?" Luella glanced up from the large stockpot of vegetable soup she was stirring, her innocent gaze making Noreen squirm.

Last week, Noreen had made arrangements with Mrs. Winslow to come in on her Wednesdays off to work an unpaid two-hour shift of dish duty after the lunch crowd left in exchange for using the old stove in the corner of the hotel kitchen to provide a meal for local law enforcement. Of course, that was before she and James had their falling out on Sunday. The deputy would likely prefer to eat his own cooking over having to share her company again.

Fine by her.

She had enough men in her life trying to tell her what to do and how to act. She didn't need James Paxton joining that club. So what if she wasn't as spiritually altruistic as the oh-so-perfect deputy? King David himself had called curses down on his enemies. She'd marked several passages in the Psalms as proof once she'd returned to her boardinghouse Sunday night. If a man after God's own heart could wish ill upon his enemies, surely the Lord would understand a slight lack of charity on her part when it came to Milton Taggert.

"Miss Noreen?" Luella set her wooden spoon aside and walked

over to where Noreen was drying a roasting pan. "Did you hear me?"

"Yes. Sorry." She tossed her drying towel on top of the counter and expelled a deflating sigh as she turned to face her friend. "The truth is, I'm not sure of the answer."

Luella quirked a brow. "Really? It wasn't a very hard question."

"You wouldn't think so, would you?" Noreen shrugged. "Unfortunately, it became rather complicated when Deputy Paxton and I had a difference of opinion the last time I took him supper."

The girl's eyes lit with interest as she backed toward the stove and the soup she was supposed to be tending. "What happened?"

What happened was that the man had butted into her business and offered unneeded and unwanted advice. Although, to be fair, his advice up until that point had been insightful and beneficial. In fact, she'd chosen not to mention the incident at all at yesterday's tea with Jane and Martha, certain her friends would have taken James's side. Especially Jane. She was always so eager to forgive everyone and see their potential for good. She would have encouraged her to pray for Taggert, too, and Noreen hadn't wanted a repeat of that particular suggestion. Martha probably would have avoided the prayer controversy, but she would have pointed out Noreen's defensive attitude. Storming out had not been her finest moment. She'd admitted that much to herself the next day after she'd had a chance to cool down. But so many emotions had rushed to the surface when James brought up Taggert, she'd doubted her ability to keep them contained. So she'd chosen escape. Better than losing her temper, or worse, crying.

"Gracious, Miss Noreen. Are you gonna leave me in suspense?"

"Sorry." She seemed to be saying that a lot lately. "There's not much to tell. Deputy Paxton offered to help me plan my temperance rally, but the conversation veered into a more personal realm, and a disagreement arose. I'm afraid I got a bit huffy with him. I'm pretty sure he'd rather not be forced to share my company again. Yet the fact that I agreed to bring him dinner two nights a week in exchange for his help still stands. Hence my quandary."

"Wait a minute." Luella stopped stirring again and nearly dropped her spoon into the pot. "You and Deputy Paxton had a *personal* conversation?" Her gaze widened with a strange mixture of intrigue and horror. "Is he courtin' you? I thought you were gonna be a spinster with the rest of us."

Heat suffused Noreen's face. "Heavens, no. The deputy is not courting me. We are merely friends. Or we were before I ran out on him." At least she'd thought they'd been friends. He probably regretted opening that particular door now that she'd slammed it in his face.

Why did he have to bring up Taggert? Everything had been going so nicely until that point.

Luella cocked a brow. "Are you sure you two aren't courtin'? You are blushing an awful lot over a *friend*. Mary Sue Crowther said you'd set your cap for him and were using your cooking skills to try to reel him in. That's why you've been visiting the jailhouse so often. I told her you were just doing the man a kind turn as an act of good citizenship, but I'm starting to think Mary Sue might have the right idea."

"Mary Sue needs to mind her own business," Noreen grumbled. Good grief. Was she really the topic of schoolyard gossip? "Deputy Paxton is concerned with keeping the town safe, and since political rallies can bring out strong reactions in people, he wanted to advise me on taking precautionary measures to ensure a peaceful protest. That is all."

"Do you think the society will support your bid for a temperance rally?" Luella resumed her soup stirring, setting aside her courtship inquisition for the moment.

"I hope so. Martha and Jane have promised their support."

They'd spent nearly all of their teatime yesterday coaching Noreen on how to present her petition to the other spinsters in a sympathetic manner. A strategy that included toning down her normal fire-and-brimstone style. She much preferred denouncing strong drink, enumerating the dangers it posed to families and communities, and challenging God-fearing folk to take a stand. Such tactics allowed her to feel strong and righteous as opposed to the plan Jane and Martha concocted that emphasized making herself vulnerable by sharing her story and relinquishing control of the outcome to the ladies of the society. She hated feeling weak. Out of control. It reminded her too much of the girl she'd worked so hard to leave behind. The girl who'd cowered in corners, struggling with all her might not to believe that she was as worthless as her father's shouting voice claimed. A voice she still heard inside her head on occasion.

A much sweeter voice pulled her from her musings this time, though.

"You have my support, too, Miss Noreen." Luella's eyes glowed with friendly fervor. "I know I'm not an official member of the spinster society, and I can't vote or anything, but I can pray for you." She lifted her chin. "More than that, I can march with you."

All concerns about her presentation to the society fled in the face of Luella's selfless loyalty. Noreen crossed to the stove in two strides, flung her arms around Luella, and hugged her tight. "You are the dearest girl."

"Miss Noreen." Luella chuckled. "The soup!"

Freeing the girl's arms, Noreen stepped back. "If the temperance movement had a dozen supporters as brave as you, we could make real change in this town."

Luella's shy smile went straight to Noreen's heart. This girl was so hungry to belong and to make her world better. Just as Noreen had been at that age. But there was a key difference. Noreen's father had already been out of the picture by then. Luella's father, on the other hand, was very much alive and in a position to retaliate against a daughter who denounced a way of life he embraced.

"Nothing would please me more than to have you march at my side, Lu, but I don't want you to do anything that might cause trouble at home."

Luella's eyes glistened with tears, yet an undeniable determination glowed beneath the gathering moisture. "I want to march with you, Miss Noreen. Because you're my friend, but also because I know how important this cause is. Not just for the people who are hurt by those who drink, but for the drinkers themselves. I love my father, and it breaks my heart to see what the liquor is doing to him. It controls him. Cripples him. I'm afraid that one day it will kill him." She rubbed her eye with the back of one hand. "He'll never get better until he puts down the bottle for good. I want to help him do that. Even if it makes him angry. He's worth the risk."

Noreen blinked away the image that sprang to mind of her own father lying on the cold ground of the barn floor. Not moving. Regret choked her. How many things would she change if she could go back in time? Could she have helped her father turn away from strong drink, helped him find his way back from the abyss?

No. She'd not tear open old wounds with pointless what-if games. She'd been a child. Her father had made his choices and paid the consequences. Yet Luella's situation was different. *Luella* was different. She was nearly a woman. A woman with her own mind, her own ability to choose her life path. How could Noreen consider herself a proponent of women's suffrage and not respect another woman's right to make her own decisions?

"All right. If the society approves the march, you can join. But why don't you ask your mother if you can stay with me that night? You can meet back up with your family at church on Sunday." Best to keep her away from her father in case his temper flared over her involvement with the rally. Hopefully, his ire would cool overnight and lower the risk of him striking out at her.

Luella's eyes brightened. "Could we make shortbread cookies and dunk them in hot cocoa?"

Noreen laughed. "Absolutely!"

Luella might be on the cusp of womanhood, but there were some delights that could never be outgrown.

"Luella Templeton! You better not let that soup scorch." Mrs. Winslow came in from the larder carrying a large crate overflowing with carrots in want of peeling, chopping, and glazing for tonight's dinner.

"No, ma'am." Luella straightened and increased her stirring speed.

"And you," the head cook said with a jerk of her chin in Noreen's direction. "I agreed to let you come in to use the old stove, not to distract my other staff. I'll thank you to keep your conversation to yourself."

"Yes, Mrs. Winslow." Noreen dipped her head. "I'll just put these dishes away and banish myself to the corner."

"See that you do." She pivoted to address the young woman who'd followed her in from the larder. "Nellie, get those potatoes peeled, chopped, and in a pot of water," she said with a nod toward the sack of potatoes cradled in the girl's arms, "then start in on these carrots. I've got to season and tenderize the beefsteak and check on the pork roast."

Noreen shot a smile at Luella, then busied herself with putting away the dishes she'd finished drying. Activity in the kitchen would only increase from now through dinner service so there'd be no more opportunities to talk. Yet as she moved to where the old stove stood in the back corner and contemplated the basket of groceries she'd brought with her, Noreen still didn't have an answer for Luella's original question.

Was she taking a meal to James tonight, or wasn't she?

Chapter
16

James paced the jailhouse floor, casting a glance into the street every few strides. He stopped and checked the time on his pocket watch. Again. Six eighteen. Noreen might just be running behind schedule, but his instincts made a mockery of that hopeful thought.

She wasn't coming.

She was hiding.

The question was why. Was she feeling embarrassed? Did she wish to avoid the awkwardness that inevitably followed a disagreement? Did she fear he was angry with her? Those motives he could deal with. He could put her at ease with a humorous anecdote—he had one picked out already involving a goat and a pair of underpants. He'd gladly offer reassurance that their conversation had done nothing to taint his opinion of her, that he still found her quite remarkable. If anything, learning more about her history only intensified his respect for how much she had overcome.

On the other hand, if she resented him for overstepping and interfering in private spiritual matters, things would be trickier to smooth over. There were plenty of people he'd upset over the course of his adult life, especially in the line of duty, and he did his best to mend the damage that resulted from those interactions. However, he'd learned the importance of letting things go when folks gave no indication of being willing to forfeit their grudges.

The situation with Noreen was different, though. He didn't want to let things go. He wanted to repair what had been broken. Regain her good opinion, if it had, in fact, been lost. Her opinion mattered to him. A lot. Enough that he couldn't just let her slip away without trying to fix whatever he'd broken.

James shoved his watch back into his trouser pocket, strode for the door, and collected his hat from the nearby coatrack. If she wasn't coming to him, he'd just have to go to her.

He ducked into the narrow alleyway that ran along the west side of the jail, choosing the privacy it afforded instead of strolling down Walnut past the courthouse. What he was about to do could technically be categorized as calling upon a lady, and while he wasn't ashamed to be seen paying a call on Noreen, he'd rather keep his intentions to himself in case she sent him packing. Besides, his insides were in enough knots already without having to stop and converse with whoever might be out and about at dinnertime.

The walk to Third Street proved too short for him to unwind any of the kinks in his gut or come up with a plan for what to say to her. He managed to squeeze in a petition asking God to guide his words, but all too soon he found himself ascending the boardinghouse front porch steps, feeling as ill-prepared as a barefooted cactus farmer.

Giving his shoulders a roll to alleviate the tightness brought on by a coat that seemed to shrink in size with each heartbeat, he cleared his throat, then rapped the door with his knuckles. He rocked from bootheels to toes as he waited for a response. It *was* the dinner hour. Not the most neighborly time to visit. Starting to regret the impulse that drove him from the jailhouse, James backed away from the door a pace and began an inner debate regarding how long politeness dictated he cool his heels on the porch before making his escape. He hadn't knocked that loud. Perhaps with the dinner commotion, no one had heard—

The click of the latch broke off his thoughts. His pulse hitched as the portal creaked open to reveal a woman scowling at him. Thankfully, it wasn't the woman he'd come to see. Although, there was a better than average chance that she'd be scowling at him, too, before this interview was over.

James fingered the brim of his hat and dipped his chin. "Evenin', Mrs. Barker. I hope I'm not disturbing your dinner."

"Of course you are, but I suppose I can make allowances for the law. What brings you to my doorstep, Deputy?"

Fighting the urge to tug on his collar, James tucked his thumbs into the tops of his trouser pockets. "I'd like to have a word with Miss O'Sullivan, if I may. Is she here?"

Mrs. Barker rolled her eyes. "What has that girl done now? I swear, I've never met a young woman so determined to run afoul of the law."

"No, ma'am. That's not why I'm—"

The proprietress wagged a finger in his face and shooed away his attempted defense. "I run a respectable boardinghouse, I'll have you know. I'll not play host to a criminal. If you're here to take her in, I'll clear out her belongings and have Mr. Clevenger come and fetch them. I don't need that kind of trouble here."

"No laws have been broken, Mrs. Barker. I assure you." Good grief. He'd come here to reconcile with Noreen, not get her evicted. "I'm paying a social call on Miss O'Sullivan. Not a professional one."

"A social call?" The woman looked so incredulous, James didn't know if he should be affronted for Noreen or himself. "Well, don't that beat all." She swung the door wide and eyed him like some kind of circus oddity as he stepped over the threshold and removed his hat. "Gentlemen callers are to wait in the parlor." She led him down the short hallway and gestured to an open doorway on the right, near the base of a staircase. "I'll let Miss O'Sullivan know you're here."

"Thank you, ma'am."

As James lowered himself onto a floral-patterned sofa, it occurred to him that taking the alleyway to get here had served no purpose. For with three little words, he'd managed to set the gossip wheel to spinning at such a high velocity that it was bound to rip through

Albany like a twister on parade. He just prayed that didn't give Noreen one more reason to avoid him.

Sitting at Mrs. Barker's dining room table and mentally berating herself for being a coward, Noreen dipped her spoon into the bowl of beef stew that stared up at her. Stew that should have been shared with James but instead had found its way to Mrs. Barker's table.

"Would you pass the corn bread, Noreen?" Velma Stafford gestured to the cloth-covered basket that had come to rest in front of Noreen. "I know I shouldn't have a second piece, but yours is so fluffy and delicious, I fear I have no willpower."

Another item that should have been shared with James. Noreen had chosen a recipe from a Northern cookbook that called for eggs and sugar, knowing how much the deputy enjoyed cake. But over the course of the afternoon, she'd talked herself out of visiting him, not wanting to see the truth in his eyes—that she'd ruined their budding friendship.

Noreen forced her mouth into a smile as she passed the basket. "I'm glad you like it. I was trying out a new recipe."

"It's delicious." Velma helped herself to a large square, then reached for the butter dish. "I envy your skill in the kitchen. I'm an utter disaster." She chuckled. "Mama tried to tell me that following a recipe is just like following a dress pattern, but when I added canned beets to a vanilla cake because I liked the pretty pink color it made, she gave up on teaching me how to cook."

"Well, I'd say you chose the right profession." As the local dressmaker, Velma had a thriving business *and* a man who intended to wed her in the fall.

"I warned John of our need to employ a cook after we wed. Can't have the dear man wasting away because he chose to fall in love with a woman who can't even bake a potato without it exploding all over the stove." Velma tilted her head as she considered Noreen. "I don't suppose you would be interested in the position, would you?"

Play cook to a pair of newlyweds who would be a constant

reminder of all she would never have? She'd rather take one of Velma's needles to the eye.

"I . . ."

Mrs. Barker swept into the dining room, saving Noreen from having to formulate a polite refusal. Although, the way her landlady's gaze roamed Noreen's face as if searching for a third eye or second nose made her dread what her salvation might cost.

"You have a caller, Noreen. A *gentleman* caller."

Velma set down her butter knife with an audible clink. "A gentleman? Oh, Noreen. How exciting! Is it anyone I know?"

"Oh, it's someone we *all* know." Excitement glowed in Mrs. Barker's gaze at that pronouncement, the kind of excitement that only appeared when she acquired exclusive rights to a tidbit so juicy it guaranteed her ascension to the top of the town's gossip ladder. "Deputy James Paxton."

James was here? Why? To collect on her food promise? No, James wasn't the type to make demands on folks, even if they had offered something and failed to deliver. More likely he'd come to check on her. Make sure she wasn't ill or something. That was more his style. Kind. Patient. Ridiculously bighearted.

Unlike her, he didn't hide from his problems.

"Noreen! I didn't know you and the deputy were courting." Velma's voice quivered with enthusiasm.

"We're not." Good heavens. As if being the topic of schoolyard gossip wasn't bad enough, by tomorrow morning the entire town would be speculating on her relationship with the deputy. "Mr. Paxton has been assisting me in planning a civic event. That's all. I'm sure he just stopped by to relate some information pertaining to that project."

Mrs. Barker shook her head and leveled a look at Noreen that spoke volumes. *Amateur. Do you really think I'll be thrown off the scent so easily?*

"He said this was a social call, not a professional one. Made that point quite clear." She tipped her head toward the dining room doorway. "He's in the front parlor. Best not keep him waiting, girl."

Noreen swallowed a groan, only half due to the fact that there was a better than average chance of Deputy's Paxton's social call making the headlines of the next edition of the *Albany News*. The other half was due to having to face James and try to explain why she hadn't brought him the meal she'd promised.

One thing was certain, however. She needed to get James away from Mrs. Barker. Her landlady was an expert eavesdropper, and whatever the deputy intended to say, Noreen preferred to be the only one listening.

"Thank you, Mrs. Barker." Noreen removed her napkin from her lap, then rose to her feet.

As she passed through the doorway, her landlady touched her arm and whispered in her ear. "Don't mess this up, Noreen. You're not likely to have another half-decent man show interest in you."

She supposed the woman had good intentions in dispensing that less-than-helpful guidance, but Noreen bristled anyway. Not because of the woman's doubt in her ability to attract a man—by Noreen's reckoning, that assessment was accurate—but because of her characterization of the man waiting in the parlor.

"You're wrong about him, ma'am," Noreen whispered back. "James Paxton is not half decent. Decency fills him to the brim and runneth over. Be sure to portray him accurately when you tell your tales."

Mrs. Barker took a step back, her eyes wide. She blinked at Noreen as if she'd never seen her before.

Taking advantage of the opening, Noreen slid through the doorway and down the hall. She paused outside the parlor to inhale a steadying breath and wing a prayer heavenward for courage, then stepped across the threshold.

Chapter 17

James shot to his feet the moment Noreen stepped into the room. "Hi. Uh . . ."

He moved toward her, then stopped, not sure of the proper protocol of a social call that fell somewhere between courtship and friendship, where both -*ships* were navigating rocky shoals thanks to some misdirection by an overzealous captain.

Noreen inched his direction as well, then blurted, "Would you like to take a walk?"

Anything to get him away from the ridiculous maritime analogies swimming through his head. He was a Texan, for pity's sake. All mental comparisons should involve horses, six-guns, and stampeding cattle.

"A walk sounds right fine."

He collected his hat from the sofa cushion where he'd left it and gestured for her to lead the way. She did, not stopping until they were a good twenty yards from the boardinghouse. At that point, she halted and spun around so fast, he nearly plowed into her front. Thankfully, he managed to rein in before he trod on her toes.

"Sorry."

"Sorry."

Their duet couldn't have been more synchronized if they'd rehearsed it. They even stepped back in unison, widening the space between them to a distance more conducive to conversation than kissing.

Where in the world had the thought of kissing come from? Well, he supposed he knew the answer. Male and female lips in close proximity tended to spawn such notions, especially when the female lips belonged to a certain spitfire who had a habit of tugging on his heartstrings. James ducked his head and gave it a subtle shake, hoping to dislodge the ill-timed idea.

"James, I really am sorry." Noreen's voice brought his head up. "And not just about our near collision." The small, self-deprecating smile that brightened her eyes went straight to his heart.

He'd forgive her just about anything when she looked at him like that.

"You're not the only one with a sore conscience," he admitted. "Mine's been aching all week. I stuck my nose in where I wasn't invited and overstepped the bounds of our friendship. I'm sorry for upsetting you like I did, and I'm extra sorry if my actions have caused you to want to avoid me."

She hung her head, hiding her pretty eyes from him. "I'm the one who got defensive and stormed out. You didn't deserve that. You also don't deserve to go hungry thanks to my reneging on our agreement. I made beef stew and corn bread, intending to deliver them to you, but I took the coward's way out and shared them with Mrs. Barker instead."

James craned his neck downward, hunting for her eyes. "You know I don't really care about the food, right?"

Her chin tipped up a notch, a vulnerability in her eyes she usually kept well hidden.

"I won't lie, I love your cooking, but there's no need to feel an obligation to feed me. I'm happy to help you with your rally or with anything else, free of charge. No strings or food attached."

Her brow furrowed slightly. "So you're not angry that I didn't bring you supper?"

"Not even a little." He grinned, glad he could put one of her concerns to rest. "In fact, if you haven't eaten too much already tonight, I'd be happy to treat you to supper at the café. Seems only fair that I should feed *you* after you fed me. Twice. And goodness knows, you don't want to eat anything I cook up myself."

"Dinner? At the café?" Her expression vacillated somewhere between flustered and befuddled.

James started second-guessing his impromptu strategy. "If you'd rather not, I completely understand. We can just take a walk around the block, and I'll return you to the boardinghouse before—"

"Dinner sounds lovely." Her posture had straightened while he'd fumbled to provide her a way to turn him down gracefully. The fire he so admired returned to her gaze and had him standing a bit taller, too. "I'm famished."

His chest expanded, and a smile spread across his face that had nothing to do with placation and everything to do with the joy found in sharing company with a woman he admired.

"Wonderful!" Not sure either one of them was ready for him to offer her his arm, he simply turned in the direction of the town square and held out his palm in invitation. "Shall we?"

She smiled and fell into step at his side, a rather comfortable place for her to be, now that he thought about it.

He turned to her as they strolled past the boardinghouse, hoping to distract her from the nosy landlady peeking through the curtains. "Did I ever tell you about the goat that kept an outlaw from escaping by eating his underpants?"

"What?" The burble of laughter that followed that word was about the prettiest sound he'd ever heard.

Noreen arrived early to the schoolhouse the following evening, nervous about her presentation to the society. She'd prepared notes, practiced in the confines of her room, and prayed over it during her shift at the hotel, but her stomach remained a ball of knots. She'd even broached the subject with James last night as he walked her back to the boardinghouse. He had no idea who she was planning to recruit—not specifically, anyway—but he still offered suggestions for her pitch.

Suggestions that would be quite a challenge to implement. Like not trying to convince people to see things her way but trying to see things from their perspective and figure out how to align the rally with ideas they already valued. Hard to do when she was still getting to know her fellow spinsters. She *did* recall from their first meeting that several ladies disliked the idea of militant women marching in the streets for the cause of suffrage. Temperance might be a different cause, but marching would likely still garner disapproval. She planned to use words like *parade* instead of *march* and to emphasize the singing of temperance hymns and the prayer meeting at the conclusion of the event in an effort to downplay any militant imagery. It might not work, especially since most people viewed her as rather confrontational, but if Jane's theory proved correct about her personal story softening hearts, she might stand a chance.

Martha glanced up from her teaching desk when Noreen entered the classroom.

"Grading papers?" Noreen asked as she walked down the center aisle, empty student desks on either side.

Visions of her spinster sisters filling those seats populated her mind as she moved. Unfortunately, the imaginary apparitions all wore frowns and censorious scowls. Noreen's steps slowed as the knots in her belly tightened.

"Going over my geography lesson for tomorrow, actually." Martha smiled as she closed her notebook and pushed to her feet. "I'm glad you came early. You can see what the room looks like from up here so it won't feel so strange later."

Noreen drew to a halt, energy suddenly draining from her limbs. "Is this a fool's errand, Martha? No one has welcomed my temperance ideas in the past. What if all I manage to do is alienate the very women I hope to call my sisters?"

Martha stepped around her desk and moved to meet Noreen in the aisle. She wrapped her arm around Noreen's shoulders and gave her a squeeze. "The Lord knows what is best. For you. For the society. For our community. Leave the outcome in his hands, and he'll take you where you need to go."

"Easier said than done," Noreen murmured.

"True." Martha laughed softly, then took Noreen's hand and led her to the head of the class. "I'm better at dispensing advice than applying it to myself."

They reached the front of the room, and Martha took hold of Noreen's shoulders as if she were a pupil preparing for a class presentation. "You are the most fearless person I know, Noreen O'Sullivan. Just because you are changing tactics and making yourself vulnerable tonight, don't forget that you've been given not a 'spirit of fear; but of power, and of love, and of a sound mind.' Strength, heart, and intelligence. You possess all three. Usually, you let your strength drive your words, but tonight let it drive your faith as your heart and mind shape your message."

Noreen pressed her lips together as she struggled to contain her rising emotion. How many times had she quoted that verse to herself in order to shove aside her concern about what others might think and follow the conviction of her soul? Yet all this time, she'd only focused on the first gift—the spirit of power. As if power was the only way to combat fear. But it wasn't. Love and a sound mind were equally potent weapons. Even now, Martha's loving support was pushing back the insecurities and doubts as she used well-crafted, logical arguments to shore up Noreen's mind.

"You're among friends here," Martha said. "Remember that."

Noreen nodded as she let that truth sink into her spirit. She might not be able to control the outcome, but she could trust her friends to have her back. And more than that, she could trust the one who *was* in control to guide the outcome in the direction that best fit his purposes. For as much as she believed in the cause of temperance, she believed in God's sovereignty more. Rushing ahead of his timing would only set her mission back, not move it forward. A hard pill to swallow for someone who had a problem with patience. But as Jane often said, how could one grow in patience unless the Lord provided opportunities for practice?

She'd never been much good at practice, either.

Noreen reached up and clasped Martha's hand. "Thank you for being here."

Martha tugged her into a hug, then blessed her with a confident smile. "You're going to do great." After stepping back, she raised a brow and shot Noreen a quizzical glance. "Now, what's this I hear about you and a certain deputy being spotted having dinner together at the café last night? Are your days as a member of our spinster society dwindling?"

"Not you too!" Noreen let out a huff of breath that sounded like a laugh that had been caught in a meat grinder. "He's just a friend, nothing more." The giddiness that roused in her belly at the mention of James threatened to call her bluff, but her growing admiration for him didn't change the fact that they could never be more than friends. Not with her past and his dreams for the future. "Deputy Paxton treated me to dinner in return for the meals I've been providing him at the jailhouse. Nothing romantic in nature, I assure you."

Martha's eyes sparkled. "'The lady doth protest too much, methinks.'"

"Leave Shakespeare out of this."

"Ooh, Shakespeare? Which play are we discussing?" Jane traipsed down the aisle, the promise of discussing literature livening her usually sedate pace.

"*The Merry Wives of Windsor*." Martha's elbow nudged Noreen's side in annoying exuberance.

Noreen shot her a glare. "You're mistaken. It was *Much Ado about Nothing*, if you'll recall."

Martha raised a challenging brow. "Are you sure it wasn't *The Taming of the Shrew*?"

"Are you calling me a shrew?" Noreen's voice raised in a fashion that was affronted but definitely *not* shrewish.

Laughter trickled out of Martha as she wrapped an arm around her jiggling belly. "*As You Like It.*"

"Oh for pity's sake."

"Now, now, ladies." Jane's bewildered gaze bounced from one friend to the other. "I have no idea what this Shakespearean battle is really about, but I assure you that *All's Well That Ends Well.*"

Noreen looked at Jane's sweetly confused face, then turned to Martha's teasing countenance, and the ridiculousness of the situation finally penetrated her guard of ruffled feathers. A host of giggles rose from her core, cleansing the tension from her spirit as they bubbled forth. Martha and Jane joined in until laughter rang from the rafters.

"Well, isn't that a delightful sound greeting my arrival?"

Noreen straightened at the sound of Hortense Lockwood's voice. She cleared her throat and stepped forward to greet their founder with as much dignity as she could manufacture on short notice.

"Miss Lockwood, I wanted to thank you for allowing me to address the society this evening."

The older woman smiled and cast a glance past Noreen to where Martha and Jane stood. "Well, you had a pair of very convincing champions arguing on your behalf."

Jane too? Noreen cast a look over her shoulder to find Martha smiling with confidence while Jane stared mostly at the floor, yet both of her friends stood behind her literally and figuratively, and Noreen's heart swelled at their steadfastness.

The rest of the spinsters filed into the schoolroom a few at a time, and the room came to life with friendly chatter. Noreen followed the plan Martha and Jane had helped develop and greeted each lady as she entered, forcing herself to make polite conversation by asking after family members and personal health when what she really wanted to do was hide with Jane in a dim corner. She learned far more about Ellie Throckmorton's goiter than she ever wanted to know, but the woman actually smiled at Noreen and thanked her for asking, as if it had been a great favor. Perhaps others understood the feeling of not being heard more than Noreen had suspected.

Miss Lockwood called the meeting to order and moved through

the agenda while Noreen did her best to lasso her nerves by sitting in the back next to Jane.

"Our first service project will take place this Saturday in the home of Parson Cowan."

Noreen's stomach clenched as the business items turned toward the monthly projects.

Miss Lockwood smiled in Jane's direction, causing her face to turn scarlet.

"Bring your sewing baskets if you will be joining the mending group. Others may volunteer to bring snacks and assist with folding and organizing the donated clothing. I will leave a sign-up sheet on the desk here at the front of the room so we can get an idea of who plans to attend and which group you would prefer to join."

Miss Lockwood's gaze targeted Noreen, and Noreen's heart oscillated like a treadle sewing machine at full speed. She swallowed—or tried to. Her throat seemed to be closing in on itself.

"Next, Miss Noreen O'Sullivan would like to propose a service project for the society's consideration. Noreen?" Miss Lockwood stepped aside and gestured for Noreen to take her place at the front of the room.

Never had a schoolroom aisle felt so long. Pulling her notes from her skirt pocket, Noreen made her way to the front, then turned to face the group. "Hello."

Was that scratchy sound her voice?

She cleared her throat and unfolded her page of notes, the paper's crinkling echoing loudly in her ears.

Make eye contact with your audience. Smile. Don't forget to breathe.

She'd written Martha's instructions on the top of her page and did her best to follow them. Her mouth curled, probably too far, judging by the strange looks on the faces before her, but she checked the item off her list anyway. Breathing proved trickier than one would expect, but she took a precious heartbeat to inhale and exhale before continuing. Martha sat in the front row, providing a friendly pair of eyes to connect with first. Even Jane sat tall and gave her a little nod of encouragement when Noreen glanced her way. Hortense

Lockwood intimidated her, so she steered her attention to Ellie Throckmorton instead.

"Many of you know that I am a member of the Woman's Christian Temperance Union. You might expect me to quote statistics about how the drinking of strong liquor leads to criminal behavior, the degradation of morality, and the destruction of families. However, I'm not here to preach to you. I'm here to share a story and seek your help.

"Before my mother married Arthur Clevenger and we moved here to Albany, my mother was married to a man known to his friends as Fiery Finn O'Sullivan. He was loud and hot tempered, but my earliest memories of my father were of a man who would tickle my ribs and carry me around on his shoulders. He had his surly moments, but he was my papa and my hero. Until the pain from his time in the war caught up to him. War takes a toll on a man, and my father began to break under the weight of the memories. He turned to strong spirits to try to forget, but the liquor took a toll of its own. It changed his temperament and led to him exacerbating an old war injury that then impeded his ability to work our farm. The more frustrated and helpless he felt, the more he turned to the saloon for succor. Yet the more he leaned on the bottle, the more his troubles expanded. He vacillated between being sullen and being angry and violent.

"My mother and I bore the brunt of his temper for years. He beat us down with derisive words, and when that wasn't sufficient, he beat us with his hands as well. Home was no longer a safe haven. It was a battlefield. One where a father broke his little girl's arm on two occasions and, even worse, broke her heart."

Noreen's voice cracked, and she rubbed her right forearm, the pain seeming to rise to the surface as she spoke of the past.

Steadying herself with a few blinks and a small sniff, she faced her audience again. Several expressions radiated compassion, sending an invisible salve into the sore places of Noreen's heart.

"Eventually, his drinking killed him, leaving my mother a widow with a mortgaged farm and no way to work it. The Lord provided for us, but we both carry deep scars from our time living with my father's drinking.

"I share my story for two reasons. First, I hope that giving you a glimpse into my life helps you to know me better. I love what this society represents, and I want to be a sister to each of you. Second, I want you to understand why I am so passionate about supporting the temperance movement. I've witnessed firsthand the power of liquor to destroy a life and damage a family. I can't abide the thought of there being another little girl or boy in our community huddling beneath their bed, hiding from a drunken father who could strike them at any moment. Our children deserve to be safe in their homes."

Heads began to nod, and Noreen's confidence grew.

"That is why I am proposing that we sponsor a temperance parade. Not only for our society to participate in, but for us to invite all members of the community to join. It would be a short parade around the square. Those who wish to carry signs may, but it is not required. We can sing temperance hymns, and those who feel comfortable can distribute temperance pledges to encourage sobriety. If all you feel comfortable doing is walking, that is fine, too. A show of numbers makes a statement all on its own. A statement I hope will convince the city council to declare Albany a dry town. Parson Cowan has already agreed to lead a short prayer meeting at the conclusion of our rally. My hope is that each of the ministers in town will announce the event to their congregations so that we might have a strong showing from the entire community. But we need a group of women to organize and lead the effort, and I can think of no better group than our society." Her gaze skimmed over the assembly, briefly meeting the eyes of every lady in the room. "Thank you for your consideration."

Feeling raw and exposed yet filled with more hope than she'd felt toward her community in quite some time, Noreen folded her notes and walked back toward her seat.

"Thank you for your impassioned presentation, Noreen." Miss Lockwood resumed her place at the front of the room as Noreen slid into her chair.

Jane leaned close and offered a smile. "You did it," she whispered. "We'll see."

Miss Lockwood looked out over the group. "As a reminder, we need a majority vote to confirm a service project. If you vote to accept a proposal, that does not obligate you to participate, but I urge you only to vote for a project that you believe will be beneficial for the society as a whole."

Was that an endorsement or a warning not to endorse? Noreen's hand fisted around her notes with painful tightness. Jane reached over and covered Noreen's hand with her own.

"All right, ladies. It's time to vote. Let's see a show of hands. How many vote in favor of sponsoring a temperance parade?"

Chapter

18

TEMPERANCE RALLY SET FOR END OF MONTH

Support the betterment of the Albany community by partici-
pating in a temperance parade and rally on Saturday, April 28,
at 4:00 p.m. Event is open to everyone. Supporters may gather
at the Albany Baptist Church at 2:00 p.m. to make signs and
practice temperance hymns. Light refreshments will be served.
Parade participants will leave the church promptly at 4:00 p.m.
and head south on Walnut to S. 2nd Street, then turn west to
circle the courthouse square before concluding by heading north on
Main. A short prayer meeting near the corner of Main and First
Streets will follow the conclusion of the parade. Players of musical
instruments are particularly encouraged to attend.

Questions may be addressed to Miss Noreen O'Sullivan.

"What do you think?" Noreen chewed on the edge of her tongue
as she waited impatiently for James to finish reading through the
draft of her newspaper article.

Last week, the society voted 11–3 in favor of her service project.
Miss Lockwood had abstained from the vote to avoid unduly influ-
encing the group, but she'd pledged her support after the meeting.

A fact that still set Noreen to reeling six days later, if she stopped to consider it for more than a moment at a time. Yet despite the show of acceptance from her spinster sisters, a part of her craved acceptance from another quarter. Hence why she'd brought her newspaper announcement to James tonight after Martha and Jane had proofread it for her during their Tuesday Tea.

His mouth turned up at one corner, and her heart did a ridiculous series of flips at his small show of approval.

"Clever," he murmured before looking up and sharing those beautiful blue eyes with her. Eyes twinkling with good humor.

Heavens, but those twinkles set her insides to dancing. One would think she'd be used to them by now, as often as they appeared, but they tickled her belly every time. She'd even started seeking them out, developing a craving for them probably not too dissimilar from the lure of liquor to a drunkard.

The dancing in her midsection halted abruptly. Goodness. Was she experiencing an *addiction*? To a man's smile? What a horrendous thought. It couldn't possibly be the same. James's smiles might invoke certain cravings, but they weren't unhealthy. They induced no stupidity or hangovers. Well, unless one counted that dinner debacle last week and the mental moping that occurred on days when she didn't see him. But never mind that. There was nothing wrong with enjoying something that lifted her spirits and lightened her mood. Except that was exactly the type of argument her father used to make.

She gave her head a little shake. It was *not* the same. James was all that was kind and gentle and peace loving. Being addicted to his smile and his company encouraged her. It didn't eat away at her insides like poison, turning her into a cruel, unfeeling monster.

His smile flattened as his brows arched. "Why are you shaking your head? This is great."

And she was overthinking everything. Again.

"Do you think so?" She nudged aside the empty plate left over from the beef dinner she'd brought to the jailhouse. "I did my best to refrain from proselytizing. I wanted it to sound like any other community event. Like the Founder's Day parade or the community picnic on the Fourth of July."

That wonderful, tummy-tickling smile returned. "You succeeded. That is exactly the impression I received as I read it. I liked the addition of the instruments, too. Makes it feel fun and festive."

"The temperance movement in England has been using brass bands in their cause for decades." She shrugged. "I thought it might help draw attention to the parade."

"I think it's a brilliant idea. Hard to resist a band."

Hard to resist you *when you look at me as if you respect and appreciate my ideas.*

Stars and garters. If she didn't get control of her mind—and fast—something embarrassing was going to slip out of her mouth and make a fool of her.

James set the paper on the table and tapped a section near the middle. "Smart to mention the street intersection instead naming the saloon outright. Taggert will know you're targeting him, but it's subtle enough that most people won't make the connection from the article alone." He leaned back in his chair, his warm gaze finding hers again. "You did a great job, Noreen. I have no doubt that you'll recruit a sizable crowd to join your march."

She dipped her chin, his pride in her almost painful to behold. How many times had she longed to hear such praise from her father, or even her stepfather? Constant disappointment had taught her to stop seeking approval from men. But having it freely given? Her shriveled heart blossomed like a drought-strained rosebud finally receiving rain.

A touch on her hand brought her chin up. He'd leaned forward and covered her hand with his. "I mean it, Noreen. This is really good."

How on earth was she to say anything intelligent when his touch scattered all her wits?

"Thank you." There. That wasn't too vacuous. Wasn't very clever, either, but she didn't have the luxury of being picky.

James turned his head sharply, and his hand slid away from hers as he rose from his seat. Only then did she notice the sound of running feet heading their way.

"Deputy!" An out of breath man with one hand holding his hat in place as he ran came into view through the doorway. "Deputy, come quick! Fightin' at the saloon. Ten, maybe fifteen, men bustin' up the place."

James strode across the room, his confidence and authority a sight to behold. He didn't let the panic of the other man fluster him. He just collected his hat, checked that his revolver was in place, and patted the fellow on the shoulder.

"I'll be right there."

He looked to Noreen, held her gaze for a precious second, and gave his head a little shake. She heard his message as clearly as if he'd said it aloud. *"Don't follow me this time."*

She gave a slight nod, knowing her presence at the saloon would only worsen the situation. The last thing she wanted to do was make things more dangerous for him.

"Be careful."

It was an impulsive thing to say. Unnecessary even. The man had been breaking up saloon fights for years. Yet her heart wouldn't allow her to keep the words inside. He'd become too important to her.

His slow smile made her heart pump a frantic rhythm that no longer had anything to do with fear for his safety.

He fingered the brim of his hat and dipped his chin in her direction. "Yes, ma'am." Then he turned and walked out the door.

The man who'd reported the fight hung back a moment, his face etched with confusion as he looked from Noreen to the deputy and back again.

Noreen blushed, certain she could guess what was going through the man's head. Why on earth would the deputy be having dinner with a sour-tempered spinster like Noreen O'Sullivan? Not completely sure of the answer herself, she ignored the fellow and focused on clearing away the dishes and packing up the leftover food. Thankfully, witnessing a saloon fight must have held more appeal than pondering a misplaced spinster, for the next time she glanced in his direction, he was gone.

Watch over James, Lord. Keep him safe.

She picked up the article she'd written, the smile he'd worn after reading it filtering through her mind and warming her heart. This town needed a man like James Paxton. A man of integrity who served his community with a cheerful spirit and a dedication to righteousness. Yes, this town needed James, but she was very much afraid that she was coming to need him, too.

James covered the ground with a long, quick stride. He glanced over his shoulder, looking for Emmett Hansen, the young cowpoke who'd reported the incident. Fellow must've been winded, 'cause he was lagging. James sighed. He wasn't about to slow his pace to wait on the cowboy, but he sure could do with a few details as to who was involved, where they were located inside, and if any guns had been drawn.

Finally, footfalls registered beside him. James twisted his neck to confirm it was Emmett before starting his questioning, but the fellow beat him to the verbal draw.

"I can't believe you're courtin' Nosy Noreen!"

James hit Emmett with a glare so fierce, the cowboy stumbled from the impact.

Emmett's hands came up. "Easy, Paxton. I didn't mean no disrespect. That's just what the guys call her. You know, 'cause she's always stickin' her nose where it don't belong."

"I'd advise you to cease talking about Miss O'Sullivan before the urge to rearrange your teeth grows too strong for me to resist."

The cowboy's eyes widened to comical proportions. "Got it."

James ground his molars, angry at himself for overreacting. He wasn't one to threaten violence. Even violence he'd never carry out. But something primal and protective had surged within him at the unexpected attack on Noreen's character.

Forcing his throat to unclench, James steadied his voice before starting his questioning. "Who's fighting?"

"Claude Templeton started it. Accused Jude Barlow of cheatin' at cards. Threw a few punches. Jude tackled him and flattened Old Coop in the process, spillin' his drink. That's when things really exploded. Last I saw, Coop was wipin' the bar with Jude's pants while Jude was still in 'em. Folks sittin' at the bar didn't take too kindly to that and startin' protesting with their fists. I think one fella conked Old Coop with a bottle to the noggin, but Coop's like a grizzly. What doesn't take him down just makes him mad."

Sounded like a free-for-all. Not his favorite. Hard to reason with a mob. Especially a drunk one.

As they neared the saloon, angry shouts filled the air along with various crashes and thuds. James turned to the wide-eyed cowboy, who looked far too young to be in a bar at all, let alone one filled with brawlers.

"Go home, Emmett. I'll take it from here."

"Are you kidding? I got me a front-row seat."

Just then, a man flew backward through the batwing doors to crash on the boardwalk, blood streaming down his face from a cut above his eye.

Emmett retreated a step. "Maybe I'll, uh, watch from the fourth or fifth row."

James clapped him on the arm. "Good choice."

Catching up to the man on the boardwalk, James grabbed him before he could stumble back into the fray. "Fight's over, Donaldson. Go home and see to that gash."

The man tried to swing at James, but the punch was sloppy and off-center. James easily evaded.

"Unless you want to spend the next few weeks in the jailhouse for assaulting an officer, you best head home, Gregor."

The sharpness of James's tone finally penetrated the man's haze-filled brain, and he blinked. "Dep'ty Pashton? Where'd you come from?"

"Doesn't matter. I'm here now. Which means the fight is over. Go home."

Gregor straightened. Mostly. He listed a bit to one side but managed to keep his feet. Unfortunately, those feet were pointing in the wrong direction. "Need my hat."

James turned him around and aimed him toward town. "Get it tomorrow."

He didn't wait to see if Gregor obeyed. He had bigger fish to fry. Pivoting sharply, he pushed through the swinging door and took in the chaos. Overturned chairs, broken glass, cards, and poker chips scattered over the floor, and about ten men engaging in various forms of fisticuffs. Between the yelling, crashing, and thumping, James could barely hear himself think. Taggert had taken up a defensive position behind the bar, guarding the expensive bottles of liquor that made up his inventory from anyone who happened to careen onto the counter. He had one such fellow by the seat of his pants at the moment, dragging him sideways until the patron toppled over the edge and onto the floor, taking out one of the few standing barstools at the same time.

James hurried over and looped his arms around the man from behind in a diagonal hold that kept him from throwing a punch. "Party's over, Rico." James raised his voice right next to the man's ear. "Time to head home."

Rico stilled and gave a nod, seeming almost relieved to have an excuse to vacate the premises that didn't reflect poorly on his manhood. James released him and gave him a little shove toward the exit.

Taggert moved to the end of the bar, his gaze darting from James to the melee and back again. "'Bout time you got here," he shouted. "They're tearin' up my place."

"One of the hazards of liquoring up your clientele."

Taggert scowled. "Sermonize later, Deputy. My taxes pay you to keep the peace, so get to pacifyin'."

If only it were that easy. James climbed up onto the bar to get to higher ground, ignoring Taggert's frown. Placing fingers in the corners of his mouth, he let out a piercing whistle. Only the man closest to the bar heard it, and when he turned his head, his opponent sucker punched him in the chin.

James started to reach for his gun, figuring it was the only thing loud enough to get people's attention, but Taggert grabbed his boot and shook his head. "My place is busted up enough already. I don't need you shooting holes in my ceiling."

James caught a glimpse of a mop in the far corner of the bar area. He nodded his head toward it. "Bring me that bucket."

Old Coop was fighting both Claude Templeton and Jude Barlow at the same time just a couple of feet from the far corner of the bar. The moment Taggert slapped the bucket onto the bar, James grabbed the handle with one hand and the base with the other and picked his way down to the far end. The water inside smelled foul, contaminated with spilled beer, tobacco spittle, and whatever else drunk men dropped on bar floors. It was perfect.

Claude managed to land a punch that pushed Old Coop back a step toward the bar. Before the big man could recover, James doused all three with the mop water.

Momentarily stunned, the three staggered apart and blinked, trying to make sense of what had happened. As three angry faces lifted to him, James gave them the *Don't test me* lawman's stare, and all six eyes widened. Taking advantage of the slight quieting of the overall din, he let out another whistle and was pleased to see punches slow and faces turn.

"Any man still in this room by the time I walk back across this bar will be spending the night in the jailhouse."

Fists clenched in shirtfronts released and raised arms lowered to more neutral positions. A dripping Jude Barlow eased toward the poker pot that had been tossed onto the floor.

"No, you don't, you cheatin' snake." Claude Templeton lunged for him.

James was about to leap from the bar to intervene when Old Coop beat him to it. Grabbing each man by the back of his collar, Coop dragged them away from the money.

"What'd'ya say, Deputy? Who gets the winnin's?"

James tipped his head toward Taggert. "I think it's only right that all winnings be forfeit to the house to cover the damages incurred this evening."

"Seems fair to me." Coop grinned and dragged Jude and Claude toward the door. He nodded to Taggert as he passed. "Best fight I've had in a coon's age, Milt. Sorry 'bout the mess, though. See ya Friday?"

Taggert nodded. "I'll be here."

After the men filed out, James hopped down from the bar and straightened a few chairs on his way to the front of the room, trying to ignore the crunch of glass under his boots. Taggert followed the last customer and closed the main door behind him. He crossed to the window next and flipped the open sign to its closed side.

When Taggert turned around, he crossed his arms over his chest and cocked a brow at James, his expression anything but grateful. "I suppose your new *lady friend* will be happy to hear that I closed down early tonight."

James cocked his own brow in return. "You antagonize everyone who tries to help you, Taggert, or just me?"

"You're not helpin' me, Paxton. You're doin' your job. Don't act like it's anything more than that."

The barb stung, but James did his best to let it go. "Judge my motives as much as you like, Taggert, but leave Miss O'Sullivan out of the conversation. Do we understand each other?"

Taggert scoffed. "What I understand is that you're going soft for the woman who wants to shut me down. She's compromised you."

James held the man's gaze, steady and sure. "If you ever have cause to believe I've treated you unfairly, you let me know. Or let Sheriff Adair know. You just better have more than a flimsy theory to back up your accusations." James tipped his hat and moved to the door. "See you at the next brawl."

Chapter
19

When the day of the rally arrived, Noreen rushed through her shift responsibilities at the hotel with an urgency that almost proved disastrous when her elbow caught the edge of the large serving tray holding all the luncheon desserts she'd just plated.

"Careful!" Luella grabbed the corner of the teetering tray just in time to keep it from clattering to the floor.

A whoosh of air exited Noreen's lungs as her culinary life passed before her eyes. "Thank you." If Luella hadn't been working the bread station on the same counter, Noreen would've been forced to create sixteen servings of an entirely new dessert, since she'd sliced the last of the pies. Baking something new, even something as simple as a custard or brown betty, would have set her back nearly an hour. Thank heaven for Luella's youthful reflexes.

"Noreen!" Mrs. Winslow's authoritative voice echoed through the kitchen.

Noreen turned to find the head cook glaring at her from over the top of a perfectly seared venison steak.

"Hang up your apron and get out of my kitchen before you ruin my lunch service."

"Yes, ma'am." She dipped her chin to hide her flushing cheeks, but she wasn't about to argue with being let go a few minutes early.

She reached behind her back to untie her apron strings, then lifted the white garment over her head as she began making her way toward the side exit.

"Oh, and Noreen?"

She pivoted to face the main kitchen area and met her employer's gaze. "Yes?"

"I look forward to your parade this afternoon." The woman didn't exactly smile, but her usual intensity softened for a moment, inspiring a burst of warmth to bloom in Noreen's chest.

"Thank you, ma'am."

As Noreen hung up her apron and placed her bonnet on her head, Luella hurried over for a quick word. "I'll be there as soon as the lunch dishes are done."

Noreen took her hand. "You are a treasure, Lu."

The girl smiled. "Mama said I could stay with you tonight, too. I can't wait." She bounced slightly at the pronouncement, widening Noreen's grin.

"I'll have your sign waiting for you at the church."

Mrs. Winslow cleared her throat. "That bread's not going to slice itself, Luella."

"Yes, ma'am." Luella hurried back to her station, but not before wrapping her arms around Noreen in an impulsive hug.

That girl. Noreen shook her head as her heart swelled with affection. Such a gift.

After securing her hat with a pair of pins, Noreen took up her bag, left the hotel kitchen, and headed to the church three blocks away. As she passed the wagonyard, she spotted a young boy handing out flyers to the men gathered there. Men who started grinning and slapping each other on the back after reading whatever had been printed on the page. Curiosity piqued, Noreen veered toward the boy as he reentered the street. His eyes met hers, but he didn't move in her direction. In fact, he turned his back and headed in the opposite direction.

"Excuse me," she called. "May I have one of those pamphlets, please?"

Thankfully, someone had drilled enough manners into the lad that he halted and turned to face her, even though his expression made it clear it was the last thing he wished to do.

"Sorry, lady. These are for menfolk only." He pulled the pile of papers against his chest, blocking her view.

Menfolk only? Noreen stiffened. Of all the chauvinistic, exclusionary . . . She forced herself to breathe. It wasn't the child's fault. He was just repeating what he'd been told.

"Well," she said, careful to keep her voice pleasant, "I happen to be heading to an event where several men will be in attendance. I'd be glad to distribute a few of those flyers for you. Save you the trouble."

His face scrunched as if he were considering the offer. After a moment, though, he shook his head. "Nah. I best hand 'em out myself. Sorry."

The boy turned and headed across the railroad tracks toward the lumber shed.

"Wait!" She took a few steps after him, then stopped.

For pity's sake. She had more important things to worry about than some male-eyes-only advertisement. She was about to turn and be on her way when a familiar figure stepped out of the carpentry shop on the corner.

James's face lit as he saw her. "Hey, Noreen. The big day's finally here. Are you excited?"

She rushed up to him and grabbed his arm with one hand as she pointed at the retreating boy with the other. "James! Thank heaven. I need you to go after that boy and ask him for a pamphlet."

"A . . . pamphlet?"

"Yes. He wouldn't give one to me. Said they were for menfolk only."

He raised a brow. "And you want to see a pamphlet intended for men because . . . ?"

"Because censorship is unconstitutional. Now go after him."

"I'm not sure this qualifies as censorship."

Why wasn't he moving? She gave him a nudge to try to get him started. "Just take your manfolk self after him and get a pamphlet."

He chuckled. "My manfolk self?"

Realizing that she was making no headway trying to force him to do her bidding, she gave up and did what she should have done in the beginning—ask. "Please, James?"

His demeanor softened before her eyes, as if those two simple words had completely disarmed him. His reluctance to fetch a pamphlet for her had been obvious, yet his shoulders dipped as if he'd made up his mind to acquiesce simply to please her. *Her.* Noreen "Troublemaker" O'Sullivan. Her insides melted in an instant.

"All right." He raised a brow and pointed a finger at her in warning. "But if there's anything offensive on that page, I'm not showing it to you."

"I agree to letting you summarize the contents for me should that be the case."

He blinked. Then laughed and shook his head. "Of course."

She worried he might be losing patience with her, but the look in his eyes exuded more fond amusement than exasperated annoyance. A fact that made her heart expand almost painfully in her chest. How easy it would be to fall in love with this man.

She touched his arm. "Thank you."

His gaze settled atop her hand for a moment before returning to her face, and when his eyes reconnected with hers, the level of heat emanating from them had doubled.

"Stay here."

Not a problem. That look had weakened her knees to the point that she'd not trust them to carry her anywhere.

She managed a nod as she reluctantly dropped her hand away from his arm, freeing him to chase down the boy with the flyers.

Noreen watched him go, strangely enamored with every move he made. A ridiculous infatuation, really. He was just a man walking down the road. The same as any other man in town. Only, he wasn't any other man in town. He was James Paxton, and she was coming dangerously close to thinking of him as hers.

James strolled into the lumber shed, scanning the area for the boy with the pamphlets. Why Noreen cared about such a thing on a day when she should be focused on her rally, he couldn't imagine. But when she'd turned those big brown eyes of hers on him and asked for his help, he'd been helpless to resist.

"Hey, Deputy." Connor Reed raised a hand in greeting.

James waved at the young lumberman. "Reed, good to see you." He glanced around the interior of the shed and frowned when he didn't find the boy. "You see a kid come through here with a bunch of flyers? I wanted to see what he was passing out."

"You just missed him." Reed stepped away from the fresh planks he'd been treating with creosote for preservative purposes. He set his brush down and reached inside the pocket of his trousers. He took out a folded sheet of paper and offered it to him. "You can take mine. I don't have any need of it. My ma would tan my hide if I showed my face inside the Salt Fork."

The saloon? James's interest instantly increased tenfold. He took the paper and scanned the contents, his gut churning. They'd suspected Taggert would pull some kind of stunt, but neither of them had anticipated such a clever move.

Forcing a smile onto his face, James nodded to Reed. "Thanks for this."

"Sure thing. See you at the parade later?"

"Yep. I'll be there." Watching out for Noreen and her marchers. Even more now that he knew to expect trouble at the end of the line. "You gonna play your trombone?"

Reed's face reddened slightly. "Yeah. Marian twisted my arm. Said she liked hearing me play."

And that's probably all the twisting his arm had needed. A man predisposed to please a certain woman capitulated easily. Shoot, some would even chase down a mysterious pamphlet in the hopes of earning a smile. Although Noreen's smile wouldn't last once he handed the flyer over.

"See you later, then," James said as he turned to go.

As much as he wanted to hide the truth to keep from spoiling Noreen's big day, he knew better than to try. She'd not thank him for prolonging her ignorance. Didn't make him feel any better about being the one to impart the news, though.

The sun hit his eyes with uncomfortable force as he exited the lumber shed. He spotted Noreen at the edge of the street, surprisingly right where he'd left her. He'd half expected her to be standing in the middle of the railroad tracks, tapping her toe impatiently against the steel. The moment she spied him, however, she abandoned her post and hotfooted her way over to him.

"Did you get one?" She eyed the folded sheet of paper in his hand with enough curiosity to kill an entire herd of cats. "Can I see it?"

He handed it to her without a word. Nothing he could say would change the truth, anyway.

Her eyes scanned over the advertisement. "'April 28,'" she read aloud absently, "'4:00–6:00 p.m. All drinks at the Salt Fork Saloon will be . . .'" She looked up at him, disbelief etched into her features. "Half price?"

The paper started to slip from her fingers, so James took it back into his possession and shoved it into his pocket.

"He's sabotaging everything I'm trying to achieve."

"Well, you *are* trying to put him out of business."

Fire flashed in her eyes. "I'm trying to save lives and make our community safer!"

James nodded. "I know. But he's trying to save something, too. His livelihood."

Her hands fisted at her sides. "I can't believe you're taking his side."

James bit back a sigh, then reached out and gently circled his fingers around her wrist. He rubbed his thumb over the end of her sleeve. "I'm not taking anyone's side, Noreen. I'm just trying to keep things in perspective."

She stiffened but, surprisingly, didn't pull away from his touch. "And you think I lack perspective?"

"Only where Taggert is concerned." He kept his voice calm and patient. "You see him as a nemesis who aims to thwart you at every turn. But he's just a man. An imperfect, somewhat cranky man who probably sees you as the villain in *his* story. Don't let him get under your skin. You don't want to show up at the church full of anger and resentment. That's not what your rally is about. It's about hope and encouragement and civic outreach. Isn't that what you've told me?"

She gave a shallow nod.

"*That's* the positive energy you need to bring to your followers. Don't worry about Taggert and his schemes. He might intend to harm your cause, but we serve a God who can take what man intends for harm and use it for good."

She exhaled a heavy breath, then slowly unfurled her fingers. James slid his hand down and fit her palm against his, his pulse kicking up a beat as he did so.

"Focus on all the people who are supporting you. Give *them* your attention, not Taggert." He gave her hand a tender squeeze, wishing he could wrap her into a hug instead. "Remember, I'll be with you every step of the way. Watching over the parade and ensuring that Taggert plays fair."

He'd add monitoring the men heading to the saloon for cheap drinks to his list as well. Hopefully, his presence would encourage them to mind their manners around the protesters.

"You're right," she said, her head bowed as she stared at her feet. "I need to focus on the rally, not the saloon. We can still sway those who . . ."

Her words faded, but her head shot upward, a new excitement sparkling in her eyes. "Oh, James! I just had the most wonderful thought. Taggert's discounted drinks will increase the number of men coming to his saloon. Men who will have to walk right past our prayer meeting. Don't you see? The people most in need of temperance pledges will be heading straight for us!"

It was all he could do not to take her smiling face in his hands and kiss her senseless. He'd always been attracted to Noreen's passion and fire, but witnessing her overflow of optimism nearly undid him. He was falling. Hard. He just prayed his heart didn't shatter upon impact.

Chapter
20

Thirty-five! Thirty-five people stood in the churchyard lining up to make the march through town. Noreen's heart felt as if it might burst from abundant fullness. Even in her wildest dreams she'd only imagined perhaps twenty people showing up for her parade, but the Lord had exceeded her expectations. Five men with instruments stood near the front. A trombone, a cornet, two clarinets, and a drum. A sixth man wore a washboard and held a pair of spoon handles at the ready. Noreen was pretty sure she recognized him as a regular saloon patron, but he'd signed a temperance pledge, so she'd agreed to let him march.

Except for the pair of ministers who'd joined their parade, the rest of the participants were women, and what a wonderful collection of women they were. Ten of her spinster sisters showed up for the parade, including Hortense Lockwood, wielding her influence with a deft hand as she recruited other ladies of her generation to join. Looking through the ranks, Noreen recognized several women from church and many others from about town. Each ready to march for the cause of temperance. Amazing! Only God could have accomplished this.

Even Jane had joined the festivities. She stood in the back of the group, flanked by her parents, but she was there, and Noreen's heart soared at her friend's willingness to overcome her fear of public attention in order to lend her support.

Noreen had tied dozens of white bows over the past few days, the symbol of purity and commitment to the cause of temperance. She'd distributed ribbons and pins to everyone who had come, and as she inspected the ranks, those white bows glimmered in the sunlight like stars shooting forth bursts of hope from every lapel or bodice.

"And they that be wise shall shine as the brightness of the firmament; and they that turn many to righteousness as the stars for ever and ever."

Oh, how she loved that verse, how she'd clung to it through the years, as if the prophet Daniel had spoken those words specifically to inspire her mission. Yet the longer she'd toiled alone, the more she'd felt her brightness dimming as discouragement and opposition cast deep shadows over her heart. But not today. Like a sputtering candle that ignites a mighty bonfire, through God's power, her flickering flame had joined with others to bring about a conflagration so bright, it would cast aside every encroaching shadow and shine hope and purpose into the darkest corners.

"Everyone ready?" Noreen peered down the rows, her heart swelling at each nod and smile that greeted her.

"Ready!" Hortense Lockwood wiggled the sign she held with enthusiasm. Black letters painted on white pasteboard proclaimed, *Prohibition Promotes Probity.*

Noreen grinned. "Excellent."

She was fairly certain the majority of spectators would have no idea what *probity* meant, but Miss Lockwood had been so proud of her alliterative accomplishment, Noreen hadn't had the heart to suggest she replace the final word with a term more readily recognizable, like *morality* or *integrity.* People knew what the parade was promoting. They'd figure it out.

She made her way toward the front of the group, double-checking that everyone had their song sheets provided by the Woman's Christian Temperance Union. She'd specifically selected songs that utilized the melodies of popular hymns or patriotic tunes to make things easier. When she reached the band members near the front, she met Connor Reed's eye. The trombone player was the most skilled of the musicians and had volunteered to take charge of the music.

"Do you feel comfortable with the song order, Mr. Reed?"

He offered a salute. "Yes, ma'am. 'Yankee Doodle,' 'The Old Hundred,' 'Happy Day,' and 'America.' That right?"

"That's perfect! Thank you for taking charge."

His cheeks reddened. "Shucks. You're the one in charge, Miss O'Sullivan. I'm just the accompaniment."

"Well, I'm exceedingly grateful you're here. All of you." She extended her smile to cover each of the musicians in turn. "Your contributions will add a level of festivity the rest of us couldn't achieve on our own. Your playing will draw attention to a worthy cause, and I've no doubt the Lord will reward you for your participation today."

Noreen stepped into position at the front of the parade block. She, Martha, and Luella would lead the pack, each bearing a sign to make their purpose known to all who saw them. Luella's sign proclaimed that *A Sober Life Is a Better Life*. Martha's urged the community to *Make Albany Dry*. And Noreen's sign exposed her woundedness for all to see. *Drunkenness Destroys Families*.

Martha handed Noreen her sign and gave her arm a squeeze. "Excited?"

Noreen nodded, even as her stomach clenched. "Nervous too. So many people came. I don't . . . I don't want to let them down."

A twinkle lit Martha's eyes. "You're far too stubborn to let that happen."

A chuckle loosened the tightness in Noreen's chest. "You're right."

Martha winked. "Of course I am. I'm a teacher. I'm paid to be right."

Luella's laughter joined the mix. "It's true. No student has ever won an argument with Miss Evans. Her rightness is quite legendary."

Nerves banished beneath the power of shared joy, Noreen checked the watch pinned to her bodice. Almost time to start.

She turned to face the group. "Five minutes, everyone!" She

eyed the single drummer of the group. "When I signal, start your cadence."

The man nodded and held his sticks at the ready.

As she pivoted to face forward, a movement to her right snagged her attention. James. His gaze met hers, and her chest grew so airy, she wouldn't have been surprised to find her feet lifting from the street to float above it. He smiled and tipped his hat, his expression abounding with pride. For her. She couldn't fully absorb the wonder of it, but it infused her spirit with a warmth that made her feel invincible.

She raised a hand to wave, but his expression shifted away from her and hardened slightly. Noreen turned to see what had caught his attention, and at first her heart leapt with joy.

Mama.

Noreen had prayed her mother would come. That she would stand beside her daughter to support a cause they both believed in. But she hadn't come alone. When Noreen noticed the frowning man at her side, her delight curdled.

After her article had come out in the paper, her stepfather had made his displeasure known, pulling her aside in the churchyard to scold her after services last week. The moment he began rehashing the familiar diatribe on the disgrace she would bring upon him by making a spectacle of herself, however, Noreen had turned her back and walked away. The cut had roused his ire, of course, but the days of her obligingly subjecting herself to his criticism had passed. The man had relinquished any right to dictate to her the moment he banned her from her mother's home.

James, bless him, put that long stride of his to good advantage as he strode past the parade block and reached her stepfather before Arthur could reach Noreen.

"Clevenger! Good of you to come out to support the community this afternoon." James positioned himself directly in her stepfather's path.

"Step aside, Deputy. I intend to have a word with Miss O'Sullivan."

"Sorry, sir. The parade's fixin' to start. Only participants are allowed in the staging area." He paused and raised a brow. "Unless you intend to join the parade?"

Join the parade? Arthur? Noreen shared an amused glance with Martha and Luella.

"Don't be absurd," Arthur sputtered. "I just, uh . . ."

Noreen swore she could hear his mind churning, desperate to find a way to outmaneuver James.

All at once, he stood a little straighter, his eyes gleaming. Noreen's stomach tightened uncomfortably.

"My wife asked me to escort her here so that she could wish her daughter good luck." He turned to Mama. "Isn't that right, dear?"

Noreen's indignation flared at the way her mother seemed to shrink beneath her husband's regard.

"I *would* like to speak to her. If I may?"

James dipped his chin and smiled at her in a way that allowed her to stand a little straighter. "Of course, ma'am. I'm sure she'd appreciate your encouragement."

As if Mama would be offering any. Noreen did her best to let go of the bitterness that threatened to spring up and choke her joy, but the weed proved resilient. She knew what Mama would say. Whatever Arthur wished. Yet it felt like ages since she'd spoken to her mother, and Noreen longed to share a piece of this moment with her. No matter how small.

Stepping out of formation, Noreen met her mother at the edge of the street. "Mama."

"Noreen." She looked uncomfortable and cast a glance over her shoulder to where Arthur stood.

The man's gaze shot a pointed look in their direction, one Noreen desperately wanted to bat away before it could impale her mother, but all she could do was take her mother's hand and distract her from her overbearing husband.

"Just relay his message, Mama. I'll not hold it against you."

Her mother turned back to Noreen, her shoulders drooping as if they'd forgotten how to hold themselves upright. "Arthur would like you to reroute your parade to circle only the south side of the courthouse square instead of looping and going down the north side twice." She kept her voice low so others wouldn't overhear. "The business owners on that side are quite unhappy about the disruption your demonstration will cause and have been pressuring him to do something about it."

Noreen bit back a sigh and did her best to remember the advice James had given her earlier. Focus on her supporters, not her detractors. It just hurt that her mother fell into the detractor camp.

"I'm sorry, Mama, but I can't do that. The parade route has already been advertised, and my marchers have their instructions. I won't derail our preparations just to please a handful of irritated shop owners." She released her mother's hand and began to step away. "It's unfair for Arthur to ask me to do so."

"Yes, it is."

Noreen halted. Had her mother just disagreed with her husband?

Mama caught Noreen's hand before it could slip away and squeezed it tightly. Tears shimmered in her eyes as her shoulders actually straightened, and her chin lifted.

"I am so proud of you, Noreen. You're making a difference. Making this community safer. Better. If I could, I'd be marching at your side. I want you to know that I will be . . . in my heart."

Noreen was so stunned it took her a moment to react. Mama must have misinterpreted her silence as disapproval, for she released her hand and dropped her head back into its cowed position. This sight broke Noreen's heart even as it broke her out of her stupor. She lunged for her mother and embraced her in a fierce hug.

"Thank you, Mama."

Her mother's arms circled her back. "I love you, sweet girl. Always and forever. Never doubt that for a moment."

"I love you, too."

A hand touched Noreen's shoulder, bringing her head up. Martha's face greeted her.

"It's time."

Noreen nodded and stepped away from her mother, giving a little sniff to clear away the residual emotion as her mother hurried back to where Arthur waited. James met Noreen's gaze for a heartbeat, a question lingering in his eyes. She answered with a smile so wide her cheeks pinched from the effort. Then she turned to her supporters and gave the call.

"Ladies and gentlemen . . . here we go!"

She looked to Connor Reed. "Let's jump into the first song right away, shall we?"

He nodded, and she signaled the drummer with a point of a finger. The cadence rang out through the air. Noreen faced forward, waited for a count of four so everyone could feel the beat, then stepped off with her left foot.

Within eight counts, the tune of "Yankee Doodle" began, and Noreen lifted her voice in the first temperance hymn of the day.

> "Now don't you know the reason why
> The temperance cause is winning?
> Our Bands of Hope resolve to try
> The pledge when life's beginning."

Her stepfather scowled as the group marched past, and for once, Noreen sought his gaze instead of avoiding it. The words of the chorus took on a double meaning as numerous voices swelled behind her.

> "That's the way to win the day,
> Wait a little longer;
> Drink shall fall with tyrants all,
> When Bands of Hope are stronger."

Chapter
21

James had trouble keeping his eyes on the spectators instead of Noreen as the parade wound through town. Never had he seen her so vibrant or confident. When he did manage to tear his gaze away from her, he remained attuned to her voice. Strange how he could pick out her alto from among all the other voices. Or maybe not so strange, considering how dear she'd become to him of late.

A good number of townsfolk had come out to see the temperance brigade and hear the band. A pair of ladies trailing the parade handed out pledge forms to anyone who would take one, targeting not only men but women and older children as well.

As they rounded the courthouse, pledge forms waving in the breeze, a new temperance song began, this one to the tune of a song he'd sung in church many times—"Happy Day."

> "All you that would be sober here,
> Come join our cause with hearts sincere;
> Forsake strong drink without delay,
> And you will surely win the day.

"Happy day! Happy day! When drinking times are done
    away.
Come sign our pledge without delay,
And live rejoicing every day.
Happy day! Happy day! When drinking times are done
    away.

"The children, too, will take a part,
And join our cause with hand and heart,
And help to send strong drink away,
So shall we surely win the day."

The chorus began again, and a few spectators joined in the song. At least the parts they recognized from church. Things could not be going better, and James thanked God for working things out for good for Noreen despite the couple of hiccups she encountered earlier this afternoon. As they turned down Main Street, however, James hurried his step to move ahead of the parade, determined to head off any trouble that might be brewing down the road. The Salt Fork Saloon stood only a block and a half away, and even from here, James could see a group of men gathered in front of the building. Praying they didn't intend anything too menacing, he broke into a jog to scout out the hostile territory.

It seemed the half-price drinks came with a catch. Taggert had propped his batwing doors open and set up a temporary bar directly inside the doorway. Chairs lined the boardwalk against the walls on both sides of the entrance, most filled with men holding pints in one hand and signs in the other. Signs that read, *My Money, My Choice*; *Jesus Drank Wine*; and *Wet Whistles Make Jolly Gents*.

"Hey, Paxton? You here for a drink?" Taggert grinned at him from behind the table he'd dragged against his doorway. "Beer's half price till six."

A hurrah erupted from the men gathered in front of the Salt Fork, followed by the clinking of glasses. Taggert smirked.

"No, thanks." James kept his demeanor calm and friendly. "Interesting setup you got here."

Taggert shrugged, his eyes glittering with cockiness. "Didn't want the fellas to miss the parade, so I decided to offer outdoor seating."

"Along with printed commentary, I see." James picked up a sign that had been leaning against the wall to the left of the door. "'Eat, drink, and be merry'?"

"What?" Taggert widened his eyes in mock innocence. "It's in the Bible. Thought all those self-righteous temperance folk liked spouting Scripture." His expression hardened. "I got just as much right to promote my views on the issue as they do." He nodded toward the approaching parade.

Noreen and her band had reached the billiard hall and were closing in on the saloon.

James turned back to Taggert, a note of warning creeping into his voice. "You're right about your freedom of speech, but I expect you to keep things civil. If any of your patrons gets out of hand, I'll shut down this little outdoor operation of yours and cite each man here for public intoxication. Are we clear?"

"You hear that, boys?" Taggert raised his voice to a near shout as his glare bored a hole in James's forehead. "The deputy here wants us to keep things civil. I say we welcome our parading friends with a cheerful song."

The patriotic sound of "America" echoed from the temperance band as Noreen and her group marched onto the scene.

> "Here let poor drunkards come,
> We'll burst their chains from rum—"

A loud, discordant harmonica overpowered the approaching voices and instigated an off-key rendition of "Old Dan Tucker" among the boardwalk throng.

> "Old Dan Tucker was a fine old man
> He washed his face in a frying pan
> He combed his hair with a wagon wheel
> And died of a toothache in his heel."

What Taggert's band lacked in musicality, they made up in enthusiasm. They belted the old folk song at the top of their lungs. A pair of grizzled fellas even decided to dance along, linking elbows and kicking up heels as boots stomped and hands clapped.

James had to give Taggert credit. The man had done his homework. Not only had he anticipated the tactics Noreen would use, he'd turned them against her. James had faith in Noreen, though. If she could manage to keep Taggert from crawling under her skin, she'd come out on top. He'd be keeping a close eye on these whiskery saloon singers, though. Drink could both embolden a man and dim his wits, a dangerous combination when one hoped to keep the peace.

What was that horrendous noise? Noreen tried to sing over the cacophony coming from outside the Salf Fork Saloon, but after marching and singing for the last thirty minutes, her voice had weakened.

As if responding to a clamorous gauntlet being thrown, Connor Reed's trombone doubled in volume. The other musicians joined suit, one of the clarinetists squeaking occasionally due to the increased airflow. The horns grew so loud, Noreen could no longer hear her own voice, let alone the voices behind her.

She pivoted to walk backward so she could signal Connor to quiet the instruments, but before she could do more than wave to get his attention, Lonnie Wilson with his washboard breastplate cut ranks.

"Is that 'Old Dan Tucker'? Boy, howdy. I love that song." He and his spoons dashed toward the saloon, his cackling voice singing out,

> "Get out of the way, Dan Tucker.
> You're too late to git your supper.
> Supper's gone and dinner cookin'.
> Old Dan Tucker's just a-standin' there lookin'."

"Lonnie!" She called after him, but only once. She recognized a lost cause when she saw one.

As they drew alongside the saloon, her heart sank. Men—lots of men—in high spirits. Clapping hands. Stomping feet. Brandishing signs. Signs that minimized the dangers of drunkenness and even justified its practice.

She fell out of step with the drum's cadence. She'd been prepared for a crowded saloon, but she'd not anticipated that Taggert would take the fight to her with song and dance and frivolity. Who wouldn't be attracted to what appeared to be harmless fun? Smiling faces, dancing feet, overloud singing. Clever man. Daring her to lose her temper and play the shrew for all to see. She knew she had to resist, but the desire to storm the saloon and bash him over the head with her sign was so strong, she handed her pasteboard weapon to Martha, fearful she'd succumb to the urge despite her better judgment.

"Take the group around the corner for the prayer meeting," Noreen instructed Martha. "I'll see if I can bring the noise down."

Martha's eyes widened as she shook her head. "Don't do anything rash. You'll undo all the good we've accomplished today."

Noreen smiled. "I won't. I promise. I'm just going to hand out some temperance pledges."

"Taggert won't like it."

"That's never stopped me before."

Martha raised a brow. "That's what worries me."

Luella leaned into the conversation. "I'll go with you."

Martha and Noreen answered in unison, "No."

"Please. My father's there." She tipped her head toward the far end of the group of chairs lining the boardwalk as she dropped one edge of her sign in order to pull a folded piece of paper from her pocket. "He needs this, Miss Evans. I'll just talk to him and no one else."

"It would be better for you to talk to him at home, Lu," Martha said.

Trusting Martha to dissuade Luella, Noreen glanced behind her and noticed her tidy ranks morphing into an indistinct blob. She signaled for the group to move past, then caught Mr. Cowan's attention. The preacher worked his way toward her.

"I'm going to do my best to quiet their singing," she said, raising her voice to be heard over what had to be the fifth verse of "Old Dan Tucker." Good old Dan must've had quite an eventful life. "Hopefully, it won't be so loud on the other side of the wall. Do you think you can make yourself heard for the prayer meeting?"

Jane's father smiled. "I've been orating sermons into dull ears and distracted minds for more than twenty-five years. I know how to make myself heard. Besides, the Lord will calm this storm. Remember, he's in control."

"I know."

She *did* know. She didn't doubt God's sovereignty for a moment. What she doubted was his willingness to intervene on her behalf. Yes, it felt as if the Lord had been more active in her life of late, blessing her with James's friendship, the support of the spinster society, and all the wonderful people who'd joined her parade. Her heart had swollen from all the gratitude swimming around inside her today. Nevertheless, memories of her childhood tempered her optimism. How many times had she prayed for God to save her and Mama from her father's drunken temper? Why hadn't he intervened then? No one had a good answer for that question. Not even Mr. Cowan.

From her own study of Scripture, Noreen had eventually concluded that while God did intervene directly in people's lives from time to time, he also worked to accomplish his will through humans. Prophets spoke his words, warriors fought his battles, and servants ministered to those in need. She'd long ago decided that she wouldn't sit back and wait for the Lord's intervention. She'd be a warrior for his cause, serving him on the battlefield. And today, that battlefield consisted of a swath of boardwalk lined with tipsy men singing a discordant melody. Surrender was not an option. At least, not one she would accept.

As Mr. Cowan led the group around the corner, Noreen turned to face her battleground and reached for the temperance pledges in the cloth bag slung across her body. Not surprisingly, James found his way to her side.

He didn't try to steer her away or talk her out of her mission, he simply stood guard beside her as she approached the men on the boardwalk.

She made her way to the harmonica player first. "Afternoon, Mr. Carter. You sure play a fine harmonica."

He removed the instrument from his mouth long enough to smile her way. "Why, thank you, Miss Noreen."

Before he could raise it back to his mouth, she pushed a pledge sheet under his nose. "Did your mother teach you to play?"

A frown marred his face, as if he couldn't quite figure out what his mama or his harmonica had to do with the piece of paper currently hindering his music making. "No, ma'am. I taught myself."

He lifted a hand to push the paper aside, but Noreen anticipated the move and shifted the paper to collide with his fingers so they would instinctively take hold.

"How talented you are. It takes a great deal of practice to master a musical instrument. A man with that kind of self-discipline has no need for liquor to dull his senses. Think how proud your mother will be to learn you've signed this temperance pledge. An answer to her prayers, I'd wager."

"My mother passed two years ago." His eyes grew slightly misty.

Oh dear. "I'm dreadfully sorry to hear that. I lost my father many years ago, too. He drank himself to death. That's why temperance is so important to me, you see. I want to save men like you from ending up like my father."

Mr. Carter lifted his harmonica back to his mouth, but instead of continuing the peppy tale of Old Dan Tucker, he began a mournful rendition of "Home on the Range."

The singing dwindled, and the dancing stopped as the mood shifted. Noreen grabbed several more pledge forms and handed them around to anyone polite enough to take one.

"You don't need to sign it today. Take it home and read it. Consider how temperance can benefit both you and your families."

A voice behind her groused, "Get her out of here, Paxton. She's harassing my customers."

James stepped back to deal with Taggert. "Your customers are on a public walkway, not inside your place of business. She's free to hand out literature to anyone she wishes."

"Think of your children." Noreen nodded to one of the older men who'd been dancing a moment ago. "Your grandchildren. Don't you want to set a good example for them? Have them be proud of you?"

A man on the end lurched from his chair and stomped toward Noreen, his face a mottled red, and his eyes narrow slits. "You got no right talkin' about our children like you know who we are. You don't know us." He swung out his hand and snatched the temperance pledge out of the harmonica player's lap. He tore it down the middle. "You think you're so much better than us, but you're not." He bunched the pieces together and turned them sideways to tear them again. "You're nothin' but an interferin' busybody"— *rip*—"too ugly to find a husband of your own"—*rip*—"so you go around punishin' other women's husbands." *Rip*.

Stunned and horribly embarrassed, Noreen froze in place as pieces of shredded paper rained down on the boardwalk. Until she felt James's hand brush the small of her back as he moved to place himself between her and the angry man.

"That's enough, Templeton." He held out a placating hand, treating him as he would a wild horse.

Templeton? This was Luella's father? A knot twisted in Noreen's chest. She recognized that look in his eyes. One that promised retribution. Thank heaven Luella would be staying with her tonight.

"Please, Papa. Listen to her. You need this."

No! Noreen swiveled her gaze down to street level, where Luella stood looking up at her father with tears in her eyes.

In a flash, his anger redirected. "What I need is for my daughter to mind her own business."

Noreen dropped her pledge forms and ran down the steps, her only thought to get to Luella before her father forgot a lawman watched his every move.

Luella, brave, loving girl that she was, stood her ground. "The drink is hurting you, Papa. Hurting our family."

Noreen reached Luella's side and immediately wrapped an arm around her shoulders and began drawing the girl away.

Mr. Templeton's gaze burned into Noreen's. "You turned my own kin against me. You'll pay for this."

Good. Keep that anger directed at me.

"Your daughter loves you. If you were sober, you'd see that."

James caught her eye and jerked his head toward the far side of the building, his message clear. *"Get the girl out of here."*

She couldn't agree more. "Come on, sweetheart. He's not ready to listen yet." He might never be.

Tears streamed down Luella's cheeks, but she finally submitted to being drawn away, even as one of the men closest to her father slapped him on the back and offered to buy him another round.

Rather ironic for a temperance woman to be thankful for the power of alcohol to sway a man away from his family, but Noreen's gratitude for the drink buyer winged heavenward as she hurried Luella back to the safety of the prayer meeting.

Chapter
22

Noreen enjoyed a bit of celebrity status at church the following morning. Several people she knew only in passing made a point to speak to her either before or after services to comment on the parade. *Positive* comments! A couple of ladies even asked about how to join the Woman's Christian Temperance Union. It felt a bit like walking through a dream. One from which Noreen was in no hurry to wake.

Besides the one tense moment with Mr. Templeton, the day had been a rousing success. Not even Taggert and his beer-drinking cronies had upset her for long. Brother Cowan's booming voice had echoed off the side wall of the saloon as he sermonized briefly on the merits of sober living before leading them in a beautiful time of prayer on behalf of those who struggle to resist liquor's lure, for their families, and for the health of the community as a whole. By the time he'd finished, even a couple of the men who'd been holding signs at Taggert's had snuck into the back of the crowd, hats in hand.

Seeds had been planted. She prayed God would bring them to fruition, that there might be a harvest of righteousness in Albany, Texas.

Not only had her parade gone better than she'd dared imagine, but afterward she'd enjoyed a wonderful night with Luella. Sharing cookies and cocoa had made her feel ten years younger, as had the bedtime whispering that had lasted until nearly midnight. The most treasured time, however, had been when they'd clasped hands and prayed for Luella's father and both of their families. Noreen had even managed to squeeze out a couple of grudging prayers on behalf of Milton Taggert. She couldn't claim any great level of altruism in the act, but she liked to think that James, and maybe even the Lord, would have been pleased with the effort.

Swinging a basket filled with fresh biscuits and two jars of preserves, Noreen walked up Walnut on her way to the jailhouse. James had volunteered to supply a half-dozen eggs and a slab of bacon for their simple, breakfast-themed supper that evening. She'd had a lovely luncheon with Jane and her parents after services but had been looking forward to her time with James all afternoon. Partly because she wanted to seek his opinion on how to go about getting a local-option law on the ballot to outlaw the sale of liquor in Albany, but mostly because she just enjoyed spending time in his company.

His ready smile and easy laughter acted like a happy contagion. The more she exposed herself to him, the easier her own smiles came. Not only did time in his company temporarily relieve her of her burdens, but when she picked them back up, they never failed to feel lighter. As if he'd taken some of the weight away when she hadn't been looking. Or maybe his theory about joy making a person stronger had some merit.

The jailhouse came into view and, with it, the handsome deputy with his smile on display as he stood in the doorway, lazily leaning a hip against the jamb. Her pulse picked up its pace at the sight, as did her feet. With her gaze focused ahead of her, she didn't see the young boy running in her direction until he darted in front of her, nearly tripping her in the process. A gasp whooshed out of her as she drew up short before plowing him in the head with her basket.

"You Miss Noreen?" The boy's chest heaved as if he'd run a fair distance. He couldn't be more than nine or ten, and the frightened look in his eyes immediately dissolved the scold forming on her tongue.

"I am." Her heartbeat took on a painful edge.

"Teacher said to show you this and tell you to get to the school-house right away." He thrust a crumpled piece of fabric toward her.

The edges of the scrap opened as she took it from him. Was that blood? A red stain in the center of the white handkerchief clenched her belly with dread. Then she spotted the flowers. *Dear Lord, Martha!* But, no, the initials by the forget-me-nots started with an *L* not an *M*. Luella!

"James!" Noreen started to run toward the jailhouse, then remembered the boy. She stopped and turned back to him. "Run and fetch the doctor."

"My brother's already doin' that. Miss Evans was helping Matty and me with our reading lessons when Lu showed up all busted." The boy's eyes shone with unshed tears.

Noreen bent down and cupped the little man's shoulder. "You did well. Thank you for finding me."

The boy shrugged and scrubbed at his eyes as if to erase the evidence of how the crisis had shaken him. "Weren't hard. Everyone knows you eat supper with the deputy on Sundays."

"Noreen?"

Speaking of the deputy . . . Noreen straightened and met James's concerned gaze. Craving steadiness in a world quickly spinning out of her control, she reached out to him, her arms trembling. He immediately clasped her elbows, offering support as she pressed one hand against his chest.

"It's Luella. She's been hurt. She's at the schoolhouse."

His face hardened, not in anger, but in readiness for whatever trouble awaited. "Then let's go."

She nodded, his stability infusing her with much-needed calm.

James acknowledged the boy, patting the youngster's back. "Thanks for fetching us, Toby. Get on home now."

Toby nodded but didn't move. "I'm pretty sure her pa's the one that done it. This ain't the first time Lu's showed up at school with a bruise, and I heard tell Mr. Templeton was good and riled after the parade yesterday."

Lord, have mercy. Noreen clutched James's forearm. Was she responsible for this?

"Thanks, Toby." James hugged her hand against his side. "I'll be sure to have a talk with him."

Talk. She knew all about those talks. The local law had talked with her father a few times, too. Never did any good. Even if there was evidence of abuse, the law wouldn't do anything about it unless someone pressed charges. That someone being the abuser's wife. A wife who'd vowed loyalty to her husband before God and who likely feared retaliation should she speak out against him. Society considered men to be the rulers of their households, and whatever happened behind closed doors a private matter. As a minor, Luella wouldn't be allowed to press charges herself, even if she wanted to, which she likely didn't, knowing Lu's tender heart. The helplessness Noreen had vowed never to surrender to again crashed into her chest like a runaway locomotive.

"Noreen? You all right?" James's gentle voice pulled her out of her spiraling thoughts.

"Fine." Not really, but she'd pretend to be for Luella's sake. "Let's go."

Still carrying the basket of biscuits, she hiked up her skirt with her other hand and ran to the schoolhouse. James loped along at her side, his sheltering presence both a comfort and a fuel that kept her moving forward.

By the time she reached the school and pounded up the stairs, her lungs ached from her heaving breaths.

"In here," Martha called from her classroom.

Noreen followed the call into the schoolroom, her heart sinking as she spotted Martha sitting on the floor in the aisle holding Luella's head in her lap. Desks had been shoved aside to widen the passage, making it easier for them to approach, but the sight of tears streaming down Martha's face had Noreen stumbling.

Martha was a rock. Always steady. Always in control. But not today. Not with dear, sweet Luella battered so badly Noreen almost didn't recognize her.

"She stumbled in here about twenty minutes ago," Martha said. "Barely able to walk. I think her right arm might be broken. Probably some ribs, too. I sent Matthew Dockins to fetch Dr. Perry. The only open wound I found is on her forehead, but everywhere I touch causes her so much pain." She stroked Luella's hair off her forehead, a sob catching in Martha's throat.

"It's all right Miss Evans." Luella's head shifted just a bit, her voice weak and broken, just like the rest of her. "It doesn't hurt so bad now."

Abandoning her basket, Noreen fell to the floor beside them, carefully covering Luella's left hand with light fingers. She watched the girl's face for any indication that she was causing her pain, but both of her eyes had swollen nearly shut, and her mouth bore a puffy split lip, making it difficult to judge reactions. The sight of her face alone broke Noreen's heart.

"Lu, I'm so sorry. I never should have let you march in that parade."

"Not your fault. I wanted to." Luella's head turned slightly toward Noreen, the slit of one eye finding her friend's gaze. "No regrets. He needed me to march. Needed to see the truth. Now he has. It'll change him. You'll see."

What Noreen saw was that being confronted with his sin had changed him into a monster who had nearly killed his youngest daughter. No repentance. No mercy. Just lashing anger.

"Is . . . is the deputy with you?"

James stepped forward and crouched next to Noreen. "I'm here, Luella."

She tried to lift her head, but the motion caused her to whimper and fall back onto Martha's lap. "Would you . . . check on my ma? She stayed behind after sending me away. I need to know . . . she's all right."

"I'll go right now."

174

"Thank you." The slit of Luella's eye closed, and her body went limp.

"Luella?" Panic gripped Noreen. She grabbed the girl's shoulder and gave her a gentle shake. "Lu?"

James laid a hand on Noreen's shoulder. "She's still breathing. Watch her chest. See?"

Sure enough, the girl's bodice rose and fell in shallow increments. *Thank you, Jesus.*

"She likely just passed out from the pain. A mercy, really."

Sweet Luella could use all the mercy she could get. Noreen reached for James's hand on her shoulder and squeezed it as she bowed her head in silent prayer.

Pounding footsteps outside brought her head back up almost instantly.

"Miss Evans?"

"In here, Doctor!"

Noreen rose and moved out of Dr. Perry's way as the man bustled in with his medical bag in hand.

"Will you be all right?" James murmured in a low voice, his hand coming to rest in the curve of her back.

She nodded. "I'll stay with Luella. Make sure she has everything she needs. Go see to her mother. Bring Trudy here, if she can make the trip. Luella will want to have her close."

She always had. After one of her father's beatings, Mama would come to Noreen's room and curl up beside her on the narrow bed, wrap her arms around her, and sing soft lullabies in her ear until Noreen fell asleep. Those moments of love and security offered just enough candlelight to get her through the dark times.

"I will." James's fingers tightened at her waist, and that old candle flame roared to life, brightening the darkness closing in on Noreen, and helping her banish her own ghosts in order to focus on helping Luella.

What Luella needed was protection, a guarantee that her father would never hurt her again.

James dropped his hand from Noreen's back and moved toward the door, but Noreen lunged out and caught his arm. "Wait."

He turned, his eyes full of questions.

"What will you do when you find him?"

James's jaw clenched. "If I catch him in the act of assaulting his wife, I'll arrest him on the spot and throw his sorry hide in jail."

"And if you don't?"

"Then I'll do my best to convince Mrs. Templeton to press charges and testify against her husband in court."

"And if she won't?" Noreen knew what his answer would be, what it *had* to be legally, but she couldn't stop herself from pushing. Turning a blind eye toward family violence had to stop. Laws had to change. People had to change.

He let out a sigh, his shoulders sagging beneath the weight of his regret. "I'll do what I can, Noreen. Maybe when I rip into him about his disgraceful behavior, I'll rile him enough that he'll take a swing at me. It would give me an excuse to arrest him."

"Well, don't purposely place yourself in danger." The last thing she wanted was for another person she cared about to be harmed today. "I expect you to come home to me in one piece."

He smiled and tugged on the brim of his hat. "Yes, ma'am."

Then he left, and the light in her world dimmed just a bit, causing her to shiver as she hovered over Luella and waited for the doctor's report. Her gaze darted toward the door several times as she tried to reignite her sputtering optimism. Dark thoughts circled her mind like wolves prowling just outside the reach of the campfire. She could feel them encroaching. Old, familiar enemies released from their cages and ready to pounce the moment her light flickered out. She tried to feed her fire with hopeful thoughts and love for her friend, but as the doctor said things like "three cracked ribs," "radial fracture of the arm," and "possible brain contusion," the icy water of her anger began dousing the flames one by one.

Chapter 23

James hoofed it over to the livery to claim his horse, then rode out to the Templeton place at a fast canter. His prayers bounced back and forth between petitioning the Lord to heal Luella and pleading for protection for the girl's mother.

His jaw clenched as he leaned forward in the saddle. Husbands had a sacred duty to protect their families. Any man who not only neglected that duty but used his physical strength as a weapon against those in his care was eligible for the millstone treatment as far as James was concerned.

Images of Luella lying broken on the schoolroom floor haunted him as he urged his mount to a greater pace. A child. A brave, loving child who wanted to save her father from his own destructive impulses. She didn't deserve this. No child did.

His heart throbbed in his chest as he thought of Noreen. Was she back in that schoolroom reliving all the times her own father had struck her?

Protect her heart, Lord.

He knew she blamed herself, and she might soon blame him if he couldn't find legal cause to arrest the skunk responsible for Luella's injuries. The thought of disappointing her flayed him like a barbed-wire whip. Too many people had let her down in her lifetime, and heaven help him, he didn't want to be added to that list. She deserved a champion. Someone who always had her back. That's who he wanted to be. Her partner. Her defender. Her . . . man.

His jaw clenched again as the realization that had been sneaking up on him for the last few days broke into the clearing of his mind. He was in love with her. In love with a woman who would complicate and disorder his life to no end. In love with a woman who might never trust a man enough to let him into her heart.

James blew out a breath and adjusted his position in the saddle. Now wasn't the time for soft feelings or romantic contemplations. Noreen was counting on him to protect the women of this community. His gut twisted as he recalled the helpless anger that had flared in her eyes as she'd questioned him about how he planned to handle Claude. How many times had the law failed to protect her and her mother? Too many. Even one time would be too many.

Don't let me fail this family, he prayed. *Help me be your arm of justice today.*

As he neared the Templeton homestead, he slowed his mount to a walk and drew his revolver. Wives rarely pressed charges against their husbands in cases like this, which meant his best chance of putting Claude behind bars entailed catching him in the act. Announcing his arrival would sabotage that endgame. So he reined in his mount near the edge of the barn, slid silently from the saddle, and hunkered below window height as he hurried toward the back of the house.

Once he reached the kitchen door, he fit his hand to the knob and eased it open a crack. He strained his ears, listening for any clues about what might be happening inside and where his suspect might be. No shouts or crashes echoed through the home. His gut knotted. Quiet didn't bode well.

The hinges creaked as he opened the door far enough to squeeze inside. The homestead wasn't large. Single story. Probably three bedrooms. If he remembered correctly, Luella was the youngest of four kids. The others had married and moved away one by one over the last several years.

Slinking forward on the balls of his feet to keep his heels from clicking on the floorboards, James made his way down the hall, checking each room he passed. An office stood to his right, but a quick duck of his head through the doorway proved it empty. He reached the front room next, and his mouth went dry. Overturned chairs, a broken lamp, a reddish stain in the middle of the rug. An image of Luella lying atop that rug, clutching her side, blood running from a cut on her head rose in his mind, making his chest ache.

"I *told* you to get out!"

James pivoted. The flash of some kind of dark cudgel snagged in his periphery. He raised an arm to block what ended up being a cast-iron skillet swinging at his skull.

The skillet swinger gasped, the sound immediately followed by the clatter of the weapon falling to the floor. "Deputy Paxton!" The horrified voice of Trudy Templeton filled the hall. "I'm so sorry. I-I thought you were . . ."

"Your husband?" James holstered his weapon, then rubbed at the dent in his forearm where the skillet had connected. He wiggled his fingers for good measure. Nothing seemed to be broken, but he'd likely sprout a prize-winning goose egg by tomorrow.

Mrs. Templeton pressed her lips together, shame darkening her cheeks. Cheeks that were already starting to bruise.

He tipped his chin toward her face. "Did Claude hit you, ma'am?"

She said nothing.

James worked his jaw. He wanted to help. To protect these women. But if they closed ranks on him, his hands would be tied.

"Did he thrash your daughter?"

Trudy's eyes lifted to meet his, desperation screaming from their blue depths. "Have you seen my Luella? Is she . . . ?" Gathering tears added a sheen to her eyes that tugged on James's heart.

"She's alive, ma'am. Dr. Perry was tending her when I left the schoolhouse."

"Thank God." The woman seemed to crater in front of him. James took hold of her arm and guided her to the sofa.

As much as he wanted to sit beside her and offer comfort and compassion, he had a job to do. "Where's your husband, Mrs. Templeton?"

"Gone."

"Where?"

Her hands shook as she smoothed the fabric of her skirt over her knees. "Don't know. Don't want to know."

Keeping his voice gentle, James sought her face. "He'll be back, Trudy."

She nodded. "I know. But Lu and I won't be here. I'm takin' her to my son's home in Abilene. Soon as she's well enough to make the trip. We can stay with Miss Lockwood until then. She came to see me after the parade. Said if Luella or I ever needed a place to stay for a night or two, she kept a guest room ready." Trudy rose from the sofa and turned pleading eyes on James. "My husband's not a bad man, Deputy. He loves us. He just . . . forgets himself when he drinks."

A circumstance that happened far too frequently of late.

"He could have killed your daughter today. Had he assaulted anyone else to that extreme, he'd already be behind bars. You need to help me protect her. Protect you."

Trudy's mouth pinched. "By shaming my husband in public? That's what brought this on in the first place. Luella spoke out against him in front of his friends. She never should have done that. Had the child minded her own business, none of this would have happened."

James's gut hardened. "What happened to Luella is *not* her fault. Not any more than the bruises on your face are yours. The blame belongs to your husband, and him alone."

The man sickened James, taking out his anger and self-loathing on women and children. Making them feel as if they were the ones to blame for his despicable actions. Endangering the lives of the precious souls God had placed in his care. The man deserved to be behind bars, preferably after accumulating a few bruises of his own. Though as much as James itched to mete out some frontier justice, he'd not dishonor his God by forfeiting his honor. Vengeance belonged to the Lord, not to man. James would have to trust the Lord to repay Claude for his wrongs, especially if Trudy refused to press charges.

The woman raised her chin, a spark of defiance and an entire bonfire of pride radiating from her tear-filled eyes. "Thank you for coming to check on me, Deputy, but I need to ask you to leave. I've no crime to report and no time for pointless conversations. You can see yourself out."

A sigh deflated his chest. Expecting her lack of cooperation didn't make receiving it any less disappointing. Yet he'd not leave her out here unprotected should Claude return sooner than anticipated.

"Yes, ma'am." He dipped his chin in deference. "I'll hitch up your wagon and have the team ready to go by the time you finish packing. Then I'll follow you into town."

She gave a disdainful sniff. "Suit yourself."

James smiled. He'd take that as a thank-you.

Trudy didn't dally. By the time James tacked up the team, hitched them to the wagon, and drove to the front of the house, a large leather suitcase and a bulging carpetbag sat waiting for him on the porch. He tossed them into the wagon bed, then found Trudy locking the front door with a third bag tucked under her arm.

James hurried up the steps. "I'll get that for you, ma'am."

She offered no protest as he relieved her of her physical burden. He wished he could relieve her of her emotional burden as well. The woman looked haggard and defeated as she turned her back on her home.

After storing the last of her luggage, James offered Mrs. Templeton a hand up as she climbed into the driver's seat. She collected the reins, her eyes focused straight ahead. James started to move away, then halted when she finally spoke.

"Would you . . ." She swallowed, probably to rid her throat of the pride obstructing her plea. "Would you arrange for the wagon and team to be returned?"

"I'll take care of it personally." It would give him a reason to plant himself in Claude's house and wait for him to come crawling back.

She nodded, her gaze meeting his for the first time since she'd asked him to leave. "Thank you, Deputy."

He nodded, wishing he could do more.

Noreen sat on a hard, ladder-back chair in Dr. Perry's clinic, next to the cot where Luella rested. The doctor had wrapped the girl's ribs, Martha said she hadn't found any open wounds. Maybe she couldn't see the gash because of how Luella was lying on the floor? where she'd hit a table on the way to the floor, and treated her smaller cuts and scrapes with iodine. Now he was in his workroom, preparing plaster of paris bandages to serve as a cast for Luella's recently set arm while Martha gently applied a cool compress to the swelling around Luella's eyes.

This never should have happened. It *wouldn't* have happened if Claude Templeton had been in his right mind. She swore she could hear the demons cackling over their victory. Another child forced to pay the price for an intemperate man's weakness.

The sound of the clinic door opening drew Noreen's attention to the hall.

"Luella? Are you here?"

"Mama?" Luella batted away the compress with her uninjured arm and tried to sit up, but Martha pressed her back against the pillows propping her up in bed.

"Stay still, Lu. She'll come to you."

Noreen made sure of it, jumping to her feet and hurrying out to the waiting area to fetch Trudy Templeton. "In here." She ushered Trudy down the hall to the small room where Luella waited.

The moment Trudy saw Luella, a sob broke from her chest. "Oh, my baby!" She ran forward and fell into the chair Noreen had vacated.

"Mama?" Tears clogged Luella's voice, too. "Are you all right?" Luella turned her head, searching her mother's face through her painfully swollen eyes.

Trudy wiped her eyes ruthlessly, then gripped her daughter's hand. "I'm fine, sweetheart. Don't you worry about me."

The woman was definitely in better shape than her daughter, but Noreen saw evidence of reddened bruising developing along her jaw and under her right eye. Her own jaw clenched in response.

Luella lowered her voice, but it still carried through the quiet room. "Did Deputy Paxton arrest Papa?"

Trudy shook her head, and the dam holding back Noreen's anger cracked.

"No, I'd already sent him away. We'll stay with Miss Lockwood for a day or two until you feel up to a train ride, then we'll go visit your brother for a few weeks. How does that sound?"

It sounded like Trudy was finally taking steps to protect her daughter, praise the Lord. Claude still needed to answer for his crime, though. To be held accountable for the pain he'd caused. To face the truth of the damage his drinking had wrought. Otherwise, nothing would change.

"But who will take care of Papa?" Luella asked. "You know how he forgets to eat when he gets to drinking."

"He's a grown man. He can take care of himself. And if we're lucky, maybe he'll remember there are other people he should be taking care of, too."

Oh, how Noreen prayed that would happen. Luella deserved a father who loved her and took care of her. But as long as he poisoned himself with liquor, Claude Templeton would never be anything more than a selfish, abusive thug.

"I don't want to leave him, Mama." Luella's tone turned pleading. "He needs us."

No! Noreen fisted her hands with such force, her nails dug painfully into her palms. Luella couldn't put herself back in that man's path. The next time he came after her, she might not survive.

Martha leaned down and stroked Luella's hair. "He needs your prayers, Lu. That's what will help him the most."

"What he needs," Noreen said between clenched teeth, "is to be cut off from the poison that's rotting his soul."

Spotting a broom standing in the corner, Noreen snatched it up and marched out of the clinic, not hesitating for even a heartbeat when Martha called out for her to stop.

There'd be no stopping this time. This was war, and there were about to be some casualties.

Chapter
24

Noreen shoved through the batwing doors of the Salt Fork Saloon without a single twinge of discomfiture. Society might deem this place forbidden for decent women, but she wasn't a decent woman at the moment. She was a warrior ready to strike at the enemy's heart.

A quick scan of the dim interior showed only a handful of patrons. A foursome played cards at a back table while two others sat at the bar. Gambling and drinking on the Lord's Day. Disgraceful. Yet she wasn't here for them.

She spotted her quarry trying to hide behind the bar. Narrowing her gaze, she strode for the gleaming mahogany counter. Voices ceased their prattle as awareness of her presence spread through the room.

Poised behind the bar with a towel in one hand and a glass in the other, Milton Taggert turned. His eyes flew wide a moment before they narrowed into slits.

"Get out of my bar, Noreen." He moved down to the edge of the bar closest to her and jabbed a finger toward the door as if she might not be aware of how to find the exit.

She tightened her grip on the broom handle and glared at her nemesis. "Claude Templeton beat his daughter nearly to death today, Mr. Taggert. Because he was drunk out of his mind, thanks to your vile brew." Her voice swelled in volume and stridency as the reins on her emotions slid from her grasp. She smacked her broomstick against the bar, and the man sitting two stools down flinched. "A child, Mr. Taggert. An innocent, loving, kindhearted young girl is lying in Dr. Perry's clinic right this moment broken, bloodied, and bruised because of your need to make a profit." Her voice broke and tears misted her eyes, but the weakness only enraged her further.

"Look, Noreen, I'm sorry the girl was hurt, but what a man does after he leaves here has nothing to do with me."

"Nothing to do with you?" she screeched. "It has *everything* to do with you." She wagged her broom near his face, but he knocked it aside with the side of his hand. "You fill these men up with poison day after day, then claim it's not your fault when they sicken? Do you have *no* care for the destruction of our community? For the safety of our children?"

Tremors beset her, but she refused to back down. Refused to surrender.

A man came up behind her and touched her arm. "C'mon, Miz O'Sullivan. Let me walk ya ho—"

"Don't touch me!" She whirled on him, nearly taking his head off with her broom.

"Whoa!" He lunged backward just in time to avoid her wild swing.

She hadn't meant to attack him, but he'd startled her. An automatic apology rose to her tongue, but she bit it back. These men could overpower her at any moment. She had to take advantage of their surprise and what few manners their mamas had drilled into their boyhood brains.

Heart thundering, hands sweating, and lungs heaving, she dodged the man beside her and ran down to the end of the bar. Taggert moved to intercept her.

"Go fetch the law, Rico," he shouted.

Using one of the bar stools like a ladder, Noreen scrambled up onto the bar and stood atop its polished surface.

"Get down from there, you imbecile," Taggert yelled. "You're gonna get hurt." He reached for her ankle, but she leapt over his hand and ran down the bar as if it were the middle of the street.

Her sensible shoes and plain navy skirt reflected in the bar's mirrors as she turned to face her Goliath. She held a stick instead of a stone, but she *would* bring this giant down.

Gripping the broom like a bat, she swung with all her might. Glass shattered as the broom handle sliced across a row of liquor bottles. The sharp smell of spirits hit her in the face, turning her stomach and bringing her tears back to the surface.

Taggert's shouts barely registered.

For Luella! Swing. For temperance! Swing. For her daddy. Swing.

Tears rolled down her face, blurring her vision and obstructing her aim. Sobs wracked her body and weakened her arms as new griefs and old ones combined.

Arms grabbed her from behind and dragged her off the bar. Someone else caught her broom and wrenched it from her hands. She kicked and struggled, but most of all, she wept.

James led the unhitched Templeton team to a trough inside the livery corral, then patted the shoulder of the horse nearest him as the animal dipped his head to drink. He'd arranged for them to be boarded until closer to sundown when he would deliver them back to the homestead. He planned to make himself comfortable in Claude Templeton's house as he waited for the man's return. He and Claude were gonna be having some serious words.

"Deputy Paxton!"

James lifted his head at the feminine call. Martha Evans waved at him as she ran down the street. Immediately alert, James ducked through the corral fence and strode to meet her.

"Hurry! You have to stop her." The usually unruffled schoolmarm looked about as ruffly as one of his mama's aprons. Loose tendrils of hair flying about, petticoats exposed from her dash down the street, eyes wide and a bit wild.

"Stop who?" He purposely spoke slowly and in a low timbre to try to calm Miss Evans. Pulling information from a flustered witness was like piecing together a jigsaw puzzle. Much more efficient to spend a moment steadying the person's pulse so he could extract the facts in an orderly fashion.

"Noreen."

The moment he heard the name, all thoughts of calm fled.

"Where is she?" he demanded. Location was the most critical information. The why and how could wait. If Noreen was in trouble, he needed to get to her. Period. The rest could be figured out later.

"I think she's heading for the saloon."

James didn't wait for more details.

"She has a weapon," Miss Evans called after him.

That tidbit turned his jog into a run. A half-formed prayer for her protection shot from his soul as his feet pounded the street. A dozen scenarios played through his mind. None of them good.

As he turned down Main, he nearly plowed into Rico Travers.

Rico grabbed James's arm. "You gotta get to the Salt Fork, Deputy. The woman's gone plumb loco."

"That's where I'm headed." Shaking off the man's hold when he didn't release him fast enough, James took off again, his gaze locked on the saloon at the end of the block.

He plowed through the batwing doors at the same time that Old Coop dragged Noreen off the bar. Jude Barlow helped, grabbing some kind of stick from her hands. A fire ignited in James's belly as he witnessed the woman he loved struggle against a gang of men twice her size. Her anguished sobs flayed him like a whip upon his back.

In an instant, his gun was in his hand and aimed at the men who dared lay hands on Noreen. "Let her go," James roared. "Now!"

Jude Barlow dropped the broom with a clatter and shot his arms straight into the air. Old Coop's reaction was slightly slower but no less emphatic. He released Noreen as if she'd suddenly morphed into a pile of hot coals, opening his arms and holding out his palms while Noreen crumpled to the floor.

James expected her to jump to her feet and start railing at the men, but she didn't. She just huddled on the floor, sobbing. Ice crystalized in his veins. Had she been hurt? Abused?

"Back away," he barked as he marched forward. He waved his gun in case the men standing around were too drunk to understand his command.

They cleared a path. All except Taggert.

"They didn't hurt her, Paxton," the barkeeper said. "They just—"

"Move." James pointed his gun at Taggert's chest. Now was not the time for explanations.

Taggert raised his hands and stepped out of the way, offering a clear line of sight to the woman lying on a floor covered with tobacco spittle, spilled beer, and mud from the bottoms of men's boots. The sight tore his heart in two.

He hurried to her side, holstering his weapon as he went. "Noreen?" He crouched beside her, gently resting his hands on her shoulders. Prepared for her to try to fend him off if she thought him another drunken cowboy, he wilted a little when she didn't so much as lift her head. Her fire had been extinguished. "It's James, honey. I'm here."

Still no reaction. His gut tightened.

"Are you hurt, sweetheart?" He exerted a little pressure on her shoulders, trying to help her unfold so he could scan for blood.

Finally, she turned her face up to his. "James?"

Swollen red eyes peered at him through wet, spiky lashes. But it was the raw grief in her gaze that told James what he needed to know. She was hurt all right, but not from her scuffle with the Salt Fork patrons. Her wounds ran deep into the crevices of her spirit.

She reached for him, twisting her body to face his as she clasped his neck with enough force to nearly pull him over. His arms circled her and pressed her tightly against his chest as he steadied them both. Slowly, he pushed to his feet, and when she sagged against him, he swung her up into his arms.

He wanted to carry her back to his quarters, hold her, and soothe her until the storm bedeviling her passed. But he had a duty to perform as well, one that couldn't be ignored.

He met the eyes of each man standing around gaping at Noreen. "I'll be back to collect statements from each of you as soon as I get Miss O'Sullivan settled. Don't be going anywhere."

Taggert scoffed as he crossed his arms over his chest. "You coddle all your criminals this way, Paxton? Or just the ones you're courting?"

James ground his teeth. "Miss O'Sullivan is no criminal."

Taggert's eyebrows rose to sarcastic heights. "No? Here I thought vandalism and destruction of private property were crimes. But I guess the high and mighty James Paxton knows the law better than a lowly tavern owner." His gaze hardened. "Or maybe that skirt you're holding has pulled the wool over your eyes and blinded you to actual evidence."

Noreen gave a tiny moan and buried her face in his coat. James tightened his hold on her, but he also lifted his head and scanned his surroundings, taking in the broken bottles behind the bar, the cracked mirror, and the smell of alcohol emanating from Noreen's clothing.

His gut soured at the evidence he could not deny.

"She traipsed in here, wielding that broomstick like a cudgel. Took a swing at Rico and another at me before she scrambled onto the bar and started smashing bottles left and right. That's at least a hundred dollars' worth of damage, if not more!"

"The little gal was upset, Milt," Old Coop said.

"Upset don't give her the right to tear up my bar!" Taggert, eyes snapping, turned on James and jabbed a finger in his direction. "If you want to get her settled before takin' statements, that's fine, but you better be settlin' her in a cell, 'cause that's where she belongs. Unless the law don't apply to gals who make sheep's eyes at the deputy."

James clenched his jaw. The man could attack his honor all he wanted, but he was getting dangerously close to besmirching Noreen's reputation, and that James would not allow.

"Watch what you say, Taggert." James's voice rumbled with a low authority that served to wipe some of the acrimony from the barkeeper's face. "I'll not have you slandering the lady."

"And I'll not have you letting her off the hook just because you've taken a shine to her."

"Enough!" James shot the man a glare hot enough to melt metal. "I made a vow to this community to administer justice without partiality, and I've never done otherwise. So instead of accusing me of something I haven't done, why don't you get of my way and let me tend to Miss O'Sullivan. The sooner I see to her, the sooner I can return and file those charges you're so eager to press."

Taggert grumbled but stepped aside. James shifted Noreen slightly in his arms, then strode for the door. A wide-eyed Martha met him on the boardwalk.

"Is she hurt?"

James didn't slow his pace. The sooner he got Noreen out of the town's view, the better. "No, but she's gonna need your help. Fetch Miss Cowan and a set of clean clothes for Noreen and meet me at the jailhouse."

Miss Evans dogged his steps. "The jailhouse? Why? We should take her to the boardinghouse."

"Can't." His armful was growing heavy and talking was becoming difficult.

"Why not?" Miss Evans demanded.

"'Cause she's under arrest."

Chapter
25

Noreen clung to James and hid her face in the crook of his shoulder, wanting to face neither the town nor the truth of what she'd done.

"She's under arrest."

His dire pronouncement had rumbled through his chest, vibrating her cheek even as it stabbed into her soul. She'd not be the first temperance fighter to spend time behind bars, yet the prospect held no allure. Not when the sentence carried a stain that would reflect poorly on her friends and family. On James.

James.

How disappointed he must be in her. A criminal, just like Taggert accused. And not even for the first time. James had stormed in to rescue her, sheltered her with gentleness and sweet endearments, all the while believing her to be innocent. She was anything but. Yet when confronted with the evidence of her misdeeds, he hadn't rejected her. Hadn't left her crumpled on the floor where she deserved to be. Instead, he'd taken her in his arms and carried her through town as if she were injured and defenseless and he her protector.

Maybe she *was* injured. Heaven knew she felt broken. Hollow. Damaged.

And tired. Tired of fighting a war she couldn't win. Tired of carrying secrets that had been poisoning her spirit as surely as Taggert's alcohol had been poisoning Luella's father.

When they finally made it to the jailhouse, James lowered her to the chair where she usually sat when she joined him for dinner. If only this were an ordinary Sunday evening where they would eat and talk and laugh together. Noreen slumped forward, not wanting to meet James's gaze or feel the stabbing pain of his disappointment.

James wasn't one to be easily thwarted, however. He hunkered down next to her feet and peered up into her face. When she tried to turn her head, the gentle touch of his fingers on her chin steered her attention back to his face.

"Look at me, sweetheart."

The endearment pierced her chest. She didn't deserve his kindness. His . . . affection.

"Are you hurt?" He took her hand in his and stroked the back of it with his thumb.

She squeezed her eyes shut and shook her head. A tear slid through her lashes to drip down her already soggy cheek.

He pushed to his feet, his hand sliding away from hers. The loss of his touch stirred a mournful ache in her belly. *This* was what she deserved. To be cast aside. Yet he didn't abandon her. He returned a moment later and began washing her face with a damp towel that had been warmed by water from the stove's reservoir. Never had she received such a humble, selfless gift. The towel caressed her face one stroke at a time, wiping over her closed eyes to clean away her tears. He took his time, soothing her with patient ministrations, yet all the while, her shame built until she finally opened her eyes and clasped his wrist.

"Don't." Her voice rasped against her throat. "I don't deserve your tenderness. I lost control. I . . . I'm a criminal."

James set the towel aside and took hold of her hand again. She tried to pull away from him, but he wouldn't let her. Stubborn man. Didn't he realize that associating with her now would destroy his career? No one would vote a man into the office of sheriff who not only consorted with criminals but allied himself with them.

"I don't see a criminal when I look at you, Noreen." Even the tenor of his voice soothed. "I see a woman who cares deeply for others, especially young girls who are suffering the same pain that she herself suffered. I see a woman who stirs my heart. A woman who is incredibly brave and a tad reckless, but only because she cares so much."

A woman who stirred his heart? Could it be true? She searched his face, finding nothing but admiration and genuine concern in his beautiful blue eyes. Yet as much as his words offered balm to her battered spirit, they also tore at her conscience. He didn't know the full truth about her. Didn't know of the stain upon her soul.

A surge of energy pushed through her exhaustion. "James." She laid a hand upon his shoulder, doing her best to forget how wonderful it had felt to rest her head within the crook of that shoulder and accept his shelter. "You have to distance yourself from me. Don't give me any special treatment. Don't you see? Taggert will accuse you of misconduct. You could lose your position. Lose your future. I'm not worth it."

I'm not worth you.

A scowl marred his features. "You *are* worth it. Worth any trouble that might come from this." He hung his head a moment, and when he lifted his face to hers again, his scowl had been replaced by a tender smile that made her want to believe that happy endings really did exist for people like her. "Whatever comes, I'll handle it. This isn't the first time someone's been unhappy with the way I've chosen to enforce the law, and it likely won't be the last. I'll carry out my duty, but I'll do it in the way I see fit. And right now, taking care of you is my top priority."

Then she had to convince him that he'd accomplished that task.

"You've taken excellent care of me." She forced herself to sit straighter in her chair, sliding her hand away from his shoulder and tugging her other hand free of his hold. "You carried me halfway across town, for pity's sake." Somehow she managed to manufacture a smile. "I lost myself for a while there, but I'm better now. I'm ready to face the consequences of my actions."

She scooted her chair back and forced herself to stand, thanking God when her legs didn't immediately crumple beneath her. James rose as well.

"Take me to the cells upstairs, James. Lock me up." When he made no move to escort her, she started walking to the central staircase that separated the office from his living quarters. "If Edna Hanover could abide the accommodations for a few nights, I'm sure I can, too."

"You know this is gutting me, don't you?" She closed her eyes at the anguish in his voice. "The thought of you behind bars . . . after all you've been through . . ."

Noreen spun to face him. "This is your job, James. I don't blame you for arresting me. I respect you for it. You have more integrity and compassion than any man I've ever met, and I am honored to have been your friend. But we must put that friendship aside. I took the law into my own hands, and I broke it. Those actions come with a price, and that price must be paid."

"I'd pay it for you, if I could."

Yes, he would. She could see the truth blazing in his earnest gaze. But she cared for him too much to allow him to do anything so foolish.

"You're a good man, James Paxton. And one day, you're going to be an amazing sheriff. Don't forget that dream."

Forget me instead.

James's jaw clenched as he marched back to the saloon, the squeal of the cell door hinge and the click of the lock ringing with deafening volume in his mind. It shredded his heart to lock Noreen in that cell. Loving someone meant protecting them, not administering pain. And what had he done? Treated the woman he loved like a prisoner. It didn't matter that she'd not held his actions against him. He still felt like a cad. The only thing that had eased his guilt was that he had locked Miss Evans and Miss Cowan in with her before he'd left.

Martha had promised him that they would take care of Noreen, clean her up, make her space more comfortable. Shoot, he'd moved half his furniture upstairs to assist. A side table and lamp, the extra chairs from around the dining table. He'd even switched out the cell cot for the mattress from his bed. Hopefully, Noreen wouldn't be staying in that cell for long, but he intended to make her as comfortable as possible for whatever the duration entailed.

The preacher's daughter had brought supper and a bag of books while the teacher had brought Noreen a change of clothes and some other personal items. He prayed Noreen would accept their friendship and support better than she had his.

She was pushing him away. He could feel it. She'd practically said as much, telling him to put their friendship aside and focus on his dream of becoming sheriff. As if that selfish goal mattered one iota to him when she was suffering. He would *not* be setting their friendship aside. If anything, he intended to deepen it. Prove to her that he couldn't be scared off by a little scandal. She meant too much to him to be set aside, and he'd not let her push him away. No matter how noble her intentions.

When James entered the Salt Fork Saloon, he found a subdued crowd, most of whom were sitting at the back of the room sipping drinks and talking in low voices.

"'Bout time you got back here." Taggert shot a glare at James from behind the bar, where he looked to be taking inventory of his damages.

James bit his tongue to keep the angry retort that jumped to mind from escaping.

"Never let 'em see ya riled. A lawman's gotta keep control of his gun, his mind, and his words at all times." His mentor, Sheriff Herron, had passed that bit of wisdom on to James early in his career. *"Can't keep the peace when you ain't got none within yerself."*

"I came as soon as I could get away." James measured his stride as he moseyed over to the bar. "What kind of numbers are we looking at?"

Taggert scowled as he jerked the end of his pencil toward a floor littered with broken glass and pungent liquor. "I'm up to twenty-eight bottles so far." He tipped his head toward the end of the bar just past his shoulder. "I expect the final count to be around thirty-five. She nearly destroyed my entire inventory. If I didn't have the beer on tap and a box of whiskey in the storage room, I'd be out of business."

James could think of worse things, but he kept that opinion to himself.

"Once you get that inventory completed, I'll also need copies of some of your past bills of sale, so the judge can get an accurate financial picture of the losses."

He'd not let Taggert gouge the system, especially not with Noreen on the other side. He'd be double-checking the inventory sheet before he left, too. Making sure there were no claims for more expensive spirits in place of what was actually damaged. But for now, he'd focus on witness statements. Pulling a small tablet from his coat pocket, he strolled over to where Rico and Old Coop waited at the back table.

It took close to an hour to take down everyone's statements and check the inventory's veracity. Thankfully, Taggert proved to be as honest as he was ornery, saving James from having to dispute any of the man's claims.

By the time he left the Salt Fork, the sun hung low on the horizon. Hungry, tired, and rather discouraged after hearing the details of what transpired in the saloon, James headed down Main toward the courthouse square. When he reached Second Steet, the sound of horses neighing at the livery a block behind him caused a groan to rise in his throat. He'd not be paying Claude Templeton a visit tonight after all. He'd have to return the wagon and team in the morning. Made it harder to run Claude to ground without the man seeing him coming, but James would make do. He'd not leave Noreen alone in the jailhouse tonight.

He really needed to hurry back to relieve Miss Evans and Miss Cowan so they could return to their homes before darkness fell, but there was one place he needed to stop first.

Five minutes later, he stood before a well-maintained house a block off the courthouse square and knocked on the front door. Arthur Clevenger opened it.

"Deputy Paxton? What brings you to my doorstep at this time of night?"

James did his best to ignore the man's disdainful tone. "Is your wife at home, Mr. Clevenger? I need to have a word with her."

The man's eyebrows immediately scrunched down over his eyes. "That daughter of hers has gotten into more trouble, hasn't she? I swear. That girl seems to be on a mission to destroy my good name."

Holding on to his patience by the slimmest thread, James met the man's gaze and held firm. "My business is with your wife, Clevenger."

"Any business you have with my wife is my business as well," Clevenger blustered.

"Perhaps." James gave a conciliatory nod. "But I still need to speak to her."

Clevenger held the door wide. "Best come in, then."

After James stepped inside, Clevenger closed the door and led the way down the hall and into a parlor, where his wife sat knitting by the light of a lamp. Ramona Clevenger looked up at James's entrance, and the clicking of her needles immediately stilled.

"Deputy Paxton?"

Arthur moved in front of James and approached his wife. He stood beside her chair and a placed hand on her shoulder. To support or restrain? Hard to judge, though James's gut told him that a man as concerned with appearances as Clevenger would care more about controlling his wife than comforting her.

"He said he needs to speak with you, my dear," Clevenger said.

James gave the man a hard look. "In private."

Clevenger laughed, the falseness of the sound grating on James's nerves. "We have no secrets from one another, do we, dear?" He gave her no time to answer. "I assure you, Deputy, anything you have to say to my wife can be said to me as well."

James focused on Noreen's mother. He'd not be taking Arthur at his word. "Mrs. Clevenger?"

She hesitated, but then her lips curved in a smile as false as her husband's laugh and nodded. "Please speak freely, Mr. Paxton. I'm quite anxious to hear what you have come to say."

He nodded and took a seat on the settee opposite her so that he might meet her gaze directly. "A young girl, a friend of your daughter's, was found beaten quite severely."

Mrs. Clevenger's eyes widened. "Oh no. Is she all right?"

James nodded. "Noreen and Miss Evans tended to her before Dr. Perry arrived and moved her to his clinic." He held Mrs. Clevenger's gaze. "The beating came at the hands of a drunken family member." He saw understanding dawn in Noreen's mother's eyes. "I'm afraid Noreen's grief and anger led her to act rashly. She stormed the saloon, smashed a large number of liquor bottles, and cracked one of the mirrors behind the bar. Milton Taggert wishes to press charges, so she's been arrested and is being held at the jail. Her friends Martha and Jane are with her now."

"I must go to her." Ramona Clevenger started to rise, but her husband's grip held her in place.

"You will do no such thing," Arthur declared. "It's high time that girl learned her lesson. She's grown far too bold, and now she must face the consequences of her actions. Maybe after spending a few nights behind bars, she'll finally start curbing her outrageous behavior."

She twisted in her chair to face her husband. "Please, Arthur. She needs me."

He didn't soften. If anything, his expression became stonier. "You heard the deputy. Her friends are with her. She'll be fine. It's much more important that we set an upright example for the girl. Show her that criminal behavior will not be tolerated in this family. Only when she has repented and turned from her obstinate ways will we associate with her."

His wife wilted.

There had been several occasions over the last few years when James had wanted to plant his fist in Arthur Clevenger's face, but never more so than at this moment.

Keeping his attention focused on Noreen's mother, James leaned forward in his chair. "I'd be happy to deliver a note on your behalf."

Her eyes lit, and she immediately set aside her knitting. Thankfully, Arthur removed his hand from her shoulder and didn't try to stop her from rising. The man was a political creature, after all, and surely realized how unreasonable he would appear should he disallow such a simple kindness.

James pushed to his feet as she gained hers.

A small smile appeared on her face—a genuine one this time. "I'll be right back."

"Yes, ma'am. Take as long as you need."

James made no effort to converse with Arthur while his wife was away. Instead, he moved about the room, studying the artwork and bric-a-brac on display as if they were the most fascinating things he'd ever encountered. He even shoved his hands into his pockets to ensure he didn't accidentally break anything. Arthur Clevenger's nose, in particular.

True to her word, Mrs. Clevenger returned in a timely fashion. Bypassing her husband, she strode straight to James and handed him a single sheet of folded paper.

"Take care of my daughter, Deputy," she whispered, her eyes pouring a trust into him he wasn't sure he deserved.

"I will."

As long as she would let him.

Chapter
26

"Y ou've never heard such a ruckus!" Martha rolled her eyes in dramatic fashion as Jane giggled quietly.

They'd arranged their three chairs into a tight circle around the provided table and shared a meal, though none of them had much of an appetite.

Noreen managed a smile, however, as she imagined a parade of pets running through Martha's schoolyard. "Did one of the children truly bring a chicken?"

"We had an entire menagerie." Martha spread her arms wide, then started ticking animals off on her fingers. "A squawking chicken fluttering about and pecking at everyone's feet. Two different bullfrogs, croaking and hopping and scaring the girls. Five dogs of various breeds and obedience levels, three cats who ran off as soon as the dogs arrived, four lizards, and one gopher snake."

"A snake?" Jane shivered and pulled her feet away from the floor as her gaze darted to the corners of the cell.

"Yes, and of course the repulsive reptile escaped and slithered under the schoolhouse, making me jump at my own shadow for the next week."

A door closed downstairs, and all three ladies jolted, which then caused them to dissolve in laughter.

Knowing what that sound meant, Noreen reached out and clasped the hands of both of her friends and squeezed them tightly. "Thank you both for coming here. I . . ." Emotion clogged her throat. "I would still be floundering in self-pity were it not for you."

Martha gave a sharp nod, in that commanding way of hers that kept even the most rambunctious child in his seat. "Never underestimate the restorative power of clean clothes, warm food, and cheerful company. All you need now is a good night's rest, and you'll be back to your fearless self on the morrow, ready to face whatever challenge awaits."

"And we'll be right by your side," Jane vowed. "Praying for you every step of the way."

"Thank you." Tears began to pool again, but Noreen blinked them away. She'd wept enough today. Time to be strong. To be the woman her friends believed her to be. Fearless. Defiant. A crusader for the cause of temperance. One who'd not let a stay in a jail cell temper her passion.

Yet when James clomped up the stairs and fit his key into the lock, a breathless panic seized Noreen's lungs. She didn't want to be alone.

Her heart pounded as Martha and Jane pulled their hands from hers, rose to their feet, and collected their belongings. Noreen stood with them, her limbs quivering. Determined to hide her weakness, she made sure not to cling as each of them wrapped her in a brief farewell embrace. But when the door clicked closed and they disappeared down the stairs, it was all she could do not to rattle the bars and call them back. Even James left, escorting them out as a gentleman should. She'd felt his gaze seeking hers, but she'd avoided eye contact, her heart too conflicted to risk letting him inside.

Biting her lip, Noreen turned away from the barred door and began to move toward the chair she'd recently vacated, but seeing the other two empty chairs beside it made her chest ache. She pivoted to the mattress that lay on the ground in the corner instead. The mattress James had taken from his own bed for her to use. She'd insisted that the cot would be fine, but he refused to be swayed. Paid her protests absolutely no mind. Stubborn, wonderful man. Maybe if she curled up on the tick and drew the blanket over her head, she could imagine he was holding her. That she wasn't alone.

Encouraged slightly by her plan, she grabbed the back of her chair and dragged it closer to the mattress. Then she sat down and started unlacing her shoes. Jane had brought her a Bible and several novels to help pass the time, but Noreen doubted she'd be able to concentrate enough to absorb anything she tried to read. Right now, all she wanted to do was close her eyes and pretend the last few hours hadn't happened.

She had one shoe removed and the other halfway unlaced when the soft sound of footsteps on the stairs stilled her hands.

"Noreen?" James's voice floated up from the stairwell. "Are you decent? I have something for you. From your mother."

Mama? Her stomach fluttered.

Ignoring the tightness around her left foot, she yanked the shoe off and stood in her stockinged feet.

"Yes, I'm presentable." *Decent* no longer seemed an apt descriptor after her escapade at the saloon.

She smoothed her skirt and lifted a hand to her hair as if she were about to meet a beau, then caught herself and clasped her hands together at her waist and waited for James to emerge.

When her eyes met his, a longing rose within her of such magnitude, she swayed slightly toward the barred door. She hungered for his comfort. To feel his arms cradling her against his chest with a strength capable of shouldering all her burdens. To hear the rumble of his voice defending her and promising that all would be well. To bury her face in his neck, close her eyes, and let the rhythmic thumping of his heart calm the riot inside her mind. Yet a wall stood between them. Not just the physical wall of steel bars but one of secrets and shame.

The compassion in his gaze only twisted her guilt into a tighter knot in her stomach. He reached through the bars and extended his hand to her, palm up. Unable to resist the lure of his touch, she fit her hand to his. Physical warmth enveloped not only her hand but her heart as well. Her grip tightened, and she barely resisted the temptation to draw his fingers to her lips and press a kiss to his knuckles.

"I stopped by your mother's house after taking statements at the saloon." James shifted his weight, his gaze seeking and finding hers. "I thought it might be better for her to hear the facts of what happened from me before someone ambushed her with a distorted account."

As much as she hated the idea of him telling her mother about her disgraceful behavior, she recognized the kindness inherent in such an action. Hiding the truth from her mother would be a futile effort. Noreen's storming of the Salt Fork was far too juicy a tidbit not to be cranked through the rumor mill.

"Thank you."

His thumb caressed the back of her hand. "She wanted to come to you the moment she heard, but your stepfather wouldn't allow it."

Of course not. Arthur was nothing if not consistent in his disdain for her temperance work. Her arrest had provided him the perfect justification for cutting her completely out of their lives, something he'd been trying to do for ages. Noreen knew her mother would never outwardly defy her husband, but her capitulation still hurt. Didn't her daughter deserve some familial devotion, too?

"She penned you a note, though, and I promised to deliver it to you." He reached into an interior coat pocket with his other hand and extended a folded sheet of paper through the bars. "I'll leave you to read it in private, but I'll be downstairs if you need anything." He squeezed her hand. "I'm here for you, Noreen. If you want to talk, I'll listen. If you want to hit something, I'll volunteer as a punching bag." His eyes twinkled. "My stomach's much softer than the wall."

She wasn't so sure that was accurate. Nothing about James Paxton was soft. Except his eyes when he looked at her. And his touch when he stroked her hand or caressed her hair.

Needing to keep herself from thinking too much about those soft spots, she quirked a small grin of her own. "Do you offer yourself as a punching bag to all your prisoners, Deputy?"

He winked. "Only the pretty ones."

Heat suffused her cheeks, even as delight filled her heart. Yet the delight couldn't withstand the growing weight of her circumstances.

This was no drawing room where a gentleman might flirt with his lady of choice. This was a jail cell. A place of punishment and confinement for lawbreakers. A purgatory for those awaiting judgment. Guilt clung to its walls, her own culpability thickening the very bars that separated her from James.

Slowly, Noreen tugged her hand free of his hold and stepped backward. "Thank you for delivering the note."

He nodded, his eyes losing a bit of their light as he withdrew his hand and shoved it into his trouser pocket. "We'll get through this, Noreen. Don't lose hope."

We.

How she longed that there could be a *we* with this marvelous man. But some gulfs were too wide to span.

Slowly, Noreen turned her back on him and walked toward her mattress. When the sound of his boot falls finally echoed in the stairwell, the tears she'd been holding back rolled down her cheeks.

Crumpling atop the mattress, she braced her back against the wall and hugged her knees to her chest in an effort to manufacture the comfort that eluded her. Perhaps her mother's letter would help. Taking out her embroidered handkerchief, she dabbed her eyes and wiped her nose, then opened the note.

My precious girl,

Arthur will not permit me to visit you in jail, but please know that my heart is with you. I will pray for you without ceasing until this nightmare is over. I understand better than most the burning fire of impotent rage. Watching those we care about suffer and being helpless to stop it is a torture like no other. Yet we cannot give in to that rage, for all it produces is more hurt. Forgiveness is the only thing that heals. There's a reason the Good Book teaches us to put away all bitterness, wrath, and anger and replace it with forgiveness and kindness, and it's not just to help folks get along together. It's because bitterness, wrath, and anger poison the soul. Trust me, I know. My soul's been shriveled for more years than I care to admit. It was only after I forgave your father that I started to heal. Now I must forgive Arthur as well. It's not easy, and there are definitely days when I want to shout and break things, just as you did at the Salt Fork, but following the Lord's wisdom always pays better dividends than following our own, so I'll keep practicing. I pray you will, too.

Forgive Mr. Taggert for running a saloon. Forgive Mr. Templeton for beating sweet Luella. Forgive your father for hurting you. And, Noreen, forgive yourself. Guilt belongs at the foot of the cross, not locked in the secret places of your heart.

With a gasp, Noreen flung the letter onto the mattress as if it had suddenly caught fire in her hand. Mama knew? No, she couldn't. Noreen had been so careful not to let anything slip. All these years . . . Mama had never said anything. If she had discovered the truth, wouldn't she have said something to her . . . accused her . . . forgiven her?

The dam that had started crumbling in the saloon gave way completely. Noreen grabbed the pillow near her hip, held it to her face, and screamed into the feathers again and again until her screams morphed into sobs and left her utterly broken.

Chapter
27

James sat on the bottom stair, his forearms braced on his knees, his head in his hands. Hunger gnawed at his empty belly, but finding food held no appeal. Not with Noreen in the cell upstairs. His spitfire was sputtering, her inner light dimming right before his eyes, and he could do nothing about it. Worse, he'd contributed to the snuffing of her flame. His hand balled into a fist, and he drew it back with a violent jerk but stopped himself short of crashing his knuckles into the wall. He slammed them into his thigh instead, and pain radiated through his entire leg from the force of the blow. He welcomed the ache, wishing that increasing his own pain would somehow diminish hers. Too bad life didn't work that way.

How do I help her when I'm the one hurting her? Show me what to do, Lord. Open my eyes—

A muffled cry echoed softly from upstairs. James straightened, his ears at full attention. The sound came again, but it was softer this time. James stealthily pushed to his feet, wincing slightly at the soreness in his right leg. He tilted his head. He couldn't make out any words, but that didn't hinder the message. Each faint sound reverberated with agony, despair, and grief.

His heart throbbed. He took three quick steps up the stairs, then drew to a halt. Would she want him to go to her? Or would his presence embarrass her? She was obviously trying to hide her distress, muffling the sounds against the mattress or with something covering her mouth. Perhaps preserving her privacy would be best. He retreated a step, taking pains to silence his movements so she wouldn't know he was there. Yet even as he did so, the tone of her muted cries shifted from primal to heart-wrenching. His own heart cracked in response. No one should be alone with that kind of devastation.

Setting his jaw, he climbed the rest of the stairs. If she sent him away, so be it. But he'd give her the choice instead of trying to guess what she needed.

Upon reaching the landing, he strode down the side of the cell, angling his gaze to peer around the privacy blanket draped over the first section of bars. The sight that met his eyes hit him like a bullet to the chest. His beautiful Noreen, who'd always carried herself like a towering force of nature, sat huddled in a tiny ball in the middle of his mattress. Knees pulled to her chest. Head bowed. Face pressed into a pillow. Shoulders trembling from the violence of her sobs.

He didn't call to her. Didn't ask her permission to enter. He just fit the key into the lock as fast as his trembling hands could manage and let himself in. He could no more stay away from her now than he could separate his arm from his body.

She gave no indication that she heard him as his bootheels clicked against the stone floor, but when he lowered himself to sit beside her on the mattress and jostled her slightly, she stiffened and tried to stifle her sobs.

Blinking back his own tears, he wrapped an arm around her quaking shoulders and pressed his cheek against her hair.

"I'm here, sweetheart. Cry as long as you want. I'll hold you till you're done."

His words seemed to unlock something inside her, for before he could fully brace himself, she rolled toward him and clumsily scrabbled to secure her hold on his torso, as if she were drowning and he was the last piece of driftwood in the sea. The pillow she'd been using fell away as she traded it in for his chest. Her knees knocked against his hip, an elbow jabbed his belly, and the top of her skull conked against his chin before he took charge and hooked an arm under her bent legs and settled her across his lap.

A shuddery sigh exhaled out of her as she nestled into him, one arm twining around his waist as the other rested against his chest. He rubbed her back and leaned his head against the wall, praying that the Prince of Peace would calm her storm.

The Lord answered his prayer, for Noreen's shudders gradually stilled. Her weeping quieted, and her body relaxed into his. She shifted a few times to wipe her face with the embroidered handkerchief she held in the hand that rested against his chest, but even those movements ceased after a few minutes. She made no effort to separate herself from him, which suited him just fine. He'd hold her all night if she'd let him.

Neither of them spoke, for words would only dilute the comfort found in physical closeness. Reality would arrive soon enough. She'd have to appear before the judge and face the consequences of her actions. He'd stand by her side through it all, but tonight wasn't about facing consequences. Tonight was about shoring up crumbling foundations. An emotional tornado had torn through Noreen's life today, shattering her control, ripping away the structure of her moral boundaries, and twisting her through an emotional vortex of new outrage tangled with old hurts. They needed to clear away the debris, find their footing, and prepare to rebuild. But first, they needed to rest.

Noreen's breathing grew heavier and deeper, and her hold on him loosened. As if her lethargy were contagious, James felt his own eyelids grow heavy. Bending his neck forward, he placed a light kiss atop Noreen's hair before tipping his head back and letting his eyes close.

He dozed off and on for probably an hour, maybe longer, judging by the full dark that filled the cell. His back had started to ache, and his right foot had gone numb from Noreen's weight pressed upon that leg, but he didn't care. The pleasure of holding the woman he loved outweighed any discomfort.

Love did strange things to a man. Changed his priorities. His career goals. Had him skipping dinner and napping at uncomfortable angles—in a jail cell, of all places. Apparently, his big brother had been right, after all.

Four years ago at their baby sister's wedding, Joshua had predicted James would be led on a merry chase when he finally lost his heart to a woman. He'd never been one to take the easy path, after all. The siblings had gotten a kick out of making pretend wagers on what type of lady would capture his heart. Judith forecasted that a trouser-wearing cowgirl would lasso him and drag him to the altar. Jethro claimed James would give in to matrimony when he finally got tired of eating his own cooking and would choose a bride based on his favorite dish from the church potluck. Joanna insisted James would play the hero and fall for a beautiful damsel in distress after rescuing her from a fate worse than death. Of course, Joanna had been awash in her own romantic glow at the time, so no one paid her overly romanticized fairy tale much attention. Josh had accrued the most agreement when he prophesized that James would fall for a female outlaw.

Now that he thought about it, they might have all been right. Noreen might not wear trousers, but she'd roped him in to helping her with her parade easily enough. She cooked like a dream, and while she was far too feisty to be anyone's damsel, he had to admit that her distress stirred his protective instincts like no other. He wanted to be her hero. To be a man she could rely on. One she *wanted* to rely on. Unlike the father and stepfather who'd failed her time and again.

Shoot. Why else would he be sitting in a dark jail cell with a crick in his neck and a lawbreaker cradled in his arms? He swore he felt the point of Josh's elbow jab his ribs and heard a triumphant whisper in his ear. *"Outlaw."*

James smiled, then leaned forward and kissed his favorite outlaw's head.

"You shouldn't do that."

Her quiet voice startled him. "Sorry," he mumbled as he jerked his face away from her hair. "I wasn't trying to take advantage. I promise."

"I know." She sighed as she lifted her face away from his chest. "That's not why I said it."

He struggled to see her face through the dark, to gauge her expression so he could deduce what she might be thinking, but the deep shadows made details nearly impossible to discern.

"Why *did* you say it, then?" he asked.

"Because a future between us is impossible, and I need to quit pretending that it's not." She pulled her arm from his waist and rubbed her neck before shifting off his lap to sit beside him.

Instinct screamed at him to grab hold of her, to stop her from slipping away, but he kept his hands to himself, respecting her need for distance. But allowing her to think he was also accepting her pronouncement about their future without a challenge was a different matter.

"Nothing's impossible, Noreen. What happened at the Salt Fork hasn't changed how I feel about you. If anything, it's made things even clearer in my mind. I love you."

A mewling sound emanated from her throat that put him in mind of a wounded kitten. Then her head wagged back and forth. "No. You can't."

"Sorry. It's done happened," he said with a smile in his voice. "Might as well get used to the idea." He'd hoped his teasing tone might offer reassurance and lighten the mood, but her head fell forward in such a dejected manner, he immediately regretted the choice.

"You don't understand. You can't love me, James, because you don't know me. Nobody does. Not even my mother—at least I didn't think she did, but after reading her note, I'm not so sure."

He fumbled for her hand in the dark and clasped it tightly. "*God* loves you, Noreen. And he knows everything about you. Even the secret things you've locked away from everyone else." Did she believe that? He prayed she did.

"But you're not God."

He smiled. Of course she'd use the one argument he couldn't

counter. "True. I'm just as flawed and sinful as the rest of humanity." He twisted his face toward her. "Yet despite my imperfections, the love I feel for you is real and deep and strong. I might not know all your secrets, but I know *you*, Noreen. You're a passionate crusader, determined to make the world a better place. You're a devoted friend and a devout woman of faith. You're intelligent, kind, and courageous. You've overcome adversity and use what you've learned to help others overcome their own trials. *That's* who you are."

"I'm also a murderer."

The words echoed through the stone chamber like a gunshot. James's ears rang from the concussive blow, leaving him disoriented as he tried to make sense of what had just happened. The feel of Noreen tugging her fingers away from his grasp broke through his confusion in an instant and brought one truth into stark relief. He couldn't fail her. Not in this.

He chased her fingers and reclaimed them, squeezing them tightly against his palm. Her head lifted, and for the first time since he'd entered the cell, her eyes met his. Praying the shadows hid the remains of his shock from her, he held her gaze.

"I'm not one to be swayed by sensational headlines," he told her. "I'll make no judgment until I hear all the facts. Besides, I have a strong character witness who insists that the woman in question would never take a life without unavoidable cause. She's no cold-hearted killer."

"That's where you're wrong, Deputy. On the night in question, my heart was as cold as ice."

Chapter
28

Noreen hung her head. The moment James had stepped through that cell door, she'd known what she had to do. For his sake.

A sudden chill beset her, and a tremor worked its way through her limbs. James, collected her blanket and draped it around her shoulders, then drew it forward like an overlarge shawl that surrounded her arms and pooled in her lap. So solicitous. So tender. So . . . loving.

Merciful heaven. He loved her. He'd said so, but more than that, he'd shown her in a hundred different ways. And how had she repaid him? By keeping secrets. Letting him believe her to be an honorable woman when she was anything but. How she wished she could accept his love and never look back, but he deserved better. He deserved honesty. Love built on selfishness and lies was no love at all.

"Would it be easier to talk if I lit the lamp?" There he went again, extending thoughtfulness and patience. He'd probably sit at her side all night whether she found the nerve to tell him the truth or not.

"No." She'd rather confess in the dark. Protect herself from seeing his disappointment.

Grasping the edges of her blanket, she pulled it tight, as if it could insulate her from the jagged memories tumbling from the box of sharp-edged shards she'd hidden away after the night her soul shattered.

"My father . . . he was not an easy man to live with, even when he wasn't drinking." His face rose in her mind. Handsome. Strong. Eyes that matched hers. The broken glass of regret slashed her conscience. "He was quick to find fault and slow to offer affirmation. He criticized Mama despite her constant efforts to please him. I hid whenever he came home from the saloon, afraid I'd accidentally stir his anger. And his fists."

She shrank within her blanket. "I grew to hate him." Her voice cracked.

Strange to both love and hate someone at the same time, yet she had. Though as her hatred piled higher, the love became harder to find. Until it was too late.

"There were times when he rode off to the saloon that I wished he wouldn't come back." Saying the words out loud tore a piece of her heart open. She'd never admitted her darkest thoughts to anyone.

James sat quietly, offering no judgment. At least no verbal condemnation. She had no idea what he might be thinking. His arm still pressed up against hers. He hadn't pulled away. But then, his kindhearted nature probably rooted him in place. Either that or shock.

She closed her eyes. Inhaled. Exhaled.

"Some nights he stumbled home well after dark, but that night he was later than usual. I made my final visit to the outhouse and noticed the barn door was open. Worried that our cow might have gotten out of her stall again, I went to check on the animals. I found Papa's horse, saddle still on, standing in the tacking area. Then I found Papa. Passed out on the barn floor. Too drunk to tend his mount. Or himself. Particularly ironic since he had backhanded me earlier that afternoon for sloshing milk out of the pail onto the fresh straw he'd spread in the cow's stall. Accused me of carelessness and said a girl who couldn't properly care for her family's stock didn't deserve to eat her family's food. The hypocrite.

"I despised him in that moment. I can still remember standing over his unconscious form and feeling my heart turn to stone. I felt no compassion. No honor for my father. Only disdain and disgust."

"You were a child, Noreen."

She shook her head, unwilling to accept youth as an excuse. "I wasn't an infant, James. I was twelve, closer to being grown than not. Old enough to know right from wrong. Even in that moment, I knew that I should return to the house and tell Mama what I'd found. But I didn't. Instead, I unsaddled Papa's horse, brushed the animal down, and settled him in his stall, feeling quite superior all the while. After finishing that task, I strode back to Papa's crumpled form. His clothing askew, his face flat against the same dirty floorboards where manure fell. He deserved to pass a night with the rest of the animals. Maybe Mama would finally get a good night's sleep without having to tend to her drunken husband and clean up his messes. The mud he dragged in, the things he knocked over in his inebriated state, the vomit that invariably came when his body tried to rid itself of the liquor's poison. Let him sleep off his drunk in the barn for once. Maybe waking in a pool of his own vomit would teach him a lesson."

Noreen adjusted her grip on her blanket shawl, knowing what came next, yet wishing she could fend off the truth. But one couldn't escape truth. It could be denied, ignored, or even buried for a time, but it never perished. It stood ready to testify at a moment's notice, to exonerate or condemn without preference. Noreen had carried the weight of its condemnation in her soul for fifteen years, made all the heavier by her choice to wrap it in secrets. The weight pressed in on her with crushing force. She had to get out from under it before she collapsed.

"He never had a chance to learn from his mistake because . . . he never woke up." Her voice cracked along with her heart as the truth tore free of the coils of secrets that had held it prisoner. "I killed him, James. My malice and derision killed him." Her body folded forward as the confession clawed its way out of her throat in a raw rasp. "The doctor said Papa choked on his own vomit. He declared it an accidental death, but I knew the truth. It hadn't been an accident. It had been murder. I could have saved him, but I left my father to die."

A warm arm encircled her exposed upper back, and tender fingers stroked her right shoulder. How could he stand to touch her after what she'd confessed? She didn't deserve his kindness, his understanding. She deserved outrage and scorn.

"You didn't know he would die, Noreen." His gentle words rained down on her like a shower of needles, pricking and poking and drawing tiny beads of blood all over her body. "There has to be intent for a person to be charged with murder, and you didn't intend—"

"But I did!" She pulled away from his comfort with a jerk and scooted forward on the mattress. Pressing up onto her knees, she turned to face him. "I wanted him gone. Out of our lives. I didn't have Luella's pure heart. I didn't pray for my father's healing, for him to break free of liquor's hold. Maybe I had once upon a time, but I gave up on those petitions when they went unanswered. I prayed selfish prayers instead. That God would protect me and Mama. That he would take Papa away. I even prayed for God's wrath to strike him down. What is that, if not intent?"

Shadows hid most of his face from her, but she could feel him lean toward her. "Those sound like the desperate prayers of a young girl trying to survive. Even David prayed for the destruction of his enemies."

Oh, she knew the psalms he spoke of. She'd used them for years to try to justify her actions, but her soul had never accepted them as an adequate excuse. "'Whosoever hateth his brother is a murderer.'" She quoted the verse that she'd never been able to rationalize away. "'And ye know that no murderer hath eternal life abiding in him,' First John 3:15."

"'There is therefore now no condemnation to them which are in Christ Jesus,' Romans 8:1," James countered. "Paul counted himself a murderer, too, yet once he accepted Christ's redemptive grace, that sin was forgiven and washed away. Just as yours was."

James reached for her hand again, and this time she didn't pull away. She craved his acceptance too much. Even if only offered for a single night.

His thumb caressed the back of her hand. "I'm not saying you don't bear any responsibility for the choice you made. We all have to heed the convicting voice of the Holy Spirit and admit our wrongs if we want to be forgiven. Yet I heard deep remorse in your recounting. You've already sought the Lord's forgiveness, haven't you?"

Noreen bit her lip and nodded. "Yes, though it took several years for me to believe that he would actually grant such a favor."

All those tearful nights kneeling by her bed, telling God how sorry she was and begging for forgiveness. She'd prayed over and over again, her guilt and shame drowning out the sweet whisper of Jesus promising pardon. Leaving the farm had made it easier. Not having to walk through the barn every day and see the place where her father's body had lain allowed her to heal to some extent and finally accept the Lord's forgiveness. But trusting the Lord proved much easier than trusting people.

She'd never told her mother about that night because she feared her mother would cast her out, and she'd be left with no one. She'd not told Martha or Jane for the same reason. Friends had been exceptionally difficult to come by for a bristly girl with a chip on her shoulder and a crusade in her heart. She couldn't risk losing them. So she'd buried the truth deep inside and turned her attention to Jesus's command to go and sin no more, pledging to make restitution for her sins by fighting the good fight of temperance.

Until today, when the good fight had been tarnished by anger, pride, and vengeance. The compulsion to bend others to her will and punish those she deemed in the wrong had driven mercy out of her soul, the very trap she'd sworn never to fall into again. Yet here she was, back in the pit.

"I thought I had put it behind me. But when I saw what Mr. Templeton had done to Luella, something dark seeped back into my soul. It offered a false sense of power and strength when I felt vulnerable and helpless, so I welcomed it. Fed it. Justified its existence. And when I realized that Luella's father would not be brought to justice,

I unleashed the rage, believing the lie that I could command my enemy's surrender and regain some measure of control." Her posture slumped. "All I managed to do was forfeit what little control I possessed. Control over my actions, my thoughts, my words. *I* was the one who surrendered to the enemy, and now I'm paying the price." A moan vibrated in her throat. "I thought I was smarter than that!"

James gripped her hand more firmly and tugged her toward him. She went willingly, if awkwardly, since her twisted skirt lay trapped beneath her legs. He caught her and hugged her to him before settling her beside him within the crook of his arm. Her face rested against his chest, so when he spoke, the words vibrated against her ear.

"We all have areas of weakness and woundedness that the enemy exploits. Heaven knows, I fall prey to his wiles when it comes to pride and plotting my own path. Paul had his thorn in the flesh, too, and the Lord's answer to him applies to us as well. His grace is sufficient. There is no limit to his forgiveness, sweetheart."

Sweetheart? How could he still think of her in endearing terms? Was there no limit to *his* forgiveness, either?

"Whatever comes tomorrow, Noreen, we'll face it together. God will never leave you nor forsake you, and neither will I. You have my word."

What could she say to that? It was the most beautiful promise she'd ever been given. Which was precisely why she was afraid to trust it. She'd been let down so many times by the very people who were supposed to love her. Yet she wanted to believe that things would be different with James. He was a man of honor. A man of principles. A man of God. However, he was also a man of duty. A man who might feel obligated to stay by her side because he had declared his feelings before she'd revealed her secrets. She couldn't allow him to be trapped by his sense of honor.

"You're a good friend, James, and a man I respect above any other." She sat up a bit and looked into his face. This close, she could see his eyes, and she forced herself to hold his gaze. "I appreciate your steadfastness more than I can say, but I need you to know that I have no expectations of our relationship extending beyond friendship. I'm a spinster and plan to be one the rest of my days. I'm married to the cause of temperance, and that is where my allegiance will always lie."

He said nothing for a long minute, just peered into her eyes as if trying to discern if a message existed behind her words. None did. She meant what she'd said. She wasn't good for him, and they both knew it. Hadn't he told her from the very beginning that allying himself with her would be bad for his career? She'd pushed anyway, like she always did, valuing her own objectives above those of anyone else. Well, no longer. Time to put his needs ahead of hers. She cared about him too much to do otherwise.

"Allegiance is a funny thing," he finally said. "It is not a finite commodity. It can be given to multiple recipients without ever diminishing the amount originally bestowed. It's rather like love in that regard."

Love? Her heart pounded with pleasure at his less-than-subtle message, but she still opened her mouth to protest.

"No more talking, Noreen," he interrupted before she could form a cohesive argument. "We don't have to solve every problem tonight. We can save some for tomorrow." He cupped her head and drew her back down to his chest. "Close your eyes and get some rest. Dawn will be here soon enough."

Perhaps she was giving in to weakness again, but she submitted to his direction, closed her eyes, and relaxed against him. It didn't take long for sleep to claim her, and when it did, it brought dreams of a handsome deputy speaking words of love.

Chapter
29

James snuggled Noreen while she slept, enjoying the feel of her nestled into his side. Treasuring the trust she bestowed by letting her guard down enough to relax in his arms. It felt right to hold her. As if they belonged together—had always belonged together—though he had to admit he was less than objective about that particular belief. The trick was going to be convincing Noreen that spinsterhood wasn't her only option.

He'd been analyzing her declaration over the last thirty minutes, and he'd come to a few conclusions. First, she intended to free him from any obligation he might feel toward her. She hadn't said she didn't *want* something more than friendship, just that she had no expectations of such. Second, she held him in some level of esteem. An encouraging confirmation that his feelings weren't entirely unreciprocated. Yet her affection was a double-edged sword, for it also drove her to protect him and safeguard his career. A fact he would appreciate if her methods didn't include putting herself out of his reach. Third, and most critical, he strongly suspected she didn't believe herself worthy of marriage. She might have accepted the Lord's forgiveness, but she still referred to herself as a murderer. Still defined herself by her worst day. A fact that made his heart bleed.

How do I help her heal, Lord?

He exhaled a breath and lightly tapped the back of his head against the stone wall a few times as if he might be able to knock some wisdom loose inside his skull.

Her story had left a deep ache in his heart. She'd been so young. Vulnerable. Subjected to abuse on a regular basis, either from harsh words or bruising blows. Yes, she'd made a poor choice that night. A sinful one, even. But to James's way of thinking, her father bore more blame for his death than she did. He'd chosen to drink to excess that night, and the consequences of that choice culminated in the stupor that killed him. Had he not brutalized his daughter for years, she might have had more compassion when she found him. Finn O'Sullivan hastened his own demise, yet Noreen paid the price. Her father was still leaving bruises, just not on her skin. These marred her soul.

James bent down and pressed his cheek against the top of her head. Perhaps finally sharing her secret would ease her burden. He prayed so. He'd do anything in his power to support and encourage her, but his loyalty could only go so far. As much as he would like to, he couldn't reach inside her heart and bind her wounds. Only her true Father could do that.

You sent your Son to heal the brokenhearted and set at liberty those who are bruised. Noreen needs that healing tonight, Lord. Her heart is broken, and her soul is bruised. Grant her liberty from the shackles of her guilt and create in her a new heart. One that can find rest in your forgiveness and receive the gift of your love. And mine.

Taking care not to jostle her any more than necessary, James slid out from under her and lowered her sleeping form to the mattress. He held his breath when she rolled onto her side, but she didn't wake. Thankful for his strong night vision, he moved away from the mattress, taking care not to kick any of the extra items that cluttered the usually sparse quarters. Moonlight filtered through the barred windows as well, allowing him to see her face. Eyes that usually sparked with spirited fire rested behind lashes clumped together in spikes from long bouts of tears. The delicate pointed chin that

220

jutted with determination and courage had been retracted to tuck against her collar.

How he wanted to lay beside her and wrap her in his arms, shelter her from the past as well as the present. To whisper reassurances in her ear and rub the shivers from her arms. But he'd not risk her reputation any more tonight. The jailhouse rarely had visitors after dark, but an emergency could arise at any moment. If someone came to summon the law and found him spooning with his prisoner, not only would his career be over, but Noreen would be left to pay the price for another man's poor choice. He'd not let that happen.

Collecting the edges of the fallen blanket, he arranged it over her. A flash of white caught his eye as he pulled the blanket toward her chin. He picked up a damp wadded handkerchief, shook it open, and draped it over the edge of the table so it could dry.

He turned to go, but something about the handkerchief nagged at a memory. Taking it in hand, he walked over to the window to examine it in what little light the moon had to offer. A cluster of flowers had been embroidered in one corner. Nothing unusual about that. Except that he'd seen the exact pattern earlier that day on a different handkerchief. One stained with blood. That one had borne Luella Templeton's initials. This one bore Noreen's. It seemed odd for them to have identical handkerchiefs. Odd but not particularly significant, seeing as how the two were friends.

James returned Noreen's handkerchief to the table, then exited the cell. He clicked the door softly closed behind him and turned the key, each scrape sounding loudly in his ears. His prisoner didn't awaken, however, so after one long final look, James made his way downstairs to the uncomfortable prison cot waiting for him in his bedroom. Not that he'd sleep much anyway. A man who wanted to be his woman's hero while stuck being her jailer had more than a few mental knots to untangle.

Jane Cowan showed up bright and early with oatmeal fixin's, a teapot, and what looked to be a book in her apron pocket. After showing her to the stove, James climbed the stairs to check on his guest.

"Noreen?" He announced his presence before he cleared the top steps. "Is it all right if I come up?"

"Yes." Her voice sounded stronger this morning, as if she'd regained a bit of her fiery spirit overnight.

A grin traveled from his heart to his face as he hopped up the last few steps to the second-floor landing. "Good morning."

She set a book aside that she'd been reading, then rose from her chair. A shy smile curled the edges of her mouth as her chin dipped and pink painted her cheeks. Was she remembering how he'd held her last night? The feel of his lips pressed against her hair? The thundering of his heart beneath her cheek? He certainly was. Every delicious detail.

Slowly those lashes lifted, and her gaze met his. "Good morning." Warmth radiated through her greeting but so did caution.

The key to her cell lay heavy in his pocket. He longed to open the door and go to her. To clasp her tightly to his chest and assure her that the light of day had not changed his feelings. Unfortunately, the light of day had changed other things. Like the number of people traipsing in and out of the jailhouse.

"Miss Cowan is downstairs making breakfast. She knew better than to trust me with the duty."

Her smile widened slightly, and his own joy doubled in response.

"It's nice to know I'll have more to eat than bread and water."

James rested his forearms on one of the crossbars. "I probably could have managed biscuits and water since I rescued your basket last night. The jam jar had dented a few of the biscuits, but I figured they were still edible. Unlike the eggs I burned this morning."

"You should have waited for Jane."

He wagged his head slightly. "I would have if I didn't have business to attend to first thing this morning."

Her eyes shuttered slightly. "Oh?"

"Yep. I'm heading out to the Templeton place. Gotta return the wagon and team."

Noreen's arms wrapped themselves around her midsection. "Is that all?"

His jaw tightened. "Thought I'd do a little hunting while I'm out there. See if I can track down the troublesome coyote that attacked one of my citizens yesterday."

Her arms lowered as she moved forward to stand directly in front of him. "Be careful, James. Wild animals are unpredictable—and dangerous." She reached out and touched his hand.

He twisted his palm, laced his fingers through hers, then brought her knuckles to his lips through the bars. Her eyes slid closed, and her breathing changed, matching the leap in his pulse, but then she tugged her hand away and retreated a step, clasping her hands at her waist.

James exhaled, doing his best to ignore the disappointment that spiked through him. She'd not be won over by spoken promises until he proved to her that he could be trusted to follow through. It would take time to convince her that his feelings would not be easily uprooted and planted elsewhere. That he'd chosen to plant himself at her side for all time.

"I'll stay alert. Don't worry." He offered a wink that earned him a raised eyebrow. A chuckle rumbled in his throat for a moment before he grew serious. "I'll check in on Luella, too, and let you know how she's doing."

Noreen's expression instantly softened. "Thank you."

He wished he could do more, but it would have to be enough for now. Unless his hunting trip turned up a prize he could gift wrap for her.

James had returned the wagon to the Templeton homestead and was unhitching the horses when the coyote attacked.

"What'd you do with them?" Claude Templeton charged out of his front door, cocking his lever-action rifle as he came. "Where's my wife and kid?"

James turned slowly, keeping his hands well away from his

weapon. No need to give the man a reason to shoot. "You don't remember?"

Claude stumbled a bit as if his feet weren't fully operational. Not surprising. The man looked half dead. Dirt and blood stained his trousers and untucked shirt. His suspenders drooped low over his hips. His hair stood out at all angles, and dark smudges circled his eyes. "Whaddya mean, 'remember'?"

James glared at the sorry excuse for a human. "You beat your little girl nearly to death, Claude."

The man's face paled before he hardened his expression. "Liar!"

"Am I?" James prowled forward, the fire of justice burning in his gut. "Then why are your knuckles raw and swollen? You're wearing her blood." He gestured to the man's filthy clothes. "Took a couple swings at your wife, too, when she tried to stop you. Thank God your girl got away. Dragged herself as far as the schoolhouse before she collapsed. You could have killed her, Claude. Killed your own kin."

His grip on the rifle loosened, and James snatched it from his hands.

The man made no protest, just stared at his hands as if he'd never seen them before. He curled one into a fist, winced at the pain the movement brought, then let his fingers unfurl. "I . . . I didn't mean to hurt her. I just . . ."

"Just what, Claude? Wanted to teach her a lesson? With your fists?" James tossed the rifle aside and got up in Claude's face. "That girl loves you. Even lying on the schoolroom floor, broken and bleeding from the beating you gave her, she believed in you. Believed that you would change. That you would *want* to change. Your wife wasn't so sure. When I got here, she was packing up her things so she could take her child somewhere safe. Somewhere away from you."

"Trudy wouldn't leave me."

"You gave her no choice."

Claude stumbled over to the wagon and leaned his back against it for support. His hand shook as he combed back his unruly hair. Then he reached into his pocket and pulled out a dented silver flask.

James lunged forward and knocked the flask from his hand. "I need that!"

James grabbed him by his filthy shirt and pinned him against the wagon bed. "What you *need* is to sober up and become the man your daughter believes you can be. A man who protects his family instead of destroying it."

James released him with a final shove and walked away. He might not have been able to make an arrest, but maybe he'd made an impression. Hopefully, one that would spawn change. Not that it would be easy. Once liquor got its claws into a man, it was hard to break free. Hard, but not impossible. Especially if you weren't alone.

After swinging up into his saddle, James nudged his horse up to where Claude sat huddled against the wagon wheel. At least the man hadn't crawled after his flask.

"I'll stop by a few times this week to check on you."

Claude made no response, just stared into the air.

"Anything you want me to convey to your wife or daughter?"

The big man hung his head. "Tell 'em . . . I'm s-sorry." Tears choked his words as the reality of what he'd done finally started to seep into his brain.

"I will, but it'll be up to you to show them how much you mean it."

Chapter
30

Noreen had never realized how slowly time could crawl until she found herself incarcerated. By Thursday evening, she'd read through three of Jane's novels, mended every tear or missing button from James's wardrobe, and had even written a letter of apology to Milton Taggert. Thank the Lord for good friends, or boredom might have stolen her sanity. Jane stopped by every morning with breakfast, fresh reading material, and cheerful conversation. Martha came by after school let out each afternoon and chatted while she graded the day's assignments. James checked on her every few hours during the middle of the day and again at night before he turned in.

Trudy Templeton brought Luella by to see her yesterday before they left town. Luella's bruises had turned a deep purple, but her smile carried a beauty lit with hope. She had reached through the bars, clasped Noreen's hand, and promised to pray for her. Dear, sweet girl. Noreen had vowed to return the favor, an easy promise to make since she'd already been praying for Luella with great fervency. She'd been praying for her father, too, ever since James had told her about the conversation he'd had with Claude Templeton. Praying that the man would finally find the motivation and strength to break free of liquor's hold.

Strange how forgiveness changed a person. A few days ago, her heart would have been too crusted with anger to allow her to pray for Claude Templeton. But after confessing the truth of her past to James and receiving his grace-filled response, the scabs on her soul finally fell away. The morning after he'd held her with such tender acceptance, she'd awakened refreshed and, in some ways, reborn. The weight of the guilt she'd carried since childhood had been replaced with a buoyant gratitude. The Lord had set her free from the chains she'd stubbornly clung to despite his forgiveness and mercy. And with their constriction released, her heart stretched wide, gaining the space necessary to extend grace to others. Even her enemies.

"Miss O'Sullivan? You have visitors." James's call from the stairwell scattered her musings. "May we come up?"

Miss O'Sullivan? Her visitors must be someone other than Jane or Martha for him to use such a formal address. Perhaps the parson had decided to pay a call.

Noreen rose from her chair and smoothed her skirt. "You may."

Martha emerged first, but her expression wilted Noreen's smile of welcome. Apologies gleamed in her eyes. Exactly who was climbing the stairs behind her?

"Martha, dear. Give me a hand, would you?"

"Of course, Miss Lockwood." Martha hurried back to the stairwell to assist the spinster society's founder.

Noreen's belly buzzed like a freshly kicked hornets' nest, and her hand immediately moved to her hair. Ridiculous impulse, that. As if a tidy coiffure could erase the fact that she'd been arrested for vandalism.

A loud huff announced Hortense Lockwood's official arrival on the second floor. "Gracious! I didn't expect the climb to be quite so arduous."

"Shall I fetch you a chair, ma'am?" James emerged behind her and quickly offered his arm as Miss Lockwood lumbered down the walkway that stretched along the length of Noreen's cell. "Or perhaps a glass of water?"

"Thank you for your kindness, Deputy Paxton, but that won't

be necessary. This visit won't be lengthy in nature. And remember, you promised that Martha and I would be allowed privacy for our conversation with Miss O'Sullivan. I trust you won't be eavesdropping from the stairwell."

"No, ma'am. You have my word."

James glanced at Noreen, and his smile shone with the warmth and tenderness she'd come to crave over the last few days. However, something wary flickered in his gaze, as if he anticipated trouble. The buzzing in her belly increased.

"Thank you, Deputy." Miss Lockwood released his arm once she'd reached the section of bars directly in front of where Noreen stood. "You may leave us now."

James nodded. "I'll be in my office if you need anything."

He caught Noreen's eye and tipped his head as if to indicate that his words were meant more for her than her visitor. An infusion of encouragement seeped into her veins and gave her the courage to face the formidable Miss Lockwood.

James disappeared down the steps, the quiet clomp of his bootheels tracking his movements from stairwell to office as the ladies waited in silence.

"Martha, check the stairwell, just in case." Miss Lockwood waved her hand in that direction.

Noreen inwardly bristled. James had given his word. If he said he'd give them privacy, he'd give them privacy. A defense rose in her throat, but she swallowed it. The truth would be evident in a moment, and in her current compromised state, it seemed wise not to challenge the woman who held her fate in the society in her hands.

Martha returned with the all clear, and Miss Lockwood's gaze peered through the bars with a sharpshooter's precision.

"I've always believed it kindest to speak truth plainly, so I'll get right to the reason for this visit."

That did not sound promising. Noreen swallowed.

"The society met this evening, Miss O'Sullivan, and voted to revoke your membership due to your violation of the charter. While Miss Evans and Miss Cowan argued quite ardently on your behalf and explained the unfortunate circumstances that led to the incident at the Salt Fork Saloon, the fact remains that you blatantly, and with intent, broke the law. Not only that, but you did so by entering a place of vice, a place whose threshold no woman of good character would dare cross."

Noreen's throat seemed to close in on itself. She'd known there'd be a price to pay for her reckless actions, but she'd expected her society sisters to rally around her, to show support for one of their own.

"Is there to be no grace, then?" she choked out. "One mistake and a member is cast aside? I thought the society was to be a sisterhood. Isn't that how you described it, Miss Lockwood? A group of ladies who support and encourage one another? Yet the first time you come to visit me, it is not to offer sisterly support but to inform me that I am no longer welcome in your fellowship."

Miss Lockwood diverted her gaze, her mouth twisting in something that almost looked like chagrin.

Martha stepped closer, her intelligent gaze darting from one friend to the other. "Perhaps instead of a full revocation, we can move Miss O'Sullivan's membership into a probationary status," she suggested. "For example, she would not be permitted to chair any committees or vote on society business for a period of, say, three months. Then, if there have been no further incidents during that time, her full membership could be reinstated."

Bless Martha and her problem-solving prowess! But would Miss Lockwood entertain such a solution?

"I . . . had not considered a probationary option." Miss Lockwood turned to face Noreen once again, her expression softer, though not completely sympathetic as she straightened her shoulders. "It seems I owe you an apology, Miss O'Sullivan. In my zealousness to protect the reputation of our society's members from your scandalous actions, I charged forward to have you dismissed from our ranks, justifying my actions with the knowledge that you broke your pledge and acted in a manner that brought disgrace upon yourself. However, what I failed to consider was the pledge we made to form a sisterhood that stands together and supports one another in times of need."

Miss Lockwood let out a sigh and raised a white-gloved hand to tentatively curl around one of the cell bars.

"You are right. I did not think of you as a sister should. I did not offer comfort or support. I offered only judgment without mercy. For that I am sorry. I opened my home to Trudy and Luella Templeton. I witnessed the damage done to that poor child. And while I cannot condone what you did, I can understand a little of what must have driven you to such a drastic demonstration."

Some of the tightness within Noreen's breast unfurled. "I do regret my actions, ma'am. For many reasons. I was overwrought and let the pain of my past overrule my good sense. But the Lord has been working on my heart while I've been confined. Truth be told, there's not much else to do here in the evenings other than confront the demons that led me to this place." With the help of a particularly patient deputy whose love and acceptance continued to amaze her. "I've begun to make peace with my past, Miss Lockwood, and with the Lord's help, it will no longer hold sway over me. The society has come to mean a great deal to me, ma'am, and I would gladly serve a probationary term to earn back my good standing. If you and the others would permit me the chance."

Miss Lockwood held her silence for a long moment before stepping back from the bars and brushing her gloved hands together. "I will speak to the other spinsters. If a majority agree, I will revise the revocation to a period of probation. Though I will recommend six months instead of three, due to the severity of the incident. You did break the law, Miss O'Sullivan."

"I understand. Thank you, Miss Lockwood." Noreen dipped her chin, some of the tightness easing from her chest.

Miss Lockwood shook a finger at her. "It's not accomplished yet, mind you. The spinsters must agree."

"Yes, ma'am." But if Hortense Lockwood advocated on her behalf, few of the spinsters would voice opposition.

The society's matron tugged on her cuffs and shifted her reticule to a comfortable place at her wrist as if readying herself to depart. "I understand you are to go before the judge tomorrow for sentencing. Is that correct?"

Noreen nodded, a few of the knots returning to her stomach. As much as she wanted out of the jailhouse, she was not looking forward to facing Milton Taggert in court and admitting her guilt. Humility had never been a trait that came easily to her, but four nights behind bars had proven an effective teacher.

"I'll plan to attend. You'll find me in the gallery. Offering my support. Something I should have done before now."

Martha reached a hand through the bars and clasped Noreen's palm tightly against her own. "As will I."

Noreen's heart leapt. "But what of your class? I am to appear at ten o'clock tomorrow morning."

Martha shrugged. "I've arranged for a guest speaker. Dr. Perry agreed to teach a science lesson. The children are quite excited about seeing all of his equipment."

Noreen's eyes misted. Martha never missed a day of class. Ever. Yet here she was, volunteering to miss a period of instruction so that she could help a friend. No gift could have meant more.

"Thank you," Noreen murmured, her voice rasping. "Thank you, both."

Chapter
31

James unlocked Noreen's cell at nine forty-five on Friday morning. She'd been pacing when he arrived but now stood by the door, eyes large in her face, hands clutching the sides of her dark blue skirt. The high-necked ivory blouse she wore enhanced her prim and proper appearance while the cameo brooch pinned at the base of her throat added a touch of femininity that would hopefully play to the judge's sympathy. The local schoolmarm had lent her the brooch and recommended Noreen leave off the temperance ribbon she always donned, but true to her uncompromising nature, she wore the white temperance bow as well, pinned to the left side of her bodice, over her heart. She'd tamed her curls into a tight, unforgiving knot at her nape, and while James agreed that the conservative style would help her look more contrite and less likely to cause trouble in the future, he missed the uninhibited nature of the curls that matched the feisty spirit of the woman he loved.

James swung the door outward and stepped inside. "Are you ready?"

She hugged her arms around her. "Ready to have this behind me, but not ready to face Judge Lynch."

Smiling, James moved close and rubbed one of her arms. "Despite his name, JC's not a hangin' judge. He'll give you a fair hearing. The man's got three daughters similar in age to you. That should soften him a bit. He's a deeply religious man, as well, and one who is quick to help those in need."

Noreen's gaze dropped to the floor. "He's also a leader in the Masonic lodge, and many of his Mason compatriots frequent the Salt Fork."

Not sure what to say to calm her nerves, he stroked her arm a final time, then held his hand out to her. She hesitantly fit her palm to his, and he tugged her toward him. Bending close, he placed a kiss on the top of her head.

"It's going to be all right, sweetheart. Whatever the outcome, we'll handle it together."

She leaned forward until her forehead rested against his chest. "There is no *we*, James. There can't be." She lifted her face, that spark of passion he'd been missing from her eyes flickering back to life. "God has called you to the life of a lawman. I know it in my soul. He's made you a gifted peacemaker. Honorable, courageous, and just. You are already making a difference here in Albany, and that impact will multiply when you are sheriff. But the townsfolk won't give you the chance to make that difference if you tie your name to mine. You need to let me go."

Not a chance. He tightened his grip on her hand as a wave of arguments rolled through his mind, eager to combat her assumptions. But Noreen didn't need him to argue with her right now. She needed him to help her find peace.

Loosening his grip on her hand, he brought her knuckles to his lips and brushed a kiss across them before releasing his hold and stepping back.

"We can discuss my career prognosis later."

Her eyebrows dipped low over the bridge of her nose, and he figured she had a few arguments of her own running through that head of hers. He grinned and gave her a wink, earning a huff from her that sounded as if it were disguising an involuntary chuckle. His grin widened. Mission accomplished.

"May I escort you to the courthouse, Miss O'Sullivan?" He sketched a brief bow and held out his arm. "Being cognizant of my career, as you are, I know you wouldn't wish for me to arrive late to the proceedings."

"Indeed not, Deputy Paxton." Her eyes danced as she pointedly ignored his proffered arm and maneuvered around him to exit the cell on her own. "Nor would I wish to add tardiness to my list of charges." She marched down the walkway to the stairwell. "Are you coming?" she called over her shoulder as she descended the stairs.

James chuckled as he pushed the cell door closed and hurried after her. "You can't get rid of me that easily." For today or for a lifetime.

Noreen managed to hold on to her independence until they reached the courthouse steps. James led her around the back to avoid the people streaming in the front doors, and when he offered his arm to steady her as she climbed the steps, she didn't refuse. Heart pounding against her sternum like a frenetic woodpecker, she latched on to his bicep. The strength evident in the hard muscle proved a comfort as she struggled to grasp the mental strength she'd need to face what lay ahead.

Once inside, James led her to the back staircase near the door, keeping her arm securely tucked against his side. She ran her palm along the dark, polished handrail, seeking to steady herself in any way possible. When they reached the first landing, however, he pulled her next to the wall and bent his face close to her ear.

"Dear Lord, give Noreen peace and help her to feel your presence beside her throughout these proceedings. In Jesus's name, amen."

Then, as if he hadn't just done the most beautiful thing any man had ever done for her, he led her up the remainder of the stairs to the second floor. The men in her life usually spoke demands and criticism over her, not prayerful blessings.

She was accustomed to men trying to bend her to their will, but time after time, James had bent his own will in order to serve and support her. Taking her in when others cast her aside, helping her plan a temperance march, rescuing her from her own folly, climbing into the depth of her despair to offer comfort, and standing by her side today and reminding her that another stood beside her as well.

God was with her. How she'd needed that reminder. Her true Father would never leave her or forsake her. Even when she stumbled and made a mess of things.

She lifted her gaze to the ceiling, her heart pulsing with gratitude. *Thank you for being here. And for sending James.*

"Ready?" Her deputy's soft voice echoed in her ear as he paused outside the courtroom's private entrance.

Noreen peered into his warm blue eyes and absorbed the encouragement he offered so freely. She straightened her shoulders and lifted her chin. "Ready."

James escorted her inside. A loud hum of conversation filled the space and set her nerves to buzzing. In all the years she'd lived in Albany, she'd never actually been inside this courtroom. The ceiling stretched upward to cathedral heights, shrinking her to insignificance. The room itself was as large as the church she attended. The gallery section boasted three rows of wooden benches on an inclining floor, backed by large windows framed in dark wood that contrasted with white walls. Stained glass winked at her from the top of the windows, adding to the cathedral feel. Floral carpet runners cushioned the walkways and aisles, muffling footfalls as people entered to witness the spectacle of Noreen O'Sullivan's fall from grace.

Goodness. Had everyone in town turned out for this event? Milton Taggert sat in the front row of the far-left section, his pointed glare finding her in an instant. Men she recognized from the Salt Fork surrounded him. Witnesses to her crime and others who were frequent patrons of his establishment. Wait . . . was that Arthur? Her own stepfather sat among Taggert's supporters? Her cheeks warmed. At least her mother wasn't sitting beside her husband. Had she come? Noreen scanned the other two sections of benches. She failed to find her mother, but other dear faces met her gaze and smiled encouragement.

Martha and Jane sat together in the front-center row and nodded to her when her eyes found them. A bit of the weight lifted from her shoulders. Hortense Lockwood and two other spinsters from the society sat near the aisle on the right, chatting quietly among themselves, not yet aware that she'd entered the room. They were here, though, and she felt herself grow a little stronger simply from their presence. Even her landlady had come. Though Mrs. Barker's appearance likely had more to do with collecting gossip fodder than supporting her troublemaking tenant. Noreen recognized a few people who had marched in her temperance parade scattered throughout the gallery along with several scowling business owners.

So many people.

A warm hand settled at the small of her back. "You have friends here, Noreen," James murmured softly. "Focus on that and ignore the rest."

Right. Noreen took a breath and allowed him to guide her to a chair at a large table positioned directly in front of the judge's bench. A half wall of dark balustrades hemmed her in from behind but did nothing to protect her from all the eyes peering at the back of her head as she took her seat.

"I'll be right over there the whole time." James tipped his head toward a chair to her left that afforded him a view of the entire room—judge, audience, and the accused. Her.

She nodded to him, yet the moment he stepped away from her, she longed to call him back.

You're not alone, Noreen. You're not alone.

The clock tower directly above their heads bonged out the ten o'clock hour, the sound vibrating her bones and quieting the on-lookers.

A court official called the session to order and announced the arrival of Judge Lynch. Noreen rose to her feet as the gray-haired man entered the room from a side door. He wore a simple black suit with a white shirt and black string tie and carried a paper file in his hand. Thankfully, he wasn't a man she recalled ever seeing in the Salt Fork.

Judge Lynch climbed the dais to the judge's bench and sat in the black leather chair positioned between two narrow windows. "Have a seat, folks."

Shuffling ensued as everyone, including Noreen, took their seats.

The judge opened his file and arranged the papers within to his satisfaction, then lifted his face to regard first Noreen and then the gallery. He had a very sober bearing, but he didn't strike her as harsh or rigid, just . . . serious.

"The matter before the court today pertains to events transpiring on April 29, 1894, at approximately 7:25 p.m. when the accused entered the Salt Fork Saloon and destroyed numerous bottles of expensive spirits and cracked one mirror for an estimated total of one hundred fifty-two dollars and seventy-five cents in damages."

At least he'd left out the details about her running up and down the bar, swinging her broom handle like a stickball bat. The man had at least a little kindness in him.

"I have before me witness statements verifying these happenings, an investigation report by the arresting officer, and a charge of malicious mischief for damaging property belonging to Mr. Milton Taggert of Albany, Texas."

Judge Lynch looked up from his papers and made eye contact with Noreen. "Miss O'Sullivan, how do you plead?"

Pushing back her chair, she rose to her feet as James had coached her and faced the judge. "Guilty, your honor."

A murmur broke out in the gallery, but one glare from the judge brought silence. Turning back to her, he nodded, rather like a grandfather encouraging one of his grandchildren. "Before I pronounce your sentence, would you care to address the court?"

"Yes, your honor." She took a deep breath, wishing she could seek out James or one of her friends for courage. Instead, she imagined the Lord coming beside her and squeezing her hand. "I deeply regret my actions last Sunday. Earlier that evening, a young girl who is quite dear to me was found severely beaten and in need of medical attention. She'd been beaten by a man too drunk to recognize the severity of his actions. When I learned that he would not be held accountable because he was a family member and his victims refused to press charges, I became overwrought and attacked the only other thing I could think to blame—the liquor. My situation does not excuse my actions. What I did was wrong, no matter my state of mind at the time. I offer the explanation only to demonstrate the extraordinary circumstances surrounding the incident. This destructive behavior was completely out of character for me, and I assure you it will not happen again."

"Thank you, Miss O'Sullivan. You may be seated." Judge Lynch's gaze moved beyond Noreen to the gallery behind. "Mr. Taggert, do you wish to address the court?"

Noreen twisted in her seat and saw the saloon owner rise to his feet.

"I do." He pointed a finger at Noreen, his eyes narrow and jaw tight. "This woman has been trying to ruin me for months. She harasses customers outside my door on a regular basis, organizes parades to protest the *legal* sale of alcohol, and lays the responsibility for all of society's ills on my doorstep. She might claim to have been *overwrought* when she vandalized my saloon, but I say she's been building up to this attack for months. It was only a matter of time before she became violent."

Noreen shook her head, her heart racing. That wasn't true. But what if the judge believed him, believed that she was a danger to the town?

Judge Lynch raised an eyebrow. "Has Miss O'Sullivan ever threatened you or your establishment with violence prior to this incident, Mr. Taggert?"

"Not directly," Taggert hedged. "But she's threatened my ability to run my business the way I see fit."

"By exercising her First Amendment rights."

Taggert had no response to that, and Noreen's pulse slowed just a tad.

"I also have it on good authority that she wrote you a letter of apology. Did you receive such a letter?"

"Well, yes, but I'm sure it was . . . some sort of . . . ploy."

"Miss O'Sullivan has shown remorse for her actions and taken steps to atone. She has no prior arrests, and according to these character references . . ." He held up a stack of papers. "She is a model employee, a regular church attendee, and someone who wishes to better her community."

People had written character references for her? She peeked at James from the corner of her eye. Had he arranged that?

Judge Lynch motioned to her. "Miss O'Sullivan, please rise."

She stood.

"Miss Noreen O'Sullivan. You are hereby released on your own recognizance. You are sentenced to make restitution to Mr. Milton Taggert in the amount of one hundred fifty-two dollars and seventy-five cents. The amount may be paid in a lump sum or in payments of ten dollars a month over the course of the next fifteen months. The first payment is due on June 1, 1894. Should you fall delinquent, you will be found in contempt of court and will face jail time."

Before she could ask any questions, he banged his gavel and exited the courtroom.

Ten dollars a month? She barely made fifteen dollars a month at the hotel. How would she live?

A bigger question filled her mind as she heard Milton Taggert behind her, complaining about the ruling. How would she live with the knowledge that two-thirds of her salary would be going to purchase the very thing she'd dedicated her life to eradicating?

Chapter
32

After Judge Lynch's ruling, Noreen's mind whirled with conflict-
ing thoughts and emotions, leaving her unsteady on her feet.
James appeared at her side in an instant, his hand going to her elbow
as if he could sense the turmoil inside of her.

"Guess this means I can have my mattress back." He grinned as
he made the quip, and her internal spinning slowed.

"I don't know." Her lips turned up at the corners. "I might need
to take up residence there. It's cheaper than the boardinghouse, and
it seems I'll be running short on funds for a while."

His gaze ran over her face, and his thumb caressed the inside of
her elbow. "Don't worry about the money, Noreen. It'll work out.
You'll see."

She wished she shared his optimism. She believed in God's
provision—the fact that an ally like James stood with her in this
moment was evidence aplenty of that blessing—yet the wrong she'd
committed deserved the punishment she'd received, and she didn't
see how a just God could ignore her responsibility. Still, she offered
James a smile and a nod, not wanting to dim his confidence.

"Noreen!"

She turned to find Martha and Jane waving to her over the top of
the short railing that separated the gallery from the official section

of the courtroom. Stepping away from James, she hurried to her friends and gladly opened her arms to accept their dual embrace.

"Praise the Lord you'll not have to serve any more jail time," Jane murmured in a soft yet fervent voice.

Noreen nodded. "Yes, a blessing, indeed." She'd not miss the bars nor the boredom, but she would miss having James so near. Now that she bore the label of *convicted vandal*, he'd need to distance himself from her to protect his upright reputation. A task he seemed disinclined to accept, which meant she'd have to help him.

Martha patted Noreen's shoulder, her expression one of unswerving confidence. "We will dedicate our next Tuesday Tea to making a financial plan for the restitution. I have a nest egg we can dip into at any time, if you need a loan. All you have to do is ask."

"I'm not touching your nest egg, Martha. Though it is sweet of you to offer."

She knew how Martha scrimped to set aside money to provide for herself when the time to retire arrived. Spinsters without family members to lean on had no one to depend upon but themselves for financial security in their later years. She'd not risk depleting Martha's funds. If something happened and Noreen lost her job or became injured or half a dozen other undesirable outcomes, Martha would be left paying the price for Noreen's foolishness. She'd not take that chance.

Martha looked like she wanted to argue, but Hortense Lockwood approached with two other spinsters in tow. Personal discussions would need to wait.

"Miss O'Sullivan, I was impressed with the forthright way you conducted yourself in court today. I respect those who take responsibility for their actions and learn from their mistakes. I believe you have done both."

Noreen dipped her head. "Thank you, ma'am."

"I had some rather fruitful visits yesterday." Her eyes glowed with depth of meaning. "I look forward to seeing you at our Thursday gathering." Miss Lockwood dipped her chin, and Noreen caught her breath.

She'd been approved to continue as a probational spinster? The nods coming from the ladies flanking Miss Lockwood seemed to indicate as much. Noreen's eyes misted as she glanced at Martha and Jane. Both her friends beamed at the news, reassuring Noreen that she hadn't misinterpreted the subtleties of the conversation.

Pulling her handkerchief from her skirt pocket, Noreen raised her arm to wipe away the accumulation of happy tears from her eyes, but someone jostled her forcibly from behind. She grabbed the railing at her side to keep from falling. Her handkerchief fluttered to the floor.

"Oh my goodness! So sorry, my dear. Here, let me help." Her stepfather took hold of her arms and pulled her upward, then bent to retrieve her handkerchief. He whipped it open, then draped it over his arm in a gesture that was probably intended to appear courtly and chivalrous, but knowing his true opinion of her, it felt contrived and ridiculous.

All sentiment drained from her in an instant, leaving her eyes dry and no longer in need of a cloth. Taking hold of the plain white corner nearest her, she gave it a tug, but Arthur failed to let go of the opposite end.

"These embroidered flowers are quite lovely, Noreen. I'm glad to see your skill with a needle has improved." He chuckled and looked to Miss Lockwood. "She had no patience for needlework when she was younger, always running off when her mother tried to teach her. Perhaps it is *your* influence that has motivated her improved domesticity. A woman of superior style, like yourself, would be an admirable model for a young woman with unruly tendencies."

Miss Lockwood did not deign to reply to his blatant pandering with anything more than a raised eyebrow. The sisterhood between Noreen and Hortense Lockwood solidified in that moment. All previous differences of opinions were forgotten.

Take that, Arthur.

"Do you intend to keep your daughter from her belongings, Mr. Clevenger?" Miss Lockwood glanced pointedly at the handkerchief corner he continued to hold.

He released it at once. "Of course not." A strained laugh bubbled from him, but no one joined in, so he lifted a hand to his mouth and morphed the sound into a cough instead. "In truth, I wished to offer Noreen a word of fatherly caution." He turned his attention to Noreen. "I overheard Mr. Taggert commiserating with one of his cronies after the ruling, and I'm afraid he's quite bitter about the mild sentence you received. I know how impassioned you are about your temperance work, my dear, but as I've warned you many times, it's not safe for you to pit yourself against a man like Taggert. He's sworn to have you prosecuted to the full extent of the law should you cause any further harm to his establishment, and I believe Judge Lynch will be much less sympathetic to a repeat offender. It will be difficult, but you must put your hatred of Mr. Taggert aside should you wish to recover from this scandal."

Noreen's brow furrowed. "I don't hate Mr. Taggert. It's the liquor I—"

"That's the way." Arthur patted her arm as he interrupted her with a condescending smile. "Keep repeating that claim to yourself. In time, it will no doubt become the truth."

As if Arthur Clevenger knew anything about truth beyond how to twist it to suit his purposes.

"Ah well, I must be going." His eyes widened slightly as if he saw an approaching predator and, as rats are wont to do, decided it was time to scurry away. "Your mother is anxious to hear news of the judge's ruling." Arthur lifted a hand in parting, then beat a hasty retreat toward the opposite door.

"Everything all right over here, Miss O'Sullivan?"

James.

So that's what had Arthur fleeing. Noreen smiled, feeling lighter than she had in days. "Improving by the moment, Deputy Paxton. Thank you."

His eyes danced with suppressed humor. "Glad to hear it, ma'am. Today's a day for counting one's blessings, to my way of thinking."

"I couldn't agree more." Especially when the man before her made about a hundred different blessings pop to mind.

Chapter 33

The jailhouse felt empty without her. James sat at the office table sipping coffee and pushing his sorry excuse for scrambled eggs around on his plate. Back to eating his own cooking on Sunday and Wednesday nights. Yet it wasn't Noreen's culinary talents he'd missed most this past week. It was her company.

Setting aside the half-finished plate of overcooked eggs and burnt toast, he hunched over his coffee mug and sighed like a lovesick polecat. Shoot. No *like* about it. He *was* a lovesick polecat. If Jethro and Josh could see him now, he'd never hear the end of their ribbing. Judith, though . . . Judith would tell him to quit moping and do something about it. Either get on with his courtship or pick a new project to pursue. No lollygagging in the middle. Decent advice. Just one problem—he wasn't ready to pick a new project, and Noreen wasn't ready to accept his courtship. Which left him stewing in the inescapable middle.

He'd helped Noreen move out of the jail last Friday, carting her things over to the boardinghouse after her sentencing, but the hug she'd offered him in appreciation of his *friendship* during her incarceration had felt an awful lot like a good-bye sort of hug. He'd told her straight out that he still intended to pay court to her, but she'd shook her head and said something ridiculous about not wanting to be the millstone around his neck that drowned his career.

The worst thing about it was that it was his own blasted fault. When she'd first come to him for assistance, he'd tried to put her off, reciting his goal of being sheriff and explaining how allying himself with her temperance mission would likely turn voters against him. Now that their relationship had taken an intimate turn, she was trying to give him what he'd said he'd wanted. But his goals had changed. He wanted *her* more than he'd ever wanted that sheriff's badge. A fact she refused to believe. Obstinate woman.

It didn't help matters that finding time to talk to her had proven nearly impossible. Noreen had taken on extra shifts at the hotel to increase her earnings. Those extra shifts came mostly in the evenings as she filled the vacancy left by Luella Templeton. Working such long hours left her exhausted by the end of the day, so even when he paid a late call at the boardinghouse, she turned him away. He had half a mind to trump up a false charge so he'd have an excuse to arrest her again. Get her alone. Make her see the truth about his intentions. The situation might even call for some radical convincing techniques. He could think of a few he'd like to try. None of which involved talking, though lips would definitely be required.

Shaking his head at himself, James got up from the table, scraped his cold eggs into the scrap bin, then washed his dishes. Maybe tomorrow he'd buy dinner at the hotel and see if he could wrangle a conversation with a particular staff member. At least he wouldn't be stuck eating his own cooking that way. He couldn't afford to let her out-stubborn him. Not with something as important as their future on the line. He'd just have to find creative ways to circumvent her defenses. Not that different from laying siege to an outlaw den. With a much better reward waiting at the end of the operation.

Any ideas you'd like to offer would be much appreciated, Lord.

A Jericho walk around the boardinghouse. A parting of the mill-pond. A pair of stone tablets appearing on his doorstep with inspired instructions. He'd be open to any of it at this point.

Unfortunately, by the time he turned in for the night, he was no closer to finding a solution than he had been hours before. He fell into an uneasy sleep, dreaming of trying to find passage across an ever-widening chasm, until the clanging of a loud bell jerked him awake. He sprang from bed, threw on his pants and boots, and grabbed his gun belt on the way to the door.

The instant he stepped outside, his gut knotted. A dreadful glow lit the dark sky as the acrid smell of smoke filled his nostrils. Ducking back inside, he dumped the contents of his slop pail onto the floor, then grabbed the handles of both it and the water bucket in the corner. These weapons would serve him better against tonight's enemy than his gun.

James ran down Second Street, past the courthouse, then cut the corner to Main, thankful that the fearsome glow led him away from Noreen's boardinghouse. A man ran down the street in the opposite direction shouting news that choked James as much as the thickening smoke.

"The Salt Fork's on fire! Save the saloon, save the town!"

James couldn't claim any particular fondness for Milton Taggert, but the man had certainly had more than his share of trouble lately. Praying that there would be no loss of life this night, and minimal loss of property, James charged toward the fiery furnace.

A pounding on the boardinghouse door awakened Noreen from a deep sleep. Rubbing her eyes, she pushed back the covers and rose to a sitting position. The pounding came again, and Noreen's heart adopted the thundering cadence.

"The Salt Fork's on fire! Save the saloon, save the town!"

Fire. Noreen's stomach clenched as the deadly announcement swiped the cobwebs from her mind. She had to help. It didn't matter that she wished the saloon gone. Fire was no respecter of persons. Sparks could jump from building to building, taking out homes, churches, or schools. The Albany Hotel where she worked stood only a few buildings away from the Salt Fork. If the fire reached the hotel, she could lose her livelihood. And what of the people staying there? She prayed they were being roused from their sleep as well. That no lives would be endangered by the fire.

Noreen hurried to the armoire, grabbed her oldest work dress, and pulled it on over the top of her nightgown. After snatching a pair of stockings from a drawer and her shoes from the end of her bed, she sat on the edge of the mattress and attired her feet. Once shod, she hurried to the dresser, where she shoved the items she always kept with her into her pocket. Her key, coin purse, and handkerchief. She flinched a bit when she grabbed the plain white cotton square. She still couldn't believe that she'd misplaced her spinster society handkerchief sometime over the last few days. She kept hoping it would turn up, but even after a thorough search of all her drawers, pockets, and handbags, it remained missing. Probably a casualty of her longer work hours combined with the mental stress of trying to discourage James's attention when, in truth, she craved his company.

James. He was probably already out there, organizing a water line and making sure everyone was safe. He'd need help, and she intended to see that he had it.

Leaving her sleeping braid to flop against her back, Noreen exited her room and ran down the stairs.

"Somehow I knew you'd be fool enough to charge into the fray." Her landlady met her by the door, a white sleeping cap covering her hair. She clutched a robe closed beneath her chin with one hand.

Noreen bit back a groan. She didn't have time for a lecture on propriety or the unsuitability of women in firefighting endeavors. James needed her. The town needed her. And she'd not let a stuffy old busybody like Mrs. Barker stop her from—

"Here." Mrs. Barker extended her arm toward Noreen, a milk pail dangling from her fingers. "Can't have ya showin' up empty-handed."

"Thanks." Noreen clasped the pail's handle, though it took a moment to get past the shock of her landlady's unaccustomed charity.

"Just don't lose it, or I'm adding the cost to next month's rent."

And just like that, the world tilted back onto its normal axis. Noreen smiled. "I won't."

"Go on with ya, now." Mrs. Barker opened the front door, and the chill of the night air sent a shiver coursing down Noreen's nape. "Just mind yer skirt," Mrs. Barker called as Noreen hurried down the porch steps. "Don't let a stray spark catch hold of ya."

It was almost as if her landlady cared.

Now that she thought about it, Mrs. Barker had made no protest when Noreen returned to the boardinghouse after her stint in jail, either. She'd fussed at her about not letting her rent payments slip now that she had additional bills to pay, but she'd not made good on her oft-made threat to toss Noreen out if she ever ran afoul of the law. Could it be that the woman's starchy manner hid a kind heart?

Noreen paused at the street and turned to lift a hand in parting. "I'll be careful."

"See that ya are" came the crotchety response.

The faint smell of smoke in the air urged Noreen not to linger. Turning in the direction of the saloon, she set off at a trot, her bucket swinging at her side. The air thickened as she passed the hotel, and shouting voices drew her closer to the building that seemed to glow from within. She'd often thought of the saloon as an evil place, but tonight it looked truly demonic. Fiery eyes taunted from broken-out windows. Undulating creatures locked inside hissed and snapped as they demanded release.

God help us.

Dozens of people swarmed the road in front of the saloon. Men in lines passed water-filled buckets both into the saloon and over to the blacksmith shop next door in an attempt to keep the blaze from spreading. She spotted James at the front of one of the bucket lines, a blue bandanna pulled up over his mouth and nose. Once he had a full bucket in his hands, he ran inside the burning building, doused something, then exited with the empty bucket. He took a moment to catch his breath while a second man took a turn running inside, then reclaimed his place at the head of the line, accepting the next bucket and dashing back inside. He'd not be able to keep that up for long before the smoke overcame him.

Noreen glanced around, trying to figure out how best to help without interrupting the rhythm of the bucket lines. Picking her way to the source, the water pump and trough at the side of the carpentry shop across the street, Noreen called out to Mr. Freeman, the blacksmith who manned the pump.

"How can I help?"

He didn't even bother to look at her, just jerked his head toward the front of the carpentry shop, where a group of women huddled together, watching the goings on. "Stay out of the way."

He stopped pumping long enough to fill two buckets at the trough and heave them up to the start of the line. A young boy ran up with four empty pails clanging in his hands. He dropped them at the trough, then ran back out to join the other school-age boys in charge of retrieving the empties.

"Freeman!" Connor Reed, soot streaking his face, ran down the line, not stopping until he stood before the blacksmith. "I got word from Paxton. Fire's spreadin' to the back side. If sparks catch the field behind the saloon, we might not be able to contain it. We need to wet down the rear."

Mr. Freeman swiped his forearm over his brow as he scrutinized the line in front of him. "Take a few of the boys. Give 'em wet blankets and put 'em on ember snuffing duty. I can't spare any of the men."

"But you have plenty of able-bodied women," Noreen said, chin jutting forward as she stepped around the back of the trough. "There's a cistern behind the hotel. I can form a line of women to bring water to the rear of the saloon from there."

Mr. Freeman glared at her, but Noreen held his gaze without flinching.

"Fine. But stay well away from the building. I don't want any injured women on my conscience." He waved at Connor. "Go with her, Reed." He shot another glare at Noreen as he started working the pump again. "He's in charge. Got it?"

"Got it."

Now was not the time to argue about a woman's capability. If having a man at least five years her junior taking charge allowed her to help James and the rest of the town, she'd accept those terms.

Spotting Mrs. Winslow among the women spectating in front of the carpentry shop, Noreen hurried over to her. "We're going to bring water from the hotel cistern to protect the rear of the saloon. Connor and a few of the boys will help with wet blankets, but if we can dampen the back of the building, we can keep the fire from spreading."

Mrs. Winslow gave a sharp nod. "I'll get some of the maids to help and pull extra ice buckets from the pantry. They're a little smaller and will be easier to carry."

Martha came up alongside Noreen and held up the bucket and empty coal scuttle she carried. "I've got a couple vessels we can use as well."

"Wonderful." Noreen smiled at Martha, then turned to the other ladies relegated to the role of spectator. "Anyone who wishes to help will be welcome. Those who wish to stay here can spread the word to others who come later."

Noreen didn't wait to count volunteers, she just headed off to the hotel, dropped her bucket by the cistern, and started working the hand pump.

"Here." Connor Reed shooed her away from the pump. "I'll fill the buckets, you set up the line."

"I don't know that we'll have enough to stretch all the way to the saloon from here." She met Connor's gaze. He looked about as confident as she felt, which was not at all, but somehow it helped having an ally.

"Just space 'em out at first," he said, "then when more people come, they'll fill in the gaps." He shrugged. "That's what Mr. Freeman did, at least."

As sound a plan as any, she supposed. Noreen surrendered the pump to Connor's greater strength and turned to survey her troops. More than she'd expected. At least fifteen women stood nearby awaiting instructions. And Mrs. Winslow would bring more from the hotel.

"All right, ladies. Leave your buckets here at the cistern, then follow me to form a line to the saloon. We'll likely have to cart the water between each checkpoint, but we'll get it there. That's what matters."

"Ain't no differ'nt than totin' water on wash day," one woman called from the back.

"Or carryin' a mop bucket from room to room."

Noreen's chest expanded. "Exactly right. We're more than capable of stopping that fire in its tracks." She turned to Martha. "Will you oversee things on this end while I take a group down toward the saloon?"

Martha nodded. "Of course."

Purpose vibrated in Noreen's veins as she waved to her crew. "Let's get to work, ladies!"

They had the line in place in mere minutes and buckets passing soon after. Connor left his position at the pump to take charge of the water toss at the end of the line, insisting Noreen stay a good ten feet away from the saloon's back door. A pile of crates filled with liquor bottles, a handful of chairs, two framed pieces of questionable art, and a lockbox of some kind sat in a heap at the edge of the field. No doubt Mr. Taggert had attempted to salvage what he could of his inventory and belongings before help arrived.

The two teen boys they'd recruited darted through the field, squelching small fires and stomping on embers before they had the chance to ignite. They'd not be able to stay ahead for long if the fire spread to the exterior or the roof.

"We have to keep the blaze contained," she shouted to Connor over the snapping and crackling that filled the air. "We should focus the water on the building, not the field. At least for now. Do you agree?"

He nodded, and his first bucketful splashed over the doorframe of the rear exit. They worked in tandem without words after that. She fed him bucket after bucket, trading empty for full until her arms ached from the strain. Connor grew braver with each toss, venturing up to the open doorway and tossing the water inside. Flames drew back with a steamy hiss, but like a relentless army, they returned to encroach from another side.

Noreen pulled her handkerchief from her skirt pocket and dunked it in her bucket before striding forward to meet Connor. "Here," she said. "Tie this around your face. It will help with the smoke."

"Thanks." He knotted the corners behind his neck, then pulled the fabric up over his nose. He reached for the bucket.

She relinquished it but placed her hand on his arm. "Don't go too far inside, Connor. It's dangerous."

His face took on a mulish cast that didn't bode well. "I can hear the others when I'm in the storeroom, ma'am. On the other side of the wall. We're close to puttin' this monster down. The dogie's in the chute, and I ain't gonna let him squeeze past me."

He pulled away and headed back into the fight. Knowing she couldn't stop him, Noreen did the only thing she could to help—hurried back to the line to collect the next bucket.

Before she made it back to her designated handoff point, though, the deep groan of weakening lumber echoed through the night.

Her gaze locked onto the doorway, but she saw no evidence of Connor. Her stomach spasmed.

Come on. No time to be a hero.

A loud crack exploded, shaking the building.

"Connor!" Noreen sprinted forward, water sloshing down the front of her dress. Had the roof collapsed? "Connor!"

Before she reached the door, Connor emerged, bent in half and coughing but alive.

Thank you, Lord!

She moved to his side just as a second man burst from the door. Instinct more than conscious thought dictated her reaction. Or maybe a divine hand set her arms in motion before her brain registered the flames. Either way, a wave of water arced out of her bucket onto the back of the man rushing past her. The man whose coat was on fire.

The instant the water hit him, he fell to his knees and clawed the coat from his body. He tossed it to the ground, then stretched a shaking hand down to the muddy earth to steady himself.

252

Noreen crept forward. "Are you all right?"

"Thanks," he said at the same time, then craned his neck around. The gratitude softening his gaze hardened to spiked iron the moment his eyes met hers. "You!"

Noreen flinched. She'd just saved Milton Taggert's life, and he looked ready to end hers.

Chapter
34

W as burning my building not enough for you?" Taggert rasped.
"Did you have to sneak around back here to destroy what
little I managed to save?" The soot blackening his face did nothing
to mask his rage.

Noreen retreated, wagging her head in denial of his irrational
charge. "I didn't touch any of your belongings. They're all there.
Look." She pointed, hoping the evidence of her veracity would calm
him. "I'm just here to help. Like everyone else."

"Help me into an early grave." Taggert grabbed her wrist. "You're
a she-devil who needs to be stopped."

Her bucket fell to the ground as his grip tightened. Connor
shouted a protest and latched on to Taggert's shoulder from behind.
Taggert whirled and slammed his fist into Connor's face. The young
man toppled backward.

"Connor!"

Noreen tried to go to him, but Taggert reclaimed his hold on her
arm and jerked her backward. Jaw clenched, he dragged her toward
his pile of salvaged goods. Did he have a gun there? A knife? Would
he kill her in front of witnesses?

"Please," she begged as she pulled against him. "I only came to help."

Taggert grunted, continuing his march undeterred. Until a shadowed figure stepped into his path and slapped him full in the face with a wall of water.

"Shame on you, Milton Taggert. Takin' your anger out on a woman like that. Let her go."

Taggert wiped a hand over his eyes, which only served to smear the soot around. "Irma?"

"Yes, it's me, you dunderhead." Irma Freeman, wife to the blacksmith whose business stood next door, planted her hands on her hips. "Out here trying to save your stinkin' swill hole before it burns to the ground. Had I known you'd be this ungrateful, I woulda just doused the smithy instead."

The manacle of his fingers loosened, and Noreen yanked free of his grasp. Taggert squinted past Mrs. Freeman to another figure emerging out of the night.

"Irma? What's going on?" Rebecca Hunter, who lived a block behind the hotel, walked onto the scene with the next bucket, her eyes wide.

Taggert looked from woman to woman, his forehead scrunching. "How many women you got out here, Irma?"

"A couple dozen, I reckon. Though they ain't here because of me. Noreen's the one who organized us. Got my stubborn husband to agree to lettin' the womenfolk run a bucket line from the hotel. You should be thankin' her, not yellin' at her."

"Her quick thinking put out the fire that caught on your back when that beam cracked, too," Connor said as he joined the group, his glare hot enough to cause sparks of its own as he rubbed his jaw. He stepped past Taggert and took the full bucket from Mrs. Hunter. "Now, if you'll excuse us, we've got a fire to put out." He looked to Noreen. "Miss O'Sullivan? You coming?"

Eager to get away from Taggert, she nodded and hurried to Connor's side. Taggert circled his gaze from person to person as if trying to piece together a puzzle that didn't fit.

"Feel free to join the effort after you check the status of your belongings," Connor called over his shoulder, then marched up to the rear of the saloon and tossed the water along the side wall that faced the smithy.

He handed the bucket to Noreen, and she jogged it back to Irma, taking a path that kept her well away from Taggert as he dug through his salvaged things.

"Keep it." Irma strode up to meet her, a new bucket in hand. "I'm tradin' places with you. You can work my section. Unless you want to head back to the hotel. No one would blame you for wantin' to put some distance between yourself and that hothead." She tipped her chin toward Taggert. "You might not think so, but the man's a good neighbor. Kind to us and the kids. I never had a quarrel with him until he put hands on you. I know it's no excuse, but it's gotta be hard on a man to see everything he's worked for turn to ash."

Noreen peered through the dark to where Taggert hunched over his pitifully small pile of belongings, taking stock of the few things he had left in this world. A good neighbor. Kind to children. She'd never thought of him as a regular person with noble qualities. He'd always been the enemy. A purveyor of poison. Yet no person was just one thing, were they? Everyone had strengths and flaws, traits to admire and others to endure. If she wished for him to see her as more than the woman who vandalized his business, perhaps she should try to see him as more than an impediment to her temperance mission.

"I suppose you're right." Noreen moved past Irma and slid into her vacated link of the firefighting chain. "Let's get this done."

By the time she made it back to Rebecca's station, there were two buckets waiting for her.

"They're starting to stack up." Rebecca hiked up the path carting a third bucket. "Rose has about five more waiting for me back there."

Noreen dropped her empty bucket. "I'll take two at a time until we get caught up, then."

Easier said than done when her arms felt as limp as melted meringue, but she was determined to prove to Taggert, and herself, that she cared more about preserving the community than beating him in the temperance war.

Irma took one bucket from her and handed over an empty. "Just leave that one there. I'll come back for it."

Noreen did as she was told, but when she turned to head back, Taggert stepped in front of her.

"I know you set this fire," he growled in a low voice, "and your Sweet Susie routine isn't going to save your neck when the truth comes out. I've got proof, and I'll make sure your besotted deputy doesn't sweep it under the rug."

Heart thumping, she stood rooted to the spot as Taggert stepped around her, picked up the extra bucket, and trudged toward the saloon. Once he was out of sight, she exhaled a shaky breath, then headed back to the checkpoint to collect the next buckets. She'd not let him rattle her. He was upset. With good reason. If he needed someone to lash out at, she had plenty of practice being the target of his scorn. She could handle it. He'd learn soon enough that she didn't set the fire. Whatever proof he thought he had would be easily rebuffed with logic because the truth was the truth. She'd not gone anywhere near the Salt Fork Saloon tonight until the call of "Fire!" pulled her from her bed.

"Last bucket, Paxton."

James accepted the final bucket from Alfred Cooper and tossed its load of water onto the charred remains of the Salt Fork's bar. The cherry finish Taggert always kept polished to a high sheen stood blackened, cracked, and burnt beyond saving. Sad enough sight to turn even a nondrinking man melancholy.

He tugged his soggy bandanna down around his neck and picked his way back toward the entrance.

"Come on, Coop. The roof's not stable." One of the ceiling beams had cracked not twenty minutes ago. "We shouldn't linger."

The man who'd been handing him buckets for the last hour stood in the center of the tavern near one of the few tables that hadn't been turned to kindling. He ran his fingers over the scorched surface. "I played poker at this table just a few hours ago. Now look at it. Everything's just . . . gone." His shoulders dropped, more than physical weariness sapping his strength. Such devastation and loss took a toll on a man's spirit.

James clapped him on the back and urged him toward the door. His own boots dragged as he moved through the depressing surroundings. "Taggert's gonna need his friends to rally around him in the coming days."

Old Coop sighed. "I'll gather the fellas. Maybe we can take up a collection or something. It wouldn't be much in the face of all this," he said as he paused at the doorway and turned back to survey the fire's damage, "but maybe it'll let him know there are people who care."

James looked back over the large room as well, seeing details he hadn't noticed when he'd been focused on dousing flames. An odd burn pattern marked the floorboards. Darker edges outlined a lighter, curved pattern that seemed to spread outward from beneath one of the windows facing the alley, almost as if something had spilled onto the floor. Something that had protected the wood beneath from the flames. At least initially.

Making a mental note to come back in daylight for a closer look, James passed through the doorway and tossed his bucket onto the pile that tired neighbors were picking through to find the ones that belonged to them. Mr. Freeman moved among the men, shaking hands and thanking folks for their hard work. The wall of the blacksmith's shop showed evidence of scorching, but no real damage had been done. A reminder that there had been victories this night as well as tragedy.

James searched the crowd for Taggert, wanting to offer some meager encouragement, though he doubted words existed that could make this moment any less demoralizing. He'd need to interview the man as well, see if he knew how the fire had started. But that could wait until the morning. Which apparently wasn't too far off, judging by the strip of pale gray sky hovering above the eastern horizon.

Not finding the man he sought among the bleary-eyed townsfolk who were starting to make their way back to their own homes, James approached the blacksmith, who seemed the most likely person to have the information he needed.

"Hey, Freeman. You seen Taggert?"

The man looked like he'd been swimming instead of fighting fires, drenched from head to toe as he was from his bucket work at the pump. "One of the boys said they saw him working the bucket line with the women at the rear."

"The women?" First he'd heard of a rear bucket line. Though, he did recall seeing Connor Reed inside the building a time or two and had wondered where the kid had come from.

"Yeah, that O'Sullivan woman pulled a bunch of women together to cart water from the hotel cistern. My wife among them. Reed was supervisin', making sure none of 'em got too close to the building."

Noreen was out here? James's sluggish pulse picked up its pace as he scoured the crowd for a different face, wanting to see her and reassure himself of her safety.

"Oh, hey." The blacksmith pointed at the far side of the saloon. "That might be him there." His bushy brows arched. "Them womenfolk don't look none too happy, though."

James turned and spotted Taggert, his head standing several inches above the group of ladies circling him and slowing his steps. James strode that direction, his gaze searching for a head of dark curly hair. Freeman followed, no doubt concerned about his wife. The schoolteacher seemed the one most determined to impede Taggert's progress, planting herself directly in his path and shaking a finger in his face. He knocked her arm aside and pushed past her, finally revealing the woman James most wanted to see.

Taggert had Noreen by the wrist.

James's jaw clenched, but he forced himself to hold his tongue. Fisting his hand to keep from drawing his gun, James picked up his pace. Taggert had lost nearly everything tonight, he reminded himself. He deserved compassion. Yet no amount of loss gave a man permission to mistreat a woman. Even one who'd pitted herself against him.

Drawing to a halt a few yards away from the group of women actively giving Taggert a piece of their minds, James raised his voice to be heard above their voices. "I suggest you release her, Taggert. No need for a bad night to get any worse."

Milton Taggert pulled Noreen forward and flung her toward James. "Arrest her, Paxton. She set the fire."

James steadied Noreen with gentle hands and did his best to portray a calm he didn't feel.

"Hold on there, Taggert. I know you and Noreen have had your differences, but that doesn't mean she set the fire. From what I hear, she helped put it out. Organized an entire water line to guard the rear."

"That's what we told him," Martha said, shooting a dark scowl at the bartender. "Mr. Reed told us she even saved Mr. Taggert's life by extinguishing a fire that caught on his clothing."

James caught a movement from the back of the group. Connor Reed stepped forward. "That's right, Deputy. I saw it with my own eyes."

Taggert waved his arms about in a wild fashion as he turned to address the people clumped around him, focusing on James and Mr. Freeman. "It's all a ploy, don't you see? She showed up to help as a pretense. To hide the truth of what she did. But I have proof that it was her." He started digging in his coat pocket.

James stepped in front of Noreen and drew his pistol from his holster. "Easy, Taggert. Let me see your hands."

"She's wanted me gone for ages." Taggert raised his left hand, but his right remained in his pocket. "And when I wouldn't give in to her little terror tactics, she took matters into her own hands."

He pulled his hand free of his pocket, and James raised his gun. The ladies around him gasped, but Taggert held no weapon in his hand. Instead, a white square danced in the night breeze like a flag of surrender. But Taggert was surrendering nothing.

"I got proof!"

James holstered his gun and stepped closer. He pulled the handkerchief from Taggert's hand. Black letters painted across the cloth proclaimed motive for all to see. *FOR TEMPERENCE*, it read. Yet that wasn't the most damning piece of evidence on the cloth. For directly below the lettering was a familiar cluster of blue embroidered flowers and Noreen's initials.

Chapter
35

How was that possible? Noreen stared at the handkerchief in James's hand. *Her* handkerchief. How had it come to be in Mr. Taggert's possession? And who had painted that blatantly misleading message upon it?

"I . . . I don't understand. Where did you find this?"

Taggert glared at her. "Tacked to my front doorframe. Right where you left it."

Noreen shook her head. "I didn't. I swear."

She looked to James, who was rubbing the pad of his thumb over the embroidered forget-me-nots, obviously remembering when he'd last seen them. In her possession while she'd been behind bars. A place to which Taggert seemed determined to have her return.

"James, I didn't do this."

He had to trust her. He *had* to. If he looked her in the eyes and believed her guilty of this atrocity—believed her capable of such a disgraceful act—her heart would shrivel like a tomato left to rot on the vine.

Taggert had no difficulty scoffing at her claim of innocence. "Bat your lashes all you want, darlin'. It's not gonna change the facts. You're the only one in town with motive. And this hankie proves your involvement. You're guilty as sin, and I got witnesses. You might have this gaggle of women on your side, but Freeman will hold Paxton's feet to the fire. Won't you, Freeman?"

The blacksmith peered at her, eyebrow raised, then crossed his large arms in front of his chest and grunted. Hard to tell if that was an affirmative grunt or a contradictory one, but his opinion wasn't the one that mattered to her at the moment.

James finally glanced up from the handkerchief, his blue eyes bright against the soot streaks on his face. He peered at her for a long moment, and her pulse fluttered like a trapped bird as she waited for his verdict. However, the longer he held her gaze, the more she became aware of what wasn't there. No disappointment. No doubt. No condemnation.

He believed her. Noreen's pulse slowed, and a shaky sigh slipped past her lips.

"There will be a thorough investigation, Taggert. I'll keep you and Mr. Freeman apprised of my progress. But in this country, a person is presumed innocent until proven guilty."

"There's no presumption about it." Taggert jabbed his finger at the handkerchief. "She left her calling card."

"Or someone else did, wanting her to take the blame."

Noreen's legs quivered to the point she worried they might fail to keep her upright. Did someone hate her so much that they'd burn down the saloon just to be rid of her? If she was found guilty, she'd be sentenced to time in prison. Or had it been an enemy of Taggert's who found her an easy scapegoat to hide behind?

"Do you believe this, Freeman?" Taggert let out a humorless laugh. "He's already makin' excuses for her. He can't be trusted to run this investigation. Someone needs to fetch the sheriff."

"Sheriff Adair is trailin' rustlers," James offered, his voice as calm and friendly as ever. As if his integrity had not just been slandered. "No one knows precisely where he is. You're welcome to go hunt for him, if you like. In the meantime, I'll be gathering evidence and conducting interviews."

"You mean picking through the evidence to try get your girl off the hook."

James's gaze hardened. "I'll examine *all* evidence, Taggert. As should you, if you want to know what really happened here. Think about it. Why would the person who set fire to your building announce their identity to the world? Miss O'Sullivan is passionate about temperance, but she's not lacking intelligence. And after the few days she spent in the jailhouse, I can guarantee she's not eager to return to incarceration."

"Never would be too soon," Noreen agreed, her nape growing cold at the thought of being behind bars again.

Martha moved forward and pointed at the handkerchief. "Not only that, Deputy, but Noreen would never misspell *temperance*. I've personally witnessed her write that word on numerous occasions, and never once has she spelled it incorrectly. Yet whoever painted that message spelled it *-ence* instead of *-ance*."

Taggert waved off her observation. "As if that matters. Anyone can make a mistake."

Martha centered her best teacher's glare on the man. "Just as you are making one now by jumping to unfounded conclusions."

"Look, we're all tired," the blacksmith said, his arms uncrossing as he moved toward the group. "Let's go home, clean up, and catch a couple hours of shut-eye. Taggert, you can bunk at our place." He thumped the saloon owner on the shoulder.

Taggert jerked away from his friend's touch. "Thanks, Freeman, but I think I'll stay around here. See what I can salvage." He shot a scowl at Noreen. "Make sure no one breaks any more bottles."

James must have been rubbing off on her more than she realized, for Taggert's jab failed to stir her defensiveness. She was too busy puzzling over the way he'd shied from the blacksmith's friendly touch. Could be lingering anger, but visions of his coat covered in flames brought another hypothesis to mind.

When he failed to get a rise out of her, Taggert stormed off. Mr. Freeman jogged after him, saying something about clearing out some space at the back of the smithy so Taggert could store his belongings.

The others dispersed as well, though many of the ladies who had defended her so adamantly a few minutes before now cast sideways glances in her direction, their uncertainty blaring bright. No doubt they were questioning her innocence thanks to that infernal handkerchief. Even Irma failed to meet Noreen's gaze as she passed by on her way to the road.

"Irma, wait." Noreen hurried after her.

Thankfully, the woman halted and didn't make Noreen chase her down. She still didn't look her in the eye, though, when Noreen drew alongside. She chose to stare at her feet instead. "It's been a long night, Noreen. You can plead your case tomorrow."

"It's not that." Though the fact Irma thought she needed to plead her case stung. "I think . . ." She stopped and straightened her posture. "There's a good chance that Taggert was burned by the fire that lit his coat. The way he jerked away from your husband seemed more like pain than anger. He'll not be able to doctor it himself. Perhaps you or Mr. Freeman could check on him."

Irma lifted her chin, surprise glimmering in her gaze. "Marcus keeps a medicine box at the forge to treat burns. They're a hazard of his trade. I'll have a word with him before I head back to the house."

Noreen nodded, her confidence wilting a bit beneath Irma's scrutiny. Suddenly craving the company of those who harbored fewer doubts about her character, Noreen turned and headed back toward James and Martha.

"Noreen?" Irma called.

She turned.

"Thanks."

It wasn't exactly a ringing endorsement of her innocence, but it was a gift of respect—one she appreciated. Noreen dipped her chin in acknowledgment, then resumed her retreat.

As soon as she came within reach of him, James placed a reassuring hand to her back. "Are you all right?"

Noreen shook her head slightly, too tired to pretend she hadn't been gutted by Taggert's accusations. "I still don't know how my handkerchief ended up tacked to his doorframe."

She glanced at Martha, knowing she'd understand the hidden layers of this particular betrayal. Swallowing the idea that someone in the society might have started the fire was like swallowing broken glass, but she had to consider the possibility.

"It's been missing for a few days," Noreen admitted. "I've been so busy with the extra shifts at the hotel that I assumed I mislaid it somewhere. I never considered someone might have taken it deliberately." She looked from Martha back to James. "I know I tend to ruffle feathers, but to think that someone committed such a heinous crime just to implicate me . . . It tears me up inside."

James reached for her hand and clasped it tightly. "Nothing that happened tonight can be laid at your feet, Noreen. Whoever did this, whatever their motive, it was *their* choice, *their* crime." He pulled her hand up to his chest and held it against his heart. "I'll find the true culprit. I'll interview everyone in Albany if I have to. Not just to protect you but to protect the town. There's an arsonist out there. One who put his own agenda ahead of people's safety. I won't let him get away with what he's done."

"It could have been a woman." Noreen hated the thought but needed to give it voice. James was right. More than her future hung in the balance. An arsonist on the loose posed a threat to the entire town.

"Can't say that I've heard of many female arsonists, but you're right. I shouldn't make assumptions." He raised her hand to his mouth and laid a quick kiss on her knuckles, not caring that she was covered in soot and grime. Not caring that someone might see.

Merciful heaven. How was she supposed to resist such a man?

Martha touched her other arm, drawing Noreen's attention away from James. "I'll let Jane know what happened. We can make inquiries as well." She raised her chin and peered at James. "Women might be more willing to speak to another woman than a lawman."

He nodded without hesitation. "Good thinking. Just be sure to keep me updated on what you learn. Easier to put a puzzle together when you've got all the pieces."

"I will." Martha turned her attention back to Noreen. "Would you like me to walk you back to the boardinghouse?"

"I'll see her home," James said. "I doubt Taggert will try anything, but I'll feel better walking her to her door just in case." He stroked the back of her hand with his thumb. "If that's all right with you."

A strong, independent woman would see herself home. That's what she'd believed for years. That it was weak to lean on a man. To lean on anyone, really. If a woman wished to be considered a man's equal, she must prove herself capable, cunning, and courageous. Yet the society had taught her that she was stronger when she *wasn't* alone. And in the dimness of predawn, when shadows outnumbered stars, alone was the last thing she wanted to be.

Noreen dipped her chin. "Yes, thank you."

James smiled, pleasure lighting his eyes and banishing all the dreary seriousness of the last half hour. Her heart expanded at the visual reminder that joy persisted, even in the midst of trials.

A loud clanking sound had all three of them turning in time to spy Connor Reed dropping a collection of water buckets on the pile of those that had been left behind.

The young man waved to them. "These are the pails left from the rear water line. I figured it'd be easier to add them to main pile."

Martha walked over to join him. "Very thoughtful of you, Mr. Reed. Thank you." She picked out the two items she'd brought with her, then glanced back to Noreen. "You know what Jane would say."

Noreen grinned, hearing her friend's soft-spoken voice in her mind. "The Lord has a plan."

"And with God all things are possible." Martha came alongside her and squeezed her arm. "We'll get through this, Noreen. Together."

"Together." She was really coming to appreciate the beauty of that word.

Martha moved off in the direction of her home near the schoolhouse while Noreen and James collected their respective buckets and headed down Main. Neither of them spoke much as they walked, weariness slowing their steps. She couldn't even find the energy to fret over her predicament. Perhaps having her hand tucked into the crook of James's arm helped her release the worry. Or maybe she was finally learning to let go of her need to control everything and trust the Lord to provide. Heaven knew she couldn't control this situation, even if she wanted to. Every aspect of it was out of her hands.

As they neared the boardinghouse, a movement on the front porch had James releasing his hold on her in order to move his hand to his gun.

"You get that fire put out, Deputy?" Mrs. Barker rose out of her rocking chair, and James moved his hand away from his holster.

"Yes, ma'am. It's safe to go on back to bed."

"Good. I'll expect Miss O'Sullivan to follow me inside directly."

Noreen chuckled softly. No one could accuse her landlady of subtlety.

James winked, his own amusement dancing in his blue eyes. "Yes, ma'am."

Noreen moved to the porch steps, placed her hand on the railing, then stopped. "James?"

He closed the distance between them with one long stride. "Yes?"

"Thank you for believing in me tonight."

He cupped her face and ran his thumb along her cheek. Her breath caught at the tenderness of his touch, and her eyes fluttered closed. "Always," he said, the low rumble of his voice rolling through her until it reached her heart and made itself at home.

"No matter what happens with the investigation," she murmured, her eyes opening to peer into his, "know that I believe in you, too."

And love you with all my heart.

The words begged for release, but she held them back, not wanting to burden him with the weight of them. He put enough pressure on himself already. When her name was cleared, she'd speak them. And if her name wasn't cleared? Well, some truths were less painful when left unspoken.

Chapter
36

J ames didn't go back to bed that morning. He heated enough water for a bath and a shave and soaked in the tub longer than usual, trying to get his thoughts in order. He needed a plan of action. One free from partiality—which would be tricky since he was anything but impartial in this case. He believed Noreen innocent, and he intended to prove that fact to Taggert and the rest of the community. Yet Taggert already assumed he'd favor the evidence that supported Noreen and ignore the rest. He couldn't do that. All facts must be examined. All testimony documented. He must seek the truth, not simply what he wanted to find.

The truth would exonerate Noreen. Of that he had no doubt. Yet the fact that someone had laid a trail of deceit to obscure the truth made him nervous. The easy evidence pointed to Noreen, and if he didn't uncover the true culprit in a timely fashion, Taggert and others would demand her arrest.

After pouring himself a cup of coffee, James settled at the table and pulled out his Bible. If ever a day needed to be started with a dose of wisdom and encouragement, it was today. Craving the words of Jesus himself, James turned to the book of John, his eyes scanning for underlined passages. A pair of verses on opposite sides of his current opening jumped off the page and into his heart. One from chapter fourteen. The other from chapter sixteen.

And I will pray the Father, and he shall give you another Comforter, that he may abide with you for ever; Even the Spirit of truth; whom the world cannot receive, because it seeth him not, neither knoweth him: but ye know him; for he dwelleth with you, and shall be in you.

Howbeit when he, the Spirit of truth, is come, he will guide you into all truth: for he shall not speak of himself; but whatsoever he shall hear, that shall he speak: and he will shew you things to come.

He meditated on the words. Closed his eyes so they could soak into his soul. The Spirit of truth. Sent from the Father at the request of Jesus. To his disciples. Those who know the Lord.

James bowed his head over his Bible, his fingers tightening on the handle of his cup, though he made no move to lift the coffee to his mouth.

The Spirit of truth dwelled in him. Lived in him. Right now. Today. Ready to help him see what the world could not see. A discerning Spirit. One sent to guide him into all truth.

All truth. Not just spiritual truth but physical truth as well. At least he hoped that's what *all* meant, for he could really use a guide as he sifted through fact and fiction.

Lord, I need your help. You know who set the fire, for you see everything. Guide me with your Spirit of truth today. Stir my mind to ask the right questions, and help me make sense of the answers. Foil the deceiver's plot, and bring justice to our community. To Noreen. Guard her heart as speculation spreads about her involvement and . . . encourage Taggert as he faces this staggering loss.

He sat in silence, sipping his coffee, and preparing his mind while he waited for the sun to rise above the horizon. Once the sky was fully light, he rose from the table, retrieved his hat, and set out for the saloon. Or what was left of it. He wanted to take a closer look at that burn pattern he'd noticed on the floor before neighbors and friends started traipsing through the place.

An oppressive mood settled over James the moment he stepped inside the Salt Fork. Memories of boisterous crowds, rowdy laughter, and friendly card games tried to surface, but they seemed trapped within the blackened walls, overshadowed by smells of smoke and wet ash.

"You're gettin' an early start."

James turned at the sound of Taggert's voice and found him behind the charred bar, separating broken glasses from unbroken ones. The clothes he wore were clean, but they hung on his frame as if they belonged to a larger man. Probably Marcus Freeman. The soot had been washed from his face and hair, but no amount of scrubbing could remove the gloom from his bearing.

"I could say the same for you." James crossed to the bar and braced his boot on the brass rail that had lost its shine and some of its shape.

A soot-darkened glass clinked softly as the barkeeper placed it in a crate. "Can't get an early start if you never actually stopped."

"I'm sorry this happened, Milt." The words felt inadequate, yet James said them anyway. They were true, after all. The man's livelihood had been wrongly stolen from him. James might not approve of all the goings on that had taken place within these walls, but Taggert was a victim of a crime, and he deserved compassion and patience.

Taggert heaved a weary sigh. "Me too." He set aside the crate of glassware and met James's gaze. "I appreciate all you did to try to save it. Not many men would enter a burning building that didn't belong to them. You, Connor, and Old Coop did that, and I owe you my thanks."

"And I owe you justice for what happened here."

Taggert rolled his eyes but didn't lash out with disparaging comments about Noreen. Probably too worn out for fit-throwin', yet James hoped it might be a sign of an improved mindset.

James retrieved a notepad and pencil from his coat pocket. "When did you first realize something was wrong?"

Taggert blew out a heavy breath and pushed the crate aside. "I closed down around two in the morning. Was in bed by three. I hadn't been asleep long, maybe an hour, when I heard a noise in the alley. Some kind of crash. Thought it was just a coon or cat or somethin', so I didn't investigate. Just rolled over and pulled the pillow over my head." His mouth flattened in a tight line. "If I had just gotten out of bed . . . maybe I could've . . ."

The road of *could haves* was a painful path that circled in on itself and led a man nowhere. Best to reroute Taggert before he got mired in that unproductive mud.

"When did you notice the fire?"

Taggert gave his head a shake, then cleared his throat. "Not sure how long I slept. Long enough that my room filled with smoke."

James jotted a note. "Is that what woke you? The smoke?"

"Don't think so." Taggert's brow furrowed. "There was a noise, I think. Something banging against my window."

"Which side of the building is that window on?"

"The side facing the alley."

Same as the window above that burn pattern he'd noticed. Interesting.

"It took me a minute to wake up," Taggert said, his face thoughtful. "I'm a sound sleeper, but I felt groggier than usual."

"Probably from the smoke you'd been breathing."

"Maybe." Taggert shrugged and ran a hand down the front of his face. "All I know is when I finally dragged myself out of bed, I started coughing. I noticed the smoke and hurried to open the windows. When I got to the one facing the alley, a stick of some kind knocked against the glass. I threw open the sash and yelled out the window. The stick clattered to the ground, and someone ran off. I heard the footsteps, but it was too dark to see anything. I threw my boots on and ran down the back staircase to the storeroom and tried to give chase, but by the time I made it to the street, it was empty. That's when I turned back to the Salt Fork and realized it was on fire. I ran up the boardwalk and found your girlfriend's hankie flappin' in the breeze."

James frowned but made no comment about the handkerchief. "It sounds like whoever started the fire wanted to make sure you didn't die in the blaze. They made a point to wake you."

Taggert raised a brow. "That supposed to make me feel better?"

"Just trying to get an accurate picture of who might have done this."

"We already know who *might* have done this, and she looks a lot like Noreen O'Sullivan." Taggert bent down, grabbed another crate filled with glassware, and slammed it onto the counter. "You aren't going to convince me she's a saint just because she couldn't stomach barbecuing a man in his bed. She destroyed my saloon. Could've burned down the entire town. She needs to be locked up."

James had expected the accusations and chose to ignore them instead of arguing. Taggert wouldn't be convinced until they had another suspect in custody. Defending Noreen wouldn't help him accomplish that goal. Gathering evidence would.

"Could you tell where the fire started?"

Taggert pulled a glass from the crate, frowned at its chipped rim, then used it to point across the room to the far side of the saloon. Directly at the area with the lighter colored floorboards.

"Over there. When I ran back inside, half the floor was on fire. I grabbed my mop bucket and started tossing water on it, but it made it worse. It spread even faster. I didn't know what else to do, so I abandoned the bucket and started carrying anything of value outside. That's when the church bell rang and the alarm sounded."

The fire spread when he tried to douse it? But later when they'd worked the bucket lines, the water had extinguished the flames. A memory flashed in James's mind from when he'd been a kid and knocked over a lantern in the yard. He'd gone to fetch water to put out the spreading fire, but his father had stopped him. He'd kicked dirt onto the flames instead. Said oil fires needed to be smothered, not doused.

"Did you notice any odors?"

Taggert raised his head, his brows scrunching together. "Now that you mention it . . . I did smell something. Kerosene, maybe?" His expression cleared. "That's why I couldn't put it out. That she-devil poured kerosene all over my floor!"

"Somebody did. I'm going to hold off on naming anyone until I have more details." James made another note, then moved over to the section of floor where he'd noticed the markings. "See how the floor is burned less over here?" He pointed with his pencil to the wavy outline that matched the pattern of a spilled liquid. A *lot* of spilled liquid.

Taggert followed and peered over James's shoulder. "Yeah."

"I think that's where the kerosene was. It protected the floorboards underneath while the flames combusted on top. After it evaporated, the wood was no longer protected, but by then it had spread to other areas, and we were able to extinguish it with our water line."

James stepped to the window at the center of the spill area. The glass had broken out from the heat, just like the rest of the windows. Unless it hadn't. He hunkered down. Shards of glass lay on the floor along the wall. James moved to the next window. No broken glass. The heat had broken the panes outward. He found the same pattern at the next window.

"What're you lookin' at?"

James moved back to the first window and kicked the glass shards with his boot. "This is the only window that broke inward. The rest broke outward. Do you remember if this window was broken when you first found the fire?"

Taggert wagged his head. "I just remember the fire, not the window. Why does it matter?"

"Because I believe our arsonist broke the window from the outside and poured the kerosene through the opening."

Excitement spurred his pulse and his feet. James hurried out of the saloon, hopped down from the elevated boardwalk, and jogged down the alley until he stood in front of the window. A window that stood even with his shoulders.

"You there, Taggert?"

The bartender stepped up to the window, the bottom of the frame sitting at about his waist. The floor of the saloon stood higher than the alley. He peered down at James through the broken panes. "What are ya thinkin', Paxton?"

"I'm thinking that whoever lit the fire probably emptied a five-gallon can through this window. That would explain the large spill area."

"And?"

"And five-gallon cans are pretty heavy. Thirty to forty pounds, wouldn't you say?"

Taggert scowled. "So?"

"Pretty heavy for a woman."

Taggert crossed his arms over his chest. "She lugged those buckets around easy enough."

"But she didn't pull those up to her shoulder. Look." James moved close to the wall. "To pour that kerosene through this window, someone would have to prop it on their shoulder, and they'd need to be fairly tall." James mimicked hefting a large can up to his shoulder. "Seems to me a woman several inches shorter than I am wouldn't have the right angle. Even if she did manage to get it to her shoulder."

"She could have stood on something. Used smaller cans."

James raised his eyebrows. "You think carrying a stool and a bunch of clanging cans around in the dead of night makes sense? Much easier to believe a man did this. In and out in one trip. Quiet. Unnoticed."

"I *did* hear a crash. Remember?"

That's right. What had he heard? James looked around the narrow alley. A long thin tree branch had been snapped in half and kicked aside. Probably the stick Taggert remembered banging on his window. But what had made the crash before that? He glanced the opposite direction, then turned slowly to peer behind him. A stack of paint cans. A couple fallen on their sides. Had the arsonist backed into the stack during his retreat?

There were too many footprints in the mud from all the traffic through here while people had been working to put out the fire to distinguish anything helpful. Still, James bent to examine the can closest to the window. Brown paint ran down the side of the metal cylinder, as if it had poured out when it had been kicked over. Between the water diluting everything and the brown paint blending with the mud, there was no trail to follow.

But maybe he didn't need a trail. The water and mud wouldn't have been there when the arsonist set the fire. The ground would have been dry. The paint wet. If the criminal had stepped in the paint, there might be incriminating evidence to be found on the guilty party's shoes.

It could be a way to clear Noreen's name! He just had to find a brown needle in a giant shoe stack.

Chapter
37

Never had her shift at the hotel felt so long. Noreen released her grip on the wooden masher handle and shook her arm out. She'd never get the potatoes smooth before the dinner service at this rate. Blowing a strand of hair out of her face, she tried to rub some life into her limp muscles. She wasn't the only tired person in the kitchen today. Everyone was moving slowly after fighting the fire this morning. Even Mrs. Winslow.

Thank heaven Mrs. Winslow hadn't witnessed Mr. Taggert's accusations and handkerchief flaunting after the bucket line disbanded. Noreen couldn't afford to lose this position. Especially with court-ordered damages to pay. Yet she'd heard whispers among the serving staff and intercepted several suspicious glances from the other cooks and dishwashers.

She tried to armor her heart and pretend she didn't care. But she did. She'd come to crave the support and friendship of others. Spinsters from the society. Fellow temperance advocates from the parade. Her bucket-wielding partners from the fire. Passion for reform still blazed inside her, but she'd come to realize that being bold and brave didn't have to mean being abrasive and unyielding.

Reclaiming the masher, Noreen set back to work. Her sore

muscles complained, but idle hands gave her mind too much freedom to roam. And today, her mind seemed determined to roam
shadowed paths where gusts of doubt left her hope flickering.

Think positive thoughts, Noreen. Cling to God's promises.

The Lord was faithful and just. He was mighty to save. With God
all things were possible. He would never leave her or forsake her.

Then one of Jane's favorite verses floated into Noreen's mind, one
that had her grip tightening on the masher's handle.

*"And we know that all things work together for good to them that love
God, to them who are the called according to his purpose."*

How many times had she read that promise? How many times
had she doubted its truth? All things *didn't* work together for good
in this world. Just look at Luella. A sweet, devout believer in Jesus.
And her father nearly beat her to death. How was that good? Even
the author of those inspired words suffered greatly while on earth.
Shipwrecked, beaten with rods, stoned, put in prison. *Prison.* Noreen's chest pinched.

She and the Lord must have different definitions of *good.*

Her mashing slowed as a light dawned inside her. A different
definition of *good.*

She'd always defined *good* as the absence of bad. Protection from
harm. Healing from sickness. Restoration of broken relationships.
Removal of difficulty. The only way she'd been able to make sense
of that verse from Romans was to assume the promise referred to
heaven—a place free from sin, sickness, grief, and pain. A place
where bad did not exist. But a future heaven offered little comfort
for a young woman enduring struggles in the here and now.

What if that promise entailed more than heaven? What if God's
good had a power all its own, a power undiminished by the bad
that existed around it?

Pausing to add another dash of cream to her potatoes, Noreen
scoured her mind for more details from Romans chapter eight in
an effort to decode the type of good to which verse twenty-eight
referred. Brother Cowan had preached a sermon on the chapter not
long ago, talking about how many beautiful promises lived in that

passage. No condemnation for those in Christ Jesus. Nothing could separate us from the love of God. With God for us, who could be against us?

She could think of several people standing against her at the moment, with Mr. Taggert topping the list. But that wasn't the point, was it? If God stood beside her, her body might not always be protected from harm, but the eternal part of her—her soul—would always be safe.

"Walking not after the flesh but after the Spirit." Mr. Cowan's voice echoed in her head as she recalled the theme he'd repeated several times during that sermon. Her potato mashing resumed with new vigor as her thoughts picked up speed. Being in Christ meant not walking after the flesh, but after the Spirit. What if his promises also focused not on the flesh but on spiritual blessings? What if the good God was working pertained to the spiritual plane, to things of eternal significance? Bringing people into deeper relationship with him, healing spiritual wounds, opening new hearts to the gospel message? Hadn't he accomplished many of those things in her life over the last weeks? She'd caused her own hardship by vandalizing the saloon, yet God had still worked good from it. Teaching her humility and reliance on him, healing her guilt over her father's death, drawing her closer to James. So much good. One just had to have eyes to see.

Noreen's hand trembled as she removed the masher from the pot and settled the lid over the mostly smooth potatoes.

I'm sorry I've doubted your goodness, God. For holding a grudge and blaming you for not protecting me and Mama. Blaming you for Daddy's weaknesses and my unhappiness. You've been by my side the whole time, haven't you? Giving me purpose, giving me friends, giving me compassion for others who have suffered. I don't know what my future holds, but I trust you to bring good from it. Help me to walk after the Spirit and not the flesh. To see your good and rejoice in it no matter what trials I endure.

"Noreen? Did you hear me?" Mrs. Winslow's voice yanked Noreen from her prayer.

She turned toward her approaching supervisor. "Sorry. What did you say?"

The head cook raised a brow. "I asked if those potatoes were ready. The first dinner orders are coming in."

Noreen nodded toward the large pot. "Yes, ma'am. They're ready."

"Good. Turn in your apron and take the rest of the shift off."

"What?" Noreen's stomach twisted. She dropped her voice to a whisper. "Are you firing me?" She'd just vowed to trust God to bring good from whatever trials came her way, but that didn't stop the trials from hurting her heart.

Mrs. Winslow shook her head and touched Noreen's shoulder. "No. You're one of the best cooks I have. I'm not giving you up without a fight."

Had that been what she'd been doing when Noreen saw her talking with the hotel manager after the lunch service? Fighting to keep her employed? Noreen's throat clogged with unexpected gratitude.

"I know you're tired and have a lot on your mind, though," Mrs. Winslow continued, "and we have all the prep done for tonight's dinner service. We can spare you."

Noreen swallowed and fought to keep her voice steady. "I don't mind finishing the shift."

"You might when I tell you that Martha Evans is waiting for you by the back door."

Martha was here? Noreen's gaze shot to the rear of the kitchen.

"She said it was important. Something about your mother."

Mama? Noreen's stomach cramped.

Mrs. Winslow dropped her hand from Noreen's arm in order to give her a little push from behind. "Go on. Get out of here."

"Thank you." Noreen abandoned the stove and hurried for the back door, untying her apron strings as she went. She pulled the apron over her head, then traded it out for the straw bonnet currently hanging on her assigned hook. Without taking the time to pin the headpiece to her hair, she clutched it by the brim and exited the kitchen.

A woman paced across the yard not far from the cistern that had supplied their bucket line last night.

"Martha?" Noreen hurried to intercept her friend. "What's happened to my mother?"

"I'm not sure. She showed up at Jane's house with a flour sack bundle and asked to speak to Parson Cowan. Jane's mother offered to take her bag for her, but she refused to let go of it. She was visibly upset and only calmed when the preacher invited her into his study for a private conference. Before she went with him, though, she asked us to fetch you and Deputy Paxton. Miss Lockwood and I were at the house going over our findings with Jane when your mother arrived. Miss Lockwood volunteered to fetch the deputy, and I came after you." Martha's gaze caught on Noreen's hat. "Are you able to leave?"

"Yes. Mrs. Winslow is covering the rest of my shift."

"Wonderful. Let's go. I'll fill you in on our findings along the way." Martha headed for the road, and Noreen matched her pace, eager to see her mother.

What had upset her? Had Arthur stepped out of line?

"She didn't look hurt, did she? My mother?"

Martha shook her head. "No, she looked fine. Just . . . troubled."

I don't know what Mama is dealing with, Lord, but take care of her. Bring her peace.

Martha turned east on First Street, taking the most direct route to the parsonage. "Miss Lockwood and I conducted inquiries all morning, paying calls on our spinsters as well as other ladies of the community, to see if we could ascertain any clues to the real arsonist's identity. Most people had been asleep at the time the fire was set, of course, and had little to offer. However, Wilma Berry recalled hearing someone run down the street past her house while she was up feeding her baby. She didn't see anything, but the fact that the perpetrator fled down Jacob Street indicates the arsonist likely lives on the west side of town. You live on the east and would have had no reason to run past Mrs. Berry's house had you set the fire."

It wasn't much, but it was something.

"We also did our best to solve the mystery of your missing handkerchief. Miss Lockwood and I both recalled seeing it at the courthouse after your sentencing hearing when your stepfather made a nuisance of himself."

Noreen raised the hem of her skirt to better navigate the train tracks crossing First Street. "Yes, but he gave it back to me."

"He did, but he also made a point of calling out your dislike of Mr. Taggert in a public place. Someone could have overheard, seen the handkerchief, and concocted a plan to incriminate you."

She hadn't considered that. "I suppose that's possible. But how would this person gain possession of my handkerchief? I keep it in my skirt pocket most of the time. No one would be able to take it from me without my knowledge."

"Except on wash day."

Noreen stumbled to a halt outside the yard of the parsonage. Mrs. Barker came into her room on Mondays to fetch the bed linens and towels. She didn't launder her tenants' personal items, but Noreen had soiled her handkerchief on Sunday thanks to Mrs. Stephens's heavy application of rosewater. Noreen had always been allergic to strong floral scents. She'd washed her handkerchief that evening and hung it up to dry on her washstand. Had Mrs. Barker accidentally taken it when she'd collected the towels?

Martha backtracked to where Noreen stood. "We spoke to your landlady. She remembers seeing your handkerchief among the linens while she was washing, but she has no recollection of folding or ironing it. Someone might have taken it from the clothesline. It's not enough on its own, but hopefully when we combine what we've learned with what the deputy has uncovered in his investigation, it will be enough to exonerate you."

"Martha, I . . ." Noreen took a breath to steady her shaking voice. "Thank you. This is so helpful."

Martha smiled. "You'd do the same for me."

"I would. In a heartbeat. Though I pray there's never a need. One spinster falsely accused of arson is quite enough."

Her friend chuckled softly, then her eyes danced as she caught sight of someone coming up behind them. "One spinster who might not be a spinster much longer."

Noreen knew who she'd find when she turned, but her heart fluttered anyway. James strode toward her with purpose, his gaze filled with concern as it locked onto hers. She had no idea how a mere meeting of the eyes could produce such a strong feeling of kinship, but she had to fight to keep from throwing herself into his arms.

"I came as soon as I could." He drew alongside, his hand finding its way to the small of her back as if she wasn't the only one craving connection. "Miss Lockwood said your mother was upset, and I needed to come right away. Do you know what happened?"

Noreen shook her head. "No, I just arrived. I'm worried, though." Forcing herself to move away from the warmth of his hand, she headed toward the parsonage. "This isn't like her. She's usually home making supper at this time of day. Something must really be wrong for her to risk Arthur's displeasure."

Jane had the door open by the time they reached the porch. "They're in the parlor," she directed.

Noreen hurried to the front room she knew well from their Tuesday Teas and stepped inside. "Mama?"

Her mother rose from the sofa, her face crumpling as she met Noreen's gaze. "Oh, Reenie, I'm so sorry." A sob burst from her, and she began swaying on her feet.

Alarmed, Noreen rushed forward, wrapped an arm around her mother, and eased her back down to the sofa. Tossing the hat she carried aside, she took a seat beside her. "Whatever it is, it'll be all right. You'll see. We've been through worse."

Her mama clasped her hand and fought to get her emotions under control. "I swore I'd never let him hurt you, but I failed."

Was she talking about Daddy? "That's behind us, Mama. Daddy can't hurt either of us anymore."

She shook her head. "Not your father. Arthur."

Noreen stilled. "What do you mean?"

Her mother didn't answer right away. Instead, she looked to Parson Cowan, who gave a small nod of his head. Her gaze shifted to James next, and her body stiffened.

"Deputy Paxton, my daughter did not start that fire."

James nodded. "I agree." He pulled his hat from his head and fiddled with the brim. "I don't suppose you know who did?"

She inhaled a shaky breath, then lifted her chin.

"My husband."

Chapter 38

James nearly dropped his hat. Clevenger set the fire? What possible motive could he have? The man made a habit of pandering to all the business owners in town in hopes of advancing his political career. By all accounts, he got on well enough with Taggert. He'd even been seen supporting the saloon owner at Noreen's hearing.

A sick swirling churned his gut as Ramona Clevenger's words began to make a horrible sort of sense. If she failed to protect her daughter from her husband, that would mean . . . Arthur Clevenger set the fire, not to harm Taggert but to destroy his stepdaughter. James couldn't fathom such cruel selfishness. How could a man live with himself after such an act? Harming his own family? Endangering the entire town? The man deserved to be thrown into a rattlesnake den.

Color drained from Noreen's face as her mother slowly rose from the sofa, clutching the flour sack she'd been guarding to her chest. Three wobbly steps brought her to stand in front of James.

She couldn't meet his eyes. Her chin nearly touched her chest as she pressed the sack into his hands.

"I never thought he'd go this far." The broken murmur of her admission made his chest ache. "For years he's blamed Noreen for his inability to convince the city council of his suitability for an appointment. Her outspoken ways and disregard for his authority reflected poorly on his ability to manage his household. And her increased temperance work angers the people with whom he's cultivated alliances. Things were better for a while after he severed ties with her, making her unwelcome in our home." She lifted her head, her gaze overflowing with regret. "I should have done a better job of standing up to him, but I went along. Wanting to keep the peace. But I'm not going along any longer. Not when my daughter would be the one paying the price."

Her shoulders straightened, and for a heartbeat, James recognized the same fire in her that he so often saw in Noreen.

Mrs. Clevenger nodded toward the parson, standing quietly in the back of the room. "Brother Cowan assured me that obeying God takes precedence over obeying one's husband in situations where the two authorities come into conflict. The Lord commands that we speak truth and act justly. I can't do those things if I hide what I know."

James hung his hat on the back of a nearby chair, then took the sack that likely held evidence of Clevenger's guilt. He waited to open it, though. Better to keep the witness talking. Get as much of the story as possible now in case she lost her nerve later. He wouldn't put it past her husband to try to intimidate her into recanting. "What do you know, Mrs. Clevenger?" He set the flour sack near his feet and retrieved the notepad from his pocket.

Her throat worked up and down as she swallowed. "Arthur never came to bed last night. That's not like him. When the fire bell awakened me, the sheets were cold on his side of the bed. I searched the house for him, but he wasn't there. I didn't see him until after the fire."

"How did he look when he came home?" James asked. "What was he wearing, and what was the condition of his clothes?"

Mrs. Clevenger paused, her expression growing thoughtful. "He looked tired. That's what I remember most. And he was in a foul mood. Snapping at me whenever I asked a question."

"Were his clothes wet? Dry? Clean or dirty? Did he smell of smoke?"

"Dry and clean. And different from the clothes he'd worn the day before. There might have been a faint smoke odor. I don't recall."

If the man had fought the fire, his clothes would have reeked of smoke. Heaven knew his own clothes had spread their stink through his entire bedroom. If Mrs. Clevenger didn't recall a smoky smell, Arthur had kept his distance from the blaze.

"When I asked about the fire," she continued, "he told me that the saloon had burned but that he'd guarded the emporium to ensure it remained unharmed."

Yep. Tended his own needs instead of helping others. A true public servant.

"I assumed his clothes hadn't been soiled because the fire hadn't reached the emporium, but then I found other clothes in the laundry pile." She nodded toward the flour sack. "The clothes he wore yesterday are in there. They smell of kerosene, and there's some kind of brownish stain on the hem of his trouser leg and one of his socks."

James's gut tightened as he looked up from his notes.

Noreen's mother wrung her hands in front of her. "When I took him his lunch today, I asked him about it because his clothes had looked and smelled normal when I'd bid him good-night. He said he'd returned to the emporium to work on a project in the storeroom and spilled paint thinner on his trousers. But when I asked what he'd been working on, he snapped at me to quit wasting his time. I had laundry to do, and he expected his clothes to be pristine when he returned. A future city councilman needed to look his best. That's when I first became suspicious. He made the claim as if it had already happened."

James crouched and opened the bag. The sharp smell of kerosene hit him in the face and wrinkled his nose. He pulled out the clothing items, one by one. Sure enough, a brown stain that could easily be paint lined the bottom edge of one pant leg, the color identical to what he'd found in the alley. A second smear of paint stained the ankle section of a gray ribbed sock. Certainty gripped James by the throat. Arthur Clevenger was the arsonist. Yet a few dirty clothes wouldn't be enough for a conviction. He needed more. He needed to connect Clevenger to the handkerchief.

Ramona Clevenger twisted slightly and nodded toward Miss Evans. "When Martha and Miss Lockwood came to see me and asked about Noreen's handkerchief, I knew what had happened. Arthur started the fire and arranged for my girl to take the blame." She shook her head as tears pooled in her eyes. "His ambition has twisted his mind. He's convinced himself that Noreen is his only impediment to achieving his goals. He must believe that with her gone, his success would be assured."

Mrs. Clevenger bit her lip and moved hesitantly toward her daughter. "I should have stood up to him sooner, Reenie. I never challenged him, even when he expelled you from our home." Her voice trembled as she tried to hold back her tears. "I didn't see what he was becoming. I didn't *want* to see. I'm sorry, Reenie. S-so sorry."

Noreen rose from the sofa and pulled her mother into a hug. "You're here now. That's what matters. I love you, Mama. Always and forever."

The ladies huddled around Noreen and her mother, murmuring comfort and encouragement. James hated to interrupt the tender moment, but he needed to ask a few more questions before he could seek out his suspect.

He cleared his throat. "Mrs. Clevenger?"

The ladies parted in front of him. Noreen's mother wiped her eyes and nose on a lacy white handkerchief, then turned to face him. "Yes, Deputy?"

"Did you ever see your husband with your daughter's embroidered handkerchief?"

Her brows scrunched together. "I-I don't think so, though I wouldn't recognize it if I had. It's been quite some time since I've been privy to the nature of Noreen's personal items."

Jane Cowan pulled a fabric square from her pocket, unfolded it, and handed it to Mrs. Clevenger. "It would have looked like this."

What was it with these hankies? First Luella, then Noreen, and now Miss Cowan. All with identical patterns on their handkerchiefs. Was this some kind of new fashion trend?

Mrs. Clevenger ran her finger over the blue embroidered flowers but shook her head. "No, I haven't seen one like this at our home."

James frowned. He'd hoped to connect Arthur to the handkerchief. It would have strengthened his case.

"Martha thinks he took it from the clothesline behind the boardinghouse." Noreen met his gaze, and James's heart pounded a little harder.

Her eyes glistened with unshed tears, yet the shock of her mother's revelation had faded, allowing the feisty grit he loved to flare back to life.

The schoolmarm nodded. "We questioned Mrs. Barker, and she recalled washing the handkerchief when it got mixed in with the towels she'd collected from her boarders' rooms, but when she took the linens off the line, there was no handkerchief. She'd forgotten about it since she doesn't usually wash personal items, but our questions sparked her memory."

James made a note to stop by the boardinghouse and ask Mrs. Barker and the other boarders if anyone recalled seeing Mr. Clevenger in the area on wash day.

Miss Cowan turned to Noreen. "Don't you do your washing on Wednesdays, when you aren't working at the hotel? How did your handkerchief get mixed in with the towels?"

"You probably don't remember, but Mrs. Stephens was wearing a heavy dose of rosewater last Sunday. The scent aggravated my allergies. I used my handkerchief all through services." Noreen met James's gaze. "Mrs. Stephens sits in the pew directly behind the Cowans."

Mrs. Cowan braced a hand on the back of the sofa. "I remember that. Louise doesn't usually wear such strong perfume. I hinted that she might have applied it too generously, and she mentioned being obligated to wear more than usual. She'd received a free bottle in exchange for wearing the perfume to church and telling everyone who asked about it where they could purchase it for themselves."

James raised a brow. "And who supplied the free bottle?"

The preacher's wife bit her lip, a pained expression on her face. "Clevenger's Emporium."

James looked to Noreen. "I assume your stepfather is aware of your allergy?"

She nodded. "When he and Mama were first married, he bought her a vial of expensive French perfume. It was a fancy blend of rose and lilac, I think. Whenever she wore it, I ended up with a headache, red eyes, and a runny nose. One time, I even had trouble breathing. After that, Mama never wore the scent, and Arthur grumbled about wasting his hard-earned money."

Ramona Clevenger's forehead scrunched. "How did he even know about your handkerchief?"

"He saw it at the courthouse," Martha explained, "after the hearing. Noticed her initials. Knew it could be used to incriminate her. He couldn't have known when Noreen would launder the handkerchief, but creating a situation where she'd be likely to soil it would increase the likelihood of her washing it. All he'd have to do is watch the boardinghouse clothesline and snatch it whenever it appeared."

"Sounds like he'd been planning this for quite some time." James frowned. "Premeditated arson of an inhabited building is a capital offense."

Punishable by life in prison with hard labor or hanging depending on the mood of the judge. An outcome Clevenger had tried to force upon Noreen. James clenched his jaw and forced himself to breathe. As much as he wanted to yank Clevenger from behind his counter and pound his fists into the man's paunchy stomach, he couldn't afford to let rage have its way. If he was to prove Noreen's innocence, he needed a cool head and a calculating mind.

Forcing a bland expression onto his face, James pocketed his notebook and collected his hat. "I think it's time I had a word with Mr. Clevenger."

The preacher strode forward. "I'll come with you."

"I'll be fine, Parson." He waved the man off, but the clergyman kept walking.

When Brother Cowan reached James's side, he clapped him on the back and offered a friendly smile. "I know you will, son, but sometimes it helps to have a witness to corroborate one man's story over another. Clevenger has powerful friends in this town. If it's just your word against his, he could bring your character into question, claim you manufactured evidence to protect your sweetheart. It might help to have an objective third party bear witness to your conversation."

The suggestion rubbed a raw spot into his hide. He shouldn't have to defend his character when he had a proven record of acting with integrity. But Taggert had raised a similar concern earlier, which validated the parson's point.

James shrugged. "Suit yourself." He couldn't afford to let his pride get in the way of Noreen's best interests. He repacked the flour sack with Clevenger's dirty clothes, then handed it to Miss Evans since she stood closest to him. "Keep an eye on this evidence until I return."

"We will." Martha voiced the vow, but everyone in the room nodded. Everyone except Noreen. She stared at him in a way that set his pulse to throbbing.

He swallowed and forced himself to turn away. Those eyes, glowing with admiration, trust, and something else he dearly wanted to explore, threatened to distract him more than the imaginary target painted on Clevenger's belly. He needed his wits about him, and imagining how it would feel to hold her and kiss her in a proper manner was not helping matters.

Focus, Paxton!

He made it halfway to the door when Noreen called to him.

"James. Wait."

He halted, of course. He'd have the entire walk to the town square to get his head on straight. If Noreen needed something from him, he'd not deny her.

As he pivoted, he almost failed to get his arms out of the way before she threw herself against his chest and grabbed hold of his waist. Blood pumping through his veins at a dizzying rate, he closed his arms around her and hugged her tight. Man, but he loved this woman. Fire and sunshine, sass and sweetness, courage and compassion, all rolled into one amazing package.

He leaned his cheek against the top of her head, then dropped a kiss onto her hair, wishing they were alone so he could soothe her worries more thoroughly. Shoot, his own worries might need a little soothing, too.

"It's gonna be all right, darlin'," he promised.

She lifted her face. "I know. Even if the worst happens, it'll still be all right. God will work it out for good."

That's when he recognized what had changed in her gaze. Peace. Somehow, in the middle of a tornado-level storm, she'd found peace. His heart swelled as he traced the curve of her face with the edge of his finger. God was indeed at work, and James prayed that work would include justice. For as much as he trusted God's plan, he really didn't want to court Noreen through steel bars.

Chapter
39

James strolled through Clevenger's Emporium while the owner completed a sale with a customer at the counter. James smiled and tipped his hat to Clevenger upon entering, not wanting to alert the man to his suspicions. Clevenger had nodded in return, though his thin mustache grew twitchy as his gaze followed James and the preacher into the store. His voice pitched high with false cheer as he exchanged pleasantries with the middle-aged matron purchasing what looked to be shaving soap and hair tonic.

"I know it's not much," she said, "but Mr. Taggert lost everything, and the ladies from our church decided to put together a basket of some basic necessities. Toiletries, clothing items, some baked goods. Anything to help relieve his burden."

"I'm sure he'll be most grateful, Mrs. Malloy."

The man was smooth. Even sounded sympathetic.

James turned down an aisle stocked with candles, lamps, lanterns, and the item he'd been looking for—kerosene. Most of the inventory consisted of one-gallon tins, but larger cans sat upon the floor. James crouched down to examine the five-gallon tins and noticed a dust-free circle on the floor behind one of the cans.

"Looks like one is missing," James said as he straightened.

The parson shrugged. "Could have been sold."

"Maybe, but the sale would've had to have been recent to account for the lack of dust. I'll check his inventory lists, though it's pretty easy to forge those."

The tinkle of a bell announced the departure of Mrs. Malloy and signaled James to make his move. He strode to the front of the store and cornered Clevenger near a display of kitchen implements.

"Deputy!" Clevenger chuckled nervously as he backed away from James while trying to look busy tidying the position of a nearby teakettle. "What can I help you with today?"

For once, James didn't offer a smile. "I need to ask you some questions regarding last night's fire." He nodded to the door. "You might want to close up shop for a bit. Keep our conversation private."

"Goodness. That sounds ominous." Clevenger laughed again, but when James simply raised an eyebrow, he coughed and turned belligerent. "Look, Paxton, you've no right to barge in here and make demands. My taxes pay your salary."

"It's not my right, it's my *duty*." James stepped closer to Clevenger and noted the sweat beading on his forehead. "And I take my duty very seriously. Which is why I'm here. I've come into possession of some evidence that implicates you in the burning of the saloon."

His face grew red. "That's ridiculous!" He retreated a step, then narrowed his eyes and went on the offensive, advancing toward James instead.

James held his ground and let him come.

"I knew you were sweet on Noreen, but I didn't think you'd go so far as to implicate an innocent man. It's disgraceful." He tried to shove James out of his path, but James refused to budge, so Clevenger huffed and navigated around him on his way to the door. He opened it wide. "I have nothing to say to you, Deputy. But I'll have plenty to say to Sheriff Adair when he returns. I might have a few words for the editor of the *Albany News* as well. I'm sure he'd be very interested in running a story on corruption in the local constabulary."

Unimpressed, James ignored the open door *and* the threats. He retrieved his notepad instead and flipped to a clean page. "Where were you between four and five o'clock this morning, before the alarm bell sounded?"

"Do you not understand plain English, man?" Clevenger stomped forward until he stood directly in front of James, then jabbed a finger toward the door. "Get out of my store."

Avoiding the question. Yep. The man was definitely hiding something.

"If you prefer to conduct this interview at the jailhouse, I'm happy to oblige. Fetch your coat and we can be on our way."

"Fetch my coat? I'm not going anywhere. You are. Get out!"

Clevenger's shout drew the attention of those outside. A crowd began to gather outside the door. Faces peered through display windows. Quiet murmurs gained momentum.

Brother Cowan stepped out of the candle aisle and strolled toward the front of the store. "Let's keep things civil, shall we?"

Clevenger glared at the preacher. "You're in on this ambush, too, Parson? And here I thought you were a man of integrity. Guess I was wrong." He gave a disdainful sniff. "You afraid your sweet daughter will be tainted by association? Is that why you're willing to railroad me with false accusations? Everyone knows Noreen set that fire. She hates the saloon. Hates Taggert. Hates men who drink. She was bound and determined to close the Salt Fork one way or the other. I'm just glad she didn't burn down the entire town in the process."

Now he was pointing fingers. So they were getting under his skin. Good. The more off-balance he was, the more likely he'd let something slip.

Thankfully, the parson didn't rise to Clevenger's bait. "I'm just here to observe, Arthur. And what I'm observing at the moment is a man making a scene in order to avoid answering a few questions. Spawns a question or two in my own mind. Like what are you trying to hide?" He nodded toward the half-dozen people loitering on the boardwalk. "Perhaps they are wondering the same thing."

Score one for the preacher. James had to fight to keep a smug grin from overtaking his stony expression.

Clevenger peered into the street, his complexion paling slightly. In a blink, he'd donned an ingratiating smile and sauntered to the shop's entrance.

"Sorry, folks, I'm going to have to close the emporium early today. Deputy Paxton requires my assistance to solve his arson case. After our town suffered such a tragedy, I feel it my civic responsibility to help any way I can. I'll be open first thing in the morning. Be sure to return then."

Good grief. Snake oil ran in the man's veins.

Clevenger closed the door, flipped the sign to *Closed*, and turned the lock. When he pivoted to face James, his oily smile slid right off his face.

"I'm not going to let you pin this fire on me, Paxton. I warned Noreen to stay away from the saloon, pleaded with her to cease her tiresome temperance crusade, but she refused to listen. My wife is devastated by Noreen's radical actions, but we agree that she has gone too far. She's a danger to this town and must face the consequences."

"I've spoken with your wife," James said, a muscle in his jaw ticking. He'd expected Clevenger to cast blame on Noreen, but the man's callous self-righteousness had James's blood simmering. "She's definitely devastated, but not because of Noreen's actions. Because of yours."

Clevenger blinked. "Ramona would never betray me."

"Betray you, how? By telling the truth?" James stalked forward. "She said you were not at home at the time the fire started. That you never came to bed last night."

"I-I fell asleep in my study."

"She told me she checked the office. Checked the entire house, as a matter of fact. You weren't there."

His eyes darted back and forth as if seeking a credible excuse. "That's because I came here . . . to the emporium. To work on a project in the storeroom."

"In the middle of the night?"

Keep digging, Clevenger. Maybe you'll bury yourself.

The man jutted his chin. "I often come up here to work when I have trouble sleeping."

James raised a brow. "I thought you said you were sleeping in the office."

"I was! Until I woke and couldn't go back to sleep."

Time to call the man's bluff.

"Let's see this project you're working on." James pivoted toward the counter and the doorway that likely led to the storeroom. "Through here, right?" He didn't have a warrant to search the man's business, so he needed Clevenger's permission. "Unless the project doesn't exist, and you're lying to an officer of the law."

"Of course it exists." Clevenger reacted to the goad as expected and shoved past James to lead the way into the storeroom. "See? Right there." He stomped to the back wall and gestured to a section where someone had slapped a few swipes of brown paint on the plaster.

Clever. Covering his tracks with more paint. Only, this color looked a shade lighter than what James had found in the alley.

"The storeroom's been needing a new coat of paint."

"So you decided to get started in the middle of the night?" James didn't bother to hide the incredulity in his voice. "Rather hard to see, isn't it?"

Clevenger crossed his arms over his chest. "Yes, well, I used lanterns."

James glanced around the room. "Where are they? The lanterns?"

"I, uh, put them away."

James strolled over to where a paint can sat next to the wall, an unwashed brush lying across the top. "You put away the lanterns but didn't clean the paintbrush?"

"Well, once the alarm bell sounded, I became distracted. I guess I forgot about the brush."

James hunkered down to fan the bristles and found the interior ones still wet with the paint. Had it been used at four in the morning, it would be dry by now. However, if it had been used, say, after a particular conversation around lunchtime when Clevenger's wife asked unwelcome questions about the state of his laundry . . . well, then, a wet brush would fit the timeline.

James wiped his fingers on a rag hanging from a nearby shelf and ignored the brown residue left behind as he made another note in his book. A few feet away, tucked in a corner stood a five-gallon can of kerosene. His pulse picked up its pace as he stepped over to the can and lifted it by its handle. Empty.

James looked to Clevenger. "You know, when I spoke to Taggert this morning, he recalled smelling kerosene when he first discovered the fire. We believe whoever set the fire used kerosene as a burning agent. And here you are storing an empty container."

"This is an emporium." Clevenger bustled forward and snatched the empty can away from James. "I sell kerosene to my customers all the time. In fact, I was using this just yesterday to distribute smaller portions of kerosene to customers who prefer that I refill their stoppered glass bottles instead of purchasing new cans every time they run low."

"Thought you used barrels for that. A heavy can would be rather difficult to pour from without making a mess."

Clevenger forced a laugh. "Yes, well, you're right about that. I did end up spilling some on my clothing yesterday."

"Interesting. Your wife said your clothes looked and smelled normal when you came home after work last night."

The man's gaze hardened. "My wife is not the most observant woman. She failed to realize that I ducked in the back and changed clothes before coming to dinner. A gentleman doesn't come to the table in soiled clothing."

James offered a smile. "I'm sure she appreciates your fine manners."

Completing his scan of the storeroom, James spotted a desk along the interior wall. Atop it stood a set of ledgers stacked neatly between a pair of cast-iron bookends. He'd need a warrant to examine them and prove that there were no records of kerosene sales on the books for yesterday. At least not enough to account for an empty five-gallon canister. He couldn't leave Clevenger free to falsify his records, though. James needed clean evidence. Best way to ensure that was to remove the suspect from the scene.

"Here's the thing, Clevenger." James tucked his notebook into his pocket and moved his hand to hover over his gun. "We have evidence that kerosene was used to start the saloon fire. You have access to large quantities." He nodded toward the empty canister. "We also have clothing worn by you yesterday that smells of kerosene and carries traces of paint found near the crime scene."

"I explained all that!" Noreen's stepfather glowered even as he started edging toward the back door.

Parson Cowan, bless him, moved in front of the exit, blocking Clevenger's escape.

"You have no alibi to corroborate your whereabouts at the time that the fire started and a well-established dislike of the intended target."

"What kind of fiction are you spinning now?" Clevenger glanced behind him, spotted Cowan, then eyed the passage leading back into the store. "I have nothing against Milton Taggert. He's an upstanding member of this community."

"I'm not talking about Taggert. I'm talking about Noreen." James braced his feet apart and dared Clevenger to try to get past him. "You intended to rid yourself of Noreen by planting that handkerchief so she would be found guilty of a capital offense. Your own stepdaughter." He shook his head, making no effort to hide his disgust. "You're despicable, and you're under arrest."

The man's gaze darted to the door and back. "You can't arrest me! All you have is supposition and a pile of wishful thinking. Noreen's guilty. The whole town knows it. She nailed her handkerchief to the front doorframe, for crying out loud."

"Did she?" James stalked forward. "That's an interesting detail. Not common knowledge. How did you come to learn that tidbit?"

Sweat dripped down Clevenger's forehead. "Taggert told me," he blurted, his panic making him careless.

"Is that so?" James's chest swelled with satisfaction at finally catching him in a provable lie. "I'll be sure to ask him about that. Now, are you going to come in a peaceable manner, or do you prefer I parade you across the town square with your hands trussed behind your back?"

Clevenger might be a coldhearted dog, but he wasn't stupid. He knew he couldn't outrun James or best him in a fight. Surrender was his only viable option.

"I'll have your badge for this, Paxton. You're gonna regret tangling with me."

James stepped forward and took hold of Clevenger's arm. "Nope. I don't think I will."

Chapter
40

James hated to disturb Judge Lynch at home, but he had to collect evidence before Clevenger had the chance to taint it, which meant he couldn't afford to delay. If Sheriff Adair returned and failed to agree with James's decision to arrest a prominent citizen, Clevenger could be released in time to attend services at church tomorrow.

Thankfully, James caught the judge before suppertime, and the man granted him an audience. Even better, he granted him a warrant to search Clevenger's home, business, and, at James's request, his shoes. James spent the next two hours collecting anything that might help exonerate Noreen. Clevenger's inventory log, the empty five-gallon kerosene can, the paint and brush from the emporium's storeroom, and a sign advertising some slightly dented tinware at a *Temporarily Reduced Price*. The first word on the painted sign bore a striking resemblance to the misspelled *temperence* lettering painted upon Noreen's handkerchief.

There wasn't much to collect from the Clevenger home since Noreen's mother had already retrieved the clothing bearing traces of both kerosene and brown paint. However, James uncovered a letter in Arthur's desk signed by a city councilman stating that Clevenger would gain his support for a future council appointment if he found a way to rid the town of their prohibition problem. It bore the date of Noreen's temperance parade.

Now all he had to do was track down a witness that could place Clevenger at the boardinghouse on laundry day and check with Taggert about any post-fire conversations he might have had with Arthur. It was too late to interview boarders or neighbors, so that left Taggert. James had promised to keep the man apprised of his investigation anyway. Might as well kill two birds with one visit. He just needed to stop by the jailhouse first to lock up the evidence he'd collected.

Before he could reach the calaboose, however, Connor Reed pushed away from the jailhouse wall and hurried across the road to intercept him.

James's gut immediately hardened. "What's wrong?" He'd left the young man in charge of his prisoner while he'd been out collecting evidence. "Is it Clevenger?"

Connor shook his head. "It's half the town."

Half the town? What did that mean? James made to skirt around Connor and investigate the jailhouse himself, but the kid stopped him with a hand to his arm.

"Hold up, Deputy. Sheriff Adair's back. He caught his rustler and was making his way back when he caught sight of the smoke cloud over Albany from his campsite this morning. He backtracked to Abilene, left his prisoner at the jail there, then rode for home. He got in about an hour ago."

James swallowed a groan. He'd wanted to have all his evidence logged and organized before presenting his case. Adair was a good lawman, but he could be a tad impatient when he was tired. And spending hours in the saddle with the fear of finding his town decimated by fire would be enough to leave any man on edge. Clevenger would've been sure to whine about his unjust imprisonment, too, making himself out as a victim while accusing James of gross misconduct.

"He didn't release Clevenger, did he?" *That* would be a disaster.

Connor wagged his head, and James released a breath.

"No, he insisted on talking to you first. But after examining the charred remains of the saloon and tracking down Taggert to get his accounting of what happened, he brought Miss O'Sullivan in for questioning. Unfortunately, bringing her in brought half a dozen others, too. Mrs. Clevenger, the schoolmarm, the entire Cowan clan. Mrs. Barker must've sniffed out what was happening, too, for she showed up not long after the first wave, dragging Velma Stafford with her. So many people were clucking for attention that the sheriff lost his temper and shouted at them all to be silent. Then he whisked Noreen into your personal quarters to question her in private, allowing only Mrs. Cowan to accompany them for propriety's sake, though she had strict instructions not to utter a sound."

Noreen was being interrogated by Sheriff Adair? James nudged Connor aside and stretched his stride as he hurried to the jailhouse. Adair had never been a fan of Noreen's outspoken ways, nor the way she challenged his authority. If she got too feisty with him, he might lock her up just to get her out of his hair. The thought of Noreen behind bars again tore at his heart. He had to convince the sheriff of her innocence—now.

Opening the jailhouse door acted like a gunshot at a horse race. People rushed toward him as if his appearance had released them from invisible restraints, their voices rising to be heard over one another.

Noreen's mother grabbed his arm, her eyes filled with tears. "You can't let him arrest her. Please. She's done nothing wrong."

Martha Evans sidled close to his other ear. "Mrs. Barker found a witness. Velma saw Mr. Clevenger near the boardinghouse on Monday afternoon."

Hope sparked inside his chest only to be dampened when Taggert growled behind him. "We finally got an unbiased lawman to take care of business. You might as well hang up your badge now, Paxton. You're about to be out of a job."

Noreen held her chin high as she met the sheriff's penetrating stare. She'd spoken the truth, and she'd not allow him to cow her into a shame she didn't deserve.

"Mighty convenient for your handkerchief to go missing a few days before the fire." Skepticism laced his voice.

"On the contrary, I found it quite *inconvenient*. That handkerchief holds special meaning to me." She traced the lacy edge of her spinster society handkerchief that Sheriff Adair had tossed down upon the table between their two armchairs. "It caused me a good deal of anxiety when I couldn't find it."

The linen looked so ragged and abused. Smears of soot and slanderous black paint had turned the pristine white into a dingy gray. A rip at the top where it had been torn free of a nail left loose fibers dangling broken and disconnected. Yet the promise embroidered into the fabric remained as strong as when it had first come into her possession. She had a sisterhood standing with her. And not just the spinsters but others, too. Friends. Family. Her heavenly Father. James. No treachery could diminish that promise. Let the sheriff make his accusations. She'd not tremble in the face of adversity.

"This isn't a game, Miss O'Sullivan." Adair slammed his hand against the wood of the table and leaned forward in his chair, his scowl fierce.

Despite her inward bravado, her fingers *did* tremble just a tad as she pulled them away from the handkerchief and back into her lap. "I'm very aware of that fact, Sheriff. I have no interest in ever seeing the inside of a cell again."

"You'll see more than the inside of a cell this time. Arson is a serious crime. Coupled with attempted murder since Taggert was inside at the time, you could be facing a hanging."

Mrs. Cowan stepped away from the cold hearth and positioned herself at Noreen's side. "That's enough, Sheriff. She's answered your questions. I'll not stand silent while you frighten her half to death."

The sheriff turned his anger on Jane's mother. "It's past time somebody scared some sense into her. Maybe if I had done it earlier, she wouldn't have acted so rashly."

Noreen fisted her hands in the fabric of her skirt. "I told you. I didn't set that fire."

"Your hankie tells a different story."

"No, my handkerchief confirms my story. I would never disfigure an item of such sentimental value. Plus, the word *temperance* is misspelled and not written in my handwriting. All these facts lend credence to the supposition that someone other than me nailed this to the saloon wall. Taggert and my stepfather are the ones telling a different story, and you're choosing to believe them because it's easier, not because it's right."

Adair's brows arched. "Now who's making assumptions?"

Noreen blinked. Was he saying that he *hadn't* decided she was guilty?

"Tell me about the fire." A bit of the heat had drained from his voice, but his gaze continued to bore into hers.

A sigh slid from her. They'd already gone over this. "I was awakened by someone pounding on the boardinghouse door and shouting about a fire. I—"

A loud commotion erupted from the other room, interrupting her thought process.

Sheriff Adair pushed back his chair, snatched the handkerchief from the table, and stormed to the door. "For the love of Pete. I told them to hold it down." He jerked the door open. "What in tarnation— Paxton! 'Bout time you got here. You left me quite a mess."

James?

Noreen leapt from her chair, hurried to the doorway, and did her best to peer around the sheriff's bulk to find James. He was carrying a sack and an odd assortment of other items, including a kerosene tin, a paint can, and what looked to be a pair of men's shoes.

"Sorry, sir. I'd hoped to have everything straightened out before you returned, but I think I can put things to rights if you give me a few minutes to organize the evidence I've collected." James's gaze darted to her, and Noreen's stomach gave a leap.

"You got a warrant for that stuff, I assume."

"Yep. Signed by Judge Lynch himself."

"Let's see it, then." The sheriff moved into the office, and Noreen followed.

Martha waved her over to where she and Jane stood near the parson, and Noreen gladly rejoined her friends. They flanked her immediately, clasping her hands and infusing her with strength as a hush fell over the gathered crowd.

"I'm just missing one thing." Metal clanked as James set down the cans he carried. He turned to Noreen's mother and held up the shoes he had tucked beneath his arm. "Are these the shoes your husband was wearing last night?"

Mama shook her head. "No, those are Arthur's Sunday shoes. He was wearing his business shoes. The ones he had on at the shop today when I took him his lunch."

"I figured as much." James set the shoes on the desk, then turned to Adair. "Would you mind fetching Clevenger's shoes from the cell upstairs?" He pulled a folded piece of paper from inside his coat. "The warrant specifies the collection of Clevenger's footwear."

The sheriff scanned the page, then grunted. "This better be worth it, Paxton."

"It will be."

The moment the sheriff trudged over to the stairs, Martha released Noreen's hand and joined James near the desk, whispering something that made James nod. Probably filling him in on what she'd learned during the investigation she and Miss Lockwood had conducted.

A new hand fit itself to Noreen's vacant one, and she glanced up to find her mother at her side. "He's a good man," she murmured, nodding her head in James's direction.

Warmth seeped through Noreen's chest. "Yes, he is."

"He cares about you."

Noreen dipped her chin. "Heaven knows why. I've caused him no end of trouble."

Mama squeezed her hand. "He's wise enough to recognize your value. A pearl of great price is worth a little trouble."

A pearl of great price? What a ridiculous notion. Yet the words bathed her soul in sunshine just the same.

Boots stomped against floorboards, and all talking ceased as Sheriff Adair returned to the crowded office. "Got the shoes." He banged them onto the table. The frown he wore made it clear that Arthur had not been an overly cooperative participant. "Now make your case."

James took a minute to organize his odd collection of items on the table next to the shoes, then asked for the handkerchief. The sheriff handed it over, and James placed it on the desk away from the other items. Then he pulled out his notebook, flipped through a few pages, and moved to the center of the room.

"Taggert reported that the fire started between four and five o'clock this morning. He smelled kerosene, and when he attempted to douse the fire with water, it spread, indicating the presence of an oil-based accelerant. While the heat of the fire broke most of the windows outward, one window facing the alley broke inward, indicating the arsonist used it as an access point for pouring the kerosene into the saloon before igniting it. After being awakened by a scratching at his window, Taggert ran downstairs to attempt to catch the fire starter, but the perpetrator escaped. When Taggert returned to the saloon, he found the handkerchief nailed to his doorframe. After that, the alarm sounded, and townsfolk came to help battle the blaze."

James moved toward the desk and pointed to the handkerchief. "The evidence against Miss O'Sullivan includes this handkerchief, that she admits belongs to her, and her practice of promoting the cause of temperance. No witness or evidence can place her at the scene of the crime until she arrived to help fight the fire. Many witnesses, however, have testified to her courageous actions in organizing a water line of women to keep the fire from spreading. In fact, her fast thinking extinguished a fire that had caught on Taggert's clothing, likely saving the man's life."

Sheriff Adair's gaze shifted to Taggert, who simply scowled as he crossed his arms over his chest.

"Doesn't mean she didn't start it," Taggert groused. "Probably only helped because she felt guilty."

The sheriff didn't bother with a response to that comment, just turned back to James. "Since Arthur Clevenger is the one behind bars and not Miss O'Sullivan, I'm guessing you found a few holes in that theory."

Taggert scoffed. "I told you, Sheriff. Paxton's sweet on her. He'll bend the evidence however he pleases to make her look innocent."

Sheriff Adair spun toward Taggert and planted himself nose to nose with the saloon owner. "James Paxton is as honest as the day is long, and I don't cotton to anyone castin' aspersions on his character. Now, I know you've had a hard day, Milt, but if you don't shut your trap, I'm gonna toss you out on your ear. Got it?"

Taggert gave a sulky nod, and James stood a little taller. Noreen smiled. Sheriff Adair was starting to grow on her.

The sheriff backed away from Taggert and waved an arm at James. "Get on with it, Paxton. We ain't got all night."

James nodded. "I examined the alley where the arsonist started the fire. The saloon stands above street level, and whoever poured the kerosene through the broken window would have had to lift a forty-pound can to roughly the height of my shoulder. A difficult task for a woman. I also discovered a paint can that had likely been kicked over by the perpetrator in his haste to get away. An escape that was overheard by Mrs. Berry, who'd been up tending a fussy child. Mrs. Berry lives on Jacob Street, indicating that the arsonist fled west, the opposite direction Miss O'Sullivan would have fled to return to her boardinghouse on the east side of town."

James stepped away from the desk, and the sheriff shuffled out of his way as he approached the table.

"Now the evidence against Arthur Clevenger." He gestured to the table that overflowed with miscellaneous items. "He stocks kerosene in his emporium, and I found this empty five-gallon can in his storeroom. Clevenger claimed he used it to fill individual orders from customers who brought in their own containers, but when I checked his inventory list and sales ledger, I uncovered only one such sale for the past week. The lack of dust where the canister once sat in the store indicated that it was recently moved, which is why I focused my attention on recent sales.

"Mrs. Clevenger provided me with clothing belonging to her husband that smells strongly of kerosene. He was wearing these clothes when she had dinner with him last night, so the kerosene had to have spilled on them sometime between the time she went to bed last night and this morning when she found them in the laundry pile."

James opened the flour sack and pulled out the clothing. The sheriff's nose wrinkled as he gave them a good sniff.

"Not only do they smell of kerosene but there is dark brown paint staining the hem of the pants as well as the ankle area of one sock. A paint color that matches the paint I found in the alley." James pointed to the old, dented can with dried paint smeared down its side. "A darker shade than the paint Clevenger was using in his storeroom." He indicated a newer can sporting a slightly lighter shade of brown around its rim.

The sheriff compared the pant leg to both paint cans. "Clevenger could have kicked over the alley paint while fighting the fire."

James shook his head. "Not if he never showed up to fight the fire. By his own admission, he chose to guard his emporium instead of joining the water lines. Mrs. Clevenger has also stated that her husband never came to bed last night, leaving him with no alibi during the time the fire started."

James picked up Arthur's business shoes and began examining them. The soles looked exceptionally clean, and the leather had been freshly polished. Covering up evidence? Noreen frowned. But as James pulled apart the laces, a triumphant grin spread across his face. He pulled the laces completely free of one shoe, stretched the string out upon the table, and pointed to a discolored place near the center.

"There. The same paint color. He tried to clean it away, but it's hard to clean out every crevice."

Sheriff Adair straightened from examining the shoelace and scratched at his beard. "You got a motive?"

James handed a letter to the sheriff, one Noreen hadn't seen. "He wants a council seat. According to his wife, he blames his step-daughter's temperance crusade for his lack of political success. This letter promises aid if Clevenger puts a stop to the local temperance problem. Having his stepdaughter arrested would certainly curb her activities." James turned and sought out Velma in the crowd. "I've been informed that Miss Stafford can place Arthur Clevenger near the boardinghouse when the laundry was on the line, giving him access to Miss O'Sullivan's handkerchief."

Velma's eyes widened as attention shifted to her, but she nodded. "That's true. I was working in the herb garden when I heard the gate squeak. I stepped around the side of the boardinghouse and saw Mr. Clevenger yank something off the clothesline. I asked him what he was doing, and he claimed the wind had blown his handkerchief over the fence, and he was just retrieving it. I found it rather peculiar but had no reason to doubt the veracity of his statement until Mrs. Barker questioned me about it this evening."

"Thank you, Miss Stafford." James pivoted back to the desk, picked up the handkerchief, then laid it next to a hand-painted sign that looked like it came from the emporium. He turned his attention back to the sheriff. "Notice how the lettering on this sign is similar to the lettering painted on the handkerchief. Similar enough to sup-pose that the same hand fashioned both of them."

James closed his notebook and placed it on the table. "Both cases are circumstantial, Sheriff, but when you weigh the evidence, the case against Clevenger is far stronger."

Taggert's arms dropped to his sides as his gaze scoured the col-lection of evidence. "Clevenger did this? For a council seat?" His hands bunched into fists. "Fool man could have burned down the entire town." The saloon owner pushed out of the corner by the stove, where he'd been standing, and strode for the door. Halfway there, he stopped and turned a haggard face toward Noreen.

"I owe you an apology."

"Well, I owe you one hundred fifty-two dollars and seventy-five cents." She smiled as she shrugged. "I'm not exactly blameless in this."

He smirked. "Finally, something we can agree on." He chuckled softly, then dipped his chin, "I'm sorry for jumpin' to conclusions and blaming you for something you didn't do."

An unseen heaviness lifted from within Noreen's breast. "Apology accepted."

Taggert tipped his hat to her, then strode out into the night.

Sheriff Adair clapped his hands and rubbed them together. "Well, Paxton, if you can convince Taggert, I don't think you'll have any trouble with the judge. As for the rest of you . . ." Adair made dramatic shooing motions. "Get out of my jailhouse. My deputy and I got work to do."

Noreen let herself be swept along with the others, accepting hugs and well wishes as everyone made their way outside. But when Mrs. Barker invited her to walk back to the boardinghouse with her and Velma, Noreen shook her head.

"I have something I need to do first."

She turned back to the jailhouse, where James stood silhouetted in the doorway.

What did one give the man who saved her life? She hoped her heart would be enough.

Chapter
41

J ames pulled the door closed behind him, his eyes locked on Noreen as the people around her dispersed. Brother Cowan shepherded his womenfolk and the schoolmarm back toward the parsonage. Mrs. Barker and Miss Stafford strolled toward the boardinghouse. Connor Reed—after shooting a wink James's way—offered to escort Mrs. Clevenger home, creating a blessed moment of privacy James refused to waste.

He moved toward her and she toward him, the pull between them stronger than ever. He ached to hold her, touch her, kiss her until he could no longer breathe, but she'd been through an emotional storm tonight, and what he wanted didn't matter as much as what she needed. So he restrained his desires, only allowing himself to take her hand and caress it with the edge of his thumb.

"Are you all right?" He searched her face for clues to how she was faring, but her dark brown eyes glistened with such adoration that all those desires to hold her rushed back with renewed ferocity.

"I am. Thanks to you." She stepped closer and placed a hand on his chest. "You're amazing, James."

The muscle beneath her fingers twitched, and his heart took off at a gallop. "I, uh, had a lot of help. Your mother. Martha. Even Mrs.

Barker . . ." Her hand smoothed the fabric of his shirt, and he lost his train of thought.

"Yes, they all played a role, and I'm incredibly grateful. But you, James, *you* pieced everything together. You convinced the sheriff." Amusement twinkled in her eyes. "Gracious, you even convinced Mr. Taggert." Her gaze grew serious. "I owe you my life."

"I was just doing my job, Noreen. You don't owe me anything."

"I disagree. I do owe you something. The truth." Her lashes dropped over her eyes, and James's gut twisted. "I've been keeping a secret from you."

Well, he wasn't about to let her tell him here. The sheriff could barge out of the jailhouse at any moment. James hooked her fingers onto his arm and led her away from the building, not stopping until he was sure they were out of earshot and even eyeshot. Whatever her secret was, he'd find a way to handle it. Find a way to support her, protect her.

He turned to face her, bracing himself for her revelation. "You can tell me. Whatever it is, we'll face it together. You have my word."

She smiled, an expression so tender, it left him a bit bewildered. No guilt or shame darkened her gaze. No embarrassment. A bit of nervousness was in evidence as she nibbled the edge of her lip, but Noreen had never been one to let a few nerves derail her.

"And you have *my* word." She slipped up to him and cupped his jaw in her hand.

His pulse leapt, and his breathing grew ragged.

"My word that I will love you for the rest of my days."

Love him? She loved him?

"I should have told you sooner, but I was afraid I wasn't good enough for you. That I would damage your career or blacken your good name. But love is supposed to cast out fear, not succumb to it, so I'll not hold mine captive any longer. I love you, James, with all my heart."

"Noreen. I . . . ." Anything resembling intelligent thought drained straight out of his brain.

She loved him! He couldn't think past that remarkable statement.

His chest expanded as his joy swelled so rapidly that he struggled to draw breath.

Wrapping an arm around her waist, he tugged her even closer, splaying his fingers wide upon her back as he pressed her to him. Her hand slid from his face and came to rest directly over his heart.

Man, but she felt good. Soft and warm. And the way her breath caught in her throat as they came together? His pulse might never recover.

"I think I started falling in love with you the first time you fixed my supper at the jailhouse." He smiled as he tucked a stray curl behind her ear, then let his fingers linger on her face, tracing the silky skin of her cheek. "I'd always admired your spunk, the way you never backed down from a fight you believed in. But when I got to know you and saw the tender heart hidden behind the bold reformer, I fell hard."

Bending his head, he inched his way down to her slightly parted lips, craving a taste more than he'd ever craved anything in his life. Stopping a hairsbreadth away, his gaze met hers, and his gut tightened at the desire shining in her glossy brown eyes.

"I love you, Noreen." His voice grew husky. "Always and forever."

Her eyes widened slightly at the use of the phrase she and her mother shared, then the edges of her lips turned upward as she reached a hand to the back of his neck and drew him the rest of the way down.

His mouth met hers, and it was all he could do not to moan at the bliss that shot through his core. Everything about her was perfection. The way her body fit against his. The bold way she met his kiss with an eagerness that heated his blood. The way her fingers twined in the hair at his nape, sending delightful shivers coursing over his skin. The way she clung to him as if she had no doubts that they belonged together.

James deepened the kiss as his heart resonated with certainty. He wanted to spend the rest of his life with this woman. Teasing her until she laughed, walking hand in hand by the millpond, sharing quiet meals in a home all their own, guarding her back as she worked to change the world.

Loosening his hold slightly, he lifted his head. Her moist lips glistened, tempting him to return for another taste, but he resisted, another matter pressing in with more insistence.

"Noreen?" He stroked her arm and waited for her eyes to flutter open.

Her lashes lifted.

"Marry me?"

She tilted her head and shot him a look full of sass that almost distracted him from the hint of insecurity lingering in her gaze. "Are you sure you want to tie yourself to a temperance lady? I'm bound to cause you no end of trouble."

"I've never been more sure of anything in my life." He tightened his hold on her. "A little trouble now and then keeps life interesting." He winked, earning her grin. "I'd marry you tomorrow if you let me."

Her expression grew serious as she slid her hand down the lapel of his coat in a terribly distracting manner. "We might need a long engagement."

"How long?" He'd wait as long as necessary and spend the time courting her properly. Convince her that he'd not change his mind, no matter how much trouble she got herself into. Still, the sooner he could make her his, the better.

"Long enough for me to finish paying my debt to Mr. Taggert." She jutted her chin in that stubborn way of hers that warned she'd battle if he tried to argue.

He immediately swallowed the offer to pay the fine for her. As his wife, she'd have access to his bank account, and he'd happily provide for her in that way.

"When I marry you, I want no blemishes on my lawful record. Once I've paid my debt with my own earnings, I'll take your name. Not a moment before."

She'd said *when* not *if*. James grinned, too happy to fret about how long he might have to wait.

"Guess I better start payin' you for the suppers you bring to the jailhouse, then. I plan to tip generously."

She giggled and shook her head. "You scoundrel. I'll take payment for the ingredients and not a penny more."

"Nope. You gotta charge for your time and the delivery fee. I insist."

Her eyes danced as she swatted his arm. "You're ridiculous. Who argues to pay a *higher* price?"

He waggled his eyebrows. "A man who doesn't want to wait fifteen months to marry the woman he loves."

A pretty pink colored her cheeks. "I'm hoping it won't be more than seven or eight months. My mother and I were talking at the Cowans' earlier today. If Arthur is convicted, she wants me to come live with her. I'm thinking of taking her up on the offer. Allow the two of us to get to know each other again." She grinned up at him. "Plus, it would save on boardinghouse fees."

"Sounds like a brilliant plan."

Speaking of boardinghouses, he really needed to get her back to hers before tongues started to wag. He pressed a kiss to her forehead, then loosened his hold and extended his arm. She tucked her hand into the crook of his elbow, and he hugged her hand against his ribs. This was what he wanted. To walk through life with Noreen at his side.

"So are you going to get a new spiffy handkerchief with those embroidered flowers that you and your friends seem to like so well?"

A smile tugged at her mouth that hinted at secrets he might never understand. "No," she said. "I think I'm ready to retire that particular design. I'll just keep on with my plain ones until I have new initials to embroider."

His chest puffed a bit. "So in six months?"

She nudged him with her shoulder. "Eight."

James chuckled. "We'll see."

EPILOGUE

FIVE AND A HALF MONTHS LATER

I can't believe you are getting married a week from Saturday."
Martha set her empty teacup on its saucer, then leaned back in
her chair, her head shaking slightly. "It seems like only yesterday
that we were pledging our fealty to the spinster society, and now
you're running off to get married."

Noreen chuckled as she lowered her own cup. "I'm not running
anywhere. James and I are staying right here in Albany. And my
fealty to the spinsters, to my *sisters*," she said as she looked pointedly at Martha and then Jane, "is unwavering. My marrying James
isn't going to change anything."

Martha raised a brow to challenge that remark. "You're far too
intelligent to utter such nonsense. Getting married changes everything."

Noreen reached out and covered her friend's hand with her own.
"Not the important things. Not our friendship. James knows how
deeply I care for the two of you. He's even encouraged me to offer
to host our Tuesday teatimes at our home after the wedding."

"Your home. In the jailhouse."

Noreen ignored Martha's wry tone as she lifted her cup back to
her lips, hoping it would hide her amusement. "Hanging curtains
on the windows upstairs will hide the bars, and I thought to lay

down a rug or two. Install a stove. Bring in some furnishings. Turn the space into a proper parlor. What do you think?"

Jane's eyes widened.

Martha looked aghast. "You can't be serious!"

Noreen released the grin she'd been holding back. "Of course I'm not serious. James has a perfectly normal sitting area downstairs in his personal quarters that we can use."

"You're terrible." Martha snatched the napkin from her lap and tossed it at Noreen a heartbeat before all three ladies burst into laughter.

Noreen wiped at her watering eyes and caught a glimpse of her mother standing in the doorway, a smile on her face.

"I'm sorry, Mama. Did we disturb you?"

"There's nothing disturbing about the sound of laughter ringing through the house." Her smile erased years of hardship from her face. "I just wanted to let you know I'm heading to the emporium. I told Mrs. Saunders I'd cover the end of her shift so she could get home in time to bake her husband a chocolate cake for his birthday. She wants to surprise him."

Ramona Clevenger's eyes danced with a merriment that softened Noreen's heart. How her mother had blossomed over these last months. There was a freedom about her now, a joy that had begun to flourish after the removal of her husband's stifling influence.

When Arthur had been convicted of arson and sentenced to life in prison with hard labor, Noreen's mother had taken over the running of Clevenger's Emporium and discovered she had a knack for business. She overhauled the inventory to cater to a more feminine clientele, focusing on groceries, dress goods, housewares, and a new line of scented soaps that had proven a top seller. Noreen assisted by polling the spinsters about what items they had the hardest time finding in town, and then gathered opinions about what would make a store appealing. Ramona took the results and implemented them within the first few weeks. She sold off farm implements, carpentry tools, and firearms and filled those shelves instead with wallpaper selections, books, and practical millinery. Word spread, and in less than a month's time, Clevenger's Emporium had become a hub for female shoppers. A store run by women to benefit women.

Noreen had left the hotel four months ago to work beside her mother in the emporium full-time. She'd drawn a salary that allowed her to increase her payments to Milton Taggert every week, until only one payment remained. The one she would send on Friday, clearing her debt and allowing her to walk down the aisle to James a free woman. Her stomach danced at the thought.

"I'll have dinner ready when you get home," Noreen promised.

Her mother nodded. "I assume your handsome deputy will be joining us. I noticed a fresh apple pie cooling on the counter."

Noreen blushed. In her hurry to get things ready for the teatime with her friends this afternoon, she'd completely forgotten to notify her mother that she'd invited James to dinner when he'd stopped by the emporium on his rounds that morning.

"You don't mind, do you?"

"Mind? Reenie, that man is welcome at our table any time. He's family." Her gaze shifted to the others in the parlor. "You girls should get Noreen to show you her dress. We finished it last night."

"Your dress?" Jane immediately set her teacup aside. "Why didn't you say anything? Where is it?" She glanced around the parlor as if expecting it to jump out from behind the sofa like a child playing hide and seek.

"In my room." Unable to contain her pleasure now that she had an excuse to forgo the rest of the tea, Noreen bounded to her feet and led the way down the hall. She pushed her bedroom door inward to reveal the ivory gown hanging from her wardrobe door.

Feminine gasps echoed around her as Martha and Jane hurried into the room and began fingering the fine wool fabric.

"Oh, Noreen. It's beautiful." A tinge of sadness colored Jane's voice despite her bright smile, and Noreen wondered if perhaps her friend harbored a secret desire to wear such a gown herself one day.

Do you have a man for her, Lord? Someone who can see past her shyness the way James saw past my prickly exterior?

She had no interest in playing matchmaker for her friends.

Noreen respected whatever choices Jane and Martha embraced in their own lives, just as she hoped they'd respect the choice she'd made with hers. But if the Almighty could find a husband for someone as stubborn and bruised as she had been, nothing was outside the realm of possibility.

"The lace at the neck is exquisite," Martha murmured.

"It's from my mama's wedding veil." Warmth filtered through Noreen's chest as she remembered the night they'd unwrapped the delicate piece. "She'd intended to pass the veil down to me to wear in its entirety, but age had yellowed the edges. The center remained in good condition, though, so we found a different way to use it."

"It's perfect," Jane declared.

Noreen moved toward her dresser, intending to show her friends the handkerchief she planned to carry with her down the aisle, the one embroidered with her new initials, but the sight of an opened envelope on her dresser top reminded her of more important news.

She withdrew the letter and turned back to her friends, handing the page to Martha. "I got a letter from Luella today. She and her mother are coming for the wedding!"

Martha's face lit as she accepted the letter and immediately began scanning its contents.

Jane clapped her hands softly. "How wonderful! It will be so good to see her and Trudy again."

Yes, it would. Noreen had missed their junior spinster immensely. "Luella wants to see her father while she's here. He's been sending her letters full of repentance and apologies. And since Mr. Taggert decided to move his saloon to Abilene instead of rebuilding in Albany, Trudy plans to use the wedding visit as a trial run. See if her husband has changed his ways enough for them to return home."

"I've seen him in church a few times," Jane said. "Always at the back so he can leave before Papa can catch him. But the fact that he's there at all shows he's trying. All God needs is a crack in order for his love to seep into a hardened heart."

His love had transformed Noreen. She prayed Mr. Templeton would allow it to transform him as well.

Martha finished reading Luella's short letter, handed it to Noreen, then turned back to admire the dress. "I still can't believe that in less than a fortnight you're going to be Mrs. James Paxton. Of all the spinsters we invited to join the society, I never expected you would be the first to suffer expulsion from the marriage clause."

Jane sputtered. "Goodness, Martha. You make it sound like she's contracted leprosy. She's not being expelled. Her membership is being retired in good standing." Jane smiled at Noreen. "Besides, you've seen how happy she is with Deputy Paxton. You wouldn't wish her to give that up just to retain her status with the society, would you?"

"I suppose not." Martha sighed in dramatic fashion. "I do want you to be happy, Noreen. I just know that things will inevitably change between us, whether we want them to or not."

"Small things might change," Noreen conceded, "but if we intentionally nurture our friendship, it will hold firm." She reached for Martha's hand with her right, then circled around to clutch Jane's with her left. "We might not always be spinsters, but we will always be sisters."

Jane and Martha squeezed her hands, and an unspoken promise flowed between them. No matter what changes the future held for each of them, their dedication to each other would never waver. What God had joined together in them, no man would put asunder.

DISCUSSION QUESTIONS

1. Noreen is very passionate about supporting the temperance movement because of the hardship she faced growing up with an alcoholic father. What are some causes that you are passionate about, and what sparked that passion in you?

2. James's career goals at the start of the story shift as his love for Noreen grows. Have you ever had a plan or goal that changed because of a shift in your priorities? How did that play out? Any regrets?

3. Noreen, Martha, and Jane have a standing Tuesday Tea date, where they meet to chat and encourage one another. Do you have special time set aside to cultivate friendships? What do you enjoy doing with your closest friends?

4. The secret spinster society is formed to support single women and empower them to see themselves as valuable and capable of serving their community and God's kingdom in meaningful ways. Hortense Lockwood sets herself up as a mentor of sorts to the other spinsters in the group. Have you ever had an older woman mentor you? What wisdom did you gain from that experience?

5. James and Noreen are opposites when it comes to temperament. James is laid back, looks at things from all angles, and approaches life with compassion and a sense of humor. Noreen is passionate and bold, and approaches life with determination and single-minded focus. Opposites can either cause friction or bring balance. Do you have a friend or loved one whose personality is the opposite of yours? How do you deal with those differences? Have there been times when experiencing those differences made you a better person?

6. Noreen worked out her anger and frustration by mashing potatoes. How do you release frustration?

7. When Noreen was at her lowest point, her friends showed up in a big way to support her, even though Noreen had brought the trouble upon herself. When has a friend or family member shown up for you in a big way?

8. Luella never gave up hope that her father would change his destructive ways, even when she lay bruised and beaten by his hand. Do you think she was naïve?

9. Noreen and her mother have a difficult relationship because of past hurts and misunderstandings, yet their love for each other endured. What could they have done differently along the way to prevent their relationship from deteriorating? How do you imagine them moving forward?

10. James refused to compromise what was right, even when it meant arresting the woman he loved. How do you think his relationship with Noreen would have been impacted if he had forfeited his honor to protect her from the consequences of her actions instead?

Read on for a *sneak peek* at

Wooing the Wallflower

Book 2 of
THE SECRET SOCIETY OF SPINSTERS

Available February 2027

Tyler, Texas
1895

"I will *not* abandon my children!" Stephen Hicks faced off with his mother-in-law in a doily-covered front parlor that felt more like a dusty street at high noon. His adversary might not be wearing a six-gun, but her narrowed eyes and the determined set of her chin rivaled that of a cold-blooded outlaw.

"No, you'll just tear them from the only home they've ever known. From the grandparents who love them. They belong here. With us. Taking them away is a cruel, heartless thing to do. But I guess I should expect nothing less from a criminal." Scorn dripped from each word that managed to squeeze through Delores Endicott's pursed lips. "You're a selfish, despicable man, Stephen Hicks, and I rue the day my daughter met you."

The woman sure knew where to aim. Stephen fought back a wince as her bullet slammed into his guilty conscience. Was she right? Was he being selfish, tearing Miranda and Cody from all they'd ever known? They would have a comfortable life with their grandparents. A nice home to live in. Enough money to ensure they had everything they could possibly need. Everything but their father.

Stephen straightened his shoulders and lifted his chin. He knew what growing up with an absent father did to a kid. Made him question his worth. Built a desperation within him to gain masculine approval from wherever he could find it. Put a chip on his shoulder and a hole in his heart. He'd not do that to his kids. He loved them too much to let them think for even a moment that he didn't want them. They were his life, and he couldn't bear to leave them with a woman whose hatred and disapproval of him would taint every memory they had of their father. Delores's poison had already started seeping into his seven-year-old daughter, turning Miranda petulant whenever he broached the subject of leaving.

Tightening the reins on his rising temper, he controlled his tone so as not to alarm his children, who were in their grandfather's study down the hall, picking out a storybook from his collection to take with them on the train. "Do you think I *want* to leave? Rebekah and I planned to make our home here, to raise our children here. But I can't do that if I can't work, and thanks to you, no one in town will hire me."

Two weeks ago, an article ran in the *Tyler Daily Courier* that tied him to the notorious Cutler Outfit—a group of outlaws wanted for train heists, bank robberies, horse thievery, and cattle rustling. The reporter had dug up evidence on Stephen's arrest in 1876 for petty larceny when he'd been sixteen. Identified him as "Kid" Hicks, a known associate of Hank Cutler. When Stephen's boss at the mill learned his history, he'd fired him. Said he was bad for business. Ten days of looking for other work hammered the point home that no one else in town was interested in hiring a former outlaw, either. He could count on two fingers the number of people in this town who'd known the truth about his past prior to that article's appearance, and only one would stoop to such tactics. The one standing in front of him.

Delores had never approved of him, despite her daughter's pleas to give him a chance. Rebekah's love had changed him, had sewn together the ragged holes in his soul with the same tidy stitches she used to make the dresses she sold in her father's mercantile. Thanks to her influence over the last decade, he'd become a man of faith, a man of family, a man forgiven. At least by his wife and the Almighty. His mother-in-law offered no such absolution. She refused to see him as anything other than a criminal and was determined to save her grandchildren from his influence. Even if it meant committing larceny herself by stealing his son and daughter out from under him.

Delores gave a haughty sniff as she tightened her hold on the shawl encircling her shoulders. "I did what had to be done to protect my grandchildren, and I won't be made the villain. It was Rebekah's wish that her father and I raise the children should anything happen to her. You know that. Had you signed the custodial order when we brought it to you, all this unpleasantness could have been avoided."

Sign an order to forfeit his kids? Not a chance. "It was Rebekah's wish that the two of you raise the children if anything happened to *both* of us. I'm still here, and despite your attempts to usurp my position, I am still Miranda and Cody's father, and I will decide what is best for them."

Done with the conversation, Stephen turned his back and headed for the hall to fetch his children.

"Rebekah never should have married you," Delores shouted at his back. "She deserved better."

The grief quivering in her voice stirred a hint of compassion in his chest. He halted and twisted to look behind him. "On that point we agree. But I thank God every day that she chose me anyway. Your daughter saved me, Mrs. Endicott, and I will love her for the rest of my days. I will tell stories about her to our children to keep her memory alive, and I'll make sure they know that she loved them with her entire being. She will not be forgotten. On that you have my word."

"As if the word of a criminal is worth anything."

His jaw clenched over the caustic rebuttal that leapt onto his tongue. Nothing he could say would change her opinion of him. Best he leave it alone and keep whatever peace could be salvaged. She was Rebekah's mother, and he'd not dishonor his late wife's memory by insulting the woman who brought her into the world, no matter how strong the temptation.

Stephen strode down the hall. "Miranda? Cody? Time to go."

Three-year-old Cody ran out of the study, a smile on his face as he stretched his arms wide. Stephen grinned and scooped the boy into his arms. "Ready to ride the choo-choo?"

Cody clapped his pudgy palms together, his glee instantly lightening Stephen's heart. "Choo-choo! Choo-choo!"

Miranda looked less enthused. She stood in the doorway, a

storybook pressed to her chest behind stubbornly crossed arms. "We want to stay here. You can't make us go!"

Stephen bit back a sigh. "Actually, I can." After shifting Cody over to his left side, he plucked his daughter off the ground with his right arm and tossed her over his shoulder like one of the sacks of grain he used to cart about at the mill. She squealed and squirmed, drawing her gasping grandmother in from the other room to demand he unhand her at once. He ignored them both, nodded to Rebekah's father—who'd never been one to engage in dramatics, thank heaven—and marched out to where his loaded wagon waited out front.

He'd already delivered their crated furniture to the depot that morning to be loaded on the freight cars while Miranda and Cody enjoyed a final visit with their grandparents. Four trunks and two satchels sat in the wagon bed, containing clothes, linens, and personal items, including a good-sized stash of Rebekah's things he hadn't had the heart to leave behind.

Keith Webber, one of the few friends left to him after the article destroyed his reputation, planned to meet him at the depot to reclaim the wagon and team he'd loaned Stephen and to give him the letter of recommendation he'd promised. Keith's cousin ran a grist mill over in Albany, and Keith had somehow convinced the man to give Stephen a job. God had opened the door, and whether Stephen's daughter liked it or not, they were walking through it.

Winner of the Christy Award, ACFW Carol Award, HOLT Medallion, and Inspirational Reader's Choice Award, bestselling author **Karen Witemeyer** writes historical romances because she believes the world needs more happily-ever-afters. She is an avid cross-stitcher, tea drinker, and gospel hymn singer who makes her home in Abilene, Texas, with her heroic husband, who vanquishes laundry dragons and dirty-dish villains whenever she's on deadline. To learn more about Karen and her books and to sign up for her free newsletter featuring special giveaways and behind-the-scenes information, please visit KarenWitemeyer.com.

Sign Up for Karen's Newsletter

Keep up to date with Karen's latest news on book releases and events by signing up for her email list at the link below.

KarenWitemeyer.com

FOLLOW KAREN ON SOCIAL MEDIA

 Author Karen Witemeyer

Be the first to hear about new books from Bethany House!

Stay up to date with our authors and books by signing up for our newsletters at

BethanyHouse.com/SignUp

FOLLOW US ON SOCIAL MEDIA

   @BethanyHouseFiction